LAND OF LIGHT

ELUDING DESTINY
BOOK FIVE

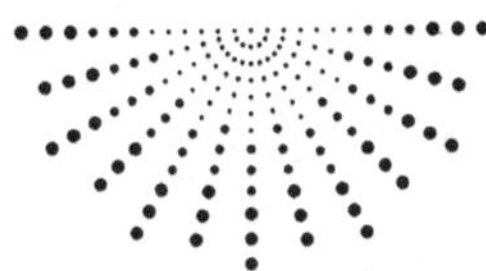

CHARLIE NOTTINGHAM

LIQUID MIND PUBLISHING

THE ELUDING DESTINEY SERIES

Eluding Destiny

The Horrors That Created Us

Aftershocks

The Precipice

Land of Light

The Quiet Army

Sacred Sins

Flash Back

The Shift

Lost to Time

Gods Among Us

The Cover Up

Blank Slate

Sign up for Charlie's newsletter and receive a free copy of the Eluding Destiny prequel, Blood Bar:

https://liquidmind.media/eluding-destiny-prequel/

CONTENT WARNING

This book contains mentions of detailed sex, drug abuse, addiction, captivity, rape, suicide, gore, violence, torture, homicide, and other adult language and situations,

It is intended only for mature audiences.
Reader discretion is advised.

PROLOGUE

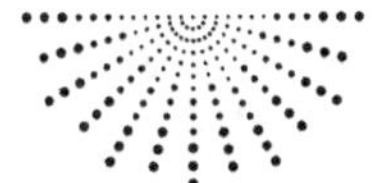

MARCH 2022 - CHRIS

"What happened, Micah?" I grasped his tiny shoulders. My wrist throbbed as the disgusting stench of charred flesh burned my nostrils.

"Is you okay?" Micah whispered. Of course. Changing the subject. As he often did when he didn't like the topic of discussion.

I clutched the electrical burn at my wrist. "Yeah, buddy. I'm okay."

His hand at my shoulder moved to my forearm. The white-hot pain pulsed through me, and I struggled to ignore the agony. I took long, heavy whiffs of the smoky, awful smelling air as it healed and tried to forget how badly I wanted to scream.

"I didn't mean to," he murmured. The wound closed and his hand pulled back.

"It's okay, buddy." I drew closer, following the sound of his voice, and took his face in my hands. He tugged my palm from his cheek and cupped it together with his. He sniffled. "It's okay, I'm not mad."

"I didn't mean to," he whispered.

Fuck, I hoped he was only apologizing for the burn he'd given me. I hoped he didn't realize what he'd just done. I prayed he kept his eyes closed like he was supposed to.

I smiled. "I'm not mad, kiddo. It's okay."

"Pwomise?" he asked softly.

I nodded, holding my smile. "I promise, buddy. I promise."

He reached his little arms out and wrapped them around my neck. His head rested against my shoulder. I raised my hand to the back of his hair. "Is he wight? Awe we leaving?"

"If that's what he said," I said. "If that's what he said, then... Then, yeah. He wouldn't have said it if he didn't mean it."

"Can I open my eyes yet?" he asked.

I fought the urge to gag at the smoking body behind me. "Not yet. Not yet, kiddo. Just hang in there."

He nodded against my chest, squeezing my back. The wind whirled outside the window. Silence crept in for a moment while I tried to retain my composure.

Fuck, I prayed he was right. I prayed they were coming. I prayed he didn't fill Micah with empty hope.

I could take the pain and misery, but my nephew couldn't. He needed out of here. Even if it was without me, he needed out of here. He needed his parents. I loved him with everything I had, but he needed what my brothers and sisters and I never had. He needed a mom and a dad.

I knew they were doing everything they could, but they needed to hurry.

Micah's tears warmed my shirt. "I'm scawd."

"Are you hurt?" I held his body tighter against my chest.

His tiny hands trembled at my back. "You has to stay 'til they get hewe."

I tucked my lips together to keep them from trembling. "I'll try, buddy. I'll try."

He nodded and squeezed me tighter.

Maybe he'd seen. Maybe he knew. Fuck, I hoped he didn't. But I had to ask.

"What did you do, Micah?" I whispered. "What happened?"

He shook his head, and his arms tightened around me. His quiet tears turned to gentle, silent sobs as his body quivered.

"Okay, it's okay," I said. "It's okay, you don't have to talk about it."

"It's almost ovew, wight?" Micah asked quietly.

I swallowed hard, nodding fast. "I think so. I think so, buddy."

"He said it was," he murmured.

A bang pounded at the door. My heart thudded in my chest, hands going clammy. But I had to stay steady. I had to keep it together for him.

His arms tightened around my body. "You can't go. You has to stay."

"I have an idea. Hold my hand, okay?"

He nodded against my shoulder and leaned back. His fingers found mine. That nails on a chalkboard sensation vibrated in my brain.

They were trying to get inside of me. I'd held them off a few times, but it was harder than ever tonight. But I held onto myself with every fiber of my being. My hands trembled as I squeezed them around his.

He was the only chance we had. He was the only reason we could get messages to them in the first place. I had to piggyback onto his abilities just to keep control of my own body, rarely even to my success.

Then, the earth beneath my feet began to quake. I gripped the cold cement for stability. Micah moved back to my lap with a gasp.

The last time I felt something that strong was when Laila blew the roof off of our cells.

"What was that?" Micah's body curled into me. "I'm scawd. I'm weally scawd."

Chris?

My stomach nearly hit the floor.

Jeremy. Jeremy's voice inside my head.

"Is it them?" Micah's hand touched my face.

Thank god. A quiet laugh left my lips.

Are you okay? Is Micah okay?

Yeah, we're okay. We're okay. I think someone's trying to get the door down, you have to hurry.

That might be one of us. Be ready to run, alright? You hear a guy with a weird Irish accent, listen to him. But we're coming. We're taking care of Peterson and Nastya then we'll be there. But if they get there first, do what they say.

I laughed. *You've got a real plan this time, huh?*

I'll see you soon.

"Uncle Chwis, I'm scawd." Micah's quiet, gentle voice shook. "I—I'm weally scawd."

"Don't be." A smile came to my lips. The ground quaked again. He grasped my shoulders and buried his head into my chest. "Don't be, buddy. Remember what we talked about? About going home? Remember those places we've shown you with the huge house and the little fountain and all the trees and the big blue sky?" He nodded against my chest. "That's where we're going. We're going home, buddy."

"You said that befowe," he whispered.

"This time's different."

A loud crack sounded outside—a gun. Micah quivered and pushed himself further into my chest as his teeth began to chatter. His shaking hand wrapped around mine, and I squeezed his body closer.

"It's almost over, buddy. We're going home." Screams erupted behind the metal wall. His little body trembled, but I held him tighter. "He wouldn't have said it if he wasn't sure."

CHAPTER ONE

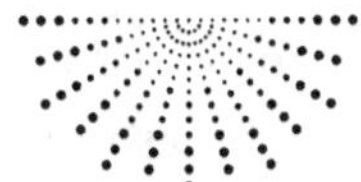

DECEMBER 23, 2020 - LAILA

Once we got inside, we did exactly as we'd done last time. We divided into our groups. We killed guards. We opened doors. We led the survivors outside where Brody began teleporting them to our closest hospital.

I should have been happy as I gazed out over the clusters of supernaturals standing around in small huddles. I should have had some remnant of pride or joy or accomplishment.

But all I felt was pain.

Micah wasn't here. Chris wasn't here. And I knew it was awful, but I would have left the rest of them there for all of eternity if it meant that I brought my son and brother-in-law home.

I wasn't sure how many people I killed that day. I know it was well over a couple hundred, but I couldn't say an exact number for certain. It's not like there were bodies left to count.

That made it easier to detach. Aside from the fact that they were the ones firing their guns at me and that I had every right to shoot back, the reality of living with the fact that I'd killed well past a hundred people is something that's difficult to accept. Tack on all the others I'd killed up until that point and you're looking at the largest serial killer the United States had ever seen besides Harry Truman when he gave notice to drop the atom bomb.

I killed more people than Ted Bundy and Jeffrey Dahmer combined in less than the time it takes most people to tie their shoes. It was as easy as blinking. It didn't feel any more difficult either.

As I watched their bodies turn to ash, I felt no remorse. I felt relieved.

After losing to Nastya, all I wanted to do was kill. I wanted to fucking end them. But I couldn't. So I took my pain out on the next available outlet that deserved it just as much.

Once upon a time, I thought that murder was always bad. That statement alone is somewhat comical. There was a time that I didn't even believe in the death penalty. But somewhere along the way, I realized that the line between death and life isn't as finite as I once believed it to be.

I once viewed living as a right. But at some point, I realized that being alive is a privilege. With a good enough reason, that privilege can —and should—be taken away.

"Here." Jeremy draped his jacket around my bare shoulders, handed me a pair of pants, and met my gaze. "I saw some steps a few halls over. No one's come up, but we've got Celena and Wyatt standing watch by them just in case."

I stepped into the sweatpants. "Sounds good. Any idea how many we got out?"

"Shit, I don't even know," he muttered. "Last I heard was around two-fifty. The closest hospital's at max capacity so we had to start moving people to another."

"Grand total's around five hundred so far then, right?" I asked. "If you count everyone I got out last time."

He gave a gentle smile. "Something like that."

I fixed the sweatpants around my hips. He handed me a shirt. I quickly threw it over my head. "Did we get any captors?"

"One," he said. "A young kid. Eighteen or nineteen, maybe twenty, I think. He's tied up in the basement."

"Sounds familiar."

"I didn't tie you up," he muttered.

"May as well have."

"That's not fair," he said quietly. "I was just trying to keep—"

"Me safe. Yeah, I know. You've said it a thousand times." I rolled my eyes. "We'll talk about this later. We aren't done here. Show me these stairs."

He pulled a ball of energy to his fingertips and started down the hallway. I walked silently beside him and took the place in for the first time.

It almost reminded me of a subway. Cement block walls curved into a semicircle above us. Mice scurried through small puddles of water beneath our feet. The area was lit only by the light we produced. There were lights on the ceiling, but they must have been shut off during the lockdown. Maybe the guards had been wearing night vision goggles. If they were, I hadn't noticed.

As I looked around, I found myself feeling somewhat relieved that I had been at the other facility. This one would have been far worse. At least I had a window in my cell. These prisoners had nothing.

The cells were slightly different than mine had been. There was still a spigot sticking out of the wall beside the toilet sink combination, there were still metal tables as beds, the floors were still concrete. But instead of steel walls, they were composed of thick concrete block. I doubted they could even communicate with other prisoners through them.

"You didn't get hit by any bullets, did you?" Jeremy asked as we turned right down a hallway.

"No, I'm fine," I muttered. "And you?"

"Yeah, I'm good," he said quietly. "I guess Wyatt got hit in the leg, but Celena took care of it."

As we continued down the hall, I said, "Why didn't I know that Lilith was a captor?"

"I thought you did."

"No, I didn't," I said. "I guess I don't know that many of them. Survivors, I mean. I want to though. After that bomb, I wasn't... Well, you know."

He gave what he could of a smile. "We can go to the hospitals tomorrow and make some rounds, if you want."

"Maybe we should go to the store and get everyone a Christmas gift. It's been a long time since they had one, and their families won't have enough time to get them any," I said. "Just something to open, you know?"

"Yeah, that sounds nice," he said.

"Oh, do you remember that little boy? The one Janis and Elijah have? I can't remember his name."

"Cage." He smiled. "His name was Cage."

"Cage," I said. "I wonder if his Dad's at the hospital. Maybe they'll get to spend Christmas together."

His smile lifted slightly. "Maybe."

Suddenly, another thought dawned on me. "Do you think Daniel's mom or dad was here?"

He nearly held his breath. "Maybe."

"I don't know what I'll say to them if they are."

"We'll tell them the truth. Peterson used him to trap you. Then you gave yourself over to him to keep Daniel safe."

The memory flashed through my mind. That look of terror in his eyes as his neck broke. As if it were happening in front of me, I instinctively pressed my eyelids together.

My head shook slightly, like shaking off the instant replay. It hit too close to home. Another little boy thrusted into a life that made no sense, tortured for some maniac's cause, then murdered for nothing.

"And then they snapped his neck," I murmured.

He was quiet for a moment. "Maybe they're already gone too."

"Maybe," I muttered. "Do you know if Liam found his brother?"

He smiled. "They're at the hospital together now."

I tried to smile. At least someone had their family back. I supposed a lot of someones would have their family back by the day's end. It did give me a touch of relief. Not really joy, but relief.

We rounded the corner to the cranny beside a narrow, metal set of steps. "Leah said she needs us to help organize people outside. You got this?" Celena called as we closed the distance between each other. Wyatt stood next to her, rolling his neck from side to side.

"Yeah, you're good," I said. "Tell anyone available to come inside and start looking. There's got to be something here that'll help us."

"Sure." Celena smiled and put her arms around me. "Congratulations, by the way. I'm so happy for you guys."

"Yeah, thanks." I forced a smile as my hand coasted over my bump. "We're really excited. But quit being such a stranger. Come visit your sister once in a while."

And I was. Truly, having my little girl meant the world to me. But I wanted my son too. I wanted the four of us to be a family. Micah, Milly, Jeremy, me. I wanted us all together. I wanted the family we'd been planning for more than two years. I wanted what was mine.

Peterson's words pulsed through my mind.

I promise that one day, you'll have him back.

Jesus fuck, why were his words my only sense of hope?

She laughed. "Yeah, coming from the one that can teleport. It's a two-hour drive for me, ya know."

"More like hour and a half." I smiled. "But you're right. It'd be easier for me than you. You guys are still coming for Christmas dinner, right?"

Wyatt's lips flapped in a trill. "Nowhere else to go."

"Oh yeah, I meant to ask," Celena said. "Is it alright if my mom comes?"

"Yeah, of course," I said. "Hey, at least our moms can bond over their exceptionally gifted daughters now."

A laugh left her lips. "Yeah, I guess so. But let us know if you need us. We're going to go outside before Leah bites our heads off."

CHAPTER TWO

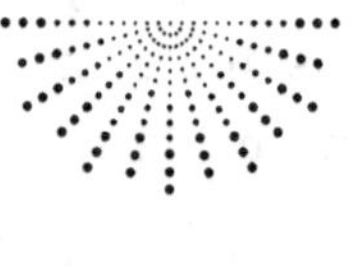

JEREMY

As we silently trotted down the dark cement staircase, I thought about what I'd say when we'd argue later. I knew that what I did was morally questionable, but I did it because I had to. It's not like I *wanted* to lock my wife in my sister's basement. It just seemed like a good idea at the time. She was moments away from losing our second child after already losing the first.

I got it. It was her body; it was her life. I shouldn't have had a say in what she did with it. But she wanted that baby. She wanted Milly as much as she wanted Micah. The reality of the situation was that I knew with one hundred percent certainty that she could not survive losing another child. She would have killed herself if she had.

That'd leave me to find Micah on my own, and I knew I wasn't strong enough. Even if I did find him, I didn't stand a chance against Nastya. Aside from that, there was no way I wouldn't relapse if I lost them both at once. I might've tried to stay strong for a while but when those months of loneliness without any inkling to find my son set back in, I wasn't sure I'd be able to keep living either.

But as usual, she was right, and I was wrong. We couldn't have taken the compound without her. Three out of eleven of us had life threatening bullet wounds and one of us died in the five minutes before Laila arrived.

As we made it to the landing at the bottom of the steps, I noted lights on under the door in front of us. I absorbed the energy back into my hand. "That's the second set of clothes I brought you so try not to catch those on fire."

"No one's here." She pulled the door open.

This hall was nothing like the rest of the caverns we'd been moving through. White drywall hung instead of damp bricks. Rather than a tunnel shape, it was like any other hallway with clean lines and corners. Dark mahogany laminate floors lined flush against the neat, freshly painted white baseboards. The recessed lights were finely aligned to the white ceiling.

It was warm. Welcoming. Virtually opposite of the floor above us. One would have thought they'd just walked into a new hospital or office building. Certainly not a futuristic madman's torture chamber.

Laila gritted her teeth together.

There were, what seemed like, a million doors upstairs. Downstairs, there were only eight. But we both knew which room we had to look in first.

Six of the doors were basic paneled white doors. The one at the end was metal with a submarine style hatch as a lock. But the one to my right was a pale blue metal door with little white clouds painted on it. Instead of a doorknob, there was a little white keypad.

"Get back." Laila took a few steps beside it.

I moved behind her. The wind picked up. Her hair spun into my face as the door quaked and fell at her feet. Once it was on the ground, she surged the wind beneath it and flung it at the wall at the end of the hall. It cracked into pieces, falling in chunks. Then we stared at it for a second.

Our baby was here. Micah was *here*. In this very room.

And then he wasn't.

I struggled to ignore the spin in my stomach.

I placed my hand on the small of her back. Instead of pushing it away as I'd expected her to, she moved into me until her hip touched mine. I kissed her hair. She let out a slow, uneven breath. Then she started through the doorway.

The walls were painted the same pale blue as the door. Little white clouds sketched along them seemed to nearly drift around the room. On the wall directly in front of us was a large faux window. Glowing bulbs laid behind a large piece of Plexiglas painted to look like the ocean, giving a false illusion of looking outside.

Pictures of letters and numbers hung on the walls in neat white frames. There were cute little stuffed animals sitting in a crowd on the small dresser to my left.

Straight ahead beneath the window sat a small, cot style bed with a single pillow and cheap throw blanket. The pillow rested at the right end flushed against the white crib. I thought it was Amy's at first.

Then, I noticed the other photos, and my stomach churned. Tears welled in my eyes and a lump formed in my throat.

Laila.

At least ten pictures of her hung scattered throughout. Some were a few years old. Others were recent. Incredibly recent. Like two months ago recent. A few were selfies she'd uploaded to Instagram. Several were photos I'd taken of her and put on Facebook.

The one that hurt the most was the one on a shelf to the right of the crib. It was from our wedding. I remembered Adam taking it. It was my profile picture on Facebook for months. My hand was resting on her hip. The side of her head laid against my chest.

But I was cropped out of it. I could see my hand and the white of my shirt. But I could have been anyone.

Beside it was another photo from our wedding. She was laughing as I grabbed her waist from behind and kissed the top of her head. Cute picture. But again, I wasn't visible. Just my arms and long black hair hanging on her shoulder.

He knew Laila. He saw her pictures. Peterson said he pointed at them and called her mommy.

But he didn't know me.

I blinked fast at tears in my eyes.

Who was he calling daddy?

That bastard that tortured his mother? The monster who cut out his uncle's eyes? The fucker that raped his mom when she was pregnant with him?

Laila walked to the crib as I continued looking at the pictures.

Then my eyes fell on one that made my heart skip a beat. It spiked me with a touch of jealousy, but it gave me hope. It sat on top of a small brown dresser.

My brother holding my son.

I pressed my lips together before they could shake. The lump in my throat got thicker. Tears spilled out of my eyes. It was the first photo I'd seen of my son aside from his ultrasound.

Chris was sitting on the floor with Micah in his lap. Micah's short waves of black framed his chubby, smiling little face. His brilliant blue eyes looked at Chris like he was the best thing in the world. I guess he *was* the best thing in his world.

Most kids would have been scared to look at Chris. But Micah didn't seem to notice, let alone care, that his uncle didn't have eyes. That told me something else that gave me hope. He knew Chris. He was familiar with him.

Maybe he talked to Micah about me. Maybe he knew who I was too, at least to some extent. Maybe he'd shown him memories of me. I was so much younger the last time my brother saw me, but maybe Micah knew something about me.

I couldn't help the tears that beaded over as I coasted my finger along the glass. Laila was right; he did look like me. But he looked like her too, if I looked closely.

His lips were as thick as mine, but the shape and width of Laila's. The roundness of his face that reminded me of her would probably thin as he aged, but that smile was her. That glowing, light up a room grin she wore better than anyone. Besides him. He wore it even better than she did which I didn't know was possible until I saw it with my own eyes.

The rest was me though. My eyes. My nose, just a tad smaller. My hair. My complexion. Those dominant Skoulda genes we all wore.

A crash sounded behind me, pulling my attention from the photo. I turned quickly. Laila yanked the frames off the wall and threw them to the mahogany-colored floor.

"Baby," I whispered.

I supposed it hurt her just as much to see that he knew her, but only the photos and idolized version Peterson hyped her into being. Not her. Not the woman behind that smile. Not the mother she wanted to be.

She grabbed another and threw it to the ground. She kept ripping them down and angrily hurling them off the walls and watching them shatter.

I set the photo down and walked to her.

As she threw another, tears glistened her cheeks. My throat grew tight. She was shattering the same way the glass of the photos did.

She moved from wall to wall until she made it to the shelf. As she grabbed the photo of Micah and Chris to toss it, I teleported to her and grabbed it before she had the chance.

"Look," I whispered, touching her back. I turned it in front of her. "Look, baby."

Her gaze travelled to it. Her hand moved to her mouth. The sound of her teeth chattering erupted before the sound of her quiet sobs. I felt the water leave my eyes and moved my hands around her shaking body.

"He's with him." I nodded hard. "He might not always be Chris when he's with him, but Peterson can't stay inside of him all the time. He's with Micah. He's not alone."

CHAPTER THREE

LAILA

The room beside Micah's was Peterson's office. A metal table with clamps and straps sat a few feet from his deserted desk. The filing cabinet was vacated. The cupboards were emptied. All that was left was the furniture.

The rooms opposite from Micah and Chris were presumably Amy's as well as Nastya's. One was painted green and covered in plants. The other was a light shade of purple with Wiccan symbols painted delicately on the walls. Different colored crystals and jewels sat neatly as decorations on the furniture.

I wouldn't describe it as creepy. It was done well. The room looked a bit mystical but certainly not scary. It was almost like the bedroom of a young college girl who bought a chakra set on Amazon and decided to go on calling herself a Witch.

The next room was strange. It was the last door in the hallway with a lock, aside from the torture room. Like Micah's, it had a keypad to enter. Nastya and Amy had normal doorknobs, but that door had a lock from the outside. Whoever was being held in this room was as much a prisoner as the rest of us had been.

But that wasn't the weird part. The weird part was the chains attached to the wall along with the awful, disgusting smell of sewage that filled my nostrils as the door came down. Chains were bolted to the wall above the bed, but the cuffs had melted to the sheets. A gray bucket sat next to it, seemingly the source of the smell.

I held my shirt over my face and looked around. This room wasn't custom decorated like the others. It was still homely but not unique by any means. The walls were white, a TV hung on the one opposite of the bed adorned with pillows and blankets. A hell of a lot more than what the people upstairs had but still wasn't much.

"Whoever was in here didn't want to be," I murmured.

"Probably the kid we have in the basement," Jeremy said.

Still looking around, I said, "We have to let him out."

He pulled his shirt over his nose. "Damn, I wish you would have left the door on this one."

"Shit, me too." I stepped back into the hallway. "We'll finish our walk through. Then we'll talk to that kid and let him go."

"He's sedated. We should probably talk to him in the morning," he said.

"We should probably sleep too," I said. "We can have someone tell us when he wakes up."

"Yeah, it's been a couple days."

I bit my lip as I started down the hall.

The moment I leaped from that cliff, I had the inkling that we weren't going to find anything here that he didn't want us to. Now I knew for sure. Any information we received, he knew about. He was planning a getaway for months. Anything important was already removed.

It was a game of cat and mouse to him. But the awful part was that we were the cat. We were Tom, and he was Jerry. We were stronger; we had the resources to destroy him. But he was smarter.

Although, I suppose it wasn't that he was actually more intelligent. It was that he knew us. He knew our story. He knew what was going to happen before we did.

While standing on that cliff side, he said something along the lines of 'don't let this one get wiped from history.' At the time, I thought he was being metaphoric. But soon enough, I would realize he was far more literal. Almost everything he said that I mistook for being figurative language over the years was the bluntest description imaginable.

Jeremy opened the next door on our right. I gritted my teeth to a line as I looked at the wall in front of us. There was a message printed in thick, black permanent marker.

One Day
But Not Today

The drawers of both dressers were pulled out to make it clear that they were emptied. Even the blankets and sheets were ripped from the queen-sized mattress.

"How did they know we were coming?" Jeremy asked. "I know that he knows the future and everything, but we could have found this place any time since September when we found the book. How did he know it'd be today?"

"Maybe the cashier at the gas station? Maybe Amy or Nastya felt our energy?" I said. "I don't know. It could've been anything. We came at this very ill-prepared. Not like we had much choice given the information we had. But still. Like you said before, we knew this could be a trap as we were walking into it."

"Yeah, but I expected it to be a *trap*," he said. "They could have taken you. But they gave you the choice. Then they gave us the compound. They knew you were going to kill all those guards, and they just let you. They handed it over to us."

"They handed it over to *me*. Almost like they knew you guys couldn't handle it and wanted to prove that I was the only one that could."

Jeremy grew quiet. "Kinda seems that way."

I paused, realizing what I'd just said. "I didn't mean that to be vain or conceited. I just meant that—"

"It's alright." He pressed his lips together. "If we would have had enough time to get more people together and form a better plan, we probably could have pulled it off. But you definitely got it done quicker and easier."

I rubbed my tired eyes. "Before we call Tina, could you and some of the guys come in and take a closer look at everything? I probably shouldn't be moving furniture, and we need to check every nook and cranny. Especially in Micah's room. It looks like everything was wiped clean, but it's worth the shot. I'd hate to overlook something like Chris's message again."

"Yeah. Yeah, we'll contact Tina after we have time to go over everything with a fine-tooth comb. There was too much oversight last time. Let's collect our bearings and figure out how we're going to go about involving the feds while we still have the time."

"Yeah, I agree." I pushed messy hair from my face. "I doubt we're going to find anything though. He took everything important."

"We should still check the test room," he said.

"At first, I was thinking we'd find a lot of things that could help. But now." I gestured to the words on the wall and looked back up to meet his gaze. "Anything we find is going to be because he wanted us to find it. Just like the book. He gave it to us. He's feeding us the information he wants us to have. Every bit of this has been planned. He knew every detail. He knew when I'd escape the last compound. He knew when we were going to find this one. He knows when we're going to get Micah back. And he knows it isn't any time soon."

Jeremy drew in a deep breath.

"Do you think you could finish up the search down here?" A yawn left my lips. "I used a lot of energy today. And this baby's kicking my ass. I need to get some sleep."

He rubbed a hand against his scruff. "Yeah, I'll finish up the search. Then I'll come home, take a shower, and get a few hours of sleep. Adam and that vamp are gonna stay guard tonight. Brody and I are gonna relieve them in the morning." He paused and rubbed his eyes. "Do you want me to wake you up if we find anything?"

"Only if it's immediately going to help us find Micah," I said. "Don't give me any false hope until I get a full night's sleep and a cup of coffee."

He gave a nod. "Alright, baby. Sleep tight."

I looked between his eyes. Then I took a step forward and put my arms around his upper back. He moved his around my waist. I struggled to ease the swell in my throat. "I'm still mad at you. I just really needed a hug."

He released a quiet chuckle, nodding against my head. His arms tightened on my lower back, and he kissed my hair. "Am I allowed to sleep in the bed? Or should I get comfy on the couch?"

I sighed. "I guess you can sleep in the bed. We'll talk about how shitty what you did was in the morning."

"I'm really sorry," he whispered in my ear.

"I'm too exhausted to have this conversation. I love you. Goodnight."

He kissed my hair. "I love you too."

After teleporting home, I put on some tea and sat on the couch with my laptop. I messaged Max on Facebook to let him know I was home but was hoping he could still cover my shifts tomorrow before we closed for the holidays. He sent back some long message I was too tired to read, saying something along the lines of how happy he was to hear from me.

Then I messaged Jenna to let her know everyone was okay. Adam already told her everything, so her response was just telling me to get some rest. I also messaged Mom to let her know that I was home and safe. I told her I'd pick up Tink in the morning unless she felt like bringing her by because I was too tired to drive.

My eyes were too heavy to keep open. There was hardly any energy left in me to be angry. I was sad. Deeply and painfully sad, but I couldn't find the energy to cry either. Even lifting the cup of warm peppermint tea to my lips felt like a task.

I wanted to take a shower. I wanted to get the smell of burned flesh off of my skin. I wanted to plan out what I would say to Jeremy in the morning. But I couldn't even find the strength to stand from the couch. Grabbing the throw blanket off the back felt like a chore in and of itself.

I fell asleep with my cup of tea on the floor beside me. It was around three when Jeremy got home and carried me to the bed.

For the first time in a long time, I didn't dream that night. I just slept. I made a mental note to use that much energy more often. It worked better than any meditation my therapist had recommended. Killing bitches, that's what helped me sleep soundly.

CHAPTER FOUR

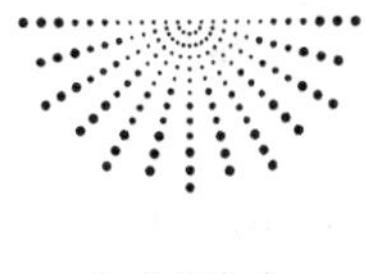

LAILA

Jeremy flipped a pancake at the stove. So like him. Cooking for me because he knew I was livid. That was the way to my fat-ass heart, food.

I leaned against the doorway into the kitchen. The backs of my hands rubbed against my eyes. The smell of chocolate and yeast filled my nose. As he turned to the bread that popped from the toaster, his gaze met mine over the kitchen island.

"Good morning, gorgeous." He gave a gentle smile.

"Morning." I stifled a yawn. "You should make chocolate chip pancakes more often. Not just when I'm mad at you."

He laughed, grabbed the bread from the toaster, and laid it on a plate. "Do you want eggs?"

"No, that's okay." I made my way to the counter. I poured a cup of coffee before turning back to the table. Plopping into the seat, I said, "I just want the pancakes."

He carried the plates to the table, sat, and met my gaze. "How'd you sleep?"

I sipped my coffee and huffed. "We need to talk about the elephant in the room here."

Jeremy licked his lips. "Just going right in there, huh?"

"Well, yeah. Locking me in a basement is kind of a big deal, Jeremy." He laughed quietly. I narrowed my gaze. "Is this funny to you?"

"No. No, I'm sorry. It's not funny. That sentence is just kind of..." He caught my unamused gaze and cleared his throat. "I'm sorry. For what I did. Also for laughing, but mainly for what I did."

I looked for his eyes through his messy hair. "That wasn't okay."

He was quiet for a moment. "It was a really shitty thing to do."

"You don't get to make decisions for me. I get why you did. And I can't say I wouldn't have done the same if I were in your shoes, but that doesn't make it okay."

He frowned. "I know that it was wrong. But you can't lose this baby, Laila. You love her, and if you lose her—"

"I know what it will do to me." My brows knitted. "I know, Jeremy. Trust me, I know. I'm living it every day. But that doesn't mean I can give up on my son. We had a shot yesterday. We had a chance. And what kind of mother would I have been if I didn't take it?"

"But we knew he wasn't going to be there," Jeremy said. "Micah and Chris weren't there. It wasn't about saving our son—"

"No, it was about saving all of the other people I swore I'd help. If it would have been Nastya, I wouldn't have gone. But I knew they were human guards. I knew I could handle it. And you didn't have faith in me. You know what I'm capable of. You know that I'm the best weapon we have, and you locked me in a basem—"

"You're my *wife*." His eyes softened. "You're the mother of my children. You're my baby. You aren't just a weapon."

I looked between his sad, loving eyes. "Baby, I wish you could be the one to fight all the battles. But we needed someone bulletproof for this one. We needed someone capable of taking down hundreds of guards in less than thirty seconds without a single casualty on our end. We needed someone to bring down a thousand-pound door and take out another fifty guards without anyone on our end getting hurt."

He frowned, averting my gaze.

"I wish I wasn't the one who killed as many people as they saved last night," I said. "I wish things were different, but they aren't. That doesn't mean I'm going to run into every battle that comes my way.

But if it's a battle I know I'll win; I have to fight it. I can't let someone I love die doing something I could've done by barely batting an eyelash."

"I know that you're right but—"

"But nothing. You almost died. Kai almost died. Wyatt almost died. Leah *did* die. Hannah also almost died. And if she would have gotten hit in the head instead of the torso, Leah would be gone forever. Both of your sisters would be gone, Jeremy. You guys had the worst plan imaginable. Hannah should have been surrounded by people with the best defensive powers or back at the hotel. Your most valuable asset who can't defend themselves shouldn't be on the battlefield unless they're heavily guarded. That's just basic strategy."

Maybe it was a bit harsh, but he needed to hear it. The fact was, he almost got his entire family killed. And fuck, I would have killed anyone to protect our kid too. But neither me nor our daughter needed protection from that fight.

"It wasn't a battlefield when we got there," he muttered.

My tone sharpened. "Are you saying it was smart to have them that close?"

Eyes drooping toward the floor like a sad puppy, he said, "No. No, the whole plan was garbage. We underestimated them. I didn't know there were going to be that many guards."

"That's what I tried to explain to you before we left," I said. "I picked a good chunk of them off just as they realized they were being attacked last time. I had the element of surprise. It sent them running the other way. You guys just planted yourselves in the middle of an open field without so much as a bulletproof vest."

He bit his lip and gave a nod. "It was stupid."

His gaze grew so solemn. And as pissed as I may have been, I did feel for him. He didn't mean for what happened to happen. He just wanted to protect *me* for once. Maybe not be the hero, but at least be *mine.*

"The only thing that would hurt as much as losing this baby is losing all of you." My voice softened as I took his hand. "Leah's my best friend. Hannah's felt like my little sister for a really long time now. Kai is my brother. You're my husband. And I almost lost all of you in one fail swoop."

He gently squeezed my palm, holding my gaze. "I'm sorry."

I moved my thumb against the back of his. "I'm going to be careful until the baby's born. I'm not going to, in your words, 'gamble her life.' But you don't get to make that decision. I have to do what I have to do regardless of whether I'm pregnant or not. *I* will be the one to decide what battles are too big for me and which aren't."

He frowned. "I get it. I don't like it. But I get it. And I'm sorry."

I believed that, and I was grateful for the apology. But it wasn't just him that I was upset with. I was fuming at the Witch who I'd given several thousand dollars to for working to find my son. Then she helped my husband lock me in the fucking basement when it came time to fight.

"And I'm pissed at Helena. That bitch owes me big. But I'm going to need her help."

"With what?"

"Training me," I said. "Only a Witch can teach me to fight a Witch. If she can't bind me, we'll find one that can. I can't be powerless again. Witch magic is different than Fae magic. I had a chance. I could use them a little. But I need to figure out how to block that cunt. At least partially. All I need is half of my abilities to stop her. And you need to do the same. I need you to be able to teleport when we get close to them. We need to be able to fight if we want to win."

He nodded gently. "Yeah. You're right."

I sipped my coffee. "We aren't ready. But we're going to get ready."

Jeremy's fingers twined between mine. He leaned forward to push hair from my face. "I know that what I did was stupid. Especially because no one knew where you were and if Brody would have gotten hit, I wouldn't have been able to let anyone know where you were. We could have all died and you would've been stuck there—"

"Actually, I was going to climb out the bathroom window," I said. "I'm going to have to pay to get that fixed."

"Of course you were. Very Beatles, *Abbey Road* of you."

I wanted to laugh, but I fought that urge. It was a good quip though; I'd give him that. The song even started playing in my head.

He chuckled. It dulled to silence after a moment, and his gaze met mine. His expression grew more serious. "But there was a reason I was so hell-bent on protecting you yesterday."

My head tilted in question. "What do you mean?"

"Before I woke up on the beach, I had this really weird dream." His gaze travelled downward. He creased his forehead in focus. "I was coughing up water in the sand, and I heard someone lecturing me. Telling me that if you lost the baby, I'd end up losing you, we wouldn't be able to save Micah, we'd both kill ourselves, and the cycle would repeat."

I arched a brow. "Who was it?"

"I..." He let out a huff. "I think it was me."

"You? What do you mean you?" I asked.

He shook his head. "I don't know. He looked exactly like me. His hair was shorter, but it was me."

"Like a premonition or something?" I asked.

"Maybe. I was asleep so that would make sense. I've never had one before. I guess it's possible though; stranger things have happened. But the weird thing was that he said, 'the cycle will repeat.'"

"What do you think he meant?" I asked.

"We don't know much about the par animos, but we do know that our souls are old. We know that we get reincarnated life after life after life because our souls can't die, right?" I nodded, and he continued, "What did Mary say before? You can't fight destiny, right?"

I paused, recalling for a moment. "Yeah. You can't elude destiny."

"What if Peterson isn't crazy?" he asked. I made a face, and he said, "Not that he isn't a psychopath, but what if he's right about the end of the world? What if we play some part in that? Maybe that's why the par animos are so important. Maybe we're here to prevent it."

The myths said a great war would come once the pairs united with their other halves. Maybe this was what it meant. Maybe some way, somehow, we were connected to the apocalypse in a more grotesque manner than Peterson had led us to believe.

"Nastya said something in that letter about Micah being so significant because of us being what we are," I said.

I thought for a moment. Then I turned my head to the side a bit and moved my hand to my stomach.

"What're you thinking?" Jeremy asked.

"Maybe Milly has a shred of destiny in all of this too," I muttered. "You said someone was healing me on the beach?"

"It wasn't whoever was in my dream though. He was wearing a T-shirt; whoever was healing you was in a hoody."

I scratched my head. "Maybe she's a part of whatever all this is. Peterson didn't want to take her, he said I 'needed this one.'"

He huffed. "I'm sick of destiny controlling our kids."

Hannah's phone began to ring on the table. I slid the answer button and put it on speaker. Before I could say hello, Leah yelled on the other end.

"Motherfucker, just calm down, dude! No one's going to hurt you —" A loud bang clattered.

"What's going on, Leah?" I stood from the table and pulled off my robe.

"Just get over here." She ended the call.

CHAPTER FIVE

JEREMY

Landing in the kitchen was like walking into a building located just outside a war zone. The room quaked, heat radiated from the floorboards beneath my feet, and the smell of smoke billowed into my nostrils. Outside, rain poured like we were in the eye of a hurricane. Lightning cracked and roared through the atmosphere, bright strikes of electric blue shining in through the windows.

Laila took off in a sprint to the basement. I trailed close behind. We bolted down the steps. Smoke floated past us, the smell of melted plastic burning down my throat. Leah was yelling as Adam tried to talk in a slow, comforting manner, but over both of them were loud, heart wrenching sobs.

As we made it to the landing, I noted Leah ducking close behind Kai. She insisted that everything was fine. The kid sat naked in the corner of the bed. It was sunken in, black and red with still burning embers. His dark blond hair was tucked against his knees. He rocked back and forth against the charred white wall.

"I just want to go home," he said between sobs, vigorously swaying into the wall before swaying outward again.

"What the hell happened?" Laila brushed past Leah and Kai to the bed.

"He woke up and started bloody screamin'," Kai said.

"We tried taking off the cuffs, but he burned the shit out of me," Adam said.

Laila grabbed a blanket from the corner that I'd brought down for her yesterday and turned to the bed. The kid was still sobbing, rocking back and forth.

She lowered herself to her knees in front of him. Her hand slowly reached out to touch his.

He continued to anxiously tremble. As their skin met, he ignited bright orange flames and pulled further into the corner. Her hand stayed on his, and the flames slowly receded.

"What's your name, kiddo?" she asked softly.

He shook his head against the back of his knees.

Laila turned to Leah, Kai, and Adam. "I got this, guys. Where are the keys?"

Adam tossed them to her and turned up the steps. "We'll be upstairs."

"Bring him down some clothes if you don't mind," Laila said.

Kai's eyes widened, flapping his lips together in a trill. Then he turned and walked past me. I chuckled. Leah rolled her eyes and started upstairs.

Once the basement door shut, Laila pushed hair behind the kid's ear. "What's your name, hon?"

He shook his head again.

She gave a nod. "That's okay. I didn't want to talk much when I got out either."

"What did you give me?" he whispered, another sob leaving his lips.

Laila met my gaze.

"I don't know what we had. Whatever we were able to get our hands on underground."

She turned back to the kid. "You might feel off for a few hours, but you'll be back to normal soon. I'm sorry this happened. We didn't know who else he was holding. We figured if he was using someone else like he was using Amy and Nastya, they might be able to help. I told my people to capture anyone that was in normal clothes. Then we saw your room and knew you were just as much a captive as I'd been."

"Just let me go," he said again. He still rocked, but his hands stopped quivering at her touch.

"As soon as you put some clothes on, you can go wherever you want. I'll even give you a lift." Laila gave a gentle smile. "But could you answer a few questions for me over breakfast first? I need all the help I can get."

He shook his head against his knees again. "I can't help you."

"You'd be amazed at how much a few—"

"You don't understand." He looked up for the first time and met her gaze. "I *can't* help you."

There was something oddly familiar about those eyes. I couldn't quite place it. It was one of those odd, 'I know you from somewhere, but I have no idea where,' kind of moments.

Familiar, and soft. Something in me immediately said to help him. To comfort him, to protect him.

He had warm, greenish brown eyes on pale skin. Loose, dark blond curls hung around his young cheeks. There was a thick black circle around his right eye. Blood vessels had popped through the whites. His lip was busted on the top left and bottom right, leaving small beads of blood trickling toward his chin. It was hard to make out much of his features behind the swelling but there was still that odd sensation of feeling like I knew him from somewhere.

And I couldn't help but notice that he didn't have the scars. They had him. He was their prisoner. Why didn't he have scars?

Laila tossed the blanket over his legs. "I helped you escape, ya know. You could help me out a little here."

He released an odd little huff of a laugh. A near smile pulled at his lips. It wasn't mischievous or condescending. It was... comfortable. Ironic, even, and so fucking familiar. I knew that smile—I knew that I did. But I couldn't place where from.

And that little chuckle. It... it wasn't the way most people in our world acted when they met Laila. Let alone when they told her no.

"We're on the same side here." He looked at Laila. Then he looked at me. "But nothing I know is going to help you find Micah or Chris. We all know there's a way to get to him. But you can't because you'll probably lose the baby if you do."

"What do you mean?" Laila asked.

It should have stuck out to me. It should have stuck out to both of us. It wouldn't though, not for another twenty-four years. Only then would I realize who that kid really was.

But only family knew she was pregnant.

He sighed, eyes shifting between hers for a moment. Then he looked at me and gazed sympathetically. "The same way you destroyed the first place. From the inside."

I furrowed my brows. "You want her to turn herself over to him?"

"I didn't say that."

I looked quizzically into the eye that wasn't swollen. "Where do I know you from?"

He looked back and forth between my eyes. A smile nearly came to his lips, but not quite. And if it were anyone else, I wouldn't have believed him. But something in me knew I had to trust that kid. "You don't."

"But you know us," Laila murmured

"Everyone knows you," he said. "Spend five minutes with Peterson. He doesn't shut the fuck up about you. Either of you."

"Then why are you afraid?" she asked.

"You killed, like, three hundred people yesterday," he said. "And I'm not giving you information that you want, so yeah, I'm a little scared."

"What did he want with you?" I turned my head to the side. "What are you?"

"Fae," Laila murmured. "It was raining pretty hard outside, the room was shaking, the bed was on fire. I can't get inside your head so you're a damn good telepath. What's weird, though, is that I can't feel your energy. But you're Elite, aren't you?"

The basement door opened. Adam brought down a stack of linens and handed them to me. "Thanks," I muttered as he started back upstairs.

The kid sighed again.

"They wanted to use you to neutralize me," Laila murmured. "The same way Kai neutralized you to keep the house from catching fire."

He looked at me. "Can I get those clothes?"

"Were you there?" she asked. "Yesterday, at the cliff. Were you there?"

The kid rubbed his good eye. "If I was, I don't remember it. They could only control me when I was unconscious."

"That's why you were strapped down and had to use a shit bucket," I said.

"I'm not a pleasant prisoner." He shrugged.

Laila smiled. "Neither was I."

"You're not going to let yourself get kidnapped again, are you?" I asked. "Because if you can keep Laila's powers from working—"

"Don't worry." The kid looked at me. "They won't be able to find me. It's safe where I'm going. Trust me. Those fuckers are never gonna touch me again."

I looked at Laila. If it were up to me, we'd keep the kid until we had Micah. He could dampen Laila's abilities, and they were already using him. But I knew Laila wasn't going to let us keep him. I could already hear her saying, "*He's been held captive by our enemy. We can't lock him up too. You don't understand what that does to someone after they've been stuck inside a box.*"

It was a useless battle I knew she'd win. There was no point in fighting it. Aside from that though, I wanted to him to be safe. And if he was sure where he was going would be, then okay.

I trusted that kid for whatever reason.

CHAPTER SIX

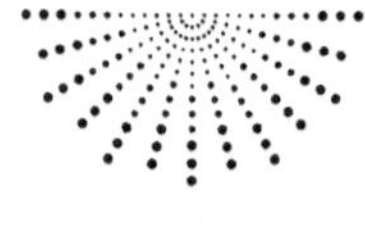

LAILA

"You just let him go?" Brody barked.

"We couldn't keep him," I said. "He didn't do anything wrong."

"He didn't tell us anything," Brody said. "We have nothing to go on."

"He wasn't going to tell us anything." I gave him the same tone he gave me. "And I wasn't going to torture information out of a kid. He was a victim in all of this too."

"We need leads," he persisted.

"We have the computer." Leah tugged her hair into a ponytail. "I got into it this morning. So far, all I have are torture documentation videos. But there's thousands of files on it. It's gonna take me some time to get through all of them."

"Anything he left on that computer he left intentionally," Jeremy said. "If it leads us anywhere, it's into a trap."

"Maybe," I said. "But we'll keep digging anyway."

Jeremy closed his eyes, rubbing his temples. "This is crazy. It's just like you said, this is a game. He knows how it all ends. We're chasing our tails for nothing."

I gazed at the countertop.

"We didn't find anything on our second walk through either," Adam murmured. "They knew we were coming. They cleared out anything of value."

"That's what I don't get." Hannah chewed her thumb nail. "If they knew we were coming, why didn't they move everyone out? Why didn't the guards at least run?"

"*They* didn't know we were coming," Leah said. "I read their minds. When you guys showed up at the door, that was their first knowledge of us being there."

"But why would he just give us his guards?" Hannah asked. "It doesn't make sense."

I thought back to the stress tests. I thought about the whip tearing my back to shreds. Then I heard his voice over the intercom telling me how beautiful my murder had been.

"Target practice," I said. "If he knew the future, then he knew I'd escape the first time. He let me kill off his people then too. Every accomplishment we've made in this was because he allowed it."

"Say that's so," Kai said from the breakfast nook beside Hannah. "He knows it all. To out whit him, ye ought to do what's not expected of ye."

"And what's that?"

"Maybe try running away from a battle instead of headfirst into it," Adam mumbled.

I rolled my eyes. "What you're saying is that to find my son, I should not try to find my son."

"I don't know." Adam rubbed his scruff. "I really have no idea. I don't have a clue what road we take next."

"Neither do I."

Jeremy ran his hand against his lips. "Well, we have to contact Tina. All those people are going to need some legal oversight."

"I want to talk to everyone first," I murmured. "Or at least spread the word to anyone who will be questioned. We weren't there yesterday. They don't know who let them out. They don't know what happened to the guards. They don't know anything."

"That's a given to most of them," Brody said. "Doesn't hurt to cover our bases though."

"Wonder what they're going to think when they see the door."

"Not our problem," Leah murmured.

I laid my head on the counter. Jeremy moved his hand gently over my back as I closed my eyes.

Everything else may have been shit, but that cool granite beneath my cheek was comforting. Relaxing. I'd have been far more relaxed if I could've killed those assholes yesterday, but I supposed I'd have to settle for a cool counter.

Brody cleared his throat behind me. "Since everyone's here, I want to tell you all something."

I smiled. At least there was something to be happy about.

I looked up from the counter and met his gaze. He shot me a nervous expression. The rest of the eyes turned to him. I knew what he was about to say, and I was glad for the lightener to the conversation.

"What's up?" Adam asked.

He ran his hand against his lips. "Do you all care if I bring someone to Christmas dinner?"

Hannah, Jeremy, and Leah creased their brows. A smile played at Kai and Adam's lips.

"Someone we know?" Leah asked.

"No, you don't know her."

"They're a her?" Hannah smirked.

Brody tried to fight the smile that came to his mouth. "Her name's Gwen."

"She's that second internship, huh?" Adam grinned.

"Do you finally have a girlfriend?" Jeremy met his brother's gaze with a grin.

"Kind of." He rubbed his mouth, laughing. "I don't know, we don't really have a title."

"Do you have a picture?" Adam asked.

"She doesn't like pictures," Brody muttered.

"Well, yeah, you have to bring her to dinner then," Leah said. "The more the merrier. Tell her to bring a bottle of wine. I can't wait to meet her."

"Sure. Of course, thanks. She can't wait to meet all of you guys too," he said with a smile. Then it fell. "Okay, so there's something you should probably know about her."

"God, she isn't human, is she?" Leah wrinkled her nose.

"I'm going to try to not be offended," Adam muttered, sitting at the bar stool beside me.

"No. Not human." He cleared his throat. Then his hand ran through his short black hair. "She's another breed, so to speak."

"What is she?" Jeremy asked.

"She's a wolf." He scratched his head. "But she's also a Vampire."

"Jesus," Adam said.

Leah shrugged. "Still better than a human."

CHAPTER SEVEN

JEREMY

As we drove down the icy gravel road, I struggled to focus on something that wasn't the deafening voice inside my head that was screaming like someone was stabbing it over and over and over.

This was useless. The past two years had been useless.

My brother was a living puppet. He unwillingly helped his captor create his prison and assisted in the emotional torment of his entire family. If we were still standing when the curtain shut on this shit show, which I doubted any of us would be, I didn't think he could live with what he'd done when that psychopath was wearing his body like a coat.

Micah was gone. He was going to die before we found him. Before I got to see him so much as take a breath. My son, along with anyone else who'd come into contact with my family in the past five years, was a pawn in this magnificent game of chess. Or perhaps, Micah was the King.

No, come to think of it, maybe he was the Queen. He was captured long ago, and the game was over. Yet, we were still chasing a goal some part of us knew we couldn't accomplish. Every day was a failure and there was nowhere left to go.

My beautiful, once gentle, and delicate wife, who should have been closer than ever to imploding, sat beside me. She gazed out the window in something of a serene daydream as we drove to her Mom's to pick up our dog like this was somehow normal. Like any of this was even close to okay.

There were dark circles beneath her eyes, maybe even a touch of redness, but also this insane level of calm that I couldn't begin to wrap my head around. There was no guilt to her eyes. There was no sadness. There was nothing.

She was okay. I'd watched her murder at least two-hundred and fifty people the day before, and she looked fine. Content. Maybe she wasn't but if so, she was a damn good actress.

The day prior, we'd lost our son once again. Then we released the only lead we had.

That's what made it harder than anything before. Losing her in March of 2019 was my biggest failure. But then I got her back. I got her back, and I pushed the thought of my dead son to the back burner. Then I learned he was more alive than either Laila or I had been in a very long time.

Peterson fooled me when he kidnapped my brother. He fooled us all. Shame on him. But then, he fooled us again. He had our son. Peterson had him in that fucking plane the moment that his mother blew the roof off of the building. He was right fucking there. And we proceeded to go on for more than another God damned year believing he was nothing more than a small rotting corpse. We wasted a fucking year.

Shame on us that time.

I was too concerned with my dying fiancé in the hospital bed to think about Brody running in a full sprint down the hallway to the sound of the fucking airplane that was carrying my child to the rainforests of Brazil.

That little, tiny room. That stupid fake window. That's where he was being carted off to. I'd only seen it for the first time and the very memory was doing something to my psyche.

"Baby." Laila's thumb coasted along the back of mine. Her other hand slid against my wrist as she looked for my gaze. "Are you alright?"

I shook my head. "No. Not really."

She moved our hands to her mouth. My knuckles touched her lips, and she squeezed her hand a little tighter around mine.

"Two years ago to the day, we were driving down this road. It looked a lot like it does now," she murmured. "There was a little more snow and a little less rain though. We were going to Mom's to have dinner and tell her I was pregnant with Micah. Do you remember that?"

I licked my lips, nodding.

"And we were so..." She gave a quiet laugh. "We were so fucking happy. I just got the life insurance money, and we were picking out paint colors for the apartment, remember?"

"I remember."

A faint laugh left her. She grew quiet for a moment. "That Laila would hate this Laila, don't you think?"

I glanced at her. "What do you mean?"

"The girl I was then." She looked back to the road. "The sweet, pathetic little dumbass that I was. Then you have the homicidal lunatic I am now." She laughed. "I don't know. Maybe in two more years, I'll be an even crazier bitch than I am now. Maybe Micah will be gone for good, and I will completely lose my shit. I don't think I can get any colder than the past two years have made me, but I never thought I could be this either. I guess anything's possible in our lives. But you know what else is possible?"

I turned to meet her gaze as we pulled into her mom's driveway. "What's that?"

"Maybe in two years, we'll be driving down this road with our two kids in the back seat," she murmured. "Micah will be almost four then. Milly will be going on two. And maybe instead of leaving your sister's house, we'll be leaving *our* house."

She blinked away tears as she smiled. "We'll stop at the store and grab some marshmallows and chocolate and graham crackers. Then we'll go home and light the fire in the living room. And we'll make hot chocolate. And you'll play your guitar while I read the kids a book. We'll all eat s'mores. Then the kids will go to bed, and we'll put the presents under the tree. And all of this will just be a painful part of our past we try really hard to forget ever happened. And we'll be happy."

I pressed my curling lip down beneath my teeth, and tears filled my eyes. It was a beautiful idea. One that I prayed would become a reality. But I'd prayed and prayed, and no gods listened. No one was going to help us bring our son home and make that Christmas fantasy a reality.

She forced a smile as tears dribbled down her fair cheeks. "We have to keep hoping that's how this ends."

"What if it isn't?" The water in my eyes overflowed and descended my face.

"I don't know. I wish I did but I—I don't. I don't know what we do if he's gone forever. But I know that we have to hold on for our daughter. She didn't choose to be born into this. We can't let her hurt like we're hurting."

I clenched my jaw to keep my lips from trembling.

"You aren't..." Laila looked between my eyes. "You aren't thinking about getting high, are you?"

I wiped my eye. "No more than usual. But you should know that. You were in my head, right? That's where that whole little speech came from?"

She chewed her lip. "I wasn't trying to invade your privacy."

"It's alright. I'd do the same in your shoes."

She turned her gaze to our hands. She cleared her throat as she wiped her cheek. "I am a great actress, by the way. Not because I want to be. Just because I have to be. If I didn't hold up this smoke screen of okay, if I let myself admit that everything might not end okay, then I'd lose my shit. I know that I should feel something for all those people I killed yesterday. But if I did, if I let myself really think about all those lives I ended, do you think I'd be able to keep going? Because I remember the guilt I felt when I first escaped. I killed a few dozen, maybe near a hundred that night. And that kind of killed me. What I did yesterday, all those people... If I *allowed* myself to feel it, I'm not sure I'd be able to allow myself to continue to live."

"I didn't mean it like that, Lai," I said quietly.

"It's okay." She cleared her throat. "I know who I am. I know what I've become. I've come to terms with it. Do you think you can?"

My gaze softened as I looked between her deep green eyes. Now, her expression was threaded with guilt. Not for the lives she'd taken but for how it made me see her. She didn't care about those people. Neither did I. But she did care about what I thought of her. She liked me seeing her as the person she used to be. The person she wished she still was. The person she could never be again.

I leaned forward and touched our lips together. My hand found her cheek as she opened her mouth against mine. I relaxed into the feel of her lips for a second before I pulled back and touched my forehead to hers.

"I know who you are too. And I love you," I whispered. "I love you so much."

"You don't care that I'm a murderer?" She gave an awkward grin.

I laughed and shook my head. "You say it like you wanted to do those things. No one has a heart bigger than yours, Lai. This isn't what you wanted. You could barely kill in self-defense until they took you. You aren't a sociopathic serial killer. You did what you had to. I know you; I know who you really are and I love you no matter what."

Her brows furrowed. She inched back. Her gaze shifted out the window. She pulled her hands away and cleared her throat again.

"What? What'd I do?"

"Nothing." Laila rubbed her mouth. "You're right. I didn't want to be this. I don't hate myself for what I've done any more or anything. Like you said, I did what I had to do."

"What is it then?" I tucked dark tendrils behind her ear.

She continued to gaze out the window. "I didn't know what he meant then. But the day that I met Peterson, I asked him why he was doing this. I—I didn't think about it until you said that but—Do you know what he said?"

"I don't," I murmured.

"A lot of things. Most of it's gibberish junk memory now. It was right before he put in my implants, so I was kind of a mess. I can't give you an exact quote."

I waited for her to go on.

"He gave me hints, you know? He told me what he was doing without *really* telling me. He said that I had to learn. I had to 'be ready.' And this is what he meant. He wanted me to become a monster. He wanted me to be jaded and murderous and… He said that the others he was holding captive, that they're part of the story too.

"He said that one day they'd be mine. I didn't know what he meant then, but I get it now. That's why he gave us the compound yesterday. His goal all along was to turn me into this. He didn't surrender them. He *gave* them to me. That's why they didn't need an airport. He was always going to give them over. He did it so the people we saved would be loyal to me."

My face screwed up as I thought for a moment. Then I remembered what he said from the zombie's lips the night of my bachelor party.

Sometimes to build an empire, you have to burn the village that once stood in its place.

This was the empire. The person she'd become. She was what he was building.

"He was building you an army," I murmured.

"He made himself the villain of my story so that I could be the hero," she said. "He said that they were a part of the story, but I was the center of it."

My hands trembled slightly. "He's from the future," I began quietly. "He… He created you an army. And he…" I cleared my throat, looking at the scars along her wrist. "He believes that the world's going to end."

Her breathing grew uneven. "And he built me an army."

CHAPTER EIGHT

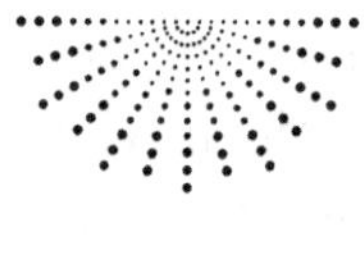

LAILA

I don't think Mom ever hugged me as tight as she did when I walked through that door. She wasn't just relieved, she was ecstatic. Her arms were like locks that wouldn't release. She squeezed so tight that I could barely breathe.

And for the first time, I understood. Because that was exactly how I planned to hold my children once I had them.

My thoughts ran in circles as she, Jeremy, and I had a cup of coffee. I couldn't bring myself to tell her what happened. Confessing to murder was hard. Confessing mass murder to my mother was harder. Especially when I didn't feel remorse for it.

After I finished my cup, I explained that we'd have to get going. We had to speak with Tina. We had to visit the survivors. And I needed to have a fucking word with Helena.

Following another long, emotionally trying hug, we took Tink back to the diner. Jeremy and I barely said a word to each other the whole way. Neither of us had a clue what to say or do next.

We had more information than we'd ever had before. But every shade of intel was laced with at least a hundred questions. Suddenly our list of a thousand unanswered questions became a million.

The real killer was that not one of those pieces of information led us to our son.

We weren't getting Micah back. Not that day, not the next or the day after that.

That dawning realization was devastating. But no more devastating than any day since I'd learned Micah was alive had been.

The grand total came to 493 people. Four-hundred and ninety-three people rescued on December 23rd, 2020. 224 in June of 2019. Together, that made 717 total lives I'd saved from this chaos.

In the video, Peterson said that I was patient 776. I could see the irony in Micah being patient 777 then. Still, I did that math. 777 minus 717 left 60 lives he had taken.

If our war was being fought by numbers, I would have won long ago. I killed hundreds more of his than he killed of mine. But there were only two lives in all of it that really mattered. Despite the five hundred people I'd saved the day before, he still held the only two that meant the most to me. That being said, he was the winner.

"Laila!" Liam's voice called as he jogged up beside me. His arms twisted around my shoulders in a physical pull from Jeremy whose fingers had been twined between mine. He squeezed my shoulder against his chest in a bear hug, gleaming with joy.

"Thank you, thank you, thank you. Thank you so much. I could kiss you, I'm so happy. I can't even put it into words. Thank you so much, Laila."

"How about you don't do that," Jeremy said. I pulled away and took a step closer to him.

Liam looked at Jeremy. "Right. Sorry."

Jeremy fought the urge to grit his teeth. "How's your brother?"

"He's great." He smiled wide and pushed up his glasses. "He's so good. He's happy and Emma can't stop crying. God, we're so grateful. To you, I mean. Not God."

My lips tugged up into a smile. "What's his name again?"

"Ben," he said. "Benny, but Ben. He'd be really embarrassed if you called him Benny. Do you have a minute? Could I introduce you?"

I forced a smile and gave a nod. "Yeah. Yeah, of course."

That was why I was there originally. To say hello to the people I'd saved.

"This room right here," Liam continued with a smile.

I followed close behind. No part of me wanted to be there after the realization I'd come to a few minutes prior. I was glad those people were home. But wasn't I the reason they were taken in the first place?

But I would say hi to Ben and Emma, then speak with my team. We'd brush up on what we'd all gathered and figure out how to go about explaining it to the masses.

As I turned into the large room the size of a school cafeteria, my stomach churned. Curtains and blue sheets hung as dividers between the areas. I expected Liam to reach for one of them, but then he spun to face me. A large, sweet grin came to his lips.

And all of the curtains simultaneously opened.

A room of nearly a thousand people turned to me with smiles a mile wide and yelled, "*Surprise!*"

The room of survivors and their families gaped up at me like I was some type of deity. They cheered like they were rooting for their favorite football team or musician. They clapped. They applauded. They smiled. They laughed.

My hand moved to my mouth, stomach spinning. Tears flooded my eyes.

"I'm going to be sick." I turned and rushed past Jeremy.

Maybe I should have been happy to see them. But all that I could think as we started down the hall was that Peterson trapped all of them with the intention of releasing them to me to pin himself a terrorist as a means to make me their hero. To tie us all together. Specifically, to tie them all to me.

Not only did it bring on a flashback of limbs flying through the air to the inside of my eyelids, but it made me feel like the villain. Stroking her own ego to her band of blind followers as if she hadn't done something awful behind closed doors.

I didn't care about those guards at the compound. I should have; they weren't the ones to blame when it was all said and done. But I cared about those people. I cared about them in a way that I cared for no one else. In many ways, they were the only people alive who could understand why I was the person I'd become.

But I was the *reason* this happened to them. I was the reason they had those scars. I was the reason people could see their brittle ribs beneath their pale flesh. We all were tortured for the purpose of becoming bound by our mutual traumas.

Jeremy caught the family restroom door with his foot as I made my way to the sink. I gripped it for stability. My breaths grew deep and labored. My shaking hands tried to steady themselves as my deep breaths turned to shallow pants.

Jeremy didn't say a word. He just put his hands around my waist and pulled my body into his. I cupped my palm over my face as my heavy pants turned to obnoxious sobs.

He didn't say it was okay. He didn't tell me it was going to get better. He just held me. He physically kept me on my feet when my entire body trembled. He let me muffle my cries into his shirt. He helped me to the ground when I couldn't stop hyperventilating.

He didn't lie and say things would get better. Neither of us were naïve enough to believe we had a happy ending any more. If we did have one, it wasn't on the horizon in the foreseeable future.

We tried hurting alone. It didn't work either. Even though it hurt to know we couldn't take each other's pain away, it was easier to hurt with someone who had a free shoulder to cry on.

It took a good twenty minutes before I was able to retain my composure. He kept holding me. He didn't let go. I think he may have cried too.

Then there was a quiet knock on the door. "Hey, Laila?" Emma's quiet voice said behind it. "I'm really sorry, I told Liam that was a bad idea. Especially after the last time. Are you okay?"

Jeremy leaned back and wiped my face with his thumbs. Then he whispered, "Do you want to go home? I can tell everyone you're having a bad morning sickness day."

I nodded quickly as tears started to roll from my eyes again.

He wiped my cheeks and kissed my forehead.

"Thank you," I murmured.

He forced a smile. "Just go relax, okay?"

A sad smile came to my lips as I wiped my crying eyes. "I love you."

"I love you too." He kissed my forehead once more.

CHAPTER NINE

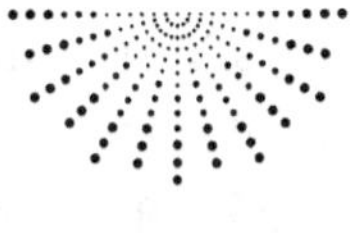

LAILA

When I got home, I sat on the couch and cried for about an hour. I had been okay. Then that massive realization set in and my composure came crumbling down.

But Tink helped. She always did when I cried. She hated seeing me in pain. She made me want to be happy. She licked the tears from my cheeks, she wagged her tail, and then she brought me a toy. Dogs and babies have this way of comforting that adult people aren't capable of. When I couldn't stop crying for myself, I'd stop crying for them.

I was just getting ready to go give Helena a piece of my mind when Jeremy came trotting up the steps with arms full of grocery bags.

"Oh, good, you're still up." He smiled and kicked the apartment door shut. He walked toward me, kissed my cheek, and extended a gray plastic bag. A huge grin played at his lips. "Go put this on."

"Jeremy, I'm not in the mood for some extravagant date right now. I need to go bitch Helena out before she cashes that two-thousand-dollar check."

"It isn't some extravagant date." He smiled. "They're pajamas."

"I'm not in the mood for lingerie either—"

"It isn't lingerie. They're footie pajamas." He laughed, holding his smile. "Helena isn't going anywhere. And you've had a hard day, you don't need more stress right now. You need a breather. And you can't have a cigarette, or a joint, or a drink. And this is the next best thing. So put your footie pajamas on, get your slippers, and let's go."

"Jeremy." I sighed.

"Laila." He smiled wider. "C'mon. You know you want to wear the footie pajamas. It's a unicorn, it matches your slippers."

"If they're footie pajamas, I don't really need slippers," I muttered.

He looked between my eyes, still smiling. "Just get dressed."

"Are you also wearing footie pajamas?"

"Mine's Iron Man." He grinned. I couldn't help the laugh that left my lips. His smile widened. "So that's a yes, right?"

Just another of the many reasons that I loved this man. He knew how heartbroken I was. And I knew that he was too. But he would do whatever it took to make me smile.

I snatched the bag.

***

"Your eyes are closed, right?" Jeremy moved his hands over them.

"Obviously I can't see with your hands on my eyes," I muttered.

He chuckled as we spun through the air. Just as he pulled his hands from my face, I took in the smell of kindling flames and moth balls. A smile came to my lips as I looked around the small cabin.

A fire crackled in the wood burner in the center of the room. Candles flickered throughout the cool space, casting dancing shadows on the old log walls. In front of the fireplace laid a pallet of blankets with a few pillows. Graham crackers, chocolate bars, and marshmallows were neatly positioned on a plate at the foot of them. A thermos sat beside it with a couple of ceramic mugs.

"I was thinking about what you said." Jeremy moved his hands around my waist from behind. He kissed my cheek and rested his head on my shoulder, voice soft and gentle. "About us doing this with our kids in a couple years. I know it's bittersweet. Everything that makes us happy is, and I know that isn't going to stop until we find our son."

I wiped a tear from the corner of my eye.

"But after you left the hospital earlier, I started talking to one of the doctors. Actually, he started talking to me," he said. I turned to face him and lifted my arms around his neck. A sad smile came to his lips. "I guess there's this chemical in our brains that we release when we're stressed. CHR? Or CRH? Something like that, I don't remember. Either way. He said that it's released when we're stressed but that it's also released during birth. It causes contractions. That's where the connection between stress and miscarriage come into play."

My voice was barely above a whisper. "Yeah, I read a study on that."

He summoned a sad smile. "I was trying to, but I know that I didn't help when I locked you in the basement. That just made you more stressed. I'm still really sorry about it."

I saw the point he was making, and I didn't disagree. This stress wasn't fair to Milly. But I couldn't just stop being stressed, not when my son was being held captive by those lunatics.

"It's okay," I said.

"No. No, it's not." He pushed hair from my face. "You need to be stress-free during this pregnancy."

I laughed quietly. "I don't think I'll ever be stress-free."

He touched the side of my neck. "Maybe not stress-free. But we need to put you under the least amount of stress possible."

I pulled away and lowered myself to the mound of blankets.

"Okay, I know our life sucks." Jeremy sat beside me. "It's been one shit storm after another for the past few years. Like you said when we got back together. We've been through a lot of shitty things, we're still going through a lot of shitty things, and we're probably going to go through more shitty things. I don't know if or when it's going to get better."

He lifted a blanket and raised it around our shoulders. I laid my head against his arm.

"We don't know what's going on with Micah. We don't know what's going on with Chris. And it hurts," he murmured. "It hurts a lot. And we're going to keep doing everything that we can. But right now, is there really anything that we can do?"

I wished he weren't, but he was right. We had no leads. We were back to square one. There was nowhere to look and nothing that could be done. It was awful, and that hurt, but it brought me back to his original question.

Was there anything we could do?

"I guess not," I muttered.

He was quiet for a few ticks. "I'm not giving up on anything or anyone. I love my son, and I want to bring him where he belongs. But I want our daughter to be okay too. We both do."

I nodded, watching a piece of burning wood fall from the log into the pile of ashes. Obviously, I wanted that too.

"So I was thinking. For the next six months until the baby comes, can we just be normal?" he asked quietly. "Can we just focus on being as close to happy as we can get?"

I turned up to meet his gaze. "If we find something that's going to lead us to our son—"

"I know," he agreed. "I know that if we have a clear shot, we have to take it. But we don't have any leads. We have nothing to chase. We don't have anything close to a clear shot."

Wasn't wrong there either.

I picked a marshmallow from the plate and popped it into my mouth.

"The moment we do, we'll go all in. Absolutely. But in the meantime, we have to focus on the things that we can control." His hand moved to my belly and his gaze found mine. "This baby. This house. The life we're creating for our family. We aren't replacing Micah, but we love Milly too. And the stress the past few days have put on you isn't healthy and it's not fair to her."

I looked down. Then I moved my hand over his on my stomach and nodded. "I wish I could say that you're wrong," I murmured. "But yeah. You're right."

"I wish I was wrong too." He pushed hair behind my ear.

"Every time we get information, any realization we come to...

Even the solid leads, all they do is leave us with more questions." I looked down at our hands on my belly. "And it hurts. It hurts so much."

Part of me wished I wouldn't have realized why he did all of it because I wanted to be happy when I visited the survivors. But I just...

"Peterson knows the story. He knows how it ends. And he hasn't been wrong yet. The only thing he did lie about was Micah being alive." I rubbed my mouth and closed my eyes. "He said that our epic battle was still in the distance. Obviously he was right because we lost. I can't beat Nastya yet. I can't bring him home because I'm not strong enough. I will be but I'm not. Not right now." I paused, chewing my inner lip. "I have to train. I have to be ready to take her on. So do you. We both have to be prepared. We have to learn to use our powers through whatever the hell the bitch is doing to suppress them. And we will," I said. "But we have to train first."

After a moment, Jeremy said, "Yeah, we do."

But there was one stone still lying face down. There was one shred of information we had that may or may not have helped us find our son. But at the very least, may have given us a better look into the bigger picture.

I turned up to meet his gaze. "But there's something else I want to do."

"What's that?" he asked.

"That dream you had. When you told yourself the cycle will repeat." He nodded, and I said, "I want to access memories from our past lives. I want to figure out what our fate looks like. We need to know what we did wrong in our past lives so we can fix it in this one. I've heard about spells to access those memories. I know they're hard, but if Helena's strong enough to trap me in the basement, she's strong enough to cast the spell."

"Yeah, maybe. We'll talk to her about it."

I dropped my head back onto his shoulder. "It feels selfish though. Trying to be happy and everything."

He kissed my forehead before he rested his head atop mine. His arm curled around my waist until it met the other at my belly. "Yeah.

In a way. But at the same time, it's kind of selfless too. It's for our daughter."

I nuzzled my head into his shoulder. "I guess."

He kissed my hair. "I want to give you one of your presents early, but I think it's going to make you cry so I'm not sure if you want it right now."

That was a good change in subject.

I smiled and tilted my gaze up to him. "What is it?"

He laughed. A small white box appeared in his hand.

"Aww, babe." My nose curled slightly. "Jewelry?"

I loved my husband. He was the sweetest, most loving, adoring man I could dream to marry. But he couldn't choose jewelry to save his life.

He rolled his eyes. "Don't worry, your sister picked it out."

"Which one?"

"Jenna."

"Oh, good. It'll be pretty." I smiled.

He chuckled. "Just open it."

I flipped up the lid to the little box. Inside was a silver pendant the size of a nickel. It was engraved with an intricate mandala and a small, single pearl in the middle.

"It's beautiful, baby. Thank you." I smiled and lifted it from the box.

"Open it up." He looked down at it in my hands. "It's a locket."

"Really?" I pulled it from the cardboard backing. He nodded as I found the clasp on the side.

Then I flipped it open. Tears formed in my eyes. Milly's ultrasound on the left and a miniature version of a picture Lydia sketched of Micah on the right.

"I made sure to get the one with the fake pearl, by the way. It's white gold though because I know how you get reactions to cheap metals," Jeremy said as I looked between the images. "I got you some other stuff too, but this was the big one. What do you think? Do you like it?"

I smiled. "I love it. Can you help me put it on?"

He smiled back, extending his palm. I handed it over and turned my back toward him. I pulled my hair to the side. He brought it around my throat and clasped it into place. He kissed the side of my neck and put his arms around my waist.

"I love you," he murmured at my ear and rested his chin on my shoulder.

"I love you too." I leaned my head into him. My gaze stayed steady on the fire as I took in a slow, deep breath.

"I'm sorry our lives are the way they are," he said quietly. "I wish things were different. But maybe one day, they will be."

I watched the flames lick the logs in the stone fireplace. "Maybe one day. But I guess this isn't so bad for now."

He moved his hand to mine. "For now."

Peterson had a catchphrase, and so did we. For now.

CHAPTER TEN

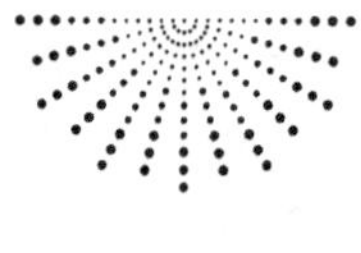

JEREMY

The rest of our evening in front of the fire was relatively quiet. Both of us tried as hard as we could to be in the moment, but it hurt. Everything hurt. It was fair to say we both felt like failures as parents.

When they say there isn't a how-to-parent book, they really aren't kidding. It's a little more complicated when you and your partner are soulmates, have a shit ton of supernatural abilities, and even more emotional baggage. It's harder to be a good parent when your first child is being held captive by a mad man who plans to execute him in order to bring on the end of the world. Add a second baby to the mix, and suddenly it's any parent's worst nightmare.

It felt arbitrary to even call myself that. I hadn't had the opportunity to be a parent yet. I wanted it more than anything which is why it all hurt so bad.

But I couldn't do anything. I tried to protect her when she was pregnant with Micah and it didn't help then either.

At that time, all that we could do was focus on Milly. It felt so fucked up to push Micah from our minds, but the pain wasn't helping anyone.

And he was with Chris. He wasn't alone. He had my brother. Family was as important to him as it was to me. I knew he would do everything he could for my son until I could. From what Laila told him, he knew that we were out there looking for them.

She said before that he wanted us to be happy. We didn't want to be. We couldn't *really* be. But we had to try.

We fell asleep curled in each other's arms on that mound of pillows and blankets. When we woke up, the sun shined in through the thin windows. I lay there for a moment and tried to imagine what it'd look like once the house was built. An article I'd read online said that a team of five workers could build a specialty home in three months if they did it right.

I was planning on waiting until after the New Year to start construction, but I needed to keep busy. If I could convince Wyatt, Adam, Brody, and Kai to help me, we could be moving in around Laila's birthday. What took a group of humans a month might take half the time for us. We'd still have to get plumbers and electricians and HVAC in, but if we worked quick, it was possible.

Laila needed something to distract her too. She wanted a room for each of the kids. If I could get the house built fast so she could start decorating, maybe she'd be a little more apt to stay away from things that could kill her. Admittedly doubtful, but possible.

"Merry Christmas, Lai." Leah handed Laila and I a large rectangle. "It's a picture collage so be careful with it. It won't fit in your apartment, but I figure you guys could put it up when you move into the new house."

"Aww, thanks." Laila smiled, looking over the photos. There was one of Tink, a few of her and me, and some group shots of all the siblings. "I wish I could hang it up now."

"Who'd you guys get?" Leah asked.

This was our tradition every year. Secret Santa. There were just too damn many of us to buy everyone a gift. Doing it this way made it possible for everyone to get one nice present they really liked rather than a bunch of shit that'd get thrown in a junk drawer.

And it was easier on everyone's wallets.

"I had Hannah. I got her a Victoria's Secret gift card and a bag of weed. Who'd you have, baby?" Laila ran her hand along my shoulder.

I sipped my coffee. "Adam. I got him a new flask. It's engraved with his name and has some fancy little collapsible shot glass that folds up on the back."

"Hey, Jeremy," Celena said behind me. I stood from my perch on the couch to meet her gaze. She extended a small white gift bag out to me. "I got you."

"Oh, cool. Thanks." I took the bag. I pulled the tissue paper out, a gift card to Guitar Center, and a pair of black boxers. I furrowed my brows before I realized they were covered in small pictures of Laila's face. I laughed. Laila cackled and reached up to high five her sister.

"She got me a pair too," Wyatt grumbled as he walked by. "With her face, I mean. Not Laila's."

"That's the best thing I've ever seen." Laila laughed, and Celena chuckled. "I love you so much right now."

"Thanks." I laughed. "Really weird gift, but thanks."

She smiled for a second. "One other thing though. Sorry for this, Lai."

I turned my head to the side a bit. Then she raised her fist and slammed it into my jaw. She may have been tiny, but she punched like an MMA fighter. As a Werewolf, that made sense.

Stumbling backward, I gripped the couch for stability. My hand went to my bleeding lip, stars appearing through my vision.

I didn't need to ask why she punched me. No one had said anything to me yet about locking Laila in the basement, and I knew it was coming. Tensions were still high the days before. Now that the dust was settling, I knew that somebody was going to punch me in the face. I wasn't particularly surprised that it was Celena either.

"Ow, bitch," Laila said, standing with furrowed brows. "What was that for?"

"You locked my sister in a basement and told us all that she chose to stay behind," Celena snapped. "Wyatt almost died out there. So did you, Kai, and Hannah. Leah did die. I get wanting to protect your wife, and I applaud you for that, but we both know that was some shady shit you pulled, Jeremy."

The room fell silent.

I blew out a slow, steady breath.

"Almost everyone we all care about nearly died because of what you did. If they would have, that blood would have been on your hands. And your dumb ass wouldn't even be alive to be pissed at.

"So moral of the story here is: if you're going to ask for my help on a suicide mission again, don't fucking lie to me about any part of it. I don't appreciate being lied to. I also don't appreciate the fact that you think it's okay to lock my sister in a cage like Joe Goldberg or something. I get why you did it, but it doesn't make it any more acceptable. Don't pull some shit like that again, dude."

Didn't appreciate the *You* reference; I wasn't a psychopathic killer. While I did lock my wife in a box, and I had killed a fair amount of people to protect her, it... Okay, there were some parallels, but it wasn't the same.

"You're right." I wiped blood from the corner of my lip. "It was a dumb move. And I'm sorry. Laila and I already talked about it, but I didn't get the chance to apologize to you guys. So I'm sorry. That wasn't cool, and I am truly, genuinely sorry."

Celena crossed her arms against her chest.

I looked around the room at my brothers and sisters. Rachel sat in an armchair with her lips pursed. Jenna was on Adam's lap with a glare my way.

"If anybody else wants to punch me, you're welcome to. I know what I did was fucked up. I know how it sounds when I say that I locked my wife in the basement, but I was terrified of losing another baby. I was terrified of losing my world again. But it doesn't excuse the fact that I put all of you in jeopardy, and I'm sorry. So, go ahead and hit me if you want to and let's move on."

"How about no one hits him because that really fucking hurt me too." Laila reached up to grab my face. She held her hand over my bleeding lip and sent white light into my skin. "And let's move on either way."

CHAPTER ELEVEN

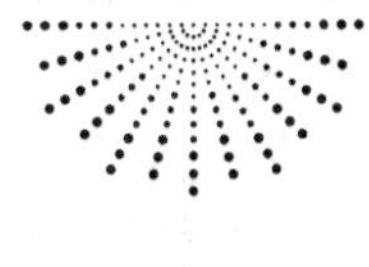

LAILA

I looked up at the twinkling stars in the sky, watching the snowflakes drift to the barren treetops ahead in the bluish light of the moon. My warm, fleece jacket caressed my bare arms. I heated my hands and rubbed them against my biceps.

Then I lifted my hot chocolate from the step below me. I took a sip and let the warmth settle in the pit of my stomach.

I wondered if Micah knew what chocolate tasted like. I wished that he did. But then again, maybe I wished that he didn't. Then I could be with him when he tasted it for the first time.

Maybe next Christmas, he and I would be sitting on this step together. Maybe I'd be holding him in my lap and letting him sip mine.

Or maybe I wouldn't.

I took another gulp.

"Hey, you." Jenna lowered herself to the porch step beside me. "Aren't you cold out here?"

I shook my head, giving a soft smile. "I raised my body temperature a few degrees, I'm alright."

She put her arms around me and grinned. "Damn, no wonder Jeremy calls you his personal heater."

I smiled and laid my head on hers.

"Are you okay?" she murmured. "Adam gave me a general synopsis of what happened down there. Do you need someone to talk to?"

"I'm okay. Just another day in the life these days."

"Killing a few hundred people is just a day in the life?"

A lump formed in my throat as I pulled away. I cleared it and ran my hands along my thighs. "Those weren't good people, Jenna. They were all taking part in a horrible scheme to torture almost a thousand people. Including me and my son and my brother-in-law."

She looked me over. Her gaze felt like a thousand knives dipped in shame before they pierced my skin. "You protested sending troops to Iraq. You made Mom take you to a rally to abolish the death penalty in freshman year."

I closed my eyes. She didn't understand. Can't say that I blamed her. If our shoes were swapped, I'd probably feel the same way.

"I know who I used to be, Jenna. I know what I stood for once upon a time. I know how soft and dainty and gentle I was once. That's not the sort of thing you forget. And yeah, part of me wishes I wouldn't have become the person I am. But over seven-hundred people that have been being held captive for months or years are free now because of what I did. A lot of people died. That blood's on my hands, and I'll take full responsibility for it. I'll carry that weight. But do you have any idea how much lighter it is than carrying that seven-hundred who deserved to be free?"

She frowned. "I get it. I never said that I didn't. But I'm worried about you, Lai. Adam told me how you jumped off a cliff and almost killed yourself—"

"Okay, now that's completely out of context. There was a Witch chasing me with some weird acid smoke that melted the skin off of my arm. Neither me or Jeremy could teleport, and it was our only way out. I wasn't trying to kill myself; I was trying to stay alive."

Jenna gave a careful nod, eyes looking between mine. "That's why Jeremy locked you in the basement?"

"Look, I could have gotten out. I put a good-sized hole in the bathroom window before Brody came to grab me. Not like that makes it okay but—"

"He wasn't wrong, Laila," she muttered. "I get that from a partner's perspective, it wasn't exactly the right thing to do. But I agree with Jeremy. Does it scare me that he knew how and figured out a way to go about doing it? Definitely. But this family's weird. I'd call it tough love before I called it controlling. He loves you, and he did the same thing that I would have done in his situation.

"You didn't see what it did to the kid when you disappeared last time. He went through hell. And you're pregnant with his kid. He already lost the first, and he's terrified of losing another. I don't blame him. I agreed that you should've stayed home in the first place, and I still do."

My sister. My bitchy, annoying big sister. Loved her with my whole heart, but I was so glad I had Celena in that moment. She had my back over anyone else. And hell, she was friends with Jeremy, but even she had my back in this. Because she knew what I was capable of, and she trusted me. Celena looked up to me. Jenna looked down on me. I supposed birth order played a part in that, but it still pissed me off.

Although, Jen had never seen me in action. Celena knew firsthand that I was beyond capable of caring for myself.

"Well, too bad it isn't up to you."

Jenna huffed. "Yeah. Too bad."

I cleared my throat and turned away. "Is that why you came out here? To tell me you think my husband had the right to lock me up and get himself and half of the people I love killed?"

She rolled her eyes. "Actually, I came out here to tell you the apple pie's almost cool enough to cut."

"Great." I stood and started toward the house.

"And something else," Jenna called behind me.

I turned. "What's that?"

She cleared her throat before pressing her lips together. "I wanted to tell you first. No one, and I mean *no one,* else knows."

I cocked my head to the side.

She looked between my eyes. Her hand lifted to her belly. "You're not the only one having a baby."

My mouth fell open. A smile came to my lips, and I stepped back toward her.

Jenna was having a baby.

"Does Adam know?"

She smiled, shaking her head. "Not yet. I just got my blood tests back from the doctor yesterday."

This was gonna be great. She was a school nurse, she had a steady income, and I knew she'd be an awesome mom. Had it not been for the fact that I was already pregnant, I would have had a giant green monster on my shoulder. But I was happy for her.

My lips pulled higher. I wrapped my arms around her. I squeezed her tight as she moved her arms around my back. "How far along are you?"

"They said barely four weeks. I guess I track my cycle really well. I don't know." She laughed. "You aren't mad, are you? Because I wasn't trying to steal your thunder or anything. It wasn't close to being planned."

"No." I smiled. "Not at all, Jen. We get to be pregnant together. Our kids are only going to be a few months apart. This is amazing."

She laughed. "What do you think Adam's going to say?"

"Probably 'holy shit.'" I grinned. "Then ramble for hours about money and how he needs to get a job."

She gave a nod. "Probably. He does though."

"Yeah, he really does." I held my smile. "But this is great. Just as my baby grows out of stuff, I can pass it down to you. It's perfect."

"Hey, are you guys coming in?" Hannah said from the glass door. "Leah's about to cut the pie, and everyone's already getting their plates ready. Oh, and I think Brody wants to introduce you to his girlfriend, Lai. She's super shy, but she really wants to meet you."

"Oh, sure." I turned and started to the door. "Gwen, right?"

"She introduced herself as Gwendolyn. But she seems really awkward. I think she got anxious and meant to say Gwen, but it came out Gwendolyn. Leah said she thinks we all hate her because of the whole Vampire thing so she's kind of freaked out but she's acting like she's not. I don't know. Seems nice though. I like her."

She didn't need to be nervous. I had no beef with vamps. The only ones I did have a problem with were ones that ended up with a blade through their heart not long after. I didn't innately hate anyone based purely on what they were.

I laughed as Jenna started in behind me. Hannah held the door. Jenna and I kicked wet snow off on the doormat. Laughter billowed from the dining room while Christmas carols played on a speaker in the living room. The smell of apple pie and honey baked ham filled my nostrils, and a smile came to my lips.

The sister I'd grown up with walked to my left and my younger sister-in-law to my right. My brother and sister, who I didn't know existed three Christmases before, sat across from each other at the large dining table sipping wine. Mine and Celena's mom sat side by side with grins as they gulped their eggnog.

My husband stood near the window with his brothers and their childhood friend, smiling and eating cold pumpkin pie. He shot me a sweet grin as I walked into the room.

I smiled back before my gaze traveled to the end of the table. My other sister-in-law stood there with the girl who coached me through the birth of my son. Leah laughed, plopping a dollop of whipped cream onto Haley's nose. Her mouth dropped, grinning. Then she leaned forward to kiss her. Leah backed away laughing, and Haley chased her with a spoonful of whipped cream.

I smiled as I took it all in. We were a good family when our life wasn't in shambles. Micah deserved to see it. He deserved to grow up surrounded by all of this love and family. He deserved normalcy.

Only two people in this room were human. But this was normal. This was love. This was what kids needed to see. Not four walls and a shrine to the mother they never met.

"Hey, you," Jeremy murmured as I reached onto the tips of my toes to kiss him.

"Hey." I smiled and circled a hand around his waist. My gaze turned to Brody. "So where's this girlfriend of yours?"

"She went to the bathroom." He glanced down the hall.

"They do that?"

He made a face. "Yeah, Laila. If *they* eat normal food, it's got to go somewhere."

"Right," I muttered. "Sorry, we're not all as familiar with the Vampire anatomy as you are."

"Just be nice, please?" His gaze was practically pleading. "Please? She's really nervous."

"I'm always nice."

"That is not true." Adam laughed and sipped his beer.

"In all fairness, you did hold a knife to her throat when we started dating," Jeremy said. "She isn't really obligated to be nice to your girlfriend."

"I'll be nice, guys, relax. I'm actually pretty excited to meet her. She's old as hell; I'm sure she's seen a lot of shit."

"That's not exactly being nice." Brody gave me a disapproving look.

"No, that's all right," a soft voice said behind me. "I'm old. Just a fact of life when you are what I am."

I turned with a smile to see the first girlfriend of Brody's I'd ever met. Gwen was absolutely stunning. She was so, *so* very far out of Brody's league. Her blond hair was cropped just below her shoulders to lay in soft, beachy curls. She had some of the softest blue eyes I'd ever seen. They were a pale, almost crystal color with hues of nearly whitish gray throughout them.

She had narrow shoulders and small, petite hips. For a born Werewolf, she was incredibly tiny. Even her bust was small. She stood a few inches shorter than me, near Hannah's height around five foot tall.

"It's nice to meet you. I'm Laila." I shook her hand.

"Gwen." She smiled. "We met once. Not really, but you opened my door. If that counts."

"I'm sorry, I don't remember. There were so many people that night."

"That's okay." Her plump lips pulled upward in a smile. "But thank you. For all of the risks you took and everything that you sacrificed to help us. I'll forever be in your debt, Laila."

No one was in my debt. I wanted to say that, but I wasn't quite ready to come out with a statement. I just didn't want people thinking of me as the hero Peterson forced me into becoming.

Maybe I was that. A hero, a savior, whatever the hell they considered me. But I'd only done what I had because it was the right thing to do. Not because I wanted anyone in my debt.

I forced a smile and cleared my throat. "I'm glad that you have your life back. But it's Christmas, you know? Let's just try to enjoy ourselves today. We don't need to think about all of that right now."

"Of course. Of course, I'm sorry."

"No, don't apologize," I said. "It's just such a beautiful night. Let's swap horror stories tomorrow."

A quiet laugh left her. "Sure."

Jeremy was right. We had to breathe. We had to try to focus on the good things. When a lead came, we'd chase it. But in the meantime, we needed to be as happy as we could be.

Milly didn't deserve the stress I was under during Micah's pregnancy.

CHAPTER TWELVE

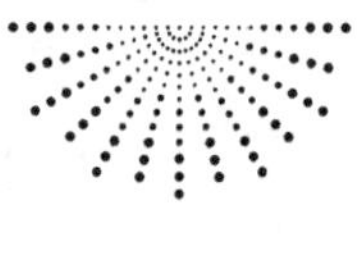

JEREMY

"Tina?" Laila said into a burner phone as I pulled on a pair of roomy sweatpants. "Yeah. It's Laila. Look, I have some good news for you. But I have no idea how to go about the legalities."

I pulled a T-shirt over my shoulders and sat beside her on the bed. She laughed, giving a nod. "Yeah, I guess it kind of is. Sorry you can't unwrap it, but I think it'll make you pretty happy either way."

I smiled as I watched her speak. "I hand delivered an envelope to your mailbox. It has GPS coordinates to the secondary location Peterson was keeping the other prisoners at. They've all been moved to a few private hospitals in the area. No other government agency has been informed so you're breaking ground on this one."

Tina's voice bounced through the speakers, but not well enough for me to make out what she was saying. "No. Micah and Chris weren't there. But five-hundred others were. Once you get everyone's transportation home sorted out and whatever interviews you guys need to conduct finished, you and I can meet up to go over the details."

There was a long pause as I leaned my head against her shoulder. "No, no casualties on our end. Quite a bit on theirs though. But no bodies left to question. You know my people aren't going to tell you how they got out either. But I know you have to do what you have to do. Better you than someone else.

"Yeah, Merry Christmas to you too. I hope you sleep better after this." A pained smile came to her lips. "Yeah. Yeah, maybe. I hope. But I've got to go. Good luck. Let me know if you need anything."

She pulled the phone from her ear and clicked the end call button. Slow breaths fell in and out of her chest. She dropped the phone to the bed beside her. I moved my hands around her waist. She pressed her quivering lips to a line. In a desperate attempt to keep it together, she moved her head to my chest and blew out a slow, shaking breath.

"We're starting the foundation on the house tomorrow." I kissed her hair. "Just digging the footing but it's a start. I talked to Adam and Wyatt about helping me work. I told them we'd pay them. Celena said she could use the cash too, and she was really offended that I didn't think to ask her."

She chuckled. "That sounds good, baby."

"Once we get the foundation finished, it'll be pretty smooth sailing from there. I'm shooting to have it done by your birthday. Or maybe mine at the latest. That way we can get moved in before the baby comes."

"That'd be nice." She fiddled with a string on her pants. "I think I want to give birth at home. It'd be nice if we weren't above the diner for that."

I smiled and pushed hair behind her ear. "Really?"

"Unless something's wrong." She turned up to meet my gaze. "Yeah, I'd like to be at home. I can't go to a regular hospital considering what happened with the light when I gave birth to Micah. Might be kind of tough to explain to a gyno if it happens again."

I laughed as she went on.

"And I did it without drugs before. I'd like to do it that way again. Hospitals make me nervous. Home seems like a better option. By the way, I was thinking about that bathroom conversation we were having. And I want a shower and a tub. I know it's kind of frivolous, but it'll come in handy with the kids. And I really want a big bathtub. Like the one that was in that hotel when we spent the night in Hawaii. You remember that, right?"

I smiled. "Yeah, I do."

That had been a nice little trip. Come to think of it, I wondered if Micah was conceived in that tub.

She rested her head back to my chest. "It'd be great if we could have it done before she's born."

I nodded, tightening my arms around her waist.

"I was thinking about bumping Max up to manager," she murmured.

"You want to stop working?" I asked.

"Not entirely. I'll still do some management. But I think I want a break."

"You love working though," I whispered.

I thought it was a bad idea. If she didn't have work, I didn't know what she'd focus on. That was her escape from reality, and I was concerned she'd fall into some nasty depression without it.

"Yeah, I guess. Sometimes. But I've intentionally drowned myself in it. And that was okay when I was single, and we didn't have a baby on the way. But I have a lot going on right now. Max does way more than he should already. I might as well just give him the title and pitch in when help's needed. And Adam needs a job. He's a good cook. I was thinking about offering him Max's."

"That might be a good idea." I gave a nod.

"I want to be able to give her my complete attention when she's born." She turned to her stomach. "And I want to help build the house too. I can use telekinesis to help you guys move heavy stuff, and I can use air to make sure no one gets hurt while they're on ladders and whatnot."

Still wasn't crazy about her working less for her mental state, but maybe building the house would have been a good distraction for her.

"I don't want to do anything to risk losing this baby," she whispered at my chest. "I want to train and perfect my abilities until she's born. Then I want to be a great mom. I might go back to work after a while, but I want to focus on her first."

68

My lips pulled into a smile as I tightened my arms around her. That was better. Working on the house may not have given her the break she needed but working on her abilities would. It'd give her a sense of pride and confidence that would hopefully help us find our son.

"You will be. A great mom, I mean."

She laughed quietly. "I really hope so."

I smiled, kissed her hair, and tightened my arms around her. She would be. She'd be the best mom in existence. In my entirely subjective view, of course.

In a manner of speaking, that was Laila's way of saying she was going to listen to me this time. Of course, she couldn't use those words. That would mean that I was right. Even if we both knew that I was, she couldn't say it aloud. But I didn't care. Being right didn't matter to me. All that mattered was keeping them safe.

CHAPTER THIRTEEN

LAILA

The next morning, Jeremy and I went about our normal routine. He took Tink outside, I fed her and made breakfast, and he poured our coffees. Then we sat at the table and ate. Afterward, he stepped into his work boots, some crappy clothes and headed to the hardware store. When he left, I put on some make up and got dressed.

Then I went to Verizon and got Jeremy and me new phones. It was about time I put him onto my plan anyway. I called Max and told him I wanted to talk to him in person before we opened up after the holidays. We agreed to meet up on Monday.

When I got home, I put away the Christmas tree. That was tough. Another year going by where I didn't share Christmas with my son. But I tried to keep it together. I only cried for about five minutes.

Then I teleported to Helena's.

I always loved her house. It was a Victorian masterpiece just outside of Burlington, Vermont. I'm sure it was a bright shade of white or maybe even blue once. But she'd painted it a soft lavender and trimmed it in deep purple. It stood out like a drag queen in a church on the small suburban street.

As I approached the doorstep, I told myself I shouldn't be too hard on her. It was a little hypocritical to be so angry with Helena when I'd been smiling and laughing with Jeremy who'd asked her to do it in the first place.

The thing about it that made my blood boil wasn't the fact that she did it. It was the fact that she had nothing to gain by doing so. Jeremy got to keep his wife and unborn child safe. Helena didn't love me nor my child.

Jeremy was only away from the hospital for an hour or so. That meant it took her a matter of minutes to make the decision to betray me. The trust between us was broken. Whether she thought she was doing the right thing or not, she went against me.

If she'd go behind my back to lock me in a cage for my husband with no thought or deliberation of how I would react, who else would she lock me up for? What would she do if Peterson threatened her life in exchange for information on me? Which lines were she willing to cross?

Jenna was right; I was a different person than I used to be. I was furious all the time. Even when my breaths were even and I had a smile pasted across my lips, I was still flaming inside. Most of the time, I kept it at bay. I remained calm. I pretended like I didn't want to burn everything to the ground.

But if I put my faith in someone and they betrayed it, I had to make it clear where my line in the sand was from there on out.

My fingers wrapped around the large metal knocker on the purple door and tapped it three times. I heard her saunter toward the door. The light even shifted through the windows as she looked out the peep hole.

Then she turned away.

"I see you, Helena," I called. "Open the god damned door."

"Only if you promise you aren't going to kill me." She peeked through the glass.

"I will if you don't open the fucking door." I leaned down to look at her through the etched window. "We need to talk."

"Alright, but I have cameras in here. I'm just warning you. If you kill me, video of it will be in the cloud," she said.

I rolled my eyes. The deadbolt clicked into the wood. The chain lock rattled as she pulled the door open to meet my gaze. She side stepped.

After I walked inside, she pushed the door shut behind me. "Alright, I know you're mad. I get it, putting a spell on you wasn't a good way to—"

I grasped her by her throat and pushed her into the wall beside the door. Her eyes grew wide. She gasped for air, and my hand got hot. The smell of burned flesh stung my nostrils as I stared into her brown gaze.

"You had no right." My eyes began to glow in their sockets as my gaze shifted between hers. I released her throat slightly to let her breathe. "You aren't my husband or my parent. You don't get to make decisions for me. You're my employee. I don't want your input and I certainly don't want your interference."

"You said." She gasped and pulled at my hand. "You wouldn't kill me."

"I'm not killing you. I'm warning you, Helena." I pressed my teeth together and stared her down. "I told you I didn't care about a price tag as long as you helped me bring my son home. You took my money. Then you locked me in a cage. While I was locked in there, everyone almost died. Leah, Jeremy, Wyatt, Kai, Hannah. They were almost blown to pieces. They were down to one healer until I got there. Because of you. Believe me when I say that if they would have died, you would be taking your last breath right now."

Her neck swelled beneath my hand with a swallow.

"All that I expected you to do was stick to your word. Help me find my son. How is locking me in a torture chamber helping me find my son?" I held her petrified gaze. When she didn't respond, I let my hand get hotter against her skin. "How was that going to help me find my son, Helena?"

"It wasn't." Her eyes stung with tears.

I let my hand cool against her neck.

"How can I trust you after this?" I asked, eyes brightening. "Jeremy's not so scary. Who else would you be willing to lock me up for?"

All she managed out was, "I'm sorry, Laila."

"I know that I'm generally a pretty nice person. But stand between me and what I have to do, and I'll have no remorse for taking your life. If you weren't a family friend, I probably would have killed you already. But this is the only warning I'll give you, Helena. Don't fuck with me again."

She nodded, eyes terrified.

White light radiated from my hand, and I squeezed her throat harder, giving her one more good 'fuck you' before I healed her. My glowing palm pinned her to the wall as she fought against the pain. I didn't want to hear her screams, so I squeezed tight enough to shut her up as the skin healed. Once I was finished, I dropped her throat and side stepped. She fell to all fours panting.

"Don't be so dramatic," I muttered as she struggled to bring air into her lungs. "You're breathing, aren't you?"

"Barely." She coughed, holding her hand around her throat.

"I could have killed you. Be grateful," I said.

Helena rolled herself to her bottom and took in slow breaths. "How am I the dramatic one here?"

I lowered myself to a chair in the foyer. "I mean it, Helena. Don't fuck with me."

"Yeah, girl, I got the message. Won't cast any barrier spells for your husband or anyone else to lock you in again. We're on the same page. Just please, don't touch my throat. I paid a lot of money for this neck."

She continued to struggle air into her lungs. A quiet laugh left her lips, and she shook her head.

My gaze harshened. "Something funny?"

She shook her head again and smiled. "You just amaze me, kid. Is that all you came here for? To remind me you're the boss?"

"No. Two other things I need to talk to you about actually."

Helena laughed again. "Had to smack me around a little before mentioning what you're really here for?"

My gaze narrowed. "You're not acting like someone who's oh-so sorry."

She leaned her head against the wall. "Get on with it then. What do you need?"

"Can you access memories from past lives?"

"That's not a simple yes or no question, Laila."

"Just tell me if it can be done."

"It can be done. But not any time soon." She gestured toward my stomach. "Has to be done on the longest day of the year. You've got to down a nasty cocktail that might kill your baby so probably best you wait anyway."

"The summer solstice."

"Yup. June 20th."

Two days before Micah's birthday. At least if we didn't have him back by then, I'd have something to keep my mind busy.

"How much will it cost?" I asked.

"Couple hundred," she said. "It's a simple spell. Not too risky."

I bit my lip and gave a nod. "June 20th then."

"So what's the second thing?"

"I need you to train me. I'm stronger than Nastya, I know I am. She can only dampen my powers now. But if I train with a Witch, I can learn how to counteract what she does. I need you to challenge my abilities until I can't be controlled."

Helena laughed again. "Let me get this straight. You come over here, threaten my life, burn the shit out of me; all for taking the control out of your hands. But now, you *want* me to take the control out of your hands."

"I never had the control," I said. "That's the problem. I'm always one step behind them. Peterson, Amy, Nastya. I'm chasing them around and around and around when I don't even have the resources to stop them yet. I wish I was the one with the upper hand, but I'm not. I will be, but I'm not. But I'm hoping doing this will give me that. If I'm strong enough to kill Nastya, I get to Peterson. I get to Peterson; I get to my son."

Helena mulled over that for a moment. "Alright, kid. Let's make you strong enough to kill one of the most powerful Witches alive."

I huffed. "No pressure or anything."

CHAPTER FOURTEEN

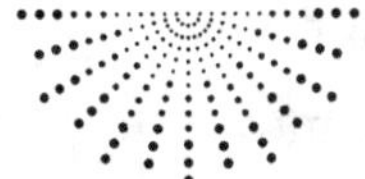

MAY 11, 2021 - JEREMY

"The couch looks awful like that." Laila frowned, propping her chin against her palm, squinting in thought. "It's blocking half the room, including the fireplace we built the house around. Sectionals belong in corners, Jeremy."

"But it looks cool like this." I smiled and leaned against it. My gaze traveled over her on the other side of the island. "When all the kids are playing hide and seek, they can hide down here."

"Yeah, and I won't be able to see them while I'm cooking," she said. "The point of an open concept is to be able to see the whole space from anywhere that you're standing."

I wiped sweat from my brow. "We just got it in here, baby. We can move it later."

Laila pursed her lips. She grumbled under her breath as she shuffled around the counter to the couch.

"What are you doing?"

She pushed her hands against the back of the cushions to no success. "If we don't move it now, it's going to stay like this for six months. And I don't like it. I'll just do it myself."

Her big belly stuck out over her vibrant harem pants, struggling against the couch that'd taken two grown men and two Werewolves to carry inside. She stood up and stomped like a toddler. I laughed, and her glare turned on me.

"This isn't funny." She pouted. "I could move it if I didn't have a ten-pound basketball on my gut."

"The doctor said she was six pounds." I smiled and made my way to her.

"That's beside the point. Just help me. It's heavier than it looks."

"Wyatt and Celena are coming back with pizza soon. They can help me when they get here, alright?" I touched her hips.

She frowned. Her hand moved to her belly and her green eyes shifted to mine. "I just want everything to be ready. You said we'd be moving in by your birthday. That was two months ago. I need to nest."

"She isn't due for another month." I smiled and pushed long hair behind her ear. "I think she'll hold off for another hour."

"But you heard what the doctor said. She's measuring pretty big. And since Micah was a preemie, she might be too. That means we should already be ready. We're not even four weeks from my due date. She could literally come at any minute."

"That is not what the doctor said." I laughed and pulled her into me. She uncomfortably shifted as her big stomach pushed into mine. "She said it was *possible.*"

She tucked her head against my chest. "If you haven't noticed, we tend to be the one percent that gets the shitty end of the stick almost all of the time."

Laila gasped and hauled away.

My eyes widened and I grasped her shoulders, ready to brace her in case she went into sudden labor. "What's wrong?"

She pawed me away and waddled across the living room to the dining table. Her hand pressed into her lower back as she attempted to bend over at the large, twelve seating table. I teleported to her when she wobbled a bit.

I reached out for her elbow. She smacked me away. Then she grabbed ahold of the table for support and crouched beside it. Struggling to her feet, her thumb and forefinger pinching a tiny silver nail extended to me.

"What if the baby got this?" she said firmly. "Babies put everything in their mouths. She could have died."

"Jesus Christ, don't scare me like that." I raised my hand to my chest. "I thought your water broke or something."

"This is serious, Jeremy. You told me the house would be ready and safe when Milly was born, and if she would have—"

"Baby." I took the nail from her hand, set it on the table, and held either of her cheeks. "We aren't done moving in yet. There's going to be a little bit of a mess. We'll clean when we're done. But Milly isn't going to be crawling for months. We're not laying our newborn on the floor under the dining room table any time soon, right?"

Laila's wide eyes gradually softened. "I guess I'm being a little neurotic, huh?"

"A little." I smiled and looked between her eyes. "Just a little. It's okay though. I know you want everything to be perfect. And it will be, baby. But you've got to give me the opportunity, alright? I'll clean the floors on my hands and knees once all our shit's moved in and all the pictures are hung and everything. Just give me the chance, okay?"

She gave a nod. "Yeah. Yeah, you're right. I'm sorry."

"It's okay. But I promised you we'd be in the house before Milly was born, and we are. We're here, we're moving in. We'll get all of the furniture in and set up before the day's over. We'll hang the pictures and TVs up tomorrow and bolt anything that could fall over on the baby to the walls. And Wednesday, we'll clean everything to make sure there's no little nails laying around anywhere."

"Does that mean we can stay here tonight?" She grinned, eyes meeting mine.

"If you want." I laughed.

A smile stretched across her lips. "I do. I do want."

I laughed again, still cupping her cheek. "Did you get everything in the garden done that you wanted to?"

"Yeah, it looks adorable. I need your help laying the rock beds though. I'm not really allowed to lift fifty-pound bags."

"No, you're really not. I'll do that tomorrow if I'm not too sore. If I am, I'll definitely get to it by the end of the week. Unless you're going to try to do it yourself before then."

She laughed. "No, it's okay. It can wait. The yard isn't as important as the house. We have all summer to get it ready anyway. Milly won't be walking for at least a year and—"

Her voice stopped abruptly. I watched her cheeks grow pink. A look of grief swept through her eyes. She was worried I'd realized she forgotten about Micah for a second.

"I'll have it done before the week's over." I leaned forward to kiss her forehead. Her gaze turned to the floor. "Hey, why don't you go try out your new tub? I'll let you know when they get back with dinner. I can work on the end tables for the bedroom while you relax for a while."

She gave a nod. "Yeah, I really wanted to try out those jets. Did we get the box of shower stuff moved in yet?"

"Yeah, it's in there. I haven't unpacked it yet though."

"That's okay, I'll do it real quick before I get my bath. What about clothes?"

"All of our clothes are in our brand new, massive walk-in closet." I smiled. "Your pajamas are on the second shelf, I think."

She smiled and gave a nod. "You're the best."

I smiled back. She kissed me once more. Then she waddled down the hallway, hand pressed into her lower back I felt the ache in.

I leaned against the table and took a look around. We'd done good.

It certainly wasn't a little shack in the woods anymore.

My gaze shifted out of the wall of windows ahead to the sweet, open front porch. That's what she wanted, a wall of windows, so that's what she got.

We'd used the original logs for the wood around them. They were too aged and corroded to stay structurally sound, so we'd placed the twelve windows that peaked to an A-line at the roof into a typical two-by-four frame, sanded and stained them a dark cherry color, and lined them like trim.

They matched the dark floors that twinkled in the light the wall let in. Aside from Tink's muddy paw prints that cascaded over them, of course.

A pretty, real flower wreath hung on either side of the white door. It complimented the white baseboards and light gray walls. The big, mahogany table I leaned against popped beside the cedar colored, butcher block countertops.

And of course, the brick fireplace in the center of the open room tied it all together, fire kindling visible from both the kitchen and the couch before the sofa.

It was the most perfect combination of modern and classic.

Our home. A great big house, with a beautiful suite for Laila and I, five bedrooms, and two baths upstairs for our babies and the ones we'd yet to think of.

It was perfect. I couldn't wait to grow old with my wife here.

CHAPTER FIFTEEN

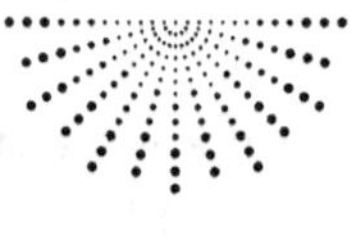

JEREMY

Life had been odd for the past five months or so. Things were good. Busy, but good. I guess that's what made it odd. We weren't used to good. We'd adapted pretty well to the madness of being who and what we are entails.

Five and a half months passed without a single shred of something that would help find Micah. Twenty weeks without a death or dramatic life-threatening event. It was refreshing to have some peace. But it was hard too.

We were focusing on Milly with everything because just thinking our son's name hurt too much. We were going on a year now that we knew he was alive with less leads than ever. I think focusing on Milly with such intent was our way of trying to prove to ourselves we weren't the shitty parents we knew that we were.

But still. Things were good. We'd been working with Helena twice a week on ways to counter Witch attacks and made a lot of progress. When she tried hard enough, Helena was still able to keep me from teleporting. It left her with a nasty nosebleed and intense bouts of vomiting, but she could do it. If she could, Nastya definitely could.

Laila had been able to break anything Helena cast on her in a few seconds for over a month now. Granted, Helena wasn't nearly as strong as Nastya. But Laila learned the basic fundamentals of fighting Witch magic. It was like learning to drive. Once she learned how to make it down the back roads, she'd have a good idea of how to go on the highway. Still be scary as shit when she went to do it but it sure as hell made more sense to tackle the big roads once she'd driven around the little ones a few times.

We'd hit some roadblocks with building permits and the septic system when we were building the house that backed up our move in date. Laila bitched daily. I didn't mind though. I'd rather hear her bitch than see her hurl herself from a cliff again.

After paying the guys, we were down a little over two-hundred grand in the savings account. Laila sold off some of the stocks that she held onto when Moe died to replenish about a quarter of it. Still though, there was a little over six-hundred thousand dollars in the account. I'd hoped I could keep it under a hundred and fifty, but Laila was all about going for the gold.

She wanted real hardwoods, a million windows, and French doors. She insisted on a grand, curving staircase with a custom-made iron handrail. She wanted a detachable baby-gate on both the top and bottom, and I agreed it was a good idea, so we splurged. She wanted hand carved crown molding and intricate, modern chandeliers.

We put three bathrooms upstairs and five bedrooms. One was an office for her, another was basically a room for my guitars and miscellaneous shit, the third was a simple guest room and the last two were Micah and Milly's. I did end up putting a small balcony on up there too. It gave us an amazing view of the rolling hills as the sun set just like I said it would. We could even see Moe's and Rachel's on a clear night.

One area we were able to cut on cost was the kitchen counters though. She didn't want granite or marble because they were "too hard and the kids could hit their head on it and die." She wanted thick butcher blocks. I was sure we'd have to replace them in a few years, but that's what she wanted so that's what she got.

I gave her full reign over everything to do with color and I. She was so concerned about nesting as if she hadn't been doing that for the last five months. It was cute though. She was overdoing it on the house a little to fill the void but so was I. It's all we really had to focus on besides the pregnancy.

Suffice to say the house was a dream come true. The view onto the front porch was amazing. Laila had planted a million flowers and laid out some cute white wicker furniture. I wanted to go with vinyl siding and simple shingles for the roof, but she insisted on stone siding and a metal roof. The roof cut back on time, but the stone added a good three weeks to our finish date.

If it weren't so big, you could say it looked like a sweet little cottage in the woods. Although we could have cut back on costs in a lot of places, it was a work of art when we were done. I'm sure if we sold it—which we never would—it'd be worth a good half million at least.

Things were soft and gentle for a while then. I couldn't say that we were the happiest we'd ever been. We weren't even close to that. Our lives were still embroidered with misery, but we were the happiest we could be.

You could say we were living in the calm before the storm.

CHAPTER SIXTEEN

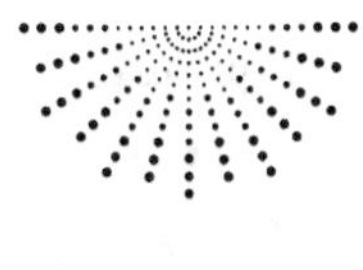

LAILA

"It really is amazing." Adam looked around the living room. "I wonder what Dad would say if he could see this."

"Bloody masterpiece." Kai laughed. "Practically a castle."

"Have you gotten it appraised yet?" Celena asked, sipping her whiskey. "You need to take out a heavy insurance policy on this place."

"Someone's coming next week. We had to go through some messy legalities to get the land transferred into our name. There's some red tape." Jeremy shrugged, and I leaned my head on his shoulder.

Hannah looked out the front wall. "God, I love these windows. Baby, can you put another window in our bedroom?"

Kai smiled and kissed her cheek. "I think that can be arranged, love."

I gazed around in the same glory. I loved our new house. It was the most brilliant idea Jeremy ever had. Everything about it screamed us. It was modern, but not fancy. It was gorgeous and big, but not in a "I'm better than everyone, look at my mansion" sort of way. Just in a big, beautiful family home sort of way. With some modern touches, of course. Like the little vacuum baseboards I made Jeremy install around the kitchen counters and heated floors.

"What does Tink think about the yard?" Hannah asked.

"She doesn't understand why there's a fence." I laughed. "She usually gets to roam free when we come to the house."

"That must suck." Wyatt sipped his beer. He sat at the oversized island with Celena's arms around his neck beside him. "From a dog's perspective, I agree that fences are bullshit."

"Well, so are coyotes and bears," I said. "You guys can take those on. My husky mutt can't."

"That's fair," he said.

"Oh my God, that balcony is amazing." Mom trotted down the steps. "I think you can see my house from there."

"Yeah, you can." I shifted to sit up.

"You have to squint pretty hard though." Jeremy gently elbowed my arm, grinning. "I told you the balcony was a good idea."

"Yeah, until we have teenagers," I muttered.

Him and that damn balcony. I mean this in the kindest way, but he never shut up about it. However, it was beautiful. I couldn't say I wasn't a fan too.

"We can both teleport; the kids probably will too," Jeremy said.

"Yeah, they won't be climbing out balconies." Adam laughed. "We sure as hell weren't."

"Lovely," Jenna grumbled, lowering herself to the couch beside me. "So we have that to look forward to."

I shook my head, smiling. Then a firm tap thudded just above my belly button. I grimaced a bit, and Jeremy smiled. His hand moved over my stomach to feel her kick. "Pretty sure she's going to be a soccer player," I said.

"Ooh, let me feel." Hannah darted across the room. She set her glass on the table, sat beside it, and put her hand to my stomach. She laughed as Milly kicked away.

"So you guys are completely moved in now, huh?" Jenna tucked her feet under her butt.

I laughed. "We have to grab a few more boxes. But yes, we're moved in. You guys can start moving into the diner now."

With Adam working at Moe's, and Jenna working at the school ten minutes down the road, and with a baby on the way, it made sense for them to get out of the main house. The apartment was small, but it was just the two of them and their baby. They didn't have pets, so it was plenty of space. Originally, we told them we didn't want rent, just to pay the utilities. Adam was cool with that—having never paid rent in his life—but Jenna insisted. I wasn't crazy about it, but it was making a dent in replenishing what we'd lost on building the house.

Nonetheless, I liked the idea of them staying there. It was a nice place to live. and I liked keeping my home in the family. And at least that sweet little Winnie the Pooh tree playhouse Jeremy made for Micah wouldn't go to waste. My nephew would love it when he came.

"Oh, thank God." Jenna smiled. "You left your bed, right?

"We did. But we took the twin from the nursery," Jeremy said.

"We got a new crib though." I forced a smile. "The old one's there for you guys. We left the boy clothes in the dressers too. Just hold onto them when you're done, in case we have a boy again."

"Are you sure?" Jenna asked softly.

I smiled and gave a nod. "We took the bigger stuff. I'm stocked on eighteen months to four T right now. We won't need the little stuff. I did take some of the gender-neutral things. You'll get more at your baby shower though."

"The house is going to feel so empty now," Leah muttered as she passed me a cup of tea. "Brody's never there anymore, you guys are living here, Adam's going to be at Moe's. Just leaves me, Hannah, and Kai." Her gaze shifted to Celena and Wyatt. "Are you guys looking for a place to stay?"

Celena laughed. "We have homes everywhere we go, huh?"

"Might take you up on it though," Wyatt said. "We're here more than there anyway."

Leah was having a hard time without having anyone to parent now that everyone was grown and finding their way. She spent a lot of time with Jeremy and me. When she wasn't working or with us, we teleported her back and forth to Haley's. But I could see how excited she was for Milly to come so she'd have someone to take care of again.

"Why don't you and Haley take the next step?" I grinned. "It's been almost two years now."

"Maybe," Leah said. "I think she wants me to go to Nevada with her though. And that's not happening. I'm not meant to live in heat like that."

That wasn't close to true. She loved summer, and she hated snow. She'd love Nevada. She just didn't want to leave us. Which I understood. We liked being close too.

"Yeah, don't do that," Hannah said.

"Are you guys ever going to have babies?" I smiled.

Leah lowered her brows and laughed. "I mean, not on accident."

"Fuck off." Jeremy laughed.

"No, really. Is that something you guys want?" I asked. "I don't think you've ever mentioned wanting or not wanting to have kids."

"I had kids. Hannah was twelve when Mom died. Brody was fifteen."

"Yeah, but they weren't *your* kids." I smiled.

"I guess its possible down the line. Not my dying wish or anything, but I'm not opposed to the idea." She glanced up the stairs behind me with a smile. "How many are you planning on having? You didn't build a six-bedroom house for nothing."

That was a good question. And the answer was, as many as we could afford. Within reasonable intervals, of course. I loved babies, and I wanted a million.

I laughed, and Jeremy smiled. "I don't know. The extra space doesn't hurt. We've got a lot of people in this family. You never know when someone's going to need a place to spend the night."

"That's fair." Celena raised her glass.

Jeremy cleared his throat. "So while everyone's here, there's something we wanted to talk to you all about."

Ah, yes. The lull in the conversation was a perfect time to bring it up. We'd been talking about it for the last month or so. Now that we were moved in, it was time to address it. Especially because Milly was going to be here soon, and I wanted it in place before she arrived.

"Uh-oh, good news or bad?" Adam asked from his perch on the other side of the couch.

"Neither really," I said. "More of a proposition."

"What is it?" Leah asked.

"There's a protection spell we want to cast around the property," I said.

Helena had mentioned it when she came to see the new house. When she saw that we had more money than she originally thought, of course. And it seemed like a brilliant idea.

"It'd make it so no one but us can get in and out," Jeremy said.

"How?" Hannah chimed in.

"And why haven't I heard of anything like that before?" Leah asked.

"Because it's expensive," Jeremy muttered.

"But we feel it's necessary given what happened to Micah," I said.

"If you guys aren't comfortable doing that to the whole property, we can just do it to an area around the house," he continued. "It'll act like a barrier from everything. Not just people, but spells. Anyone's abilities will be able to work just outside the border. But the second it makes contact with it, the spell will neutralize anything that hits it. Telepathy, teleportation, fire, bullets. Bombs, even."

"Air, light, and water can pass through it, so can we, but nothing else," I went on. "And yes, it is going to be expensive. But I'm not worried about that. It will give all of us a safe haven for the worst-case scenario."

"When you say nothing can pass through it, do you mean nothing at all? Not even humans?" Jenna asked.

"Not even humans," I said.

"Not unless they have a key," Jeremy said.

"What's the key?" Leah asked.

"A piece of quartz that's bound with either mine or Jeremy's blood," I said. "You can wear it as jewelry, or you can crush it into a powder and mix it into tattoo ink."

"Then you can't lose it," Jeremy stated.

"You don't think that's a little over the top?" Mom asked.

"I don't," I said. "It'd give me peace of mind. Might help me sleep better at night."

"What happens if you aren't wearing a necklace?" Jenna asked. "And what about our cars?"

"If you're inside the car, wearing your necklace, you'll pass straight through it," Jeremy said. "If you have a passenger inside your car, or you yourself, are not wearing a necklace, it'll feel like your car suddenly hit a wall. That's why I like the tattoo concept."

"I think it's a good idea," Leah said. "No parties with human guests then, I suppose."

"Not unless they put on a necklace," I said.

"Yeah, I agree," Adam said. "If that psycho is right and the end of the world really is coming, I like the idea of our family home being impenetrable."

"That's a good point," Hannah muttered.

Another one we'd heavily considered when Helena mentioned it. I wanted to make our entire property a safe room. Not just for us, but others too. I didn't know what was coming, but our property was big enough. If it came to it, we could build an entire community on the massive plot of land. We could set up tiny homes, possibly thousands of tents. It could be the only safe place on earth if and when catastrophe struck.

Land here was fruitful. We had plenty of streams with fresh water. Tons of trees we could use to kindle fires. In a worst-case scenario, this place could provide us with all the basics we needed to survive.

"But how do you know Nastya won't be able to get through it?" Celena asked.

"Ultimately, she could," Jeremy said. "But there's only one way that's physically possible."

"Which is?" Leah asked.

"We'd both have to die." I gestured between Jeremy and me. "That's why the crystals have to be bound with our blood. It's essentially a force field built from our energy. So yeah, if we go down, it goes back to how it is now. But if only one of us does, it'll be okay."

"Wouldn't it make sense to bind us all to it then?" Leah asked. "No offense or anything, guys. But neither of you have a great track record with not dying."

"We have a good record of coming back from the dead though." I smiled. "But yeah, if you want to connect your power to it, that can be done. It'd make it stronger too, which I think is a great idea. And if you're a part of the spell, then you don't need a crystal or a tattoo to get in and out. So anyone who wants to contribute to the spell is welcome to."

"I think it's a great idea," Hannah said.

"Is anyone against it?" I looked around. There were some head shakes followed by some shrugs.

"So no one objects? We should do it over the whole property?" Jeremy asked.

"I'll have to talk to Brody and make sure he's okay with it," Leah said. "But I'm in. Let me know when you need me to bleed for you."

"Next week," I said. "We want it done before the baby's born."

"I think it's a good idea," Mom agreed. She took a sip of her wine. "I want the tattoo though. I'll forget a necklace."

"Yeah, me too," Jenna muttered. "But what about the babies?"

"Our descendants can enter with or without the quartz," Jeremy said. "Not our entire bloodline. But the people we give birth to and potentially the people they give birth to if we all live long enough to see grandchildren. So if Adam adds his power to the spell, it won't affect your baby."

"Oh, good," Jenna said. "Well, yeah. I like the idea then."

"What if we've got to lock some bloke up in the basement?" Kai asked.

"Throw a necklace on 'em," I said.

"Makes sense," he said. "I want in on it."

"Yeah, me too," Hannah said.

"I'll join the party." Celena raised her glass again.

"Yeah, throw me in there too." Wyatt sipped his beer.

"I'm in too," Adam said.

"We all agree then?" I asked.

"I'll call Brody tonight and go over it with him. I'm sure he'll be down," Leah said.

CHAPTER SEVENTEEN

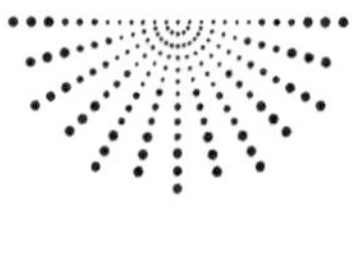

LAILA

The day after our housewarming party was my reconcile day. That's what I'd started to consider my Saturdays. Sundays were spent at Mom's where she taught me recipes I grew up on while Tink played in the creek. Mondays were for business with Moe's. Tuesdays were training with Helena then recouping from training. Wednesdays were my gardening days. On Thursdays, I did more catch-up work at Moe's. Fridays, I trained with Helena again. Then Saturday, I recouped.

I went over the things I didn't get to when one task required my attention more than another. Whether it was laundry or tax forms for the diner, there was always something I'd missed throughout the week. If there wasn't, I spent it outside in the yard with Tink.

I started writing again on Saturdays too. Doctor Williams suggested it at a therapy session earlier in the year. I told her the thought was a little disturbing. I didn't tell her it was because of the book we'd found last year, but I told her recording my thoughts for anyone else to read was an uncomfortable concept for me. Then she suggested I write a page and burn it before anyone else got the chance to read it.

It wasn't much at first. Part of me had forgotten how to construct sentences since the last thing I'd really written had been more than four years prior. But after a few tries, it was like riding a bike. The ink forming letters followed by words on the pages was practically blood flowing from my veins. I'd released more energy into the world than most people do in a lifetime, but nothing felt as relieving as putting that pen to paper.

The thoughts leaving my body in the form of language left me feeling as though a million worlds had lifted off my shoulders.

They were a jumbled mess of phrases and thoughts in my mind but as they hit that manila sheet, they created straight, organized, and maybe even rational ideas. Truth be told, it was far more therapeutic than any of the therapy I'd been paying thirty dollars a week per copay for.

That particular day, I was writing in my worn notepad as I sipped tea on the patio. Tink frolicked through the fresh growing grass chasing a blue butterfly in the open yard before me. The smell of roses and daisies danced up my nose as I smiled at the spring morning.

For a moment, I felt like I was in a fairytale. I was sitting on my patio drinking tea with a pen and paper in my lap while my husband finished assembling a crib in the periwinkle room he'd just finished building for our soon-to-be born daughter.

Life was good.

Then the damn phone rang.

Max's name lit up the screen. I raised the phone to my ear. "You're supposed to be off work today, sir. I certainly hope this isn't diner related."

"No, I'm working today because I was off yesterday. Remember? You approved it," he said.

"Oh, shit. Yeah, that's right. Sorry, I've kind of been in my own world lately." I rubbed my eyes as a yawn left my lips. "What's going on?"

"Yeah, so somebody's here. He says it's really important that he talks to you. Said you don't know each other personally but you'd want to hear what he has to say. Wouldn't tell me his name though," Max said. "I figured it probably has something to do with Micah. He's waiting in the dining area for you to get here. He says he won't leave 'til he gets to talk to you."

I sat forward. "What does he look like?"

"Late thirties, maybe early forties. Medium build, about Jeremy's height. He's black, bald. I don't know, pretty friendly guy though."

I thought hard for a moment. I hadn't exactly gotten to know the survivors. But maybe it was one of them with information on Peterson.

"That doesn't sound like anyone I know off the top of my head," I muttered. "Does he have scars like mine?"

"No. No scars, nothing particularly identifying."

Ordinarily, I would have handled it alone. But I was a few weeks from birth. And if he weren't a survivor, I had no clue who he could be.

"Okay, I'm going to go get Jeremy. I'll be there in five, ten minutes tops. Tell Adam. Ya never know, could be an ally. Could be an enemy. When I get there, I want you to wait outside until I tell you it's clear, alright?"

"Got it. I don't think it's going to go like that though, he seems nice," Max said. "But I'll do as I'm told. See you when you get here."

"Alright, bye." I ended the call.

My hands grasped either arm of the wicker chair in a trying attempt to stand. Being a mom was going to be cool. Being so fat that standing was a task was a pain in the ass. I grasped my aching back, calling Tink to the swinging, glass French door.

"Baby," I yelled upstairs as I wobbled my way toward the entryway. "Something's happening, we've got to get to Moe's."

"What do you mean something's happening?" He quickly galloped down the steps. "Is everyone okay?"

"Yeah. Yeah, I think." I lowered myself to the bench to pull my shoes over my swollen feet. "Max said there's someone at the diner who refuses to leave until they talk to me."

"You don't think it's Peterson, do you?" He hurriedly pulled his shirt over his head.

"I guess it's possible, but Max said he seemed nice. Peterson's a little more dramatic than just showing up at Moe's."

"Probably. Are you sure you want to go though? You're getting pretty close to your due date."

"Yes, Jeremy. I'm sure that I want to go to my diner—the one we were living above until about four days ago—and talk to the man who refuses to leave until he talks to me."

"Driving or teleporting?"

"Teleporting." I finished tying my shoe. I gripped the seat of the bench to hoist myself up before I stumbled back to it.

Jeremy extended his hand to mine. I took it and let him pull me up. "You ready?"

I nodded. Then we landed in the stairwell to our old apartment. I stumbled and grasped the handrail. He grabbed my elbow to steady me as I grew a little lightheaded.

"You okay?" he asked.

"Yeah." I stifled a yawn. "Yeah, just kind of tired. I'll be alright."

He nodded back. I took his hand and started down the steps into the kitchen. Max turned his gaze to mine. "Damn, that was quick."

"Where is he?" I asked.

Max nodded to the front of the house. "Corner booth."

"I'm getting a weird vibe." Adam rounded up the basement steps into the kitchen. "He's definitely not human."

"Any idea what he is?" Jeremy asked.

"We're about to find out." I waddled my way through the swinging door.

There he sat in the corner booth. When I saw him, I knew that I recognized at least some of his features from somewhere. The thick lips, the broad jaw, the squared chin. But it didn't click until he said it.

He was dressed well, but almost like he was trying too hard. Judging by the wrinkles around his eyes, he had to be around fifty years old yet wore a pair of dark washed skinny jeans and a gray V-neck that looked more appropriate for a college student. His white Jordans were in impeccable condition. Just a glance at him made it clear that he was incredibly concerned with his physical appearance.

He chomped into a burger as I approached. A splotch of ketchup spilled from his lips onto his shirt. He grumbled something to himself.

I placed my hands on my hips. "Are you who was asking for me?"

"That depends," he made out through chews. After swallowing, he turned his gaze up to me with a smile. "You're Laila, right?"

"I am."

"So you must be Jeremy." He gestured to him beside me.

"Yeah," Jeremy said. "And who are you?"

He chewed for a moment, swallowed, and licked his fingers. Then he extended his hand toward me. "I go by Don."

"I'm not shaking the hand that just came out of your mouth."

Don laughed. He wiped his hand against his jeans. "Yeah, guess that's fair."

"What's this about then, Don?" Jeremy asked.

"Why don't you sit?" He gestured between the two of us.

"That's alright. We'll stand." He tucked an arm around my waist.

Don laughed. "I'm not a threat or anything, kids. We just need to talk."

"About?" I asked.

"About the two-thousand-year-old book both you and I are prophesied in."

My heart stopped. The zombie in the basement. I quickly skimmed through the conversation, but no Don came to mind.

"The Bible, you mean?" I asked.

"Revelation, to be exact."

"I don't recall a Don being mentioned in there." Jeremy furrowed his brows.

"I said I *go by* Don. I've been called a lot of things over the years." He smiled. "You might know me by Apollyon."

There it was. "Abaddon?" I asked.

The Demon said to lead the swarm of locusts from hell. Apparently, an enemy of god.

At the time, I was still on the fence about Demons. I spent most of my early years in the supernatural world killing them. But considering how many Peterson held captive and tortured alongside me, my viewpoint had begun to shift. I knew Angels weren't my friends. But I wasn't sure if Demons were either.

"Yeah, it's a little long. Don's easier. More westernized." He mindlessly chomped on a French fry. "These are really good. Do you season them with lemon pepper?"

Jeremy's hand tightened at my hip, pulling me closer. "What are you doing here?"

He looked between us. "Alright, don't look at me like you've just seen a ghost. I know what those legends say about me, but I sure as hell ain't the leader of a swarm of locusts."

"Then why are you here?" I asked.

"Look, so I know you two are looking for your kid. I'd like to help where I can." He chewed another fry. "I don't have any idea where he actually *is*, but I do know some things that might help. Particularly how your son ties into it all."

"What do you know about my son?" My voice was low, but laced with defense.

"The lamb, you mean?" he asked.

No one outside of the family and Moriah La Fay knew what was in the letter Nastya had sent her. No one knew about Micah being a part of some biblical prophecy to bring on the end of the world outside of us. It made sense for him to know that he was mentioned, then to tie me into it through context clues and my recent fame in our world. But to refer to Micah as the lamb, he had to have more information than met the eye.

"What do you know about *that*?" Jeremy questioned.

"Oh, ya know. The part where your kid kills the planet. Or at least, that's my take on it. Not one hundred percent sure if that part's accurate yet."

"*How* do you know about that?" Jeremy lowered his voice.

"Can't reveal my sources."

I was open to leads. But not from someone who wouldn't be transparent with me. Maybe that was a little hypocritical since I wasn't exactly see-through either. But his kid wasn't riding on all of this. Mine was.

"Then I'm going to have to ask you to leave." I looked between his honey swirled, chocolate brown eyes. "But thanks for stopping by. Your meal's on the house."

"Oh, come on now. Don't be like that." He frowned. "Believe it or not, I'm really not the bad guy here. What'd Liam say about me, huh? Tell you about the thing with the cat when he was in third grade? 'Cause that wasn't my fault. I told him not to—"

"Liam?" My forehead scrunched up. "You know Liam?"

Don laughed. "I mean, yeah. Since he swam out of my left nut twenty-five years ago."

"Liam's your son?" Jeremy's expression wasn't much different than mine.

"Oh," he muttered, looking between us. "He didn't tell you that, did he?"

"No. No, he did not." I gritted my teeth together.

Liam was about to have his ass handed to him. I'd helped bring his siblings home from captivity, and the little shit didn't tell me his father was one of the oldest, most historic Demons in existence? I'd learned a thing or two about coincidences over the years. If it looks and quacks like a duck, it's probably a fucking duck.

"Oh, well shit." Don wiped his mouth.

We need to go talk to him. Now.

I nodded to Jeremy before turning my gaze back to Don.

"Well, you look mad. So here's what I'm going to do." He reached into his jacket pocket, pulled out a small business card, and scribbled on the back.

There was sincerity in his voice, and in his gaze, but I was far from at ease.

Why the fuck had Liam never told me who his father was?

"Here's my number. When you're ready, we can meet up and talk about the roles we all play in this thing. You pick the place. Let me know at least twelve hours in advance on a time so I can clear my schedule. You can give me the location five minutes before you expect me there, so you don't have to worry about a swarm or anything. Not that I'd do that, but I know that's what you're thinking." He looked deep into my eyes as he handed me the card. "But trust me, Laila. You and me? I'm pretty sure we're fighting for the same team."

"Hell?" I asked.

He laughed and shook his head. "Earth, baby girl."

CHAPTER EIGHTEEN

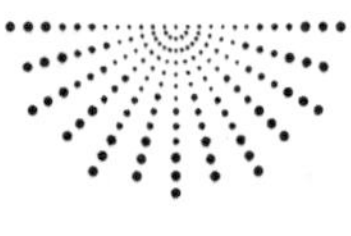

JEREMY

Laila pounded on the door of the small ranch. Her eyes were glowing bright green in their sockets. But as scary as her expression may have been, that hand holding her lower back before her giant belly kind of took away from the terrifying persona it seemed she was going for.

"Just don't kill him, alright?" I said.

"Why?" she asked. "Since when do you care about Liam?"

"I don't. But I'd rather find out what he knows than kill him and leave two preteens without a parent," I said.

She rolled her eyes and pounded on the door again. Then stomping started toward us.

His brows were furrowed as he opened the door but softened when he saw Laila.

The guy had fucked my wife, but I still sympathized with him. Whether I liked him or not, he was a good person. And he had helped in the last rescue of our people, as well as the first. I didn't think what he'd kept from her he did maliciously. It didn't help me build trust in the guy. But I did feel bad for him. It sucks to be the one Laila looks at with those furious, glowing eyes.

"Hey, what's going on?" He looked past us off the porch. "Something wrong?"

"Oh, yeah." Her eyes narrowed. "Something's wrong."

"What is it?" he asked. "Do you guys want to come in?"

"Mhmm." Laila stepped past him. I sent a nod his way, walking through the threshold.

"What's up, guys?" Liam shut the door behind me.

Before he had time to meet my gaze, a knife appeared in Laila's hand. She raised it to his throat and backed him into the door.

His eyes widened. "What the fuck are you doing?"

"Why the fuck didn't you tell me who your dad was?" Her eyes glowed in their sockets.

"My dad?" He tried to push the knife away, but she held it closer to his skin, beads of red trickling down the silver. "Jesus Christ, Laila. What's your problem? I didn't do shit to you."

"You've been giving him information on me, haven't you?" She pushed the blade closer into his throat.

"I haven't talked to my dad in four years. He didn't even show when the kids came home," he said. "I wouldn't do that, Laila. Everything that you've done for my family, I'd never betray you."

"Then how the fuck did he know about my son?"

"I don't know, but it wasn't me." His eyes were wide, and admittedly, they looked honest. "I don't talk to my dad; you know that. He's never been a part of my life. I don't know what he's up to this time, but I swear to God, I haven't said a word to him about you."

"Then why didn't you care to mention that he's one of the most significant Demons in hell?"

"When did he come up?" Liam asked. "When and *why* would I have had the opportunity, let alone the *reason* to tell you that?"

"I don't fucking know, but it can't be a coincidence," Laila said.

"Think about what you're saying. What purpose would I have in telling my dad stories about my fuck-buddy?"

"Bragging rights," I said. "Getting to say you fucked a hero to our people."

"You showed up at my doorstep," Laila continued. "I should have questioned it, but I didn't. Guess it's my own stupid fault for not using my head, huh?"

"I swear to God, I didn't do anything." Liam's hands were shaking then, but his eyes still looked sincere. He was afraid because Laila was terrifying. But I didn't think it was because he had anything to do with what his dad knew. "C'mon, baby girl. Put that knife down. We both know I'm strong enough to get it off you."

I couldn't help my chuckle. "Not a good choice of words, man."

"Oh, yeah?" Laila laughed. Her smile fell. "Try. I fucking dare you, Liam. Just try and get this knife out of my hand."

I tried not to smile at that thought. I would have loved to see that fight. But I also knew it'd end with him as a pile of ash pretty damn quick.

"Don't do this, Laila," Liam continued. "Nobody's got to get hurt, alright? Let's just talk."

"You want to talk? Let's talk." Laila nodded, pushing the blade further into his skin. "Your dad just shows up at my diner, the same place we met—ironically enough—insisting on talking to me. Refusing to leave until he does. Then he goes on to tell me about information he has in connection to my son. And he mentions you."

"What?"

"How did you know about the prophecy, Liam?" I asked.

"What prophecy?"

"Don't try to play dumb," Laila said. "I never told you. He said his sources told him. So how the fuck did you know?"

"Laila, I have no clue what you're talking about," Liam insisted with wide, believable eyes. "Just put the knife down and go in my head. Look at my memories. I haven't talked to him in years, I swear."

"Are you going to keep—"

"It was me," a quiet feminine voice said behind me. "Don't hurt him, Laila. It was me."

I turned to Liam's fourteen-year-old little sister. Tears beaded down her cheeks, staring at her idol holding her brother against a wall with a knife to his throat.

Laila turned her head. "What?"

"That letter, you had it in your purse the day you came to talk to Liam," she murmured.

"You went into her purse?" Liam snapped. Laila lowered the knife. "What were you doing going through someone else's shit, Emma?"

"I'm so sorry, Laila." Her lip quivered, fighting back a sob. "I—I was just—You can tell a lot about a girl by what she carries in her purse. And you—I just wanted to know you. I wasn't stealing or anything. I just thought that if I—I don't know, maybe if we had something in common, I could connect to you. I was—I was just curious."

The tone in the room shifted pretty quickly. It made sense. Liam cared for Laila; I couldn't genuinely see him betraying her. But a fourteen-year-old girl who idolized her going through her purse? That seemed likely. Plus, the two of us always had a sweet spot for kids.

"Emma." Liam ran his hand over his mouth, and his eyes closed.

"What did you tell him, Emma?" Laila moved across the room toward her.

Emma was practically shaking by the time Laila was close enough to touch her. Her eyes were frozen, wide in fear.

Laila's expression softened. She reached out to take Emma's hand and the other pushed tight black curls from her face. "It's okay, I'm not going to hurt you. I just need to know what you told him."

"I—I took a picture of the letter," she murmured. "I only sent it to Dad and then I deleted it."

"How long have you been talking to Dad?" Liam said beside me. "How did you even get in contact with him?"

"He came by one day when you were at work," she murmured. "I—He was gone for so long before I disappeared. And then he—He wanted to be in my life and I—I—"

"It's alright." Laila moved her hand up and down Emma's bicep. Then she put an arm around her shoulder and started down the hall. "It's alright, let's go sit down."

"That's the second time she's almost killed me now," Liam muttered beside me.

"Two's nothing. She never really means it though."

"Felt like she meant it," he muttered.

CHAPTER NINETEEN

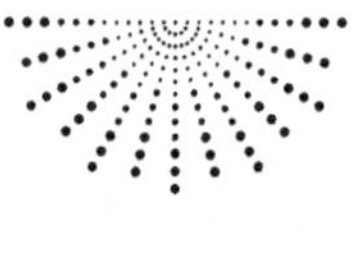

JEREMY

Emma didn't know much. She knew what she'd overheard in passing conversations. She knew rumors. But the only information she had on us was the prophecy. She didn't have anything particularly notable that would help someone working against us.

Laila went through her memories to make sure there wasn't anything she'd accidentally, or intentionally, left out. She also checked to make sure she didn't tell Don when we were planning to attack a few months prior to be sure Peterson wasn't tipped off. When there was nothing substantial in her thoughts, Laila apologized for Emma having to see that. She gave a brief description of what was at stake, and Emma grasped it. She apologized profusely before Liam sent her to her room.

Still, we didn't know much about Abaddon. He was a very old, very powerful fallen Angel. He had ties high up in Hell's hierarchy. But that was about all we knew.

"Can we trust him?" I asked. "Your dad, he said he was on our side. Is he?"

"From my experience, Dad's only side is his own. So if your goals align, then sure."

"What are his goals?" Laila asked. "Is he rogue?"

"Not really," Liam said. "He's a bad parent. But he's not a bad person. I couldn't tell you what his goals are though. Like I told you before, we haven't talked in almost half a decade."

Something about his expression said otherwise. His tight jaw, his slightly flared nostrils. When he uttered the word 'parent,' his lip curled in disgust.

"If he's not a bad person, why do you hate him the way you do?" I asked. "'Cause that face, that isn't resentment. That's hate. You *hate* him."

Liam nodded, chewing his lip. "Yeah. Yeah, I do. Can't stand the motherfucker. But I wouldn't say he's evil."

I could relate. I'd never been fond of my father either. Not because he was evil. Just because he was a selfish prick.

"What would you say then?" I asked.

"He's just a piece of shit. He wasn't always, we had some good times together when I was a kid. But things changed. They..." He rubbed his face. "He fucked us over more times than I can count. And Mom just kept letting him come back for us. She said it was important for kids to have a father, even a shitty one. She should have left him, but she didn't. He just kept going in and out of our lives like a revolving door. Then one day, he just didn't walk in again. We were better off in the long run, but yeah. I hate him."

"Was he abusive?" Laila asked.

"Not really. Definitely not physically. Sometimes emotionally, but not any more than Mom was. Nothing we all don't say when we're mad. They fought a lot though."

"What about?" I asked.

His gaze met mine, pressing his lips together. Then he rubbed his mouth. "He's an addict. And a cheater. And a compulsive liar."

Well, that explained why he hated me so much. I was two of said mentioned things. I'd done pretty good on breaking the lying habit, but the addict part would never go away.

"What's his drug of choice?" Laila asked.

"He's a gambler," Liam said. "We didn't always live in this shit hole, ya know. We had a nice little house in the suburbs when the twins came. Mom inherited it. It was paid off. We were doing alright.

"Then Dad bet it in an underground poker game. They couldn't kill him, and they were going to kill one of us if Mom didn't sign it over. So she did. Then they broke up. We moved into this hell hole. Then they got back together. And broke up and got back together. Then broke up and got back together. Then they broke up, and they didn't get back together. And I didn't see him again until the twins' funerals."

At least I never got that bad. I didn't even use money from our joint account to get high. Granted, I stole my drugs. Still though. Never bet my kid's home for a rush.

"Was that the worst of it?" Laila asked.

"Pretty much. There was other stuff too. Using the mortgage money to gamble, crashing our only car because he was too drunk to see straight, hookers in and out while Mom was at work. Lots of other shit. But yeah, gambling our family home was the worst."

So maybe Abaddon could be trusted after all. Not enough to invite for holiday dinners, but enough that a meeting wasn't so scary. I was curious about one thing though.

"I've got to ask," I said. "What happened with the cat in third grade?"

He rolled his eyes. "When I was in kindergarten, I went to this kid's house, and he had a sphinx cat. I loved it, and I wanted one. They're crazy expensive, or at least they were then, so I mowed lawns and shoveled snow for three fucking years, man. I worked my ass off for that cat."

I raised a brow. "He gambled your cat?"

Liam gave a nod. "He gambled my cat."

"Damn," I muttered.

"Yeah, piece of shit."

"Do you know why he fell?" Laila asked.

"He never talked about it. It's literally ancient history. He's a couple thousand years old. God only knows."

I licked my lips. When we met, I'd definitely be asking about that. But it wasn't vital in the moment.

"Anybody want to fill me in on that prophecy you guys were talking about?" Liam asked.

Laila looked at me as if to ask if I thought telling him was a good idea. "Emma's going to tell him anyway."

Laila bit her lip. "Remember the day that Morgan La Fay showed up at the diner?"

He nodded.

"She gave me a letter she'd gotten from Nastya," Laila said. "It was mostly nonsense. Incoherent rambles of someone who seemed to be long off their medication."

"What'd it say?" Liam asked.

"That Micah's going to bring on the apocalypse." I raked a hand through my hair. "She described him as the lamb."

Liam cocked his head to the side. "Like, the sacrifice?"

"That's their plan. Sacrifice him to bring on the full biblical apocalypse."

"But why?" Liam asked. "Why Micah?"

"The bond." Laila gestured between the two of us. "I don't understand all the details, but that's what the letter said. Only a love like ours could bring a child like Micah into the world."

Liam's brows stayed creased as he leaned back in his seat. He rubbed his hand against his mouth, shaking his head from side to side. "I guess I can see the biblical parallels. Sacrificing the first-born son and all that dumb shit."

"There's a lot of them," Laila said. "At first, I thought it was bullshit. I just thought that Peterson was crazy. And he is, I'm not saying that he isn't. But now... I—I don't know."

"You think the end of the world's coming?" Liam whispered.

"Not if I can help it. But I'm starting to think it's possible."

He leaned back in his seat and rubbed his mouth. "That's why Dad contacted you. He's one of the stars in Revelation."

"We think so," I said.

"He doesn't want the world to end, does he?" Laila asked.

"No. He's... Spunky. Dad loves being alive. He loves being on Earth. If you guys are trying to prevent the end of the world, I'd trust that he's on your side. He's a lot of things, but capable of mass murder isn't one of them. He wouldn't be able to live with himself."

"Really?" Laila asked. "He hasn't killed?"

"Maybe a few times," Liam said. "But not a whole planet, that's for sure. He probably wouldn't have had the balls to do what you did back in December either."

I thought for a moment. "I always thought that the dragon was Lucifer. But now that I'm thinking about it... Does that mean we're fighting on the same side as hell?"

"Hell isn't all bad, ya know," Liam said. "Not every fallen Angel wants to bring death to mankind. Most of them just didn't stay in line so they got kicked out the pearly gates. That doesn't mean they're evil."

"Some are," I muttered. "I've killed a lot of them. They aren't all like you."

"Maybe not," Liam agreed. "But they aren't all bad either. First gens almost never are. Every first-generation Demon I've met was pretty likable besides my dad. It's the descendants and demis that do awful shit."

"That's true," Laila muttered. "No Demon I've killed was first generation. They've all been beasts."

Liam nodded. "Even Lucifer. Pretty nice guy to be honest."

I'd heard stories about Lucifer. But they were along the same lines I'd heard of the supposed God. I never spoke with anyone who met him personally. And I wasn't sure how I felt about him. A lot of his people were responsible for some seriously shitty things. Like killing my aunt. But I was curious what he was like.

"You've met him?" I asked.

"Couple times. He and Dad did business together when I was a kid. Then he loaned me money to go to college when I graduated high school."

"Damn," Laila muttered. "See, this would have been nice shit to know, Liam. All that talk about not being defined by our bloodlines, you could have mentioned this. It would have been nice to know that you're old pals with the king of hell."

"I wouldn't call him a king," Liam said. "I'd say he's more like the head of state. He's a leader. A damn good one to be honest. There's a reason most of the things your kind kill aren't Demons. Usually rogue vamps and wolves, right? Because Lucifer keeps his people in line. That's why most of the Demons you meet are decent people. It isn't easy to get to earth if you're a Demon unless you're a mutt that's born here. Lucifer keeps them safe by keeping them from earth and keeps earth safe by keeping them from getting over."

"Yeah, well he could do a better job," I retorted. "A lot of good people have died at Demon hands."

"A lot of good wolves died at human hands." Liam asked. "A lot of good humans have died at wolf's hands. You're a Guardian, shouldn't you have prevented those things from happening? Couldn't you have done a better job?"

I saw his point. With responsibility came failures. I could have been there the day that Annie was murdered by one of those beasts. But nope, I was dope sick in my bedroom.

"Fair enough."

"You know what I don't get?" Laila furrowed her brows in thought.

"Hmm?"

"If the apocalypse isn't Hell versus Heaven, then who's fighting who?" she asked.

"I don't know. I guess we'll have to meet up with Don and go from there."

Laila made a face. Her hand moved to her tummy, and she exhaled a slow breath.

"Are you okay?" Liam looked her over.

I put my hand on hers, expecting to feel my daughter's little thump.

"Yeah. I'm okay. Probably just gas or something."

I laced our fingers together. Then Liam's eyes widened a bit. His mouth pulled in a slight smile. "No, I don't think it's gas."

Laila gave him a look. "What do you mean?"

Then, I heard it.

Plop. Plop. Plop.

My brows furrowed, turning my gaze to the source of the sound.

Water dripped from the edge of the chair she sat on.

Laila gasped, looking down.

My eyes widened. She covered her mouth and stood. "Oh, shit."

She started to the towel on the stove.

Liam shook his head. "No, I'll clean it up."

I sat there dumbfounded for a moment. My rational mind knew it wasn't piss and that I had to move, but it came as a surprise.

"No, no," she began.

He stood and took the towel from her hand.

My heart raced in my chest, and I scurried to my feet. No longer in shock, excitement filled me.

"Laila, I'm a nurse. A little amniotic fluid isn't going to kill me. Go to the hospital. I got this. Then let me know when she gets here."

Laila blinked hard. She nodded.

I couldn't help the quiet, joyous laugh that left my lips.

It was happening.

I was about to watch my daughter come into the world.

I was about to be a dad.

CHAPTER TWENTY

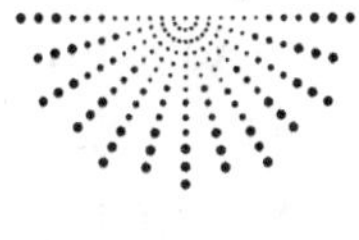

LAILA

"Yup." The doctor smiled, adjusting the sheet over my legs. "That was your water breaking. Are you feeling contractions?"

Aside from the anxious butterflies, nope. It was nothing like I had with Micah. Maybe there would have been some pain if I weren't so excited, but all I kept thinking was that soon, I'd have my baby in my arms.

"Not really," I said. "Some tension, I guess. Like mild cramps. I don't know, maybe. It feels a lot different than it did before."

"Well, consider yourself lucky." The doctor grinned. "You're a little less than four centimeters dilated."

"Already?" My eyes widened. "But I don't even feel anything."

"That happens," she said. "Some people feel almost no form of pain during labor. It's rare, but it does happen."

"Isn't it too early?" Jeremy asked. "We still have another month to go."

"No, you should be alright." The doctor pulled one glove off into the other. "I'm not seeing any signs of distress. Baby's heart rate's normal. Everything looks great."

"But she's not even close to forty weeks," Jeremy said.

"We consider a safe delivery for humans between thirty-five and forty weeks. We're at almost thirty-four weeks now. But your anatomy is a little different because of your abilities, Laila. You've used them throughout your pregnancy, I'm sure."

"Yeah," I said. "But what does that have to do with anything?"

"Well, you're a healer. Your ability makes cells regenerate faster. It's not uncommon for healers to have labors a little earlier than others. I told you she was measuring pretty big; that's probably why."

"Maybe Micah was more developed than I thought then too." I ran my hand along my stomach. That'd explain why he survived.

"Maybe." She smiled and gave a nod. "But, hey, at least she won't be a Gemini."

I laughed. "Can I still do it at home?"

"If that's where you're comfortable," she said. "There's no reason to stay here if you don't want to. I can check on you hourly until you're fully dilated. You have another teleporter who can take me back and forth so Jeremy can stay with you, right?"

"Yeah, we have a few," Jeremy said.

"Then absolutely. If we encounter any issues, we'll bring you back here. But I don't think we'll have to. Everything looks good, and you know what you're doing, Momma. This isn't your first rodeo. You've got a good birth canal for babies, your PH levels are excellent, she's facing downward. You're stretching well; I don't think you'll even need an episiotomy. You're a great candidate for home birth even without a doctor teleporting in and out."

A smile pulled at my lips. I ran my fingertips over my belly and smiled. "Yeah, I think we'll be alright. Two of my sisters are healers, they'll be at the house too. If anything goes wrong, they can help."

She smiled and gave a nod. "That's a good plan. I'm going to send you with a doppler to monitor the baby's heart rate though. If it spikes or drops, you come get me immediately. It will beep obnoxiously if it isn't in a safe range."

Just as I went to reply, my stomach tightened. My eyes opened further. But I couldn't help the little laugh that escaped me.

My first contraction. It hurt, obviously it hurt, but it made me happy. She was coming. She was about to be here. I was finally going to be able to call myself a mom.

Jeremy gasped, wide eyes meeting mine. I grimaced, hand on my taut belly, but smiled. His eyes stayed wide for a second. Then a smile came to his lips, and he chuckled.

"That feels more like last time." He squeezed my hand.

I smiled and gave a nod.

The doctor laughed. Once the tightening slowed and I exhaled a heavy breath, she continued, "I also want you to look out for any heavy bleeding. It looks like you have pretty fast deliveries. That isn't a bad thing, but it can cause some issues after birth. There's risks of the baby aspirating amniotic fluid so I'm going to have a suctioning device on hand."

"That's probably what happened to Micah, huh?" I asked.

She gave a nod. "That'd be my best guess."

"Is there anything else we should look out for?" Jeremy ran his thumb against mine. "Any major red flags we should get you for immediately?"

"If you could check her blood pressure while I'm gone, that would be helpful. I'll send you with a mobile device. All you have to do is press a button, but I'll walk you through it first."

Jeremy nodded. "I can do that."

I'll never forget that look on his face as the doctor went over how to put the cuff on my bicep. It was a gentle, yet firm expression of concentration tied up with joy and anxiety. I wished that I could have taken a picture and captured that moment.

His eyes were wide, but focused. His brows pulled together slightly, watching carefully as she slid the cuff up my arm. He listened closely to every word she said, nodding here and there.

He was excited and nervous and happy all at once.

That look was the definition of beauty. He was so eager and proud, yet still so humbly fearful. I'd known for years how badly he wanted to be a parent. But now that we were here, now that he was about to meet his daughter, reality set in and made me realize how perfect of a man I'd chosen to build a family with.

He was going to be the best dad.

CHAPTER TWENTY-ONE

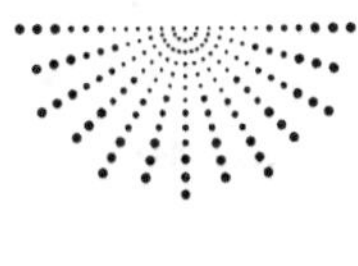

LAILA

"Baby." I closed my eyes through a contraction. My hand squeezed tighter around his sweaty fingers while a slow, shaking breath left my lips. Sweat beaded above my lips before dripping to my chin. The hair around my face started to stick to my forehead and cheeks like the back of my thighs to a leather seat on a hot summer day.

He wiped a cool rag along my clammy face. "Yeah?"

"Do you feel it too?" I asked. "The way that I do?"

He gently tucked hair behind my ear. "I don't think in the way that you do. It only hurts for a second or two."

"Lucky you." I closed my eyes again, breathing heavily through the throb that radiated into my back.

"I'm sorry, baby. I wish I could do it for you," he said.

I believed him on that one. He would have loved to be the one to carry our children. To him, it was the most amazing thing in the world. To me, it was pretty typical. Beautiful, of course. I did love it. But it'd always just been a factor of life in my eyes.

When the contraction began to subside, I closed my eyes and laid my head against his bicep. He kissed my forehead. His voice was so soft and gentle, like the melody of a pretty song. "You're amazing though, you know that?"

I laughed. My eyes opened to meet his. "Women have been birthing babies for millions of years. It isn't that special."

"Anything you do is special." He smiled, running a cool rag down my cheek. "Because you're amazing."

This was how it should've been last time too. I should have had his hand in mine. I should have lay comfortably on the soft sofa. I should have had the relief that came with his touch, his gentle voice, his strong, safe arms around me, and the feel of that cool rag down my cheek.

Another quiet laugh left me. "I'm so glad you're here."

"Me too." He moved his hand around my shoulder. I closed my eyes, nuzzling my head into his chest. He kissed my hair, and my hand found his. "I get to cut the cord, right?"

"Yeah." I smiled. "You get to cut the cord, baby."

He nearly laughed as he pulled me in a little tighter. "You know what's crazy?"

"What's that?"

"Tomorrow," he whispered, kissing my hair," or maybe tonight, we get to meet our daughter."

I smiled, tears forming in my eyes. I held his hand a little tighter.

"We get to hold her and kiss her and feed her." He squeezed me harder, resting his head on mine. "We get to be parents."

"About time," I murmured.

A long moment of silence crept up.

I was ecstatic about Milly coming too. I was overjoyed, in fact. But I was also in labor. My head hurt, I was ridiculously hot, and Milly was kicking away at my spleen. I was more excited to have her out of me than the joys of parenthood.

Aside from that, I was nervous. Not of losing her, this labor was a lot less intense than Micah's had been.

And I loved my daughter so much. But a few hours before, I had a knife to a man's throat. A little girl quaked at me in fear. And I couldn't help but wonder if I had any clue what the fuck I was doing.

"Baby," I said again.

"Yeah?" He laughed.

After a long moment, I whispered, "I'm scared."

His hand moved up and down my arm in a soothing motion. "It isn't like last time. Nothing's going to happen to her."

I lifted my head to meet his gaze. "It isn't that."

"What is it then?" His gentle eyes met mine.

"I don't think I'm going to be good at this." Tears bubbled in my eyes and began to descend my cheeks. "I want to be. And I'm going to try to be. But I'm already such a failure as a mother."

He gingerly wiped my face with his thumbs, head shaking. "That's not true."

"Yes, it is." My glistening tears turned to heavier cries. I bit my trembling lip. "I love him. And I love her. But I'm not good at this. I couldn't even keep him safe while he was inside me. I almost lost her too. I got in that van. They carried him off in the plane, and it's my fault, and I don't know how I'm going to do this." My teeth began to chatter, and I looked between his sad eyes. "And I'm a murderer. I'm not a good person. How am I supposed to be a good mother if I don't even know how to be a good person? I don't know how I'm supposed to teach another little person to be good because I'm not. I'm not good."

"Baby." His warm thumbs wiped the salty water from my skin. "Baby, our world isn't that black and white. Those people, they didn't deserve to live."

"Who am I to decide that?" I asked. "How do I explain that to my kid? How do I tell them I took hundreds of lives and feel no remorse for it? How do you tell them that?"

"You don't." He gave something between a huff and a chuckle. "It's not like what's happened is a bedtime story, Lai. What happened to you and what you did to retaliate was awful. Every part of it. What they did to you, what you had to do them. But one day, when they're old enough, maybe they'll be able to understand it all. Maybe then we can tell them. Or you can, if you want. But they don't have to know. I didn't know my parents were out there killing Vampires and Werewolves and

Demons when I was a kid. But when I was old enough to understand that they were doing what needed to be done, I respected it. I respected the lives they saved; I didn't care about the lives they took."

"And what about when they hear the survivors calling me a savior?" I asked. "What do I say then?"

"That you saved almost a thousand people. *Good* people who deserved to live. We tell them that you did the right thing because you did. You did the right thing, baby. And the fact that you're worried you didn't just proves that you're wrong. That you're good." He looked between my eyes for a moment. Then he turned and took my face in his hands. "You're the best person I've ever met, Laila."

"Because you knew me before I became this," I whispered.

"No." He smiled and shook his head. "Because I watched you grow into this. This beautiful, strong, fearless, hard-headed, pain in my ass." A quiet laugh left my lips, and his smile widened. "I loved you when you were weak too, but I love you more than ever now. Not because of the bad things, but because you're strong. Because you don't give up. Even when everything is telling you that you should, even when it looks like there's no hope left, you don't give up.

"And that's what's going to make you a great mom. That strength. That inability to throw in the towel. And because you always take up for the underdog. Because you take in lost animals and tip your server the amount of the bill every time."

He lifted our hands to turn my wedding ring toward us. "Because you had to get a lab-grown diamond. Because you insisted my sister keep my mom's ring. Because you wouldn't let that deer die alone."

As tears formed in my eyes, he smiled softly.

"You're good, Lai. You're a good person. That's why I fell in love with you and that's why I still love you. Because you're kind and thoughtful and just *good*." He looked between my eyes. "You'd kill for what matters to you. You'd kill to keep our family safe. Some people might think that's bad, but I don't. I think that's strength."

Emma's sweet little face flashed behind my eyes. That little girl who thought I was about to kill her for revealing my secrets. And I wouldn't; I'd never hurt a child. But she thought that I would because she only knew me as a murderer. I wanted her to know me as more than that. I wanted her to know what Jeremy did. Even if I didn't see myself as good, even if she didn't after knowing the whole story, I wanted her to understand my actions and make her decision about me on her own.

"She thought I was going to kill her."

"What?"

"Emma," I muttered. "That's what she was thinking when I started walking toward her. She was praying that I wouldn't kill her. And I wouldn't. I'd never kill a kid. But she thought that I would."

He frowned, gaze shifting between mine.

"All she wanted was to know me," I whispered. "That's all she wanted, Jeremy. She just wanted to know me. And I owe her that. I owe them all that. I'm the reason they were there, and I owe them the truth. They deserve to know that I'm no savior. They were put in that place for me *to* save."

"You want to tell them?" he asked quietly.

After a moment, I said, "They deserve the truth."

"Yeah, they do."

"I want to plan something for them," I murmured. "Not a party. That was bad. But maybe a banquet of some kind? Or like, maybe we could rent a hotel somewhere. And they all could come, and we can get to know each other, and I can explain it all. Or at least, the parts that I know. I—I have to do something nice for them. And they deserve to know what we know."

He gave a gentle laugh and brushed sweaty hair behind my ear. "A banquet sounds good. Renting a whole hotel might be overdoing it a little though."

I smiled. "Maybe a little, huh?"

He chuckled again. "A little. But I think it's a good idea. They do deserve to know. If the end of the world is coming and we do need an army, we'll have to be transparent with them. If they find out that you knew and didn't tell them, they'll think you played some part in it that you didn't."

I swallowed hard. "Yeah, I have to. I have to tell them."

He nodded. "Once we get Milly settled in, we'll start making the plans."

I nodded again. Then another contraction took hold.

He gently coasted his hand up and down my back.

It was like an intense ache, more in my back than my stomach, actually. But it still had nothing on Micah's birth.

My eyes closed, and he wiped the rag against my sweaty temple.

"My mom's coming, isn't she?" I asked. "She said she was going to be here."

"Yeah, she's coming." He kissed my hair. "She texted a little bit ago and said she was on her way. Celena and Brody are coming up too."

I continued to pant through the contraction. "Can you call her when this one's over? I think that enema's kicking in, and I don't want you to see that. Tink needs to go outside too."

"Sure, baby." His hand coasted over my shoulder. His lips pressed into my forehead. "Do you need help to get to the bathroom?"

"No, I'm okay. I'll just teleport," I murmured. "Thank you though."

CHAPTER TWENTY-TWO

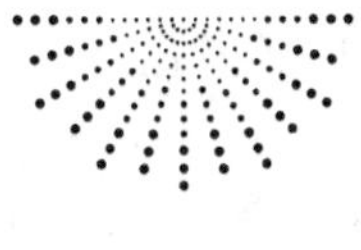

JEREMY

Warm spring air slid against my bare arms. Birds chirped in the thick foliage above as the dial tone rung against my ear. I glanced over the flowers growing in the garden off the porch. The lilies had just started to bloom, their fragrance filling my nose.

I smiled. Malina Lilly. Or maybe, Malina Lillian. We'd been torn on the middle name for a while now, but that sounded pretty. I bet that Laila would like it.

"Shit. Yeah, I'm coming, hon. I got pulled over," Rachel answered the phone. "I told the cop my daughter was in labor, and I needed to get there ASAP, but he didn't care. You know what this asshole had the nerve to tell me? 'Well, now you might miss it anyway.' I didn't miss it, did I?"

"No." I laughed. "No, the doctor just stopped by a little bit ago. She's five centimeters dilated now."

"Okay, good. Good, I'll be there in five minutes tops. Tell her to cross her legs 'til I get there."

"Don't you mean fingers?" I asked.

"No, I mean legs. Trap that baby in there 'til Grandma makes it,"

Rachel said quickly. I laughed. "I'm not missing this again. How is she? Is she doing okay?"

"Yeah, mostly," I said. "She barely flinches at the contractions."

"And emotionally?"

Chewing my cheek, I watched Tink chase after a butterfly. "I don't know. She's okay. No panic attacks or anything so that's good. But yeah, I think she'll be better when you get here. Jenna's with you too, right?"

"Yeah, I'm here," Jenna chimed in.

"Good. Yeah, that's good. She really wants you guys here," I said. "But okay, I'll see you soon. Don't speed, we have some time."

"Alright, hon, see ya soon."

After ending the call, I pulled down the notifications on the top of my screen. It'd been on silent since we went to the hospital. But I had three missed calls and a text from Ray.

Please call me asap. Not s.o.s. so I didn't call Laila but it's important.

Ah, shit.

I clicked call. His voice spoke on the other line before I had enough time to lift it to my ear.

"Oh, thank God," he answered. "I was worried something happened to you guys."

"No, we're fine. Laila's in labor though. What's going on?" I glanced into the living room as Laila waddled her way to the couch. "Is every-thing okay?"

"Shit, I'm so sorry to interrupt. She isn't crowning or anything, is she?"

"No, five centimeters dilated. I should get back in there, but I don't want to worry her with whatever this is. Are you guys okay? Do you need me to send someone to grab you?"

"Maybe. Maybe, I don't know. Something happened. Me and Lydia are fine; no one got hurt. But it's—it was fucking weird, man."

"Short on time here, Ray. Get to the point," I said quickly.

"Right, sorry. Okay, so Lydia's had nightmares since she got back. But recently, in the past month or so, they've gotten really intense. She broke four windows making tree branches climb inside. She's read my mind on accident a handful of times and started freaking out because she didn't mean to do it. I don't know."

Typical Ray, giving me irrelevant information that I really didn't have time for. "What's that have to do with nightmares?"

"Shit. I guess it doesn't. Maybe it's connected though. I don't know, either way. The nightmares are terrifying. She wakes up screaming and hysterically crying. It's always been bad, but last night was different. She had a nightmare, I calmed her down, and she went back to bed. Then I was already up so I was reading on my Kindle, but I was still in my work clothes, right?

"So I walk past her room to piss like I always do. And she always, *always* keeps the door open, and it was pushed up to the frame. Not enough that it would click shut, but just barely cracked. So I look inside, and I see somebody standing beside her bed. I didn't even think, I just grabbed my gun and pulled the trigger. But he must have heard me 'cause he turned around and just barely missed the bullet. Then he was standing in front of me and grabbed me by my throat. Then we teleported, and he had me up against a wall."

As soon as teleport left his mouth, my stomach sunk. Of course something with Micah had to happen while Laila was in labor with Milly. That was just our fucking luck.

"He—He... He didn't, um..."

"He had no eyes, and he looked a lot like me with a buzz cut," I said. "What happened? What did he do?"

"That's not the weird part," Ray continued. "It was Amy's voice. Coming out of *his* mouth."

I creased my brows in thought as Laila turned the TV on. That answered the question we'd been pondering since that day on the cliff.

Guess the bitch lived.

"What did she say?"

He fell silent for a moment. Then he said, "She said to tell Laila congratulations. Then she hit me over the head with a lamp. Lydia just woke me up. Neither of us know how she slept through the gunshot."

"Guessing Amy had something to do with that," I murmured. "Damn it. I was really hoping she was dead."

"What?" he asked.

"I don't have time to explain, but I will. Call Adam, tell him to come grab you and bring you back to Leah's. Laila needs me right now. I don't have time to play messenger boy. You tell everyone what you just told me. Make sure no one says a word about this to Laila until at least after the baby's born. We can't ruin this for her." I felt the first twinge of another contraction. "I have a Witch coming to put perimeter spells around the property. She wasn't going to come until next week, but maybe she can come today. Talk to Leah when you get here, tell her to tell Helena everything I just told you, and that she'll get her check as soon as the baby comes. She'll understand. Helena's scared of Laila. She'll push us up her schedule under the circumstance."

"Okay. Okay, I think I got all that," Ray agreed. "We'll go pack a bag."

"Okay. Only call me if it's life or death, alright?"

Celena and Brody emerged through the brush along the gravel road a few hundred feet away.

"Will do. Tell Laila I said good luck."

"Thanks. Alright, I'll talk to you later."

I shuttered the phone and started down the steps in a jog. Celena and Brody smiled up at me, waving.

"Congratulations, man." Brody grinned and tossed his arms around my shoulders. "I'm so happy for you guys."

"Thanks." I quickly pulled away. "But you guys need to know about something."

Celena's head rolled back. "Ah, fuck."

I glanced at the porch, making sure Laila hadn't come outside. Then I lowered my voice and leaned close. "Ray called. Chris was in Lydia's room last night, but Amy was in his body."

"I thought she was dead," Brody said.

"Yeah, me too," I muttered. "But apparently not. Either way. Ray shot, she pinned him to the wall, and told him to tell Laila she said congratulations."

"Fuck." Celena's hand lifted to rub her forehead. "She knows Laila's in labor."

"Doubt she would have said that unless they're going to try something. We're going to have to put up the perimeter spell as soon as possible. I told Ray to have Adam pick him up and tell Leah to get in contact with Helena. But if one of you could tell Leah what I just told you, that'd be great. Laila sees me on my phone, she's going to ask who I'm talking to. Just try and get the message out to everyone because I can't leave her right now."

"Yeah, of course," Brody said. "Where do you want me?"

"I need you both here. You can teleport the doctor back and forth, and I need you in case something happens to Laila or the baby." I gestured between them.

"Got it." Celena nodded. "We're not telling her, right? She's pushing a baby out of her twat. She can't do this right now."

"I hate keeping anything from her, but we have to on this one. If she starts to panic... I don't know. Let's just not let that happen."

"No, you're right," Brody said. "She physically can't fight right now if she wanted to. All it's going to do is send her into a panic attack. She doesn't need to know about this until the baby's born."

"Not ideal." I ran my hand against my mouth. "But we don't have a choice. This is the only option we've got. Once the baby's born and she gets some rest, then we tell her. 'Til then, we get the spell up, we keep Lydia and Ray safe, and we keep Laila and Milly safe."

"Hey guys," Laila called from the porch. "The party's in here, ya know."

Brody and Celena faked a laugh. I smiled, calling for Tink in the bushes, and started up the steps.

Lying to her was never easy. Every other time, it felt like a weight sitting on my chest. But this time, it wasn't the guilt that got to me.

It was the nearly unfathomable fear of losing another child to them. We were so close. She was almost here. She was about to come, and I'd be damned before I let them take my daughter too. I wouldn't let history repeat itself.

CHAPTER TWENTY-THREE

JEREMY

"You make childbirth look like a breeze," Jenna muttered.

Laila closed her eyes and breathed heavily through a contraction. "It isn't." She pushed her head further into my shoulder. "Micah's was harder than this time. Maybe I just handle pain better than I used to. I don't know."

"This is amazing though." Celena laughed. "A baby's about to climb out of your vagina. It's like magic."

Laila laughed, wincing through the pain. I moved my hand up and down her back as she took a slow, deep breath. My lips pressed to her sweaty forehead. I thumbed stray hair behind her ear.

Part of me was panicking a little bit. Leah, Kai, Hannah, Wyatt, Ray, Lydia, and Adam were all circling the property with shovels to bury stones that would keep the spell grounded. When Brody left next time to get the doctor, he was going to have to convince her to lie to Laila. We needed her blood for the spell, but we couldn't tell her we needed it then. Not while she was seven centimeters dilated.

But the bigger part of me was in awe. I watched her carefully wipe sweat from her brows as they creased over her closed eyes in slow motion. She looked so perfect. Pained yet focused. The beads of sweat trickled like they did after a long, peaceful run in the summer.

It was funny. People always said childbirth was the worst pain imaginable, which I don't doubt for most women.

But I'd seen Laila in agony. And birthing our daughter was anything but.

True misery wasn't the pain of the birth. Agony was building a bedroom for a child we never got to hold. Misery was birthing him alone in the dark with no pillow to rest her head on and no hand to rub the tense muscles along her spine. True, aching pain was loving and losing a child we would have given our lives for.

Physically, she was enduring pain for Milly too. Emotionally though, she was at peace. She was near happy even.

The pain of her last labor washed away the pain of this one. Once she'd lost a child, the pain associated with the next was a blessing.

That pain was love. That pain was bringing life to existence. It was beauty. It couldn't be a curse. She knew what a curse was, and our daughter's birth was farther than that than the sun is from Pluto.

I couldn't take that from her. She deserved this moment of peace. She deserved to enjoy this process. Because she was. I could see it in her expression. She was in less pain now than she'd been in since she was pregnant with Micah.

"Who all do you want in the room when it, like, actually happens?" Brody asked.

As the contraction passed, Laila cleared her throat. She cuddled against my shoulder. "I don't care. Whoever wants to be there." She reached over and rubbed Tinkerbell's head. "But I do want you in there with me, missy."

Tink panted hard, smiling. Then she dropped her head to Laila's thigh and cuddled close to her belly.

"I think I'll wait outside," he said.

"I'll be in there with you, baby." Rachel smiled.

"I am going to be in the corner with my eyes closed." Celena chuckled.

"I want to see it. All the gory details. I have to prepare myself." Jenna raised her hand. "Do you think you're going to poop on the bed? That's my biggest fear."

"I don't know, man. If I still have shit in me after that enema, I'd be shocked," Laila muttered.

I laughed and wiped the cool rag against her forehead. "You feel pretty hot, should we turn the air up?"

"No, I like the warmth. But could you guys open the windows?" She looked between Celena and Brody. Her hands tightened around my bicep, and she smiled. "I finally got comfy."

"'Course." Celena smiled, bringing herself to her feet. Giving a soft grin, Brody followed.

"Should we check your blood pressure?" I asked quietly.

"That's okay. The doctor's coming soon. We'll do it then."

I kissed her damp hair pulled into a messy bun. "Alright, baby."

Her aching back vibrated into mine. I twisted an arm beneath her and pushed my fingertips into the tight knot forming in the dimple just above her ass. When I felt relief from the pressure, a soft, gentle breath escaped her.

I guessed that was a cool feature about our bond. There wasn't much I could do to help the pain of the contractions, but I knew exactly where was sore and just the right amount of pressure to apply to soften the pain.

"I wonder what she's going to look like," Laila murmured.

"She's going to be beautiful." I smiled and rested my head on hers. "Just like you."

"Maybe she'll look like you." She turned her gaze up to meet mine. A smile stretched up her flushed cheeks. "I hope she has your eyes."

"I hope she has *your* eyes." I grinned. My thumb slid across the sweat that pearled from her forehead. "Your eyes are gorgeous."

She smiled, looking between mine. "So are yours."

"So she's golden either way." My lips curved higher as I cupped her cheek.

A quiet laugh left her lips. Then she leaned up to kiss me. I pulled her closer, feeling the warmth of her skin radiate into mine. We stayed like that for a soft and gentle moment.

Then a bright, white light flashed from the other side of the living room. "You're going to want to frame that." Celena grinned. "I'll text it to you in a minute."

I smiled, and Laila pulled back. She held her smile too.

Shit was bound to hit the fan again soon but for that moment, that brief and wonderful moment, I think we really were happy.

CHAPTER TWENTY-FOUR

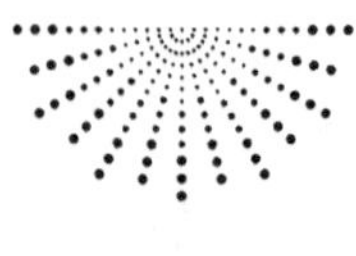

JEREMY

"I'd say another hour and you're going to be pushing, Momma." The doctor smiled, pulling off her blue nitrile gloves. "You're almost ten centimeters. A little over nine at the moment. This baby's ready to meet the world."

I laughed quietly. Laila smiled with joyous tears in her eyes.

It's really happening. We are about to be parents. We are about to have our baby girl.

"I have one more thing I have to run through really quick at the hospital. I'll be right back, shouldn't be more than ten minutes. But before I go, I'd like to collect a quick blood sample. Everything looks great; I don't want you to worry. It's just routine."

Laila pulled the blanket off of her legs and adjusted the loose, flowing night gown over them. She sat up, met my gaze, and extended her arm. Her lips curved in a smile. "We're about to meet our daughter."

I smiled back, blinking tears away. "I can't wait."

She wiped unwilling, elation-filled tears from her eyes. The doctor shot me a sad smile as she tied the tourniquet around Laila's arm.

I wasn't proud to do it either. But she'd thank me for it later. The birth was going *exactly* as she'd hoped and planned it would.

Lying is occasionally the right thing to do in medical situations. A doctor wouldn't tell someone who just had a heart attack that everyone they care about is at risk while they lie in a hospital bed. I think the doctor knew that as well as I did.

"You have Brody come grab me immediately if you start feeling the urge to push, alright?"

Laila nodded.

The doctor pulled the needle from her arm and pressed a pad of gauze to the blood.

"You got it, doc."

She smiled, fastened the tape to her forearm, and pulled away. While she started to the door, her smile lifted higher. "See the three of you soon."

Laila grinned. She looked so happy. Her smile wouldn't fall from her full lips, the warm blush to her cheeks was so joyous, and her eyes glistened with more life than I'd seen in them in a very long time. Even exhausted and pouring sweat, she was full of bliss.

I made my way to help her from the bed. She struggled a bit against the plastic lined plush. I kept my fingers twisted between hers and leaned down to press our lips together.

She smiled against my mouth, arms twisting around my back. Then she pulled her lips from mine with a laugh. "I can't wait until I can hug you again."

I chuckled, pushing hair from her face. "I can kind of hug you from behind."

"It's not the same." She smiled. "I just can't believe we're finally here. She's almost here. She's *really* almost here."

"We made it." I grinned, holding her face in my hands.

"Almost." Her lips curved higher, and her eyes brightened with excitement. "On the home stretch."

We need your blood, Leah's voice echoed in my mind.

Shit.

She was going to feel it.

Now, my lie was going to become more elaborate.

"Why don't you lie down while I go get your mom?" I wiped sweat from her cheek. "Looks like you could use some water anyway."

"Yeah, that sounds good. Standing feels good for a second or two, but it's doing something to this hip back here."

I kissed her forehead and teleported us to the top of the bed. "Less work on that hip."

I helped her sit and lifted the throw blanket from the armchair over her chest. I kissed her cheek one more time. Then I headed to the door.

"Baby?" She curled her head against a pillow.

"Yeah?" I glanced over my shoulder.

"Do we have the diapers here? Or are they still at the apartment?" she asked.

"They're here," I said, smiling. "And so are the birthday onesies you picked out and the embroidered blanket with her name on it."

Laila let out a sweet laugh. "Good."

"Hey, what do you think about Lily?" My smile lifted. "Malina Lillian."

She smiled too. "I love it."

I walked out the doorway. My gaze shifted to Jenna and Rachel at the couch, holding my grin. "She's nine centimeters now. Should be seeing a baby within an hour."

They squealed, excitedly clapped, and brushed past me into the room. I chuckled, starting to the kitchen. Celena stood over the island wringing her hands and licking her teeth.

Ah, shit. I knew that face. Something wasn't right.

I lowered my voice. "What's going on?"

"I don't know. Wyatt's worried," she murmured. "They think he's here. Fucking with their heads or something. I don't know what he meant, but we need to get that shield up pronto."

I didn't know what that meant either. But I wasn't taking any risks.

I teleported to the butcher block, grabbed a knife, and turned to the dishwasher. I opened it up and put the knife into the silverware holder.

"What are you doing?" Celena whispered.

"She'll see it through my eyes. She can't see me intentionally cutting myself, she's almost crowning," I said.

"Smart," she said.

I grabbed a towel from the sink, closed my eyes, and firmly grasped ahold of the knife in my palm. I grasped it hard so that it was deep enough to create a heavy blood flow.

"Are you okay?" Laila called from the bedroom.

"Yeah, baby, I'm fine," I yelled. "Just stupid, left a knife facing up in the dishwasher."

"Dumbass." I heard her say.

I released half of a laugh. Celena chuckled, and I wrapped the towel around my hand. Brody appeared a few feet away with a hand in his hair. "Good, you've got the blood."

I passed him the rag. He took it. Celena offered her hand out for mine. I extended it, and she began healing. "Make it quick."

"Will do. We were just waiting on you and Laila's. We're good to go now," Brody said.

I ignored the burning, stinging pain that radiated up my arm. The skin on my hand closed and he disappeared. I peddled to the sink and washed the blood from my hands. Then I went to the fridge, grabbed a bottle of water, and started back to the bedroom.

"Jeremy," Celena said quietly.

I turned to meet her gaze.

"I think something's going to happen," Celena murmured. "Wyatt's psychic. And he says he has a bad feeling. My job's to keep her safe with you, and that's what I'm going to do. But we have to get in that room, close the door, and we have to keep it shut. I don't know why; I don't know what he meant. But that's what he said."

Lovely. So we were about to be under attack. While Laila pushed a baby out of her vagina.

Ya know, just another day in the life.

"Let's get in there then."

CHAPTER TWENTY-FIVE

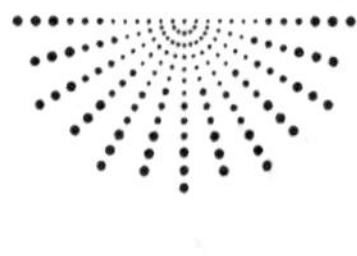

JEREMY

"Jeremy." Laila laid her back against my chest. I lifted sweaty hair from her flushed cheek as she panted out a slow, tired breath.

"Yeah?" I asked.

Her eyes shifted between mine. "Why did they need your blood right now?"

Fuck. She knew. But I was still gonna hold onto my lie. Whether shit was about to blow up or not, she didn't need to worry about that. Not right now. Right now, all she had to worry about was bringing our daughter into the world.

I managed the slightest smile. "We just wanted to get the spell up as soon as possible."

She squinted, still looking up at me. "C'mon, baby. We both know you're a better liar than that."

The cool rag in my hand slid across her forehead. "We'll talk about it after the baby comes."

Her eyes were still on me, voice barely more than a whisper. "Something's wrong, huh?"

"We're getting the shield up. Everything's going to be fine." I smiled.

"Do I need to know right now?"

"It can wait."

"Don't tell me then."

Relief washed over me as I kissed her forehead. Then Brody appeared a few feet in front of us with the doctor. He forced a smile she saw right through. "How ya doing, Lai?"

She gave a soft smile. "I'm okay."

"Feeling the urge to push yet?" the doctor asked.

"A little bit," Laila said.

The doctor smiled and sat at the chair in front of the bed. "Well, let's see what we're working with."

"Turn around, Brody," I muttered, helping Laila scoot down the bed.

"It's not like I want to see that anyway." He rolled his eyes and swiveled to face the French doors that led to the back garden.

Laila laughed, lifted her skirt, and opened her knees. I stayed behind her. She leaned back onto my stomach. Our gazes met, and I wiped sweat from her cheek. She brought a smile to her lips as she looked from my left eye to my right. "Everything's going to be okay, right?"

"Everything's going to be great."

She knew I had no way of knowing that. She was pretty sure that I was lying. But she nodded anyway. She needed hope. Even if it was false hope.

"Well, well, well." The doctor smiled at us over her knees. "Looks like Milly's ready when you are, Mom."

* * *

The moments after the doctor told Laila it was time to push were so confusing. My heart raced with excitement. My lips curved up in joy. But my stomach ached with fear, and my hands shook with anxiety.

I wanted to actually watch Milly come out, but Laila got comfy with her back against my chest, and there was no way I was going to make her move. Plus, it was kind of comforting to have my arms around her. If I had to, I could teleport us out of here in a millisecond.

"Alright, Laila." The doctor looked up at her, smile spread across her lips. "She's crowning. Next time you feel a contraction, you're gonna push, alright?"

Laila nodded, panting hard.

A sudden, curved blast of white energy shot through the air from behind us and chased through the wall in front of us.

Laila gasped.

I tightened my arms around her.

"It's okay. It's just the protection spell. The doctor has her crystal, it's okay." I held her tighter.

Trying to catch her breath, she continued the breathing exercises they'd taught her in Lamaze class. Her eyes closed, hand squeezing around mine. "It's okay."

I kissed her hair. "You're amazing."

"I'm tired," she whispered.

"She's almost here." I smiled. "You can take a nap when she is."

"I will not be taking a nap," she said. "I'm gonna be up with this baby until I pass out."

I laughed and kissed her hair again. I didn't plan on sleeping any time soon either.

Then an ear-piercing scream echoed outside the windows.

All of our eyes widened and shifted around each other's.

Tink scurried from her place by the door into the bathroom.

The feminine cry I believe Hannah released was mostly inaudible, but one part was clear.

"*Help me!*"

My heart hammered, and my stomach turned. Had my wife not been literally squeezing my daughter out of her twat, I'd already be gone. But I couldn't leave her. I *wouldn't* leave her.

I felt Laila's body temperature rise. Her eyes brightened to a glow.

My gaze shifted to Brody behind me in the chair next to my side table. "Go."

He nodded and disappeared.

"I can't do this," Laila whispered, head shaking. "I can't—What's happening? What's going on out there?"

"I don't know, baby. But you're doing great. You focus on this baby, okay? She's almost here. They can handle whatever's going on out there. You handle what's going on in here."

She breathed out a slow pant and gave a nod. "She's almost here."

I squeezed her hands. Then more screams erupted. A large thump rattled the pictures and shelves on the wall behind us. Celena teleported to the windows, closed them all at an inhuman speed, and pulled the curtains shut along the way.

Suddenly, the evening lit room grew dark, and Laila's breaths shortened. Her even intakes and slows sighs turned to quick, nervous pants on the verge of gasps.

"It's okay," I whispered at her ear. I kissed her hair. "It's okay, I'm right here."

She tightened her fingers around mine.

Jenna held her cell phone flashlight between Laila's legs for the doctor.

"Part of the head's almost out, Laila. Just a few more good pushes, okay?" the doctor asked.

Laila nodded with closed eyes.

Just as the next contraction began, the gentle drizzle outside turned to a downpour pounding on the tin roof as loud as the cries fighting to make their way from Laila's lips. The wind howled like a wolf between the trees outside.

"Is that you?" Celena asked.

Laila shook her head and continued to push.

"It's Milly," I whispered.

The doctor chanted encouraging notions to Laila while time seemed to stand still. I was scared shitless yet wrapped up in one of the best moments of my life. It was more bitter than a lemon yet sweeter than pie.

I felt her body shake as she pushed again. But that time, the push was followed by a gush of fluid and the sweetest, purest sound I'd ever heard. Just as that sound erupted, so did a familiar gold, shimmering golden light around Milly's body tied with hues of purple and specks of white.

Micah came into the world as a light brighter than the sun. Milly came into the world wrapped in a swirling, glistening smoke like aura.

Tears flooded my eyes. The doctor lifted our crying baby girl to the white towel on Laila's stomach.

Her tiny, blood and mucus covered hands reached upward. That beautiful, high pitched infant cry filled our ears. Laila released my hands quicker than lightning to touch Milly's fingers. She thumbed along hers and laughed as tears erupted down her face.

My baby. My kind of ugly, mucus, cream and blood covered little girl. So fucking weird looking, but somehow, the prettiest thing I'd ever seen.

The doctor clamped the cord close to Milly's belly and another further down the slimy, almost alien looking cord. Then she said, "You're cutting it, right, Dad?"

I froze at that realization.

There she was. My little girl. I finally was, in fact, Dad.

Then I smiled.

I shifted around Laila a bit. The doctor passed me a pair of scissors and pointed to the part that I should cut. I stared down at her in awe as the metal sliced through the piece of tissue.

Her skin was a bright white beneath the shimmering gold light and dark red blood. She had a full head of dark brown hair covered in thick, maroon colored mucus. I couldn't see her eyes or mouth that well through the cries, but that tiny chin and that little nose looked just like her mom.

Once I put the scissor down, Laila hurriedly wrapped the towel around our daughter and tugged her into her chest. That sweet cry echoed through the high ceiling above us like the sound of a fire engine coming down the street while a house was on fire.

Then I looked down at the most beautiful thing I'd ever laid eyes on wrapped up in my wife's arms. Laila laughed, face red, glistening with sweat and tears. She lifted her hand that wasn't holding her to wipe blood from her cheeks with the corner of the towel.

"Hi, Milly," Laila whispered as I reached out to touch our daughter's warm cheek. "I'm your mom."

CHAPTER TWENTY-SIX

LAILA

It felt like the world around me stopped spinning as I looked at my baby in my arms. She squealed like a pig headed for slaughter, but she was perfect. I wouldn't have traded that painful, ear piercing screech for any other sound in the world. That's all I'd wanted to hear since I birthed Micah. That beautiful, loud, begging cry.

I know that I pushed out the after birth, but I don't remember it. All that I remember is staring down at that beautiful little face. Those rosy cheeks coated in vernix caseosa. That tiny nose. Those closed, crying eyes.

Despite that blood and chunky cream all over her skin, she was the prettiest newborn I'd ever seen. She was a bit red still from the swelling of birth. But her cheeks were rounder. Her head was a bit bigger. She didn't have that shrunken, funky looking, alien appearance to her that most newborns do.

She was perfect.

It was the most beautiful moment of my life. It was a dream becoming a reality.

I forgot about the scream outside. I paid no mind to Celena healing my torn lady bits. I didn't even think about Micah for a second. All that

I heard, all that I saw, all that I felt was that ball of warmth tucked against my chest.

She was beautiful. She was my daughter. She was everything. She was *my* baby.

I was holding *my* baby.

As that realization washed over me, my glistening tears of joy grew into heavy, happy cries. Jeremy laughed, hugging me with one arm and holding Milly's hand with the other.

Those few minutes were the best of my life.

It was relief. It was love. It was joy.

I thought I'd be flooded with guilt for loving another child. Then I thought that I couldn't possibly love another baby as much as I loved Micah. But I was so incredibly wrong.

The capabilities of love are the most beautiful things imaginable. Love ultimately has no limits. One can love something so much and think that they couldn't love anyone as much as they love them. Then another and think the same. But then somehow, over time, you realize that love isn't measured on a scale.

Love is like a gaseous compound in the empty wonders of outer space. It can't be limited to one small box because it expands endlessly in every direction. There's always infinite room for it to grow. It doesn't in any way lessen the love that's already taking up space. That love simply morphs together to create something larger, complex, and even more beautiful.

My moment broke when a knock pounded at the door.

I clenched Milly closer to my chest.

Suddenly, that sparkling golden light emitting from my daughter's skin expanded in every direction until it pinged off of all four walls. It acted like a layer of luminescent, golden paint speckled with dots of purple and white.

We all stared around in amazement, and Milly's cries slowed.

Her eyes began to pull open. As they did, my jaw nearly dropped. I never hated my eyes, but when I saw them on my daughter's face, they were the most beautiful thing I'd ever seen.

"Holy shit," Celena murmured, running her hand along the force field. "It doesn't hurt or anything, but it's hard as stone. And warm."

I laughed as I looked into the glowing emerald eyes that gradually receded luminance until they twinkled like freshly polished jewels. They were a bit darker than mine, but there were streaks of dark, vibrant blue through them like Jeremy's.

"She's gonna be a little bad ass." Jenna looked over her from beside me.

The pounding at the door proceeded, growing so firm that it began to crack against the heavy force field. Pieces of wood and paint dropped to the ground on the outside of the translucent layer around the room. The cracks grew until it fell to the ground in chunks. It was being physically torn apart from the other side.

I tightened my arms around Milly, gaze locked with the shaking door. "Should we teleport?"

"I just tried," Jeremy said. "Nothing's getting in or out until Milly lets it."

"That could be a real predicament later," Mom murmured behind Jeremy.

I turned back up to Jeremy. "She's here. Now you've got to tell me what the hell's going on out there."

"Amy was in Lydia's bedroom wearing Chris's body last night," he said quickly, staring at the door as it broke to pieces. "He shot, she pinned him to a wall, told him to tell Laila congratulations and knocked him out."

"Fucking Christ," I muttered. Then I watched the rest of the door fall.

I expected it to be Chris. That'd be great actually—we could get our hands on him. Or Peterson even. Or maybe Amy. Who knew? Anyone other than who it was.

Adam.

He slammed an ax into the force field over and over and over as if it could break it. They clanged together like blades in a sword fight. He wore a smug look on his face that I didn't even know Adam's bubbly gaze was capable of. The expression alone made it clear that it wasn't him.

We'd thought that Nastya completed the possession through binding spells. But clearly, that wasn't the case.

My heart broke for a moment because I had no idea what that meant. Was Adam's dead body possessed? Would Amy, or Peterson, or Nastya, or whoever was inside of his body leave willingly if not?

Then another realization occurred to me. This was to prove a point. It was their way of saying fuck you.

Put up the spell; it doesn't matter. We can still get to you. Waste ten grand. We're still in charge. We can still torture you, even in the best moment of your life.

Just as my breaths grew short, a baseball bat hit Adam over the head. His eyes closed, and he collapsed to the ground.

My eyes met Mary's. And a joyous laugh left my lips.

She had bright red blood sprayed across her dirty gray T-shirt and dark washed blue jeans. I couldn't help but fear for who must have died to leave behind that amount of blood. But she smiled, and my worry faded.

"How's my granddaughter?"

Just as she spoke, the golden walls fell to the ground like glitter before disappearing into nothing.

CHAPTER TWENTY-SEVEN

LAILA

My heart had just stopped racing. The gentle warmth of chamomile coasted down my throat. Milly slept in my arms; little fingers wrapped around my thumb. Her sweet scent like yeast and sugar filled my nose. The sound of her little breaths drifted into my ears. One of Jeremy's arms rested around my waist, the other around Milly's hand.

I looked up and glanced around the main house kitchen. "So everyone's okay."

They certainly didn't look it, but everyone was on two feet. Each of them was covered in mud and blood. Their clothing was torn, some clearly from stab wounds. But everyone was healed and okay now.

"Everyone's okay." Leah wiped crimson from her forehead.

"What the hell happened?" Jeremy asked.

"A blood bath," Hannah said, brushing mud from her lip to take a sip of water.

"It wasn't. Everyone's fine," Wyatt said. "No one killed anyone."

"Not yet," Helena said from the breakfast nook. "Not yet, but it's going to happen. This bitch..." She scoffed. "This bitch isn't going to stop 'til she's dead. In the meantime, I'm going to work up a spell. Hey, Laila, think Moriah La Fay would give you a sample of blood? Even a lock of hair. If I get La Fay blood, I can mark all of us and keep this from happening again."

"What was *this?*" I looked around the room of brothers, sisters, friends, and family covered in damp mud and drying blood.

"They were inside of us," Lydia whispered. "Hopping from one body to the next."

"We were all turning on each other." Hannah rubbed her red, bruising neck. Kai reached out to touch her shoulder, and she flinched away. He swallowed hard, and his hand moved back to his side.

"They're fucking with us," Jeremy whispered.

"They're trying to tell us they're still in control," Brody said. "That's what this was. Their way of saying we can take away everything that you love no matter how hard you're trying to do everything right. To make it clear they didn't forget."

They weren't. There was a reason for it. But all that mattered was getting that spell cast so that it couldn't happen again.

"I'll call Moriah in the morning. I already owe her a favor but maybe she'll put it on my tab. It's two a.m. there, and I'm exhausted so I'm not doing it now. But this can't happen again. I'll get her blood one way or another."

Helena nodded.

"Where have you been, Mary?" Jeremy asked. "How'd you get through the barrier?"

"I gave her a necklace," Leah said.

"Where I've been is a long, complicated story we'll get to in the morning after the two of you get some time with your new baby." Mary smiled, looking between the three of us. "You're exhausted, Laila. And clearly that baby knows how to keep the three of you safe. You should get some rest. We should all get cleaned up. Then we'll go over everything in the morning."

Mary was right; Milly was all I wanted to focus on. Hell, even as I glanced around that room, I felt euphoric from the baby in my arms. Not in the sense that I was high, and not in the sense that Milly had some magical power that did it, just in that maternal sense that comes when a new life is born.

I hadn't been able to move that ball of warmth from my arms since I held her. I hadn't been able to focus on anything *but* her. I heard what everyone said about what had happened during her birth, but I couldn't care less about it. Milly was all that mattered.

"That was amazing, wasn't it?" I smiled, turning down to her. "She knew exactly what to do. Hadn't even taken a shit yet, and she knew how to put a shield around the entire room."

"She's a powerful child," Mary murmured. "You could do that too, you know."

"Really?" Jeremy asked. "Because we've both glowed like that before. But it just makes us feel good. We've never used it offensively."

I did. With the guards inside the last compound. But it just put them into a state of peace before I killed them.

It wasn't like what Milly did.

"*You* did, Jeremy?" Mary asked.

He nodded and brought a swirling ball of it to his hand. "I still can."

Her brow ached, smiling. "You're stronger than I thought."

"What do you mean?" I asked.

"That ability is associated with the soul. I've only known it to be associated with Angels and Demons. But it could be different with the par animarum." A smile came to her lips. "It's literally your soul vibrating out of your body."

"We lose a part of our soul?" I asked.

"No. It returns to your body as it disintegrates. But it's a very powerful ability that can be used a thousand different ways. It's very difficult to break through, even for a very powerful Witch. It's worth perfecting."

"We can use all the help we can get," I said.

She gave a soft smile and looked at Milly. "Has she eaten yet?"

"Twice." I smiled. "Twenty minutes on each boob both times."

"Jesus, that's like half the time that she's been alive," Celena murmured.

"Newborns eat a lot." Jeremy rested his chin on my shoulder. His finger traced down her nose, and he kissed my cheek.

"She latched well?" Mary asked.

"Right away," I said. "She knows exactly what to do."

"Little genius." Celena beamed with pride.

"She's beautiful." Mary smiled. "I can't wait until I get cleaned up so I can hold her."

"Mary's right though." Adam rubbed his mouth. "We should all try and get some rest. We're too shaken up to pass around a newborn anyway."

"Yeah, I agree," Hannah murmured. "I want to, but I don't think Laila's willing to share yet anyway."

I laughed. "No, not yet."

"Have you held her yet, hon?" Mom asked Jeremy.

"No." He smiled and ran his fingertip along her fingers. "But it's okay. She's here. She's healthy. She's perfect."

"And how are you feeling, Laila?" Mary smiled. "I always had this euphoric sensation for days following the births of my children."

I smiled. "It's like I'm high."

"It's oxytocin," Jeremy murmured.

"I felt like that too." Mom smiled. "Not just with Jenna. With you too, Lai."

My finger slid down her velvet soft cheek. "I already love her so much."

"Me too." Jeremy smiled beside me.

CHAPTER TWENTY-EIGHT

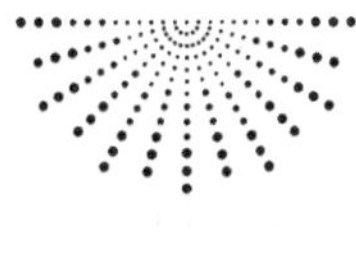

LAILA

My fingertips slowly danced down the soft black hairs that framed her soft white skin. Leaning down, I sniffed her hair and closed my eyes. I just couldn't stop looking at her. She was so pretty, so soft, so perfect. Nearly hypnotizing, really.

"We should be okay without a door for a few days, right?" A clunk sounded as Jeremy dumped broken wood into a contractor bag. "It's just you and me. We don't close doors that much anyway."

"Yeah, we'll be okay," I murmured.

"Okay, good." He nodded, sweeping the debris into a pile.

"We can worry about that in the morning." I smiled, looking up from Milly in my arms.

He kneeled to wipe up the dust. "You walk around barefoot."

"I'll wear slippers." I stood with a smile.

He went on wiping up the splinters and dust as I made my way across the room.

Once I stood in front of him, he looked up to meet my gaze. "Do you want to hold her?"

He swallowed before a smile came to his lips. "I'm kind of scared to."

I laughed. "Why?"

"What if I drop her?"

I laughed again. "You won't drop her."

"I should wash my hands though," he said.

"Actually, I'd prefer if you didn't. It's good to expose her to germs. I read an article recently about how you should wash your hands normally around a new baby. You don't have to sanitize them unless they've been soiled or unless you've gone somewhere heavily infested with germs. You haven't been around anyone with the rona, have you?"

He smiled and shook his head.

"Then hold your daughter." I smiled.

"You sure you're ready to share?"

"We can take turns."

He took in a deep breath. Then he smiled and set the broom down. "I haven't held a newborn since Hannah. You're going to have to refresh my memory a little."

"Okay, so put your arm out like this." I gestured with my own. He nodded, pulling his arm to his chest. I shifted her in my arms until I was holding her head in one hand and rested her body against my forearm. "Keep her head up with the crease of your elbow and hold her butt with your hand."

He nodded.

I rested her in the nook of his arm.

His other hand instinctively moved to her chest, and his fingers touched her sleeping cheek.

"And you're holding your daughter." I smiled.

That was the sweetest sight I'd ever seen. My arms felt empty without her in them, but she was still in the safest place in the world. Mine and his arms were always the best place for our children.

His eyes were so gentle as they moved over her sleeping face. His lips held the softest, sweetest grin I'd ever seen. He looked just as happy as I was.

He laughed, staring down in awe. "She's so warm." My smile widened and happy tears formed in my eyes. "If she has your powers, how can we check her temperature? Your usual temp is around one-oh-five, and that's high grade for most people."

"We'll ask the doctor tomorrow when we take her for her vaccines," I murmured.

He nodded, gaze steady on our baby in his arms. "She looks just like you when you're sleeping."

I smiled. The image of Micah in Chris's arms that hung on the fridge flashed behind my eyes. I cleared my throat. "One looks almost identical to you and one looks almost just like me."

He smiled. "I'm glad she got your eyes."

"There's some of your blue in there." I grinned. "They aren't *just* like mine."

"Pretty close." He smiled, finger tracing down her nose. "And she definitely didn't get my nose."

She definitely did not. Don't get me wrong, I loved that nose. But the boys pulled it off far better than the girls. Hannah was lucky and got a miniature version of the same one.

A quiet laugh left my lips. I touched her hand that stuck out of the swaddled pink blanket. "I really need a shower, but I don't want to stop looking at her."

He smiled and met my gaze. "I could hold her and sit in there with you."

My smile widened. "That's a good idea."

"Then maybe we should bath her." His finger slid along a piece of dried blood in her hair. "The nurses usually do that at the hospital, right?"

I nodded, running my fingertip down her soft nose. "Yeah, I think so."

He fell quiet for a moment, just gazing down at her in his arms. Then he turned his gaze up to mine. "I'm sorry I lied to you. You were in active labor and I didn't want to, but it felt like I had to."

For the first time, I wasn't angry at him for lying in the slightest. It could have been the hormones talking but he definitely made the right call.

"I'm glad you did," I said. "Everything turned out fine anyway. I wasn't needed on this one. And I got the experience I wanted with Micah. It was beautiful. Up until the end then anyway."

"It was." He smiled. "Beautiful, I mean."

I smiled again and gave a nod.

"You were amazing," he whispered. Then he leaned forward and kissed my forehead. "It looks so much scarier in movies."

"It can be," I murmured. "But I think I knew what I was doing this time. And there was a really great reward at the end."

He smiled wider. "The best."

CHAPTER TWENTY-NINE

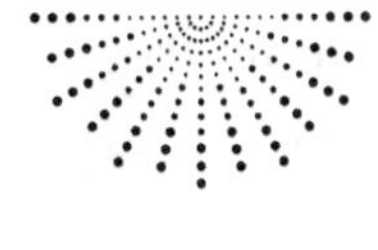

LAILA

"I still look pregnant." I looked at my naked body in the mirror. My finger poked into the squishy, bloated stomach that had been hard as a rock a few hours before.

"You literally just gave birth." Jeremy laughed. "You're still swollen and everything. Give yourself some time."

"I guess I still had a belly for a while after Micah too." I turned to the shower and spun the faucet handle. I looked at Milly with a smile, voice altering to a baby tone. "But you're worth my once cute tummy being ugly and wrinkly."

"It's still cute." Jeremy smiled. "You only have a few stretch marks anyway. And I think they're pretty cute too."

I looked over the blinking little girl in his arms. "At least I get to feel like they're worth it now."

He smiled softly. "She was worth everything."

I struggled a smile. "Almost everything."

His gaze turned back to her. "I didn't think it was possible to love someone I just met this much."

I smiled and stepped into the shower. "It's amazing, isn't it?"

"She's just so perfect." He laughed and sat on the edge of the tub.

"How did she know we were in danger? And how'd she know to take it down when she did? And did you look outside? It stopped raining."

"I don't know." I smiled. "She's got your instincts, I suppose."

He smiled as he murmured something to her that I didn't hear over the running water.

"Is this how you felt when Micah was born?" He glanced up at me through the glass shower door. "Like, more love for one person than you ever thought was possible?"

I smiled back. "The only thing that compares to how much I love him is how much I love her. You're a close second, but they're a tie. No offense."

He laughed. "None taken. I kind of feel the same way. It's a little different for me with Micah though."

I dipped my hair under the water and swallowed the swell in my throat. "Yeah. I guess it's a little different with Micah for me too."

He grew quiet then.

It wasn't that I didn't love Micah as much as I loved Milly. I loved them equally. But I didn't get to hold him. I didn't get to protect him. It wasn't that the measure of love equaled out to a different number. It was just, simply, different.

"It kind of sucks that you're breastfeeding," Jeremy muttered as we looked down at Milly sucking at my chest.

"Why do you say that?" I turned up to meet his gaze. "You're the one who went on and on about how 'breast is best' and that natural feeding is better for her."

"'Cause I can't feed her." He chuckled, his fingertip trailing down her cheek.

"Once I start getting a better milk supply, I can start pumping." I smiled. "Then you can feed her too."

"Oh, yeah. I forgot about pumping. That's a good idea."

"It is, huh?"

He smiled. Then he kissed my forehead. "I can't believe this is real."

It did feel surreal. Like it was too good to be true. Although, I supposed it wasn't. Too good to be true would've been if Micah miraculously showed up at the door with his uncle. But this was pretty great too.

"Neither can I," I muttered. Tears formed in my eyes. "We've waited so much longer than we ever should have had to for this."

"We should have had this two years ago," he whispered as Milly wrapped her little hand around his finger. "No one has the right to take this from someone."

I grew quiet.

"I'm sorry. I didn't mean to kill the mood," he muttered. "It just... It makes me so angry."

"It's okay," I murmured. "For some reason, having her makes talking about him a little easier."

"Yeah." His thumb slid along her fingertips. "Somehow it does."

"We should show her pictures of him as she gets older. The one's Lydia's made. The one of him and Chris on the mantel." I watched her deep green eyes dance over mine. "She should get used to how Chris looks too."

He was quiet for a moment. His voice was a sad, near whisper when he spoke. "Do you think we're going to find them?"

"I know that we will. I've given up on the concept of when. But I know that one day, maybe in a month, or maybe in six, or maybe in a year, we're going to find something. And when we do, we're going to be smart. We're going to have a strong, concrete plan. We're going to think out every possible outcome, and we're going to win. We're going to bring Micah and Chris home and kill the other three. I don't know how I know, but I do. I just know."

He rested his chin on my shoulder. "Have you thought about that at all?"

"What part?"

"Killing him," he said. "Have you thought about how you want to do that?"

A quiet laugh left my lips. "More times than I can count."

"And?" He turned to meet my gaze. "How are you going to do it?"

"I'm not going to kill him right away. I need answers first. I need to know why he did all of this. And I want him to know how it feels to be tied to a table."

He nodded, gaze shifting between mine.

"I'm cutting off his dick. That's a given," I muttered. "Then whatever other forms of torture I have to use to get what I need out of him. But other than that, the death itself will probably come to me in the moment. Before I kill him though, every one of the survivors that wants to is going to get a chance to torture him the way they see fit. Not enough to kill him though. I get that."

"It's a good thing she can't understand English yet." Jeremy chuckled.

I laughed. As much as I enjoyed fantasizing about killing that bastard, I also wasn't in the mood. I was in love with my new baby. She's all I wanted to think about.

So, I changed the subject. "Are you going to teach her all of the languages you know?"

"Maybe one day we'll get to all of them." He grinned and brushed black hair from her forehead. "But we'll start with English and French. Spanish will be next because it's gradually becoming the second language of the country we live in. But by the time we're there, she'll be old enough to learn to read music, and we'll focus on that before we get to a third language."

I laughed and looked over his boyish grin. "Oh, yeah?"

He nodded. "And she's going to at least know how to play *Smoke on the Water* by the time she's five."

"Sounds reasonable." I smiled.

She sure the hell would. As well as just about every other instrument on the planet. Even some we'd yet to realize existed.

CHAPTER THIRTY

JEREMY

I didn't sleep that night. Laila did between feedings with Milly, but I didn't. My eyes were heavy, and I was exhausted, but I didn't want to stop looking at her. I couldn't bring myself to put her down.

The thought of missing a single moment with her terrified me. Even if it was for something that I needed like sleep. She'd only been alive for a few hours. What if I missed something important in that time? What if I missed her first smile? What if I missed her first poop? What if she got SIDS?

I just couldn't stop looking at her. If I wanted to put her down, I had to put her in the bassinette because Laila used her powers in her sleep from time to time. Not to mention the frantic flailing during her nightmares. Milly might not be safe; she couldn't sleep in our bed. But I couldn't put her down.

She was new to this whole life thing. She'd spent the last thirty-four weeks inside the warmth and comfort of her mother's body. And it was pretty great in there—I knew firsthand. I never wanted to leave either.

Joking aside, all of the things in the new world around her must have been scary.

No longer hearing that thump-thump of Laila's heart. Swaddled in a soft blanket rather than existing inside a tiny, hot swimming pool. Feeling hunger for the first time after being continuously full since her existence came to be. Cool air touching her skin for the first time. A scratchy, restricting diaper pressed against her soft, fragile skin.

Before then, I couldn't do anything to help either of my children. But that night, I got to give her comfort. I got to give her what Laila had given her for the past thirty-four weeks. I was able to be her parent.

It was the best thing I'd ever felt.

***

"How can anything be this pretty?" Hannah laughed as she played with Milly's hand in her arms.

"Because she looks just like her mom." I smiled at Laila.

"She really does," Hannah muttered. "Did you, like, clone yourself?"

"She doesn't look *that* much like me." Laila laughed. "Look at her lips."

"Those are your lips." Hannah laughed. "Maybe a little fuller though."

"Exactly," Laila said.

"It's a Fae thing," Leah said. "We're exceptionally beautiful babies."

"And adults." Mary nodded. "It's a trait. But the babies look so much prettier because they're slightly more developed than human babies when they're born. Past that awkward stage, so to speak."

"That's true," Rachel agreed, taking a bite of her pancake. "Laila was a gorgeous baby. So were you, Jenna. But it took you a little longer."

"Thanks, Mom." Jenna laughed.

"Sorry, sweetie." Rachel chuckled. "She really does look just like you did when you were born, Laila. Doesn't she, Mary?"

Mary smiled and gave a soft nod. "She does."

Laila smiled, gazing down at Milly in my sister's arms.

"Okay, I get a turn now." Leah brushed against Hannah. "Hand her over."

Laila laughed as they passed her along. "Just be careful. Drop my baby, and I'll kill you."

"I'm not dropping any babies." Leah looked down at Milly. A quiet laugh left her lips as she looked between her eyes. "Okay, my ovaries are getting tingly. Remember when you asked if I was going to have babies and I said maybe? I was wrong. The answer is yes."

"I get to hold her next." Kai grinned.

"Then me." Jenna raised her hand.

"Well, you guys are going to have to make it snappy." Laila touched her boobs. "I think my milk just dropped."

"Oh, come on, can't you pump?" Leah asked. "I just got her."

"You can hold her for a minute." Laila laughed. "But no. I'm not pumping yet. It's important for her to get all of the colostrum in the first couple days."

"What's that?" Adam asked on the other side of the island.

"Like, super nutritious boob milk." I gulped up my cup of coffee.

"No shit," he muttered. "What's in it?"

"A bunch of vitamins and a lot of calories," I said.

"You guys are experts on this," Jenna said.

Laila managed a smile. "Well, we had a lot of time to prepare."

"Sorry," Jenna said. "I didn't mean to, ya know... Bring all of that up right now."

"No, it's okay," Laila said. "It happened. We're not going to pretend that it didn't. She's going to know who her brother is."

Kai smiled. "She should. I wish ye'd've known a bit 'bout me before we met."

"Would've made things a little easier, huh?" Laila grinned.

"Perhaps a bit." He smiled and ran his fingertips along Milly's around Leah's thumb. "This little lass's a beaut though. Wish I'd have got to see her sooner."

"That's okay; I wasn't willing to let her go 'til late last night anyway." Laila laughed. "Then Jeremy stayed up all night holding her when she wasn't eating."

"Yeah, I'm ready to share now too." I smiled.

Leah shot me a smile before looking back down to Milly. "Your Aunt Celena told me about all that cool stuff you did so I know that you and I are going to be good pals, little lady."

"It was really fucking cool," I said.

"That rain was all her too." Laila smiled with pride. "She's a really special kid."

"Those temper tantrums though." Hannah laughed.

Laila shook her head with a smile. "I'll just counter it out. She's going to learn to never use her powers against her family. She already knows how to use them to protect us though, so I think she'll grasp it pretty quick."

If only it was that simple. Milly always had a little mind of her own. She just *loved* to tear pieces of the roof to the ground when she got pissed off.

"You aren't binding them?" Jenna asked.

Everyone in the room besides Mary, Rachel, and Jenna fell silent and scrunched down their brows.

"Of course we're not binding them," I said.

Never in a million years would I bind my child's abilities. To me, and to Laila, that was the equivalent of telling our child which gender they were supposed to be attracted to. That was the equivalent of telling them which god to worship. It was a part of who they were, it was their heart and soul, and we'd never dream of taking that from them.

Even if the little shit did like to destroy my house when she got pissed off.

"And neither are we." Adam's brows fell further over his eyes.

Jenna arched one. "And that's exclusively your decision?"

"Since I have powers, and you don't, yeah. It is," Adam said.

"Excuse me?" Jenna said. "This is my baby; any decision being made about him is just as much mine as it is yours."

"This isn't something you could understand, Jenna. Ask your sister how hard it is to find out what you are later in life. You're never going to experience that; you don't get to be a judge."

"This is about the circumcision thing again, isn't it?" she said. "I don't have one so I can't possibly make an educated decision on the subject, right?"

"Exactly," Adam said.

I struggled not to laugh. If I said that to Laila, she'd have punched me in the face quicker than I could say I was sorry.

"You're ridiculous," Jenna said.

"Baby, do you know how many kids with uncircumcised penises I personally mocked in the locker room in middle school?" Adam asked.

"That is true," I muttered.

"The world's changing—"

"Kids are always going to be little pricks. That's just science." Adam raised his shoulders in a shrug.

"It's an unnecessary, painful, and traumatic event," she continued.

"I was circumcised, and I'm not traumatized," Adam said.

"Me neither," I muttered.

"Alright, guys," Laila chimed in. "This sounds like a private conversation the two of you should have as parents at a time that isn't meeting my daughter."

"Sorry," Jenna muttered.

"Yeah, my bad," Adam said.

"Laila, Jeremy." Mary glanced between us. "I'd like to give you a brief description of my last few months when you get the chance. Even the brief version is rather loquacious so you may want to get comfortable."

CHAPTER THIRTY-ONE

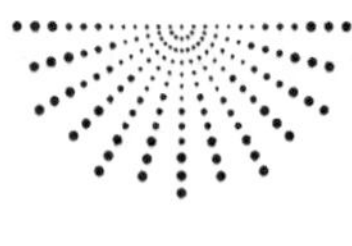

LAILA

As Milly suckled away at my chest, Jeremy and I sat on the couch in the front room. Mary sat in the adjacent armchair. Warm light shined in through the open windows, a pleasant spring breeze drifting through the air. But as peaceful and joyous as that felt, something in Mary's gaze sent a shiver down my spine.

"After the last time that we all spoke, I went..." Mary cleared her throat. "I went downstairs. I couldn't find anything in Heaven, and I was running out of places to look."

"You went to Hell?" I asked.

She nodded slowly. "Still, I didn't find much. Not at first. But I made deals. Barters for shreds of information on the supposed apocalypse."

"What did you find?" I asked.

"What kind of barters?" Jeremy said beside me.

"Unwise barters," she muttered. "But that's beside the point. What I believe, what I think that I've found, isn't easy to fathom."

"We can handle it."

Her hand ran over her mouth. "There's a more in-depth prophecy. In which, the two of you are mentioned by name."

I should have been a bit shocked. But honestly? After finding a book I'd written forty some years in the future and learning that I was written about in the book of Revelation, it took a lot to shock me.

"What does it say?" I asked quietly.

"I had to have it translated from Enochian, so it isn't easy to understand," she muttered.

"You don't speak it?" Jeremy asked.

"I speak *our* Enochian." Drawing in a deep breath, she searched for the words. "But this is different. It's more primitive. Older. Older than anything I've ever seen, which means a great deal coming from me."

"And it said our names?" Jeremy asked.

"In a manner of speaking." Mary nodded.

"What do you mean?"

She rubbed her mouth, which was odd. I'd only seen Mary show any signs of emotion a handful of times, and now, her posture wasn't perfect, her eyes were slightly widened, and she anxiously rubbed her mouth. "Do you know what your names mean? Or Micah's? Did you pick it intentionally, Laila?"

I thought back to scrolling through baby names online. Micah just stood out. Jeremy said he liked it, and it sounded good with Christopher, so that was that. "Not really. I just liked it."

"I didn't think about your name much when I named you either. It just came to me. Do you know what it means?" I shook my head, and she smiled. "The angel of conception."

Birth clearly played a big part in my story. Being a mother, having children, fertility. They were the primary components of my story, in fact.

"And Jeremy, your name means appointed by Yahweh," Mary said. "I'm not one hundred percent sure how that relates to you, but that's what it means."

He cocked his head to the side. "Yahweh is the Hebrew god. *Your* god."

"Zeus in Greek mythology," she said. "Odin in Viking tales, or perhaps Thor? Allah to Muslims, Krishna in Hinduism. Jehovah to others. Use whichever named you'd like."

I didn't know it then, but she was wrong about that part. He wasn't Odin. He was… He was closest to Loki in Norse mythology.

"What does Micah mean?" I asked.

She was quiet for a moment. "Micah means he who is like God. Christopher means bearing Christ."

My throat grew tight. He who is like god definitely aligned with the prophecy we'd already heard, as did the concept of the reborn Christ. The savior of god's chosen people.

According to myth, that's what Guardians were. God's chosen people set to help the humans pave a better way of life. I never really believed it, but that is why we answered to the Angels once upon a time.

"The prophecy referred to you, Laila, as the Angel of mothers and conception." She turned to Jeremy. "You as who god has appointed, and Micah as he who is like God and Cristo."

"That's Latin, isn't it?" I asked.

"Christ in Latin," Jeremy said. "What does that mean?"

"I don't know entirely. The tablet was complicated. Only a portion of it has even been able to be translated."

"What else were you able to get out of it?" Jeremy asked.

Mary's gaze was distant, head shaking slightly. "Mostly illegible nonsense. Words with meanings that existed long before my time. But one thing that was made clear was the meaning behind all of it in itself."

"Can you just, not speak in riddles for five minutes, Mary?" Jeremy asked.

She rubbed the corner of her eye. "It was inscribed on a circular stone tablet. The prophecy was underlined in a spiral that wrapped under every word and started where it began."

"What does that mean?" I asked.

"The cycle will repeat," Jeremy murmured.

Mary nodded.

"What else did it say?" I asked.

"The cursed divine family of resilience. I believe in reference to all of us," Mary murmured. "A loose definition. It mentioned something about eternal salvation on earth. A holy beginning, a damning center, and a holy end to cease all damnation that is and ever was. The awakening of the tree of life. An end to all pain and suffering. An end to the world as we know it after the cycle is broken."

"What does that mean?" I asked quietly.

Jeremy's breaths slowed, and his hand reached for mine. "Or the cycle will repeat."

I still didn't understand. But I did know one thing. Milly was born. The solstice was a month away. And I needed to know what this cycle was really about.

"I'm worried, guys," Mary murmured. "Heaven, Hell... Everyone's terrified. The things that they're stockpiling up there..."

"In Heaven?" Jeremy asked.

She swallowed hard. "They have weapons. Wildly dangerous weapons. And I don't know whose side they're on."

My heart picked up. "What are you getting at, Mary?"

Her breaths were far from even as she met my gaze. "These weapons... They aren't the kind Angels would use to fight Demons. These are capable of..." She let out a slow, shaking breath. Tears bubbled in her eyes. Not once had I ever seen Mary cry, and yet, there were tears across those hazel eyes. "They're strong enough to wipe this little blue planet to nothing. Bury the world alive. Burn it to ash. Bring on another great flood, so to speak."

Jeremy's fingers tightened on mine as my arm clenched around my daughter.

"I don't know why they would bring these things out after all of these thousands of years unless they were going to use them. I'm afraid for this planet. I'll still be standing after whatever they do, but I fear for those that aren't immortal."

Jeremy licked his lips. "How did you get this information on Heaven? You're lower level."

Her eyes closed. Her gaze shifted to the ground. "I broke protocol."

We all knew a thing or two about the Council and the Archangels above them. There are rules. There weren't many, and certainly not as much as there should've been—hence why she got away with Moe's murder and what she had that siren do to Jeremy.

However, there is one rule in Heaven that no Angel dare break. It's a simple one, really. Obey.

I leaned forward, heart racing. "Did you get caught?"

Slowly, she nodded.

"No," Jeremy whispered.

"It's not so bad," she murmured. "They didn't recycle me. My power will strengthen. I'm weaker than I've been in many years, but I'll be better in time. It's just going to take some adjustment. I have a fair bit of time left in this body unless something happens to it so not much has changed, really."

"You fell," I whispered.

She wiped her cheek and looked up to meet my gaze. Her deep hazel eyes stared back at me. She forced a smile. "I fell."

No longer was my biological mother an Angel.

Now, she was a Demon.

CHAPTER THIRTY-TWO

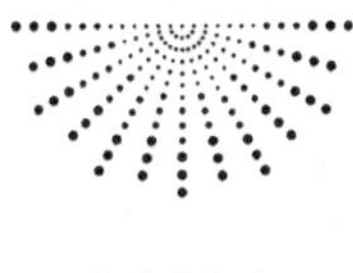

LAILA

"Laila, darling." Moriah laughed on the other end of the phone. "I'm so glad to hear from you. How is that new baby?"

"News made it across the pond that quick?" I smiled, holding the phone against my ear with my shoulder.

My hands fumbled with the diaper around Milly's hips before I nearly dropped the phone onto her head. Then I realized, I have powers. Why not use them? My gaze shifted to the tabs of the diaper. They telekinetically flipped open and laid on the waist band.

I smiled and lifted her back to my arms. Her small open mouth bobbed around in search of food, and I chuckled. Then I pulled my shirt off of my shoulder. And like that, the little chunker was back to eating.

"The shot heard 'round the world, love." She laughed. "Didn't you feel the massive surge of energy? It's all anyone's been talking about."

"I was a little distracted by the infant making her way out of my vagina so not really." I laughed and draped a blanket over her bare skin.

"Well, it was beautiful. Anyone inclined saw a gold light painted with purple stars race across the sky. Marvelous, truly. I'd love to meet the little harlot."

Smiling slightly, I said, "As long as you don't call her a harlot again, that could be arranged."

Moriah laughed again. "So what is it, darling? You didn't call me the day after your daughter's birth on a social call, I presume."

"Always business between us."

"Now that you aren't pregnant, that should change. You and I could have a wonderful time. Your abilities, my money, some very expensive wine. Oh, and my stylist. You're only ever in rags. With a body like yours, that's shameful." She chuckled again. "But business first, shall we?"

I didn't have any intentions on going out on the town in the foreseeable future. My future was the little girl in my arms. Especially not with the pretentious, extravagant La Fay Witch. But it was a sweet offer. Despite the jab at my taste in clothes.

"Always." I rubbed my eye. "Look, your sister pulled some fucked up shit last night."

I could practically hear her eyes rolling through the phone. "Of course she did. What was it this time?"

"Hopping inside my family's head while I was in active labor," I said. "Making them try to kill each other. My brother-in-law took down my bedroom door with an ax."

"Jesus Christ," she murmured. "Dramatic old cunt. What do you need from me?"

"Ideally to kill the bitch," I said. "But in the short term, I could use a sample of your blood. My Witch wants to cast a spell that will prevent her from entering our body's again and she needs DNA for it."

"That can be arranged," she said. "I can overnight it to you, if you'd like. Although, that marks two on the tally board for me. None for you, darling."

I repositioned Milly on my nipple. Or attempted to, anyway. Her mouth was like a damn suction cup. "What do you want, Moriah?"

"I've been watching the stars," she murmured. "You're written all over them. I keep doing you favors; I need to know that you'll do the same for me one day."

There it was. Selfish little bitch. Love her. But nothing comes free when working with a La Fay.

"The prophecy," I muttered. "You want immunity."

"I wouldn't say immunity," she said. "I just need to know that you'll help me when that time comes. I don't know what that means yet. But I know that I need your protection. You're stronger than anything I've ever seen, Laila. If the end of the world is near, I need to know that you and I are in the same corner."

"Help me get my son home, Moriah. Prove that you're in mine. I know how family works, and no matter how many times you tell me you hate her; I'm always going to wonder where your allegiance lies."

She practically scoffed. "I suppose family means something far different to you than me. Still, I see your perspective. I'm not sure how I can prove that in our current state, but I assure you that my assistance is yours until your son is returned. And then, your assistance may be required of me."

"Sounds fair," I said. "I can't make you any promises though. I don't know what this Apocalypse looks like either. I'm just as scared as you. I'll do whatever I can to help you, Moriah. But if you do end up going down, please don't curse me."

She laughed for a moment. "You're sweet, darling. That's all I needed to hear. Thank you."

"Sure." I smiled. "But don't worry about overnighting it. I'll send Jeremy by to grab it so we can get the spell cast as soon as possible."

"Even better. I've been dying to meet him." Her tone was almost seductive.

I laughed and rolled my eyes. "Expect him in an hour."

"I'll be waiting, darling. You know the place, don't you?"

"Jeremy does." I lowered myself to the rocking chair with Milly.

"You don't say," she murmured.

"Listen, bitch, if you try to sleep with my husband, I will rip your tongue from your throat, put it in a blender, and make you drink it like a smoothie."

"Oh, darling, never." She chuckled. "But a little eye candy never hurt anyone, did it?"

I huffed. "Bye, Moriah."

"Bye, darling."

"She's going to give us the blood?" Jeremy asked in the doorway. I dropped the phone to my lap. He ran a brush through his damp black hair and leaned against the frame.

"Yeah, she's expecting you in an hour," I said.

He nodded and turned his gaze down to Milly's. A smile played at his lips. He ran his fingertip along hers before he looked back up to me. "Do you need anything? Are you hungry?"

"I'm starving." I grinned. "I want Moe's."

He smiled. "Max called me earlier. He wants to come by and meet Milly. I can have him grab you something."

"Do you know what else I want?" My smile widened. "Sushi. And more coffee. So much more coffee. And raw cookie dough."

He laughed again. "That would taste awful if you ate them all at the same time."

"I'll use a palette cleanser between."

"I'm surprised a Crown and Coke wasn't on that list," he said with a soft, nearly curious smile.

When I was pregnant with Micah, I couldn't wait to have a drink again. But it was different with Milly. I was older, I was wiser, and inebriation wasn't as exciting as it'd once been.

"I'm a mom," I said. "In a couple months, if we go out at some point, I might get a drink or two. But I can't drink all the time like I used to. I probably will smoke weed again after I stop breastfeeding. But my binge drinking days are behind me." I looked at Milly in my arms. "She needs me. And you, too."

He smiled softly. "She does."

"And so does Micah," I said. "But until I get him, I have to be alert for her. The night I kill Peterson, I'm getting obliterated. No doubt about it. But until he's dead." I paused. "I'm going to be in control from here on out. I'm not pregnant anymore. I'm stronger than I've ever been. If these past few months have taught me anything, it's that you don't win if you don't fight with your head as much as you do with your body."

CHAPTER THIRTY-THREE

JEREMY

The La Fay mansion was exactly as I'd remembered it. Impeccable marble floors, ceilings twenty or thirty feet high, grand columns, two massive winding staircases. It was only the second time I'd been inside, and to be frank, even that was two times too many. The La Fay's weren't the type of company I liked to keep, but my grandparents felt much differently.

Nothing particularly notable in terms of the supernatural world took place my first time here. It just gave me an inside look into the world my part of the family was near exiled from. However, on an even less fortunate note, I'll never forget it because that was the night that I lost my virginity to Olivia. In the ballroom bathroom off the room I stood in waiting for Moriah.

I stayed with my grandparents over summer break going into my junior year. Olivia's dad and my grandpa were both on the Chambers, and they handled business together during my stay. I'm not sure what that business even was. I suppose I'm still not. Nonetheless, her family stayed for about a week in the guest house. At that point, we met again as adolescents rather than children.

We were young. We'd known each other since childhood, and we both started to grow out of our awkward phases. She was there, I was there; it was convenient. By that time, I had a little bit of a reputation and was starting to look the part. I'm sure the fact that I'd always had a bit of a crush on her as a kid had something to do with it too. We flirted a lot, but nothing happened in France.

While they were there, her dad asked if any of us would be attending the Meeting of Chambers at the La Fay home in London a few weeks later. And that side of the supernatural world was a piece I was glad to have been left out of.

They were always so elusive and mysterious, and I saw right through it. I watched them dress up in fancy clothes and thousands of dollars in jewelry to talk about the world's problems as if they couldn't solve them with their combined wealth and abilities in a heartbeat. Not to mention their claws that dipped deep into every major government in the world.

But Olivia was going to be there, so I went.

As much as I resented the concept, I guess that I expected a Meeting of Chambers to be some cool, top secret event. That was hardly the case. Essentially, the Men and Women of Chambers gathered and talked shit. It was just a bunch of obsolete people with a thousand accents sitting around a large table discussing possible threats of exposure and areas where our people were not acting as they should. As if they had a clue what they were talking about from their mansions and private jets.

The whole evening felt like some type of gossip circle. It didn't seem like they wanted to solve anything. They were simply keeping tabs of the goings-on around the world.

To put it lightly, seeing the supposed voices of our people in that context left an even more sour taste in my mouth for our kinds than I'd had before.

When Annie took us in, she didn't have much help financially, so I held a resentment for people that wealthy. My grandparents could have made our lives a lot easier than they were. Or more specifically, they could've made Annie's life a lot easier than it was.

One way or the other, I was pretty ready to get out of that ballroom. I didn't want to sit there and listen to those uppity, heads-up-their-own-asses dickheads bitch all night. I went out into the foyer to get a drink.

Then I ran into Olivia. One thing led to another, and, as they say, the rest is history.

Regardless, my experience with the Chambers that night had made it very clear that nothing was as it seemed with the La Fays. Nor anyone who associated with the Chamber or the Council, for that matter. Maybe Moriah was different. Maybe she really was counting on Laila to save her life and wouldn't jeopardize our future with our son. She always seemed to be the apple that fell the farthest from the tree. Yet, still too close to it for my comfort as an ally.

"Jeremiah Skoulda," a soft, dainty voice said from the extravagant staircase behind me.

I turned and forced a smile. "Jeremy's good."

That was my name, not Jeremiah. Mom wanted to name me Jeremiah, but Dad wanted Jeremie with the French spelling. Mom compromised with Jeremy so long as it was the English spelling so people wouldn't mess it up.

Her soft, billowing laugh echoed through the grand ceiling above us. She smiled. "Not one for formalities?"

"You could say that," I said.

"Well" —she held her smile— "it's nice to finally meet you. As much as I've heard, I feel like we're old pals."

I chuckled awkwardly. "We've actually met."

"No." She laughed, creasing her drawn on brows. "I'm sure I'd remember that."

"We definitely did," I said. "I was sixteen. I looked a lot different than I do now."

"You don't say," she murmured. "Where?"

"Here." I gestured around. "It was at a Chambers meeting."

"Oh." She rolled her eyes. "That's why I don't remember, darling. I'm sure I was piss drunk. That's about the only way to make it through one of those."

"Fair enough," I said.

"How is that new baby of yours?" she asked with a smile, still descending the steps.

"She's perfect." I glanced at the wall clock. "And I should probably get back to her. I've waited a good minute already."

A huff of a laugh left her lips. Her gaze narrowed, but only slightly. "Sure."

I supposed people like her weren't used to being told to hurry up.

She reached into her clutch and pulled out a vial of dark red blood. As she extended it to me, I laughed. My hand ran along my mouth. For all I knew, that blood belonged to anyone. "I think we need it fresh."

Moriah made a face. "I know the spell. This is only an hour old; it'll do just fine."

"Just to be safe."

She ran her tongue along her teeth. "Do you have a knife?"

"Your guard took it. I'm going to need it back before I leave, by the way."

A quiet laugh left her. Her gaze narrowed a bit. "Why don't you just take it? You could, couldn't you?"

"I could," I said. "But surrendering a weapon to an ally's a courtesy. Mutual trust's important."

"There's nothing mutual about it." Moriah laughed. "It's entirely the visitor's trust in the host."

I teleported a few feet away and then back to where I stood. "Not when you can't surrender your most valuable weapon."

"I suppose. More of a pretentious surrender, no?"

I gave a half grin.

A smile came to her lips. She made her way back to the guard. She muttered something to him before he handed her my knife. "Do you at least have something to catch the blood?"

I pulled a Ziploc bag from my jeans pocket. Moriah huffed. "Well, hold it open for me then, would you?"

My eyes struggled against the urge to roll as I pulled apart the thick pieces of plastic. When she raised the blade to her palm, she said, "You don't like me much, do you, Jeremiah?"

"Jeremy," I muttered.

She pierced the blade into her skin. "But I fail to see why that is. I've only ever helped you."

I tightened my jaw as Nastya's face flashed through hers. A long stream of blood dripped from her hand to the white marble floor. I moved the bag beneath it, and she met my gaze.

"Your sister has my son." I looked between her cool eyes. "Your sister helped a man torture my wife for more than three months. This blood is the reason the last two years of my life have been utter hell. Your family destroyed mine. We're allies, Moriah. We aren't friends."

Her eyes creased a bit. "Why do you think I gave Laila that letter, Jeremy?"

"Because you want her to owe you a favor."

"Sure," she said. "But it never occurred to you that the murder of a child isn't something that I support?"

Maybe that was so. But I knew these types of people. I also knew Witches. Everything they did, they did so in their own interest. Believing she was doing this out of the kindness of her heart wasn't only naïve but stupid.

"Yes, Jeremy. I'm selfish. I'm not what you could call kind. I'm certainly no savior. I'm many, many things. But evil is not one of them. Do you know how many people I've killed? None. Do you know how many lives I've threatened? Only my own by giving your wife that letter. Yes, my family matters. They're powerful and important and unfortunately, I was born into their chaos. But I'm not them. I'm certainly not my sister. Please don't suggest anything along those lines again because I find it incredibly offensive. I understand that you're close with your siblings, but that isn't the case for all of us.

"Anastasia was always an awful person, even as girls. She killed my pets as a child. She tortured other children in school. She was always a cruel and demented creature. And yes, a part of me will always care for her, but only on the primal level that she is family. I won't try to pretend that isn't true. But at the end of the day, the world is better off without her. I don't want her to live any more than you do. Do I want her dead as *much* as you do? Of course not. But I do want this to end. Whatever madness this is that she's caught up in terrifies me. If I can help you and Laila prevent what she's trying to do, even if that means she dies in the process, I can accept that."

"You realize it isn't if," I said. "We're going to kill her, Moriah. This isn't just about preventing whatever it is that she's planning. This is revenge as much as it is justice for the seven-hundred and eighty lives she played a part in destroying, not to mention the thousands of loved ones who've been affected by her actions. It isn't a matter of if. It's just a matter of when."

Moriah sighed. A small cloth shot across the room into her bleeding hand. She pressed it to her palm. "That's what I'm anticipating."

I sealed the small bag of blood.

"My point here is that I'm lying my loyalty on the table for you," she continued. "The power is in your hands, Jeremy. I can't and won't attempt to control you."

"You could," I said. "If my Witch can, so can you."

"I can't control Laila who is an extension of you."

"No one can control Laila."

"That's my point." Moriah gave a soft smile as she looked between my eyes. "Nastya is powerful, yes. But Laila is limitless. If the end cannot be prevented, she is my best chance at survival. That's what the cards, the stars, and the crystals all say. The two of you are the only chance we have. Betraying you would be suicide."

She wasn't wrong. And I still didn't like her. I never would, in fact. But with all things considered, she wasn't a bad person to have in our corner.

CHAPTER THIRTY-FOUR

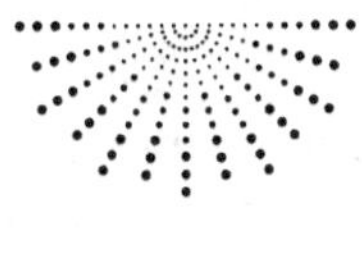

LAILA

"How is she?" Helena smiled in the doorway to the nursery.

I smiled back. "She's perfect."

"She looks perfect." She grinned. "Where's Jeremy?"

"Getting that blood for the spell. He should be back soon." I stood from the rocking chair. "How much do I owe you for it?"

"Don't worry about it, kid. I'm casting it for myself already. Whipping up a bigger batch won't be a problem. This one's on the house."

"Well, thank you." I walked to the changing table and grabbed a burp cloth. "While you're here, how's that past lives spell coming along?"

"Just about ready," she said. "I'm having an issue with one thing though."

"What's that?" I asked, wiping the spit up from the edge of Milly's lip.

"An ingredient." Helena sat on the ottoman in front of the rocking chair. "It's pretty rare. I had a guy for things like this, but he died last year. I'm working on a new contact now though. Fingers crossed; he'll be a solid connect by the solstice."

"You aren't sure if you'll be able to do it?" I asked.

"I'm doing everything I can, Laila."

"What is it? That you're having a hard time finding, I mean."

"Dried mullock root," she muttered. "I've only used it once. It's not called for often but when it is, it can't be substituted."

"I've never heard of it."

"Your brother probably has." Helena smiled down at Milly. "They use it for headaches and fevers over there."

"It's from the Fae realm?"

I'd never been but always wanted to. If Helena needed some to help me learn more about breaking this cycle, maybe I'd benefit from a little getaway to my homeland. Jeremy and I both had some time off work to spend with Milly. Disappearing to another world could be kinda fun.

"Only place it grows. It won't thrive in our atmosphere. It's got to come straight through the planes. Only has a few weeks shelf life once it touches our air."

"Let me know if you can't find it in a week," I said. "Kai got over here; he knows how to get back. We'll get it for you if need be."

"Oh, sure," she said. "I didn't even think of that."

Her gaze was steady on Milly's as she spoke. The expression over her face was layered with pain and affection. It was the same face I made when a stranger's baby smiled at me before yesterday when I had my own.

"Helena." I smiled.

She looked up to meet my gaze.

"Do you want to hold her?" I smiled a bit wider.

She smiled, glancing between me and Milly. "Could I?"

"You know how, right?"

"Do I know how to hold a baby," she retorted under her breath. Her eyes rolled. "Yes, Laila, I know how to hold a baby."

I laughed and lowered her into Helena's arms. She smiled down at her and touched her nose. A smile came to my lips as I sat in the rocking chair beside her.

"She really does look just like you," Helena murmured. "It's like a miniature version."

"I see Jeremy." I held my joyous gaze. "But I'll take that as a compliment."

"It is." She smiled. "She's powerful too. It's practically pulsing out of her. You feel it, don't you?"

The same way I felt Jeremy halfway around the world, I could feel Milly's energy.

It's like the sensation of feeling the warmth of a fire before it approaches or smelling the moisture in the air before the rain falls. But not quite the same. It's a sense that certainly exists, but there isn't quite a word for. At least, not in any human language.

"Yeah," I said. "She's pretty damn strong."

Helena moved her head in a slow nod. She smiled down at Milly. Her sleeping eyes fluttered back and forth as Helena touched her fingers. She pulled her closer into her chest.

She was smiling, but she looked a bit sad.

"Did you lose one?" I asked quietly.

Her gaze shifted up to mine. She tilted her head to the side a bit.

"A baby," I muttered. "That look, it's the same one I made when I held someone else's baby before I had her."

Helena cleared her throat. "Just the idea. I've come to terms with it, you know? It makes me wonder what could have been if things were different."

"You didn't freeze your sperm?" I asked.

She frowned. "Figured it was better not to bring kids into this shit hole of a world we live in. I'm selfish anyway. I wouldn't be a good parent. I like my life. I like no one telling me what to do. Sometimes, though..." She paused. "Sometimes I just wonder what my life would have been if I was born with two X chromosomes."

I smiled. "Well. You're an amazing woman with either set of chromosomes."

She smiled and gave a nod. "Yeah, I'm pretty great."

I laughed. "Not to mention modest."

"Modesty's just another word for low self-esteem," Helena said.

"Going to have to agree to disagree with you on that one," I muttered.

"Hey." Jeremy appeared in the doorway.

Blood dripped down his hand and out of the corner of the Ziploc bag filled with blood like a water balloon.

"Jesus Christ." I grasped my chest. "Can you not appear in an empty doorway holding a leaking bag of blood? Like, ever again?"

"Oh, shit." He cupped his palm beneath it.

I grabbed my empty coffee mug and rushed to catch the blood that dripped between the cracks of his fingers.

"Why didn't you use a bowl?" I glanced at the blood on the edge of Milly's pink rug.

He plopped it into the cup before turning for the bathroom.

"Look at this. You got Witch's blood on your daughter's brand-new carpet."

"You said it didn't match anyway. We'll get her a new one." He flicked the faucet on.

He was right; I hated that rug. He'd bought it. And I loved my husband with every fiber of my being, but not to pick out décor. He'd spent fifty bucks on it, and the fabric was absolute garbage. He said that the butterflies on it were cute. The idea was, but the execution was subpar at best.

I walked back to the rocking chair. He came back into the room drying his hands as I set the cup of blood on the end table.

As he smiled down at Milly over Helena's shoulder, I let my lips vibrate in a trill.

"Baby," I said.

"Laila." He stood up and walked toward me. Then he kissed my cheek with a smile.

"It'd be safe to take Milly to the Fae Realm, right?" I asked.

"What?" He cocked his head to the side. "Why?"

"I need dried mullock to access the memories from your past lives." Helena looked up. "Unless you know of anyone that can get it. My Fae herb guy died last year."

"Oh, I see. Well, yeah, I'm pretty sure it's safe. They have healers everywhere over there. The moment someone catches a cold, they eradicate it. She wouldn't need any vaccines first or anything. The people are pretty peaceful if we go to the right places. Neither of us will get a warm welcome because you're a hybrid and I'm not Fae, but I can't think of any reason not to go in terms of safety. Your powers will be stronger there anyway. And I've always wanted to go."

"Yeah, me too." I smiled. "I think it'd be kind of fun. We should talk to Kai about how to go about that. Maybe he could be our tour guide."

CHAPTER THIRTY-FIVE

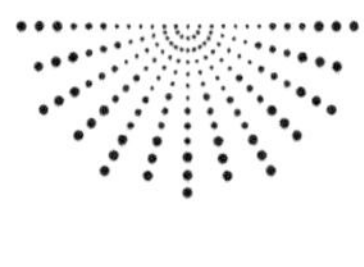

LAILA

We headed back to the main house shortly after Jeremy got back. I was antsy to test out the new stroller, so Jeremy got it out of the closet and set it up. But the road was bumpy, and Milly was bouncing around too much, so I carried her. Which left Jeremy pushing the stroller the other half mile up the drive.

Regardless, Kai and Hannah were already in the kitchen eating lunch, so we jumped straight into the conversation.

"But you could do it?" I bounced Milly against my chest to get her to burp.

"Aye," Kai said. "I'd need your help, but yes. I'd love a trip back home. How 'bout it, love?" He smiled at Hannah. "Want to see where I grew up?"

She smiled, nodding. "I would *love* to see where you grew up."

He kissed her cheek and grinned. Then he turned back to me. "Do you have coin?"

"No," Jeremy said. "We'll have to get some jewels to barter with."

"Tanzanite's cheap here, no?" Kai asked. "Because it's worth kingdoms back home."

"Cheaper than diamond and emerald," Jeremy said. "Not cheap-cheap though. How many carats would we need for the mullock?"

"Half of one would be more than enough," he said. "They might overcharge because of what we are though."

Jeremy counted on his fingers for a moment. "And how much should we bring for inns and food?"

"Hmm." Kai thought for a moment. "Well, we'll probably be there a night or two. There's four of us. For a shite stay, we could get by on a quarter karat. But for a decent place and transportation, I'd say another karat would be plenty. Should have some left over if we're frugal."

"And what about souvenirs?" I bounced with my hand patting Milly's back.

Jeremy smiled. "You want to get souvenirs?"

"Of course I want to get souvenirs." I grinned. "It's the land of my people."

Kai chuckled, giving me a once over. "Lass, you know that to most of them, the two of us are abominations? Racism bleeds through all of the dimensions."

"That's okay," I said. "No one's going to try to kill me or anything, right?"

"No, they aren't brute the way humans can be, but—"

"Then I'm not worried about it," I said.

"You do know about the wars, don't you?" Kai asked. "You've heard of the battles between Angels and Fae that wiped out millions, yes?"

"Yeah, I've heard the stories. I understand *that* they don't like us, and I understand *why* they don't like us. But I don't care. I want to witness the culture regardless of whether I'm accepted in it. Our mom doesn't have much history, you know. The Fae are the only heritage we have. I'd like to see the world my ancestors lived on."

I thought that I understood. I'd read Moe's journal where he discussed the wars between the Angels and the Fae. That the god of the Angels and the deities in the Fae Realm had bad blood dating back to the creations of both worlds. It never really detailed why, only that the races hated on another.

And I'd heard Kai talk about the way he was mistreated growing up, but he always made it sound like harsh bullying. Not to say that we were in certain danger there, but I could have prepared myself for our not so warm welcome a little more than I did.

Kai smiled. "We'll need clothes."

"Ooh, do I get to wear one of those fancy Renaissance dresses?" Hannah grinned.

"We aren't royalty, Han." Jeremy's lip curled up in a smidge of disgust. "Listen, dude, I'm not wearing tights."

"Where we're going, something like Laila's 'll do fine." He gestured toward my flowing harem pants.

Jeremy wrinkled his nose.

"Do you not like my pants?" I asked.

"They're too roomy," he muttered. "Cute on you. Easy access." I rolled my eyes, and he smiled. "Just not my thing, baby."

I laughed, and Kai shrugged. "Short sleeve, long and flowy for you two."

"So these'll work?" I gestured toward my legs.

He laughed. "Those are pants, Laila."

"Uh-huh."

"Women don't wear pants unless they're in the army," Jeremy said. "You've got to wear a dress."

"Ew," I muttered.

I wasn't sure why that was my reaction. There's nothing wrong with dresses, even men wore them there. More like kilts, but still. I supposed it was human society's conditioning. It made me believe that a dress made me fragile, or dainty. But it didn't.

Dresses are pretty. There's nothing innately dainty about them. They just aren't great in battle. Although, in fairness, neither were my harem pants.

Leah trotted down the steps. "What are you guys talking about?"

"We're going to the Fae Realm," I said. Milly finally burped, leaving a giant patch of white pouring down the burp cloth on my chest. I wiped her lip with the corner. "We need an ingredient for a spell."

"Really?" Her eyes widened with a smile. "Where to?"

"Edge of the Open Lands. The Capitol." Kai pulled himself to the counter. "Only place I ken to get dried mullock."

"Got room for one more?" Her hands moved to her hips. "I can bring my own money for rooms and food. But I have a few vacation days I could use up before the end of the fiscal year. I've always wanted to go. The Open Lands are gorgeous, aren't they?"

Smiling, Kai said, "Aye. The most beautiful place I've ever seen. I've only been where we're going twice, but it's incredible."

"I don't see why not," I said. "Hey, we should ask Celena too."

"We should make it a big family trip," Hannah said. "We should all go."

"Jenna can't," Kai said. "Neither can your mother, Laila. The portal I create isn't safe for humans. There are ways, but it'd take time that we don't have."

"We'll bring them back a keychain or something," I said.

"I don't think Adam will want to leave Jenna," Leah said. "They can't afford to lose the money. And she's so far in her pregnancy, she isn't gonna want to sleep on the beds over there."

"With us being gone too, Moe's couldn't afford to give him the time off anyway," Jeremy said.

"I don't think Brody would want to come," Hannah muttered. "Not like Gwen would be accepted either."

"No, that's not a good idea," Kai said quickly. "She'd be in the way of certain death, even in the Open Lands. They'll chew their tongues for most of us, but Vampires aren't welcome."

"So probably just us and maybe Celena and Wyatt," I said. "Wolves are cool, right?"

"Aye," Kai said. "Wolves weren't involved in the wars. There's no biased toward them. More acceptable than the lot of us."

"When are you planning on going?" Leah asked.

"Probably a few weeks," I said. "Give us enough time to get in the groove with the baby. Establish her feeding schedule, check on her weight and everything. We have to be back by the solstice so sooner rather than later. But still, at least a couple weeks."

"That'll give me enough time to get a PTO request in," Leah said.

"I have straight As. I can skip a day or two." Hannah craned onto her tiptoes to press her lips to Kai's.

"Helena's working on that spell back at our house, by the way," Jeremy said. "Everyone should come down and get their dose."

"Sure," Leah said. "Adam and Brody are at work, but I'll grab theirs for them."

"What about Milly?" Hannah asked at a near whisper. "She, uh... Her powers would be a valuable target."

"We're not doing that," I said.

"She was born yesterday," Jeremy said. "And I know you didn't see it but trust me. This baby knows how to keep them out."

CHAPTER THIRTY-SIX

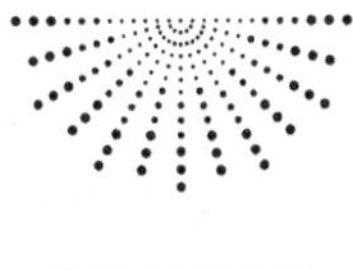

JEREMY

Max called a while later and told me he was waiting at the end of the driveway. I kissed Laila's cheek before teleporting to the iron gate we'd just installed. He laughed, smiled, and gave me a brotherly hug. I laughed too, said thanks, and then handed him his necklace.

"Don't lose it, don't give it to a girlfriend, and don't forget it before you drive through this gate," I said. "'Cause if you drive through without it, you're totaling your car."

"Damn, you guys aren't fucking around." He slid the rope necklace over his head. "But bold of you to assume I have a girlfriend."

"After Micah, we aren't taking any chances," I said. "There is an alternative though. You could crush this into a powder and tattoo it into your skin. I'd prefer it actually. Someone could just rip this right off your neck if they wanted it."

"No shit," he muttered. "Is that, like, a possibility? Because I'd be happy to just meet you here and throw a necklace on when I come in and give it back when I leave. I'd rather not carry something that valuable. I damn sure don't want to be the reason something happens to that little girl."

I couldn't help the way my gaze hardened. "Nothing's going to happen to her."

"No, I know," Max said. "But I'm not a fighter, man. Someone holds a knife to my throat for that necklace, and they're walking away with it."

Well, in fairness, I didn't disagree. I liked knowing where each necklace was at any given time. Even Mary returned hers before she left. Rachel already had Helena prepare the ink for her tattoo, as did Jenna. And I liked it that way. I wanted Max to have access to our home, but not at the expense of risking my child's life.

"You don't want the tattoo?" I asked.

"So somebody can cut it off and sew it on themselves? Graft me like some Buffalo Bill type shit? No, man. I'll pass. Thanks though. You and Laila would both kill me if something happened to one of these. Nah, I don't want that responsibility."

"Suit yourself," I said. "But Laila's really excited to see you. You brought her food, right?"

He laughed and gave a nod. "Yeah, I got her food."

"We should get up there then."

"Yeah, I'll be up in a minute." Max nodded and started back to his Subaru.

"Damn, she's beautiful." Max's grinned down at Milly. Her green eyes focused on him, just like she seemed to with everyone. Her eyes were always wide when she was awake, taking in every little detail around her.

"Just like her mom." I smiled and kissed Laila's cheek. She laughed and chomped into a French fry.

"How are her eyes so green? Aren't they supposed to be blue first?" Max asked.

"For humans," I said.

"Seems to be a Fae thing," Laila said.

"No shit," he murmured. "So what's the story with that guy who was at the diner yesterday morning?"

"Oh, fuck," Laila said. "I forgot about Don."

"Yeah, me too," I said. "We should meet up with him and figure out what he knows. I could handle it if you want to stay here with her."

Laila said, "No, I want to be there. He probably won't tell you much if I'm not. But let's wait a couple of days. I could use some rest."

I kissed her forehead. "Alright, baby."

"He was cool though?" Max asked.

"Yeah, he wasn't a major threat or anything," Laila said. "Can't say I trust him. But I don't think he's an enemy."

"Alright, guys." Helena galloped down the steps. "I've got everyone's dose ready here."

"Do you have any extra?" Laila brought herself to her feet. "Max is human, but they could use him too. I'd rather be safe than sorry."

Ah, that was a good point. One I hadn't thought of. If they hopped into Max, it could end a few ways. But the most likely would be that we'd have to kill him to save someone else that we loved. And I'd rather not.

Max tilted his head. "An extra dose of what?"

"The birth didn't go exactly as planned yesterday," I said. "That Witch working for Peterson was fucking with everyone's heads. They were all trying to kill each other. Adam beat our bedroom door down with an ax, Kai strangled Hannah, Wyatt almost killed Leah. This just prevents them from getting into our heads."

"It was pretty bad," Laila muttered. "If you don't want to take it, you don't have to. But if they did try to use you, and we had to stop you—"

"I'll take the dose," Max said. "I don't wanna be turned into another one of your ash piles, Lai."

I laughed and made my way to Helena. Then she handed us a small plastic bottle. "I do have some extra. It won't last long though, only a day tops before it loses its properties."

Laila twisted off the lid. "It's safe to breastfeed, right?"

"Just drink plenty of water," she said.

"How's it taste?" I asked.

"Probably like asshole," she said. "I haven't taken mine yet."

"Well, let's find out," Laila muttered.

I twisted off the cap and set it in my pocket. My eyes closed, I held the bottle to my mouth, and tilted my head back. Its contents dumped into my mouth like gasoline into a pit of fire. The second it touched my tongue, it felt like I'd just downed a bottle of hot sauce mixed with mud. Iron lingered on the back of my tongue as I swallowed hard and covered my gagging lips.

To say the least, I'd have rather tasted an asshole.

"Jesus Christ." Laila ran to the sink. She held her head under the spigot and drank. I darted to the fridge and grabbed the gallon of milk.

"That's awful." I poured milk into two cups.

Helena grabbed the other and chugged for a moment.

"That sure looks pleasant," Max muttered as he stood with Milly.

"Fuck me, man." Laila coughed. "I hate magic."

I rubbed my watering eyes and drew deep breaths into my numb, burning airways. "Jesus Christ, Helena."

"It's better than those fuckers making us kill each other, isn't it?" She poured another glass of milk and panted heavily into her open mouth.

"I guess," I muttered.

"You *guess*." Helena scoffed before chugging.

"Bread," Laila said. "I need bread."

"And Hannah said to give this shit to our baby." I poured more milk into my glass.

"I wouldn't have let you do that if you wanted to." Helena shook her head. "I don't cast on kids. Barrier spells are one thing, but potions are another."

"That's what I thought too," I said. "I think she can defend herself either way. She doesn't need it."

"Yeah, it seems like it," Helena said.

As the burn settled a bit, I turned to Max. "We're going to be out of town for a couple days next week or the week after. Is there any way you could watch Tink for us?"

"Leah, Kai, and Hannah won't be here either or we'd just leave her at the house." Laila walked to me and took a gulp of my milk. "You won't have a way to contact us though."

"Yeah, I'll watch her," he said. "Where's she at, anyway?"

"Who knows." I laughed.

"We barely see her since we moved in." Laila chuckled. "She has a doggy door now so she's constantly in and out. She spends a lot of time in the kids' rooms too."

"And on the balcony. Have you seen the balcony?" I grinned.

"You and that damn balcony." Laila laughed.

"It is a cool balcony," Helena said.

I loved that fucking balcony.

CHAPTER THIRTY-SEVEN

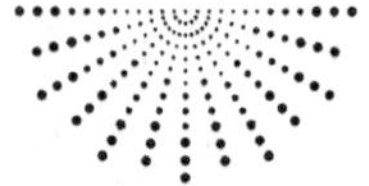

SIX DAYS LATER - JEREMY

The smell of melted cheese, red sauce, and bread filled my nose. Quiet Italian music played from the speakers in the corners. Heat from the kitchen drifted into the dining area, not helping with the nervous sweat that beaded at my forehead. My gaze shifted over the congested restaurant, but I kept a careful eye on the entrance.

"Are you sure we should have brought Milly?" I lowered my voice and leaned closer to Laila.

"What's he gonna do—Pull the baby off my tit in the middle of a restaurant?" She dipped a mozzarella stick in marinara sauce. She took a bite before lifting up the blanket that draped over her shoulder to peek at Milly. "He isn't gonna do shit anyway. But especially not with all these people's" —she raised her voice a bit, narrowing her gaze at the middle-aged man who wrinkled his nose the moment he noticed her put the blanket over her shoulder— "*Annoying judgmental stares.*"

He quickly turned his head away. I laughed and took a sip from my Sprite. "What time did you tell him?"

"Quarter 'til," she said. "He still has a couple minutes."

Meeting with a Demon like Abaddon was an intimidating concept to me. I heard what Liam said, and I'd met a few Demons over the years that weren't too bad. But Abaddon was incredibly old and abundantly powerful. Maybe not as powerful as my wife, but still powerful enough that it put me on edge.

I met her gaze. "You aren't worried about all of this?"

"Not really. I'm not saying I trust him. But I guess I can relate to him. He's not all good, but he isn't evil." Then she lowered her voice. "Since Mary fell, does that mean I'm half Demon now?"

"No. Her DNA was altered after you were born. You're still half Angel."

"That's good," she said. "Only 'cause they're stronger though. I don't care about the title. I think I'd prefer Demon actually. It sounds more hardcore."

My head moved from side to side. I chuckled. "You're silly."

She smiled and took another bite of her mozzarella stick. "I don't know why, but I don't think we have to worry. We'll keep our guard up for a while, but I don't know. I think I like him. He's peppy."

"I hope you're right," I muttered as I watched him walk in the front door. He smiled and waved, then he started toward us. "Just keep your guard up, alright?"

"Always."

He smiled wider as he approached the table. Then he sat at the chair beside Laila and pointed at Milly against Laila's chest covered in the periwinkle blanket. "Is that the new baby?"

"It is," Laila said.

"Aww, can I hold her?"

"You cannot." I picked a mozzarella stick up and bit into it.

He turned to me with his lips lowered in a frown. "Alright, point received. I get it. You don't know me; I don't know you. But trust me, man. I don't want your kid."

"No, why would you?" I narrowed my gaze slightly. "You didn't even want yours."

He rolled his eyes.

"Let's get down to business, alright?" Laila lowered her voice. "You said you wanted to talk to me. Let's talk."

"Right." Don nodded. "Alright, where to begin. Let's see."

"You said you knew something about our son." I leaned across the table. "Maybe start there."

He gave a nod. "Alright. Well, first let me make it clear that I have no idea where they are, and I have no way to help you find them. That's not the information that I have."

"Great." Laila huffed. "Then before we get to that, please explain to me why you had Emma get you intel on me."

He laughed and rubbed his mouth. "She told you about that, huh?"

"She did," I said. "Really mature, by the way. Blackmailing your thirteen-year-old with affection to spy on someone for you. Didn't occur to you that you could just make contact and ask?"

"Look, I didn't have shit to offer you." Don looked between my eyes. "I've been looking for my kid too, ya know. I didn't know he was alive either. I know I'm a shit parent, but I never wanted my kid to die. When Emma showed up at that hospital, and I learned that she and Benny were still out there, I set out on a mission to find him just like y'all did. And I didn't find shit. You did though, so thank you. I mean that. I owe you my life two times over. The both of you."

"That's why you were digging into me?" Laila asked. "To get information on Peterson?"

"Yeah, that's all I wanted. I just wanted to find my kid. Believe me or don't but that's the truth." Don met her gaze. "I know you're scared of me, alright? I know that my name has a reputation. But I've killed less people than you, Laila. We have more in common than you think."

"Why did you fall?" I asked.

He turned to meet my gaze. Asking a first-generation Demon why they got kicked out of Heaven was our world's equivalent of asking someone in prison what they were in for. It was a major social faux pas to ask at all, but especially coming from a Guardian.

Prior to me and Laila's bond, I didn't rank very high on the hierarchy. A question like that wasn't deemed necessary to answer because of how low I was on the totem poll, at least in terms of authority. The Skoulda name struck fear through any supernatural creature's body with the right tone but against a Demon as powerful and old as Abbadon, I was no one.

But not anymore. Still, I was just a Guardian. But my wife was practically royalty. I wish I were humble enough to say that it didn't change the way I talked to the people in our world I had no respect for, but it definitely did. Because I was Laila's, I was untouchable. I didn't use that card often, but I wouldn't take any risks when it came to my kid. I'd ask the questions I wanted answers to.

"Ballsy of you," Don said.

"You want us to trust you," I said. "Give us a reason to."

He sucked his teeth. "Fine. I fucked a human, alright? She got pregnant and the first Nephilim was born."

"Oh," I murmured.

"I got kicked out of Heaven because I loved someone. Happy? Can you quit looking at me like I'm the bad guy now?"

"You got kicked out of Heaven because you created a monster," I muttered.

Perhaps the Nephilim were where the racism within the supernatural world came from.

Certain races can't make viable offspring—humans and Angels being one of them. Vamps can't have kids—not once they're turned. Guardians, Elves, and Werewolves are the only races that can mix with any other race, including humans, and have viable offspring. Fae can mix with other supernatural races but cannot conceive with humans. The species differential won't allow it.

Angels, like Fae, can mix with any of the supernatural races. Although, it's said that Fae could only procreate with one another until the past few thousand years when Elvan blood started meshing with the Fae. Prior to that, Fae could only procreate with each other. They could conceive with other races, but they couldn't carry to term. At least, that was my understanding from what I'd read in the texts in our underground libraries.

But when Angels or Demons fuck a human? They *can* have children. But the children come out... malformed. As in, beasts. Also known as lower-level Demons, like the kinds I spent most of my adult life fighting.

"Yeah, and I loved that monster." He sent me a darting gaze. "Then he wiped out a village and I had to kill him."

I'll admit, a spike of guilt did course through me. Bringing a monster into the world and having to kill them couldn't be an easy thing to live with. But it lessened my respect for the guy even further. Even if my kid were a monster, even if they did destroy a village, I wouldn't kill them. I might lock them up to keep the world safe. But never would I kill my own child.

We fell silent as Milly began to fuss in Laila's arms. She lifted her from beneath the blanket on top of it to pat her back. She rocked back and forth and slid the pacifier into her crying lips. Then she broke the silence.

"I'm sorry for your loss. Losing a child's the worst pain imaginable."

"Yeah, thanks," he muttered. Then he rubbed down the bridge of his nose. "Can we get back to what's important now?"

"Sure," Laila said. "You were looking for Benny, but you didn't have anything of value to bring to us. You just wanted to know what we knew so you could find your son."

"Right." He ran a hand along his stubble. "So I did some digging. After I saw that letter, I realized how we were all connected. That's when I realized who you guys were in this. That's when I realized who your son was."

"And who is that?" Laila rocked back and forth to soothe Milly. "What does that even mean?"

"I'm not entirely sure," Don said. "But I know they're going to use him."

"Use him for what?" I asked.

"Do you guys know what Wormwood is?" He looked between us.

We sure the hell did not.

"Do you?" I asked.

He nodded. "Kinda sorta."

"What is it then?" Laila asked.

He rubbed his mouth. "Look, all I know is what Lucifer told me.

He knows more than I do. I can get you his information if you want to meet with him."

"But what do *you* know?" I asked.

He rubbed his scruff. "Okay, so Wormwood isn't a star and it sure as hell ain't no Angel."

"What is it then?" Laila asked.

"It's a them," he said. "A really, really, *really* old group of people. More like an entire civilization."

"What do you mean?" I leaned further across the table.

"I don't know the details," he muttered. "But this realm. This world, it wasn't God's. It was never meant to be a long-term home for the humans. This is where they live while they're still going through the soul cycles of reincarnation. This isn't where they belong. This is just where they learn to live for the second life."

"What are you talking about?" Laila asked. "What does that have to do with Wormwood?"

"Wormwood is the name of a group who ran this planet long before the humans got dropped off on it. The sun was new then; it was fresh to form a civilization," Don said.

"I'm not following," I said.

"Okay." He rubbed his mouth and thought for a moment. "So long before us, any of us, there was nothing habitable on this side of space, right? But there were creators. That's who Wormwood was. They made this planet livable so that they could sell it. Read the Bible, man. Genesis."

"The Bible says that God created the Heavens and the Earth," Laila said.

"No, the Bible says the Elohim created the Heavens and the Earth. But that's not the point. According to Lucifer, what they teach y'all in church is Dad's prideful version of the story. Always was an egotistical prick.

"But from his son's perspective, the only other one I know personally who was there when it went down, God created Heaven, but he renovated Earth. And since Daddy ain't around, I'm taking my brother's word," Don said. "Think about it this way. God bought the planet. He separated the sky from the water, he rose the mountains from the sea. He hung some drapes and gave it a fresh coat of paint. But he didn't build the house."

I wasn't really following. But I did know what the Elohim were. At least, vaguely. The word is debated by Biblical scholars. Sometimes, it only references the big guy—Yahweh, God, the Angel's father. In others, it references a group of deities, or another one entirely.

My brows furrowed far over my eyes. "If he bought it, then why is Wormwood coming back?"

"I don't know, maybe he's behind on the payment," Don said. "Who knows, man. I wasn't born yet. But maybe this was always God's plan. Most of the human souls alive have been recycled a million times and haven't learned a damn thing. Maybe he always planned to kill off his creations. Hasn't had a problem doing it in the past. All the villages he smote over the years, never seemed like he gave a damn to be honest."

"Clearly it was planned," Laila muttered. "That's why we're in that prophecy. 'The earth will rise up and protect her.' If that isn't predestination for what I am, then I don't know what is."

That information was a lot to take in at once, but even so, it didn't make much sense. It reminded me of the myths of the par animarum. Snippets that got misconstrued by someone who wasn't paying close enough attention.

And I wasn't crazy about the idea. Just the name sent a shiver down my spine. I was raised a strict Catholic, after all.

But clearly, the only person with information we needed was the one who was around to witness the beginning. Or at least, the beginning of life here on Earth.

No, I wasn't crazy about the idea. But I would do anything, *anything*, that would bring our son home. Or at least learn something that may help us.

"You said Lucifer would be willing to meet with us?" I asked.

"He's a pretty busy guy. You'll be on a wait list for a while. Maybe six months to a year," Don said. "But yeah. I can get you on it. He wants to meet you guys, but it'll have to be on his terms. He won't let you pick the location and set the time. He'll have guards and his own forms of protection that you can't expect him to surrender."

Not like I expected the king of Hell to put me at the top of his list.

"Sure. Fine, I wouldn't expect otherwise. But you said they're going to use Micah," I said. "What did you mean?"

"I don't know exactly," Don muttered. "But I do know that it has something to do with his soul. His soul's old too, but it was too powerful to be born for thousands of years." He rubbed his mouth. "The two of you, your soul's and bloodlines had to line up perfectly for him to be born. He's been around almost as long as you have, but the timing had to be right. His soul's more innocent than just about anyone's because it's only lived a couple lives. It's as close to purity as you can get. And there's another type of power behind purity and virtue. But he... He couldn't be born to just any parents. None of your kids could. Your kids?" He looked down at Milly. "Their souls have always been a hell of a lot like yours. Not any body could hold them. That's what Lucy said, anyway. If I had to guess, I'd say that's what they're using. The power of his soul."

CHAPTER THIRTY-EIGHT

JEREMY

I turned the music down, put the car in drive, and glanced at Laila. I listened to the cicadas buzzing in the treetops out the open window. "So what are you thinking?" I asked.

Laila pulled her seatbelt over her chest in the middle seat beside Milly. "I'm thinking we should go to Dairy Queen and then take Milly for a walk at the park. We have the stroller in the trunk, don't we?"

I glanced at her in the rearview mirror. "That's not what I meant."

After a quiet moment, she said, "I think it's going to be six months to a year until we get a meeting with the only other person who can give us some information."

"But about what he said," I said.

She swallowed hard. Her gaze shifted to Milly in her car seat. "I'm freaked the fuck out. But what am I going to do about it?" Her eyes turned back to mine in the mirror as I came to a stop light. "What can I do right now? Because I'm kind of an emotional rollercoaster. I cried at a Pepsi commercial yesterday. If I think about what he just told us, if I don't slowly let that sink in, I'm going to lose my shit."

I chewed my cheek, nodding.

I wished it were that easy for me. To just not think about it. But all I could think was the fact that Satan, the literal devil, had more information on my son than I did.

My kid was about to turn two, I'd never even met him, and my only hope to get even the slightest shred of intel on him—not even to find him, just a little bit of information—was the king of Hell.

I knew that I wasn't exactly aligned with Heaven anymore. But did I want to be aligned with the damn devil? Definitely not.

Although, in fairness, I shouldn't have judged him so harshly. Aside from scare tactics I'd been told as a child in church, I'd heard far worse about Angels and the Council than I had about him.

"And this is Milly's first time out in the world." Laila smiled and gazed over her in the car seat. "Regardless of whatever else is going on out there, I want to enjoy my daughter. Every moment I get with her is a gift and especially so if they're all right and the end of the world really is coming."

"You don't believe it, do you?" I asked after a quiet moment. "That the world's going to end?"

"I think we're supposed to prevent it," she muttered. "I think saving Micah's how we do that. I think he's the trigger that starts the end. I think Peterson is trying to start the build of a new world. But I think if we get Micah home, we prevent it, and things stay as they are."

She was right, at least to some extent. There was nothing we could do but wait. Just as we had been doing. Waiting, and waiting, and waiting. Also like she said, I wanted to focus on Milly. She was the light of my life. She was my hope. And we had to keep it together for her.

I nervously licked my dry lips and looked out the front window. "It's going to be nice to go to the Fae Realm. Get a break from all of this for a little while."

She smiled down at Milly. Then her soft gaze turned back up to me. "Yeah, I think so too. Kai was telling me about how they have all of these different animals and that the atmosphere looks like a different color. He says that there's fruits and berries everywhere. And he told me about the fairies. They call them pixies. Do you know about the pixies?"

I smiled back at her as I let off the break. "I do know about the pixies."

Bugs. That's what they were. Little tiny pests that resembled humans on a smaller scale with wings. They were beautiful, glowed iridescent colors, and stung like bees. I wasn't all that excited to see them in the flesh.

"Apparently they're really annoying, but I'm super stoked to see them." She turned back down to Milly. "Hey, do you think the Fae Realm was the Garden of Eden?"

"Huh." I tilted my head in thought for a moment. "I never thought of that. Maybe. It'd make sense, wouldn't it?"

For the record, the Garden of Eden was *not* the Fae Realm.

"I think it would," she said. "But that was a yes on the ice cream and walk in the park, right?"

I managed a smile. "Yeah, baby. We'll go get ice cream and go for a walk in the park."

If Earth as we knew it was going to end, we may as well enjoy the time we had with our daughter on it while we had it. But if it weren't going to, if everything were going to turn out fine, at least we'd always remember Milly's first trip to the outside world as eating ice cream and walking around the playground as the sun set.

We drove to Dairy Queen before heading to the park. Laila spent a good twenty minutes fidgeting with the stroller only to carry Milly around the track in the paisley embroidered sling Leah gave to her at the baby shower. Since Milly was born, she was almost always in that sling. Nearly every waking moment, Laila's gleaming eyes and arms were glued to our daughter. She had all of those glorious bonding hormones and was in her absolute glory.

I was overjoyed about my daughter too. There was nothing I loved more. But that's why I was so scared.

I'd gotten to live. I hadn't had much happiness throughout the course of my life, but I got to live it. Neither of my children had gotten that chance yet.

There was too much talk about the apocalypse for me to believe that it wasn't on the horizon. Mary fell from Heaven because she was so sure of it. Powerful Demons were reaching out to *us* for help. One of the most significant Witches in the world was doing the same. The first fallen Angel, the strongest of them all, wanted to meet with us to discuss it.

I was terrified.

The years we'd spent trying to protect and then to save our son would be nothing if they were right. What was any of it worth if the world ended before our children were old enough to see it? Why did we waste all of our energy and suffering to a cause that would ultimately be worthless when we all died anyway?

"Jeremy," Laila whispered against my chest as the TV cut to a commercial.

"Hmm?"

She turned up to meet my gaze. I slid my fingertips along her smooth bicep. Her sad eyes travelled over mine. Her hand moved from my leg to my face. Then she leaned forward and carefully pressed her lips to mine.

I lifted my hand from her arm to the side of her face. My palm held her jaw close to me as my eyes closed and my racing heart slowed a bit. A moment later, she inched back and rested her forehead against mine. My gaze shifted between hers for a second as I moved my thumb along her cheek.

"I'm scared too," Laila whispered. "But I think that we come out on the other side. I think that we make it."

I moved my fingers through her hair. "I'm not worried about us. I'm worried about her." I glanced at Milly sleeping in the swing just in front of the couch. "I'm worried about our son."

"So am I," she murmured as quiet as a mouse. "I'm terrified. But she doesn't need to feel that. She doesn't need to know what we know. All she needs is love. I want her to learn from my mistakes. I don't want her to hurt over things that can't be changed the way that I have. When we know for sure that we have a reason to panic, we panic. But for now, we just have to hold her a little closer. We finally have the opportunity to be parents. We get the opportunity to do this right. We can't fuck this up too."

I gave a slow nod.

Her lips lowered in a frown. Then she kissed me again and lifted herself onto my lap. I held her hips. She took my face in her hands and kissed me like she hadn't been kissed in a month. I pulled her closer with one hand and held her neck with the other. After a long moment she pulled back and looked between my eyes with a strong, hopeful gaze.

"We can make it through anything. We've been through some of the worst things imaginable, and we're still here. We've both come back from the dead. We don't lie down and die, Jeremy." She moved hair from my face behind my ear. "I was young and stupid with Micah. And I haven't learned it all yet, but I've learned a lot. And I'll be damned before something happens to my little girl. We'll get Micah back soon too, and when we do, no one will ever hurt him again. I won't give anyone the opportunity to take him from me again. We're *going* to fix this. But you have to keep your head up, okay?"

"Baby—" I began.

"I need you to keep your head up." Her dark green eyes looked between mine. "Your daughter needs you to keep your head up. And so does your son."

I knew what she was thinking. She saw—and felt—how stressed I was. And typically, when I stressed, I did drugs. At least, in the past couple years, that's what I'd done. But getting high wasn't what I wanted.

Now, all that I wanted was to keep my family safe. I wanted my son to know his family, to know me. I wanted my little girl to experience having a child of her own if she wanted. I wanted them to have lives worth living.

"I'm okay, Lai." I twirled her hair between my fingertips. "You don't need to worry about me. I'm just... I'm just scared. I'm not considering going out and getting high or anything, if that's what you're thinking.

It's just a lot to take in while I'm trying to enjoy adjusting to finally being able to call myself a dad. I'm gonna be fine though."

She gave a nod. Then she kissed me again, tucked her arms around my neck, and rested her head against my shoulder. "I love you," she whispered at my ear.

I kissed her hair and tightened my arms around her back. My gaze shifted over Milly dreaming peacefully in her swing. "I love you too."

CHAPTER THIRTY-NINE

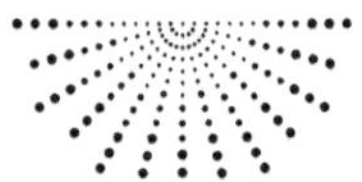

A WEEK AND A HALF LATER - LAILA

The practically intoxicating scent of Jeremy's body wash floated from the bathroom into the master. Silence—a rarity with an infant in the house—settled in my ears. I stared at myself in the wall mirror of the closet. And I frowned.

I hadn't worn a dress in so long, I almost forgot how pretty they were. But I did not feel pretty in this. Not anymore. This damn belly didn't want to give. I supposed I was only a few weeks from birth, but still. I wanted to be at least close to skinny again, damn it.

"You look gorgeous," Jeremy murmured in the doorway.

I pinched my squishy stomach. "I look like a walrus."

"You're crazy." He laughed and lifted Milly from the swing. "Doesn't Mommy look beautiful, Mills?"

A smile pulled at my lips. "Daddy just says that because he's stuck with me forever, and he knows these are the only boobs he gets to touch for the rest of his life."

"This baby looks just like you, Lai," Jeremy said. "If she hears you talking about how much you hate your body, she's going to hate hers. You don't want that, right?"

"Yeah, yeah." I waved my hand at him and took Milly from his arms. "She can't understand me yet anyway."

"You're the one who's always rambling on about positive energy." He smiled. "Try focusing that on yourself."

"Listen, pal, I just had a baby." I wagged a finger. He undid the towel at his hips and sat on the bed. "I'm allowed to be mad at my swollen uterus for a while."

He rolled his eyes as he pulled my blue, flowing harem pants over his feet. I lay Milly in her bassinet and walked back to the closet.

"It's just annoying that I have to wear a dress. I don't want to wear anything too revealing, but I need to be able to whip my tit out." I pulled out the blue spaghetti strap sun dress and looked over it.

"I don't think modesty's an issue in the Open Lands as long as you're in a dress." He stood and pulled the pants up. "The Open Lands are like the LA of the Fae Realm."

"But if I bend over, you can see my butt," I muttered.

"I don't mind. I love your butt."

I thumbed through the clothes. "I'm still bleeding a little though. What if I leak?"

"I don't know, wear an extra pad," he said.

"I'm not bringing plastic with me." I wrinkled my nose. "It's bad enough in our world. I don't want it to spread to theirs."

"What are you using then?" he asked.

"Just reusable absorbent underwear," I said. "It's not, like, a lot of blood. But it just doesn't feel right to wear a dress. I don't know."

"So if it's not a *lot* of blood, does that mean we can have sex now?" He grinned and leaned against the wall outside the closet door.

"The doctor said six weeks, and it's only been three and a half." I grinned at him around the corner of the closet doorway. "So sorry, baby. Got to deal with your hand for a while."

"Yeah, but that's for humans. You've been healed since she was born." He smiled and put his hand around my waist from behind. His lips touched my jaw as he pulled hair behind my back.

A quiet laugh escaped me. Then I turned to put my arms around his neck. "Most people don't even want sex this soon after a baby's born."

"Are you one of them?" His hands coasted from my ribs to my hips.

Another laugh. No, I wasn't one of them. I pretty much always wanted to have sex.

He smiled, leaned down, and pressed his lips to mine. My fingers traced up his firm chest. He grabbed ahold of my hips and lifted me to my vanity at the edge of the closet.

I took a glance at Milly outside the room in her bassinet. Her eyes were fluttering shut. Maybe if we were quick...

His lips drifted down my neck. My eyes closed before my head rolled back a bit. His hand snuck up my thigh and ran along the seam of my underwear. Just as warmth filled between my thighs, the front door slammed shut.

"Hey, are you guys almost ready?" Hannah called.

Then Milly erupted in cries.

My head fell to Jeremy's chest. He laughed and rested his head on mine.

"We should just kiss our sex life goodbye," he muttered.

"Yeah, I think that's what you do when you become a parent." I picked up my head and hopped from the shelf.

As I started to Milly, he brushed past me. "You get dressed. I need to chill for a second before I go out there in these pants anyway."

"You look so pretty." Hannah grabbed ahold of either side of my dress. "Green is your color, dude."

It was okay. A floor length, billowing A-line. Only thin straps held it in place over my shoulders, which I wasn't the biggest fan of with my scars considered. But it left my boob easily accessible for my daughter and seemed dress code appropriate. It also covered my swollen tummy well. And, honestly, was pretty damn comfy.

"It's not too slutty for a mom?" I pulled up the neckline.

Celena made a face. "You're a mom, not a nun."

"Would the lot of ye quit yapping about yer clothes?" Kai put his hands at his hips.

"Yeah, I'm ready to go." Leah uncomfortably pulled her shawl over her form fitting, flowing black dress. "And I don't want to talk about the attire."

"You look really pretty too though." I smiled. "I don't think I've ever seen you look so feminine."

Her gaze narrowed. "I said I don't want to talk about it."

"Give girls a reason to dress up and they'll spend half of the time you're there talking about their clothes," Wyatt said.

Jeremy laughed and fixed the blanket a bit tighter around Milly's face.

"Alright, alright," I said. "What do you need me to do, Kai?"

"Well, ye ought to hold the baby." He looked between Celena and I. "And then I need both you and you to hold my hands. I've got the rest."

I walked beside him and did so.

Jeremy passed me Milly as Kai looked between him and Wyatt. "Come to think of it, maybe the two of ye should grab ahold'a yer soulmates. The more power we've got, the longer the portal'll stay open."

"Sounds reasonable." Jeremy's hand moved to my waist, kissing my forehead. I smiled up at him, holding Milly close to my chest.

Celena took Wyatt's hand and gave a gentle grin. He stood beside Hannah with Leah to her left. Jeremy stood beside her, forming a circle in the grass of the main house's backyard.

"Now when I say jump, ye jump. Hannah and Leah will go first. Then we make our way around the circle. The last to cross will be you, Wyatt," Kai said. "Those of us with Fae blood'll feel quite close to normal when we land. But Hannah, Jeremy, Wyatt, ye all will feel relatively similar to how most feel teleporting for the first time. Laila, you hold that baby tight. It's safe but only so long as ye don't drop her."

"I'm not dropping my baby." I looked down at the beautiful little girl in my arms.

"Alright then." Kai looked around. "Everyone has their bags, yes?" We nodded, and he smiled. "Then here we go."

He closed his eyes and laced his fingers between mine and Celena's. Then he began quietly speaking a language I'd never heard. The wind picked up speed around us, and Jeremy gripped my hip a little tighter. Gray clouds rolled in, and small water droplets fell from the sky, smacking our skin like tiny BBs.

Kai's voice got louder. Then a thousand quiet whispers in the same tongue that Kai spoke filled our ears. Phrasing it that way makes it sound creepy, but it was actually incredibly peaceful. It was almost euphoric.

Warmth radiated from his palm into mine. Then the ground quivered a bit beneath our feet.

The small quivers turned to large cracks. We gazed around each other in a bit of fear tied up with wonder. Where the earth shook and formed cracks began to emit a radiance of gold speckled with bright hues of green and swirling shades of pale, yet electric, blue.

In a matter of moments, it all doubled or tripled in intensity. The wind got stronger, the rain fell harder, the whispers grew louder, Kai's hand got hotter, and the tear in the earth stretched wider in all directions until it was near flush with our feet.

I gazed in awe of the swirling colors on the ground against the cool, dew dampened grass. It danced in circles like water in a hurricane before it's left the sea. Yet it shined like the electricity of a beautiful, multicolored sun.

"Now jump," Kai yelled.

Hannah held her breath and jumped into the glowing portal on the ground. Kai went back to chanting. Leah followed close at her tail, grinned, widened her eyes, and dropped into the tear of dimensions. Jeremy squeezed my hip and smiled. Then he jumped inside.

I released Kai's hand. My arms tightened around Milly.

I took a step forward and fell.

The abyss reminded me a great deal of teleportation. But it was slower. I never saw anything when I teleported because it happened so quick.

The portal was a little different. I didn't have long, maybe around three seconds, but I got a glimpse at the threads that tied our dimensions together. Never mind the swirling sensation that left me worried I would drop Milly after all.

It was a beautiful, intricate swirl of colors. Blues, and yellows, and greens, and pinks. Suddenly, I could *see* the layers of our world.

I'd done research on sacred geometry before I knew what it was. Maybe my abilities were why I had such great interest in the odd hippy things I enjoyed in my adolescence prior to understanding how I tied into the universe.

Regardless, I was glad that I had an interest in them because now I knew that it wasn't crazy science fiction. The supposed quack scientists who'd researched the power of mandalas and the intricate swirls of the universe weren't quacks after all.

It was like floating through a tunnel that was somehow contorted to the shape of my body. Every inch of it glowed a million hues like gems in the sunlight.

That's almost how it appeared; a wall of gems that floated to my skin and held me within it. Yet, they were malleable. They touched my skin and cradled it like its own form of gravity. Those who didn't know what sacred geometry was may compare it to drifting along the light refractions of a kaleidoscope.

CHAPTER FORTY

JEREMY

My knees collapsed to hot black sand as the contents of my stomach jumped up my esophagus. I lurched forward and vomited onto the warm granules my hands sunk into. The puke felt cool compared to the ground.

"Motherfucker, that hurt," Leah said a few feet away, pulling herself to her feet.

My gaze shifted back to the portal I'd just shot out of like a geyser in anticipation of Laila. I swallowed hard, panting heavily with wide eyes. My heart hammered as I prayed that she'd use air when she made it through with our daughter.

Then she came out the other end whirling through the orange kissed atmosphere. She began to plummet to the ground desperately clutching Milly to her chest, and my breath caught. The green dress ballooned around her like a parachute. I teleported into the air, grasped her waist, and flashed back to the ground.

Laila recovered and looked around in amazement.

I fell back to the sand vomiting. "Fuck, this is worse than being dope sick."

"Oh, shit. I'm sorry, baby. Are you okay?" Laila leaned down and ran her hand along my back.

My stomach clenched once more, and I barfed again. Her hand moved along my shoulder. "Oh, yeah. I'm great."

She laughed a bit. "I was about to catch myself, you know. You didn't have to do that. It was cute though."

"Well, ya could have done it sooner." I dropped to my ass. "How's Milly?"

She looked down at her and laughed. "Still sleeping like a bear."

Kai's landing was incredibly graceful. He shot upward and caught the air around him to levitate himself near thirty feet in the air. He spun it to hold him in a standing position. Then he carefully glided to the sand beside Hannah. She was still barfing when he leaned down and pushed hair from her face.

"Jesus Christ!" Celena flew through the air. Then she plummeted to the ground. Now that I was recovering a bit, watching them fly into the world was near humorous. They shot upward like balls in those fake vacuums they make for kids.

Wyatt's reaction was almost priceless. His bulky, flailing body roared into the air yelling "What the fu-u-uck," slower than the rest of us had. He fell just as quick, slamming to the sand like a thousand-pound weight.

As I stood, I got my first good look around. All of the stories didn't do it justice. This place was a cornucopia of beauty.

Once I could take a breath without smelling vomit, I inhaled a long whiff of the most gorgeous air I'd ever taken into my lungs. Although I smelled the salt in the ocean, there was something else that made its way up my nostrils too. It wasn't comparable to anything I'd breathed in on earth. I couldn't even truly describe it. It was sweet like baked goods, but flowery like honey suckle. There was even a touch of a citrus aroma like lemon that danced up my nose, although it was not quite identical.

The world around me reflected the color of ours at sunset or sunrise. It was as if the air had been painted warm orange and yellow hues with a hint of pink. The waters of the ocean to my left lay crystal clear on the black sand. Inside the tides, I saw fish of a thousand colors and forms that I didn't know existed swimming comfortably throughout the translucent water. Vivid, neon coral reefs that rested beneath them a bit further out made the clear water appear as if it was glowing.

"This is where I should have taken you to propose," I muttered, gazing around in awe.

"You should have," Laila murmured. "Maybe I wouldn't have said no."

I wiped my smiling lips, took her hand, and touched her wedding band with my thumb. "You rescinded your no either way."

"Yeah," she said with a smile. "I guess I did."

I kissed her forehead and moved my arm around her shoulders as I looked out in wonder. Beauty wasn't enough to describe the marvels of this dimension. I knew it'd be magnificent, but now I understood all of the hype. We were standing in the most enchanting realm of pure, radiating magic.

It almost felt like home.

But I wasn't Fae, so I didn't understand why.

A few months though, and I definitely would.

CHAPTER FORTY-ONE

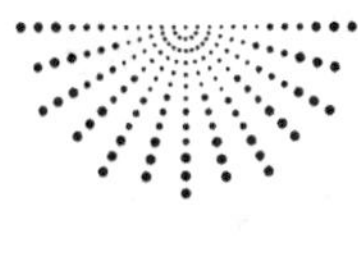

LAILA

"Seven folks and one babe," Kai said to the man over the wooden table I suppose we'd equate to a desk in our world.

"Aye, filling our whole inn for the night." The man on the other side smiled. "How're the lot of ye sleeping? Separate beds or communal?"

"Separate." I chimed in.

"Ye ken how much that's going to cost ye?" he asked.

"Will this cover it?" Jeremy set a small ring on the table. It had a white gold band and a purplish-blue gem in the center.

The man's brows raised with his eyes. "Is that..."

"White gold setting and three-quarter carats of tanzanite," Jeremy said. "So that's enough?"

"Enough..." He pinched the ring between his fingers. He studied it for a moment before a deep, billowing laugh left his lips. "This'll be plenty. How many rooms d'ye say?"

"Let's see." I looked around. "Celena and Wyatt, Hannah and Kai, me and you, and Leah so four."

"Aye." The man nodded. "Four rooms it is. Will ye need a carrycot for the babe?"

"A carrycot?" I asked.

"A cradle," Kai said. "Aye, mate."

"There's a pram shop a few paths down." The old man rummaged in the drawer behind the desk. "They got a reel back system if ye won't be staying long."

"That's great, thank you." I smiled, bouncing Milly on my hip.

"Where're the lot of ye from?" He handed Kai a few sets of old skeleton keys.

"The north tides for me," Kai said.

"The rest of ye Earth born?" he asked.

"We are," I said.

"Except for me," Leah said. "Not really sure where I was born."

"Sprite bloodline, no?" the clerk asked.

"That's what I'm told."

"An orphaned babe from the war, I'd bet." He looked over her. "Your color says it all."

"Oh yeah?" Leah put her hands on her hips. "I didn't realize they correlated."

"Oh, yes," he said. "Your race got the worst of it aside from the pointers."

"Pointers?" Celena asked. "What's that?"

Kai glanced her way. "The Elves, love."

"There's Elves." She chuckled. "Of course there's Elves."

He looked between Celena and me. "Don't ken much about yer own, do ye?"

"Neither of us knew what we were until adulthood," I said. "We're still learning."

"Well, take a gander at the print shop. Plenty of history there if ye wanna learn." He smiled, nodding toward the steps on the left. "But yer rooms are on the second floor. I'll have the cot up in a half tick as yer settling in. Check out's at the mid-day bell."

"Much thanks." Kai smiled. Then he turned away from the desk. "We'll settle in and then we'll go out. I've got an old friend working at an apothecary down the way."

"That sounds good," I said.

Everyone paired off into smiling groups as we started through the barn styled inn. Things were simple here. The entire structure was solid wood, cabin-like. There were no smoothed edges with thick coats of polyurethane and stains. Every detail was jagged and authentic.

It was like taking a step back in time. The interiors reminded me of a colonial village I visited on a field trip in seventh grade. Everything was bare. No rugs laid on the old wooden boards. There was no paint on the thick logs that formed the structure.

Candles sat along shelves that lined the day lit hallways. The wicks stuck out of fist sized mounds of recycled dripping wax from the nights before. It almost looked like a piece of art; something that might sell for a billion dollars as a contemporary piece in a New York art show. I could see where the previous candles had burned to bead past the old and off the edge of the narrow shelf to form small wax puddles frozen along the walls.

Aside from the candles, there wasn't much décor in the old inn. The windows had no glass or decorative curtains, only shutters with small iron handles. Just wax puddles and beautifully designed, purplish black doorknobs. Before we left, I made a mental note to ask Kai where I could find some just like them. I was in the market for a new doorknob after Adam's ax incident anyway.

It may have come off a bit eerie for someone who liked the finer things. Helena or Moriah would be appalled to even step foot in conditions like these. But I liked it. I certainly didn't want to stay forever; I loved the comfort of my weatherproof home. Still, I could admire and engulf myself in its simplicity for a moment.

"So this isn't where you grew up?" I asked Kai as Jeremy and Leah laughed and pointed out the window at the end of the hall.

"I wish." He laughed. "Made a few trips though. Always wanted to move this way. The Open Lands or Earth. Then I met yous and knew pretty quick where I wanted to call home."

"Was it far from here? Where you grew up?" I asked.

"Aye. 'Nother continent actually. See, the Open Lands are what our people consider the free world. The acceptance we got from that cashier, that seemed typical to you. But worldwide here? Some places won't even let people like us inside."

"That's why you came here instead of home, huh?" I asked.

"Aye," he murmured. "But I'd like to make a stop there if you or Jeremy could take me. Couple old friends I'd like Hannah to meet."

"Sure." I smiled. "But you should really learn to do that yourself, you know. Your little sister's passing you up."

He grinned and met my gaze. "How about ye fuck off?"

"Harsh." I laughed, beaming up at him. "I'm going to need you to show me to that pram shop first thing. And we aren't renting, I'm taking that baby home."

"Sure."

"And thanks for this, by the way. I really appreciate it."

He smiled. "Thanks for etting' me show ye round."

CHAPTER FORTY-TWO

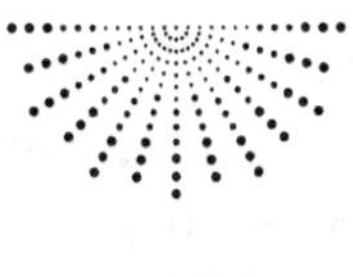

LAILA

Milly lay in the crevice of my bare chest while I gazed out at the city in wonder. It was located at the edge of a peninsula. From the view out our inn's window, I could see the entire city as well as the ocean behind it. I could take in all of its beauty from one perspective.

Where we'd stood on the beach, I couldn't make out much of what I saw of the waters from that window. The shore's sands were as black as night against the clear water that crashed onto them, creating large clusters of thick white foam. The most awe-striking of all was the coral reef that framed the entire peninsula. It was painted a thousand neon colors, some I cannot describe because I didn't know the colors existed until I saw them with my own eyes.

Near the right side of the land, my gaze slowly took in the magnificence of the largest mountain I'd ever seen. After squinting for a moment, noting some purple magma at the top, I realized mountain wasn't the word to describe the monstrosity. It was a volcano—a beautiful volcano—but the purple lava is what threw me.

What I first believed to be a thick cloud of smoke began to morph. I squinted further and stood to peer out the window. When I watched the colors around it reflect a color between obsidian and violet from the glow of the volcano, my eyes widened.

"What—Is that what I think it is?" I looked at Jeremy.

"What is it?" He stood and walked to me.

I stared out the window. Then, bright violet light shot from its mouth. My heart skipped a beat, and Jeremy laughed.

"You knew they were real, didn't you?" He put his hands to my hips from behind.

My gaze couldn't shift from the beautiful creature flying around the mountain like a snake to a tree. It was beautiful, yet terrifying, and somehow, incredibly tranquil all at once. It could have been the most fascinating dance of elegance and terror I would ever witness.

Jeremy laughed. "They don't bite." He kissed my hair.

"No, I know," I muttered. "It's just... I've seen the drawings in the books. I know about the bonds they form with the Fae. But seeing one in real life..."

"It won't hurt us." He smiled, gazing out the window from behind me. "Dragons here are like cats to the Egyptians."

"I'm not scared. I'm mesmerized."

"It is beautiful, isn't it?" He rested his head on mine. "All of this is just so beautiful."

"I wonder if Earth would look close to this if we didn't destroy it," I muttered.

"Maybe. But it isn't all like this, baby. Different climates have different landscapes just like back home."

"Yeah, but on the way here from the beach, did you see a single piece of garbage on the ground? Or the beach?" I turned up to meet his gaze. "Because I didn't."

"These people take pride in their planet," Jeremy said. "It supplies them with life, it's where their gifts come from."

I nodded, looking out over the city. That much was evident in the landscape.

Some buildings were wooden, like the one we stood in. There were simple cottages and barns. Others were stone. Some glowed like fire, leaving me wonder if they were encased in some form of magma or composed of it entirely.

A few were even shaped in half globes of water. There was a large structure toward the edge of the city designed the same way. It was the size of a stadium or sport's arena, yet appeared to be a giant water droplet sitting within the town.

Near the far left of my view, I looked out over the other side of the peninsula. I would call it a rainforest, but it didn't look like one I'd ever seen. It looked like that coral reef in the distance, practically glowing with fluorescent colors. No two trees' leaves were the same hues. It appeared as though a flower garden had been blown up and placed within the city's confines. Some were pink, others were blue, some were yellow, and others were purple. It was almost like our leaves changing in Autumn, but the colors were vibrant rather than warm. The most important difference wasn't their colors but their liveliness. They were luminescent, glowing like millions of fireflies.

Intricate systems of rope ladders and bridges connected them to huts and larger structures scattered throughout. Within some of the larger towering trees shined candles around brilliantly colored curtains and drapes. People walked along them as if wandering the streets of the cities themselves.

The harder I squinted, the more I saw the elements of the planet used to create the metropolis. The fire coating some buildings. The trees holding others above the ground. The water that flowed through canals to form domed shelters.

Just as I was done taking it in and beginning to adjust to the city's marvels, my jaw fell open once more.

The dragon flying around the volcano was nothing in size when compared to the structure slowly orbiting into view. It was hidden by the mountain's wonder at first, but now I could see it.

A magnificent castle floated around the mountain like the Earth to the Sun. It was like something out of a fairytale. I couldn't make out much detail, but a few elements were clear. Like the crystal-clear tube of water beneath that nearly cradled it.

The large structure had ten or more towers jutting up into the sky.

Some walls were thick black stone while others were elements. One appeared to be a wall of purple magma, dancing off the side and sliding off the water that swirled beneath.

"That, I did not see in the books," Jeremy whispered as it slowly oscillated around the mountain.

I remember thinking something as I breathed in the reality of this beautiful world.

Why does this feel so familiar?

CHAPTER FORTY-THREE

JEREMY

"Oooh, look." Laila bounced with excitement, shifting an old-fashioned stroller back and forth. I smiled at the grin that came to her lips, rocking Milly in my arms. The three of us stood inside the old shop off the main road while the others looked through the ones nearby. "Isn't this one pretty?"

"It is." I smiled as she inspected the wooden basket lined with layers of brilliantly colored linen. Instead of metal wheels, the four were composed of twisting wood and vines that I'm sure someone who controlled Earth created by hand. Beautiful ivy climbed through the thinner pieces that connected to the bassinette on the top. "But the wheels don't look very durable. They'd probably do okay here, but on cement back home, they'd fall apart so quick."

"Yeah." She frowned. "I guess so, huh?"

"Whatchye looking for today, loves?" A sweet old woman made her way to us with a big smile. "A pram for the new babe, ay?"

She reached out and smiled down at Milly. Her fingers grazed my daughter's, and Laila's jaw tightened a bit. I squeezed Milly a little closer to me, and the woman turned to Laila.

"Ma'am?" she asked. It came out sounding closer to 'Mum.'

"Right." Laila cleared her throat. Then she pulled a smile to her lips. "Sorry, yes. Yes, we're looking for a pram."

"From the Earth Realm, I take it." The old woman put her hands to her hips. "Got to concur with yer lord then, dear. This beaut idn't what yer looking for. Won't hold up to a lick of use in that world."

"What would you recommend?" I asked.

"Hmm, well." She put her fingertip to her chin. "Stone would be ideal."

"A pram made from stone?" Laila asked.

"Metal," I said.

"Aye, I've got just the one," the woman said. "Ye short on coin? I'd hate to show it to ye if ye can't swing it."

"Coin isn't an issue," Laila said.

"All right, this way then." She turned and made a gesture for us to follow. We trailed after her through the nooks and crannies of the tiny shop. "Me and my master invested a pretty coin into this beauty for a lord in the rolling hills. The mistress came to collect once the babe came and blew her lid. Wouldn't pay a bloody shilling. She insisted nothing of it was right. Gods smite me if it wasn't everything she asked for and more. She wanted stone wheels, so we gave 'em to her. She wanted a triple sealed umbrella, and that's what she got. We even double padded the bed for the little tot. If ye ask me, she'd probably taken on a number of shops like ours to build her pram and wanted to see which one she liked the best before she bought it."

Laila chuckled as the woman made it to the corner. Then she pulled a thin white sheet off of a stroller and looked back to us. But once I heard the gasp leave Laila's lips, I knew we were walking out with it.

It was pretty. I liked the one we had back home because it was convenient. Milly's car seat fit inside of it perfectly, there was a big basket on the bottom, cup holders on the top, and a net on a zipper to keep out bugs. But she was in awe of that handmade pram.

The two wheels and handle were a dark metal that appeared dark purple with other iridescent hues when the light hit it just right—the same metal I kept seeing over and over in this land.

The bed was lined in exquisite white fabric embroidered with vines and bright colored flowers. Even the hood was a wondrous shade of white with beautiful flowers.

It reminded me of the mural of tattoos on Laila's back. I'm sure she thought the same thing when she saw it.

"It's perfect," Laila whispered as her fingertips slid along the metal. "It's absolutely perfect."

"What do you think, Papa?" The woman smiled at me. "Want to make your missus the happiest woman alive?"

I laughed. "It's her money, ma'am. If she wants it, she'll take it."

"I want it." Laila grinned. "We'll take it."

Another laugh left my lips. The woman beamed. "All right then. That'll be four-hundred shillings."

"Here." I adjusted Milly in my arms before reaching into my pocket. Then I handed her a small stone of tanzanite, just barely a half carat's worth.

A gasp drew into her dropped open mouth. She flung her hand to her chest, and her eyes widened. "This is far too much, master. I can't take all of this."

"Sure you can," Laila said as she pulled out the stroller.

"No, no," she said. "I couldn't, missus."

"You could, and you will." Laila smiled. "Please."

She looked at Laila, eyes still wide. Then she turned to me. "This is all right with you, sir?"

I really had no say in the matter. But I recognized the way men controlled certain things in this world.

I laughed and gave a nod. "Yes, ma'am."

Slow breaths left her lips as she looked down at the jewel in her hand. Then she turned back up to look between us. Quickly, she turned away hollering, "Stay here a moment, loves!"

My gaze turned back to Laila as her fingers stroked the fabric. A soft, gentle smile painted across her lips and brought one to mine. She'd been so happy recently.

Her smiling green eyes met mine. "Isn't it perfect?"

"Mhmm." I smiled back.

Her smile widened. Then she walked to me. She put her hand against my chest and brought herself onto the tips of her toes to touch her lips to mine. Then she reached for Milly in my arms.

She had the most priceless gaze of joy as she lifted Milly up and set her in the pram. I couldn't help but grin as I watched her enjoy her moment. It was such a simple thing, but it brought her so much happiness.

"Ah, here we are." The woman came into view with a plate of food. "If ye won't give me less, I've got to give ye more. This is me mum's recipe; been in the family for centuries. Take a few, please. Throw 'em in that sack over your back."

"That's okay—" I began.

"Ah, rubbish," she said. "Take the cakes. And these, these too."

The woman reached into the pocket of her flowing skirt and pulled out a few plucked flower buds. They had yellow, rounded, powdery centers that almost appeared translucent. The pedals were white toward the center and faded to pink on the ends.

"Ye can harvest the seeds or just have at them." She laughed and looked back up at us. Then she tapped Laila on the nose. "New mums need a breather once in a while."

Laila opened her hand. "What is it?"

"Lotus." The woman sat them in her palm.

"Really?" I leaned down to look at them.

Damn it. Always wanted to try one of those. But I was clean and serene.

"Aye, they are. Plenty of 'em grow round these parts. Wouldn't recommend taking 'em back with ye though. They can have some not-so-pleasant effects on humans."

CHAPTER FORTY-FOUR

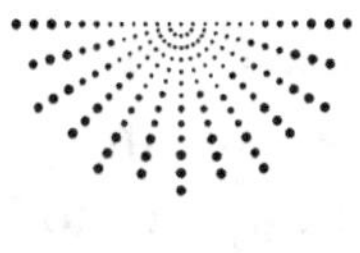

JEREMY

"That is the prettiest stroller I have ever seen," Hannah gushed. "It looks just like your wedding dress."

Leah stroked her finger down the embroidery. "Yeah, even the lace."

"A little more colorful though," Celena said.

"That's why I got it." Laila grinned beside me, gazing down at Milly inside of it. Then she reached into the pocket of her dress to pull out the flowers. "Oh, and the lady at the shop gave us these."

Kai nearly gasped. He reached out and took one from her palm. "These are impeccably grown."

"No shit." Leah grinned, snatching one from Laila's hand. "I've wanted to try one of these forever. Can I have it?"

"What's in them?" I asked Kai. "I know they get you high, but what is it?"

"It's nitrous oxide," Wyatt said. "Inside the little yellow bubble, right?"

"Right," Leah said.

"But an incredibly high concentrate," Kai said. "Only lasts for a moment or two but well worth it if ye ask me. And it tastes amazing."

"You could try one, Lai," Celena said. "Laughing gas is used during labor anyway."

"No, no. I'm good."

"No peer pressure or anything, but you should definitely try it," Leah said.

"Got to agree," Kai said. "It's just a moment, but it's a moment of bliss."

Laila looked up at me with an expression that was hard to place. I'm not sure if it were because of guilt or worry that I'd eat one and plummet back into addiction. But her gaze was almost asking for permission—not something I was used to from her.

"Go ahead." I smiled. "I'll stay on baby duty for a minute or two."

"Are you sure?"

"Yeah, of course." I lifted Milly from the cradle into my arms. Then I let my smile widen. "I got her, go ahead."

"How many of those do you have?" Celena grinned.

She looked down at her hand and counted for a moment. "Five."

"Well, I've had plenty of 'em." Kai smiled.

"And I'll pass," I said.

Truthfully, I really wanted to try that damn flower. I'd heard about how much fun they were. I knew that they were culturally appropriate here, and I knew that nitrous oxide wouldn't send me falling off the wagon.

But I also knew that Laila would think it would. And that she really wanted to try it. She wouldn't if I did because then no one would be sober for Milly.

So I just gave her a reassuring smile.

"So we can each have one." Laila began handing them to everyone. "We just eat them?"

"No. Put it on yer tongue and close your mouth. The petals'll melt in a moment. When they do, clap your tongue against the roof of your mouth to pop the bubble and inhale. Gives ye the best flavor that way."

Everyone placed their flower on their tongue and closed their mouths.

Laila looked up to me with a near embarrassed gaze. A quiet pop sounded behind her lips. Then a giant grin pulled up her cheeks. Her eyes glimmered for a second, and I laughed. Then quiet chuckles left her mouth. She leaned onto her tip toes and pressed her lips to mine.

As she did, a magnificent flavor touched my tongue. It was floral but not strong like a perfume. Instead, it was sweeter than any sugar I'd ever tasted. It had earthly aspects that reminded me of tea or honey but most of all, it was sweet and flowery.

Her hands cradled my face as her lips brushed mine. I smiled against her lips. Then she leaned back and smiled childishly down at Milly.

"Holy shit," Leah murmured followed by an echo of laughter.

"It tastes so good." Hannah smiled wide, put her arms around Kai's neck, and kissed him.

"Damn." Wyatt snickered.

"I totally get the hype." Celena giggled.

"What's it feel like?" I ran my hand along Laila's jaw.

"Like floating." She smiled as her gaze shifted over Milly. "Not flying, but floating. And really, *really* happy." I laughed as she turned her gaze up to me. She held her smile but huffed. "And now it's gone."

"That was fucking quick," Leah grumbled.

"But it was beautiful," Hannah whispered with a dazed grin and kissed Kai again.

I laughed. "Alright, you guys got your buzz. Let's find that apothecary so we can get what we came here for."

We all waited a moment as Hannah continued to kiss Kai.

"Maybe it lasts longer on some people," Celena mumbled.

"Clearly." Laila gave an awkward glance over Hannah as she pushed her body into Kai's. Her hands slid from his chest to his shoulders, squeezing hard. Then she arched her chest even closer.

I turned back to Laila. "Alright, so this is a little weird."

Kai laughed and pulled away from my sister. "You're tiny, you'd feel it longer than the rest of us."

"Well, thanks," Laila muttered.

"Yeah, kind of offended to be honest," Leah said under her breath.

"Apothecary, Kai." Celena clapped her hands.

"Right." He laughed. "Everyone follow me."

Walking the pathways of the city was like walking the streets of a mystical version of Los Angeles. Some roads were composed of thick pavers like the ones I'd seen in Europe while others were mere dirt paths. Some were even lined with moss. Laila commented once more on how it was nature's carpet, took off her sandals, and walked along it barefoot.

The earthy aspect of the metropolis astounded me. Clearly, it was a city. There were thousands of people everywhere we turned. But if I kept my gaze on just one thing for a moment, I felt like I was in the forest.

Literally every area was covered in foliage of some kind or another. Whether it was a stream to my left or a tree to my right, nature ruled this place. Instead of fighting against it, the Fae embraced it. They used it to create the most glorious, majestic, urban reality.

The only intimidating dragon we'd seen was that massive one flying around the mountain castle in the distance. But we saw at least a thousand smaller ones while walking to the apothecary. Some were the size of robins, others the size of hawks, and a few were the size of a large dog with wings. It made me wonder what Tink's reaction would be to seeing them soar above.

There were dozens of other animals as well. Almost all of them were bright colors, which made sense for camouflage in the brilliantly colored forests. They didn't look real; they looked like super realistic stuffed animals hopping and scurrying the streets. A lot of them reminded me of Pokémon, actually.

But that was another thing that fascinated me. The animals didn't act like pigeons and ground hogs back home. They didn't scurry away from us as we walked past. They glanced our way, then went back to whatever they were doing. Either that, or they didn't look up at all. They had no fear of us, because the people here hadn't given them a reason to be afraid. And that mystified me. I wished animals back home would've done the same, but I couldn't blame them. Our species came in and destroyed their ecosystems.

What intrigued me the most was the people rather than the surroundings themselves. I knew that the Fae realm had other species of creatures similar to humans and myself, but some of them left me a bit perplexed. There were people with massive fangs protruding from their closed lips on blue skin. Others had horns and markings that looked like tattoos on their green flesh.

People stood on barrels in the streets playing instruments, many I couldn't identify by name but could probably play if I had a few minutes with them. Some blew fire from their mouths while others created floating balls of water for people to climb inside of and roll like a bowling ball. I could see it giving Laila and Celena some ideas for future battles.

Some type of festival was going on during our time there. I couldn't tell you for sure what they were celebrating. Truthfully, I'm not sure *they* knew what they were celebrating. There were no signs that specified. Nonetheless, the streets were loud and busy, full of life and vibrancy that made it nearly impossible to feel anything besides excitement and intrigue.

Most women wore skirts and petticoats, but there were a few that didn't. The one's who didn't wore the type of clothing I'd seen every woman in every video game ever made wearing. Extremely tight pants or shorts, open back and stomach with a skintight bra.

Almost all of the men were shirtless in a pair of harem pants like the ones I wore. Some wore loose shirts that I'd describe as pirate-like. However, there were a few in armor. They had thick breastplates and shoulder pads and carried a heavy shield with large swords tucked at their hips. But again, they weren't silver or bronze. They were the blackish purple color, the same thing the pram I pushed was made from.

I hadn't thought about Micah in a day or two, but when I saw those men in armor, he flooded back into my thoughts. A wave of grief washed over me as I thought of how beautiful it would have been for him to witness. Especially at his age. Getting to see a real-life knight would have been a dream come true for me as a young boy.

Then I pushed the thought from my mind and focused on the little girl gazing at the orangish sky above us. She hadn't been a very fussy baby, although she was never the quietest either. But there, she was peaceful. Maybe even happy.

They all were. The four Fae in our group couldn't stop smiling. I'm not sure that they even realized how joyous they were. Wyatt, Hannah, and I could see it though. There was no denying that they were in their absolute glory.

Honestly, so was I. And I couldn't have begun to understand why.

Things weren't as soft and beautiful when we arrived at the apothecary though.

CHAPTER FORTY-FIVE

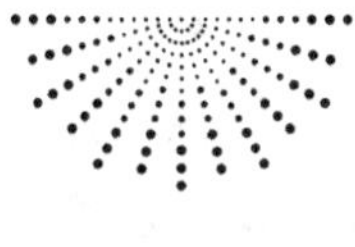

JEREMY

The apothecary was set up a lot like the pram shop had been. It sat at the corner of a busy street. Unlike the pram shop though, the building was built from glistening purplish black stones. That same substance I was seeing everywhere on this world.

"I'll go ahead on in," Kai said as we approached. "Probably best if the lot of us don't go in at once. We'd like to fill up the whole space."

"Sounds good." I handed him a gem from my pocket. He started inside, and the rest of us gazed around in wonder.

Laila gestured to a woman dancing with fire on the street corner parallel from us. "There's plenty of entertainment out here."

The woman wore nothing but a black chain mail bikini. At first, I thought it was a bit grotesque for that place considering there was an entire crowd of people able to see her nipples and bare ass. But then, she blew purple fire downward while mid-jump in the air and I understood. She couldn't wear clothes doing a dance like that. Metal was the only, and most conservative, option.

The fire oscillated in a circle beneath her feet before she jumped onto it in a summersault and used it as something of a brace. As it spun in the circle, she floated along its interior and allowed it to encase her within it. The fire continued to spin as the woman pulled her knees into her chest. In a matter of seconds, her body was doing constant spins inside a giant ball of swirling violet fire.

"Why am I so attracted to someone who could kill me that easily," Leah murmured. Her gaze was locked on the woman who erupted from the ball of fire and landed in a pose with either arm outstretched to the sky.

"Cause that's a part of the allure." I smiled and tucked my hand around Laila's waist. She turned up with a smile and pressed her lips to mine.

"...outta my shop, I say!" a man's voice yelled from the store behind us. All of our heads turned around. A hefty bald man held the back of Kai's shirt, ripping him from the door he'd just entered. After making it through the threshold, he tossed him to the ground like garbage.

Hannah gasped and ran to help him to his feet, but the man pushed her too. "I said *out!*"

My heart hammered, and I handed Milly to Laila. Leah rushed to help Hannah to her feet. Wyatt had already started toward the man.

"What the fuck's wrong with you?" Wyatt snapped. "You think it's okay to hit a woman?"

I helped Kai to his feet as he wiped blood from his forehead.

"I din't hit nobody." The man curled his nose, spit splattering from his thin lips. "Don't matter if I did though. Yer kinds ain't welcome here."

"This is the Open Lands." Kai wiped the blood that streamed from his forehead down his cheek. "We've got as much right to be here as you."

"Ye don't have no right!" The man stomped closer.

He was looking at Kai, but he pushed me to get closer to him. I let out something of a scoff, putting a hand in front of Kai. I didn't particularly want to fight anyone either, but I knew my brother-in-law wasn't one to throw punches. And this guy clearly already had.

"Let's all take a deep breath," Laila began behind me. "We can all—"

"Ye and that thing damn sure ain't allowed in my shop. Away from my store, all of ye!" the man urged, side stepping so that he wasn't directly in front of me. Laila clenched Milly closer to her chest. "May as well bash its head off the ground and give it what it deserves like yer kind did to—"

"Are you talking about my daughter?" I felt my hands began to shake and sweat. My heart's race nearly doubled. I stepped between him and Laila. "Because that didn't sound like an insult to me, that sounded like a threat."

"Jeremy." Kai put his hand to my chest. "It idn't worth it, we'll find the herbs elsewhere."

"Yer daughter." The man scrunched up his nose, gaze narrowing up at me. "More like a bloody abomination. Mixing races, all that power ain't meant for one babe—"

"Go fuck yourself," I snapped. "Hate like yours is the problem, not my daughter's DNA."

"He's just a bigot, Jeremy." Leah put her hand to my chest, but I pushed it away.

"Aye, how's about I go fuck that whore wife—"

I didn't even think. My hand just raised into a fist and clapped into his jaw. His head whirled to the side, crimson flying from his lips and splattering bystanders. The music slowed to a quiet as he turned back to me. The burly little man's teeth grinded together, blood spilling from a cut on his lip. His eyes started to glow an iridescent shade of blue.

"Call my wife a whore again," I said.

"It doesn't matter, baby." Laila put a hand on my bicep. "Let's just—"

"Your. Whore. Wif—" I raised my hand to punch him again. He flinched back. Wyatt grabbed my shoulders and pulled me away.

"We're leaving," Wyatt said beside me.

A crowd was forming around us. At least fifty people had their eyes locked on us—the group of foreigners, half of which had the blood of their greatest oppressors in their veins. I knew what these people were capable of when someone hurt their people. My wife was one of them. I'd rather not end up a pile of ash.

I released my tight jaw and sucked my teeth. The man smiled.

"C'mon, baby," Laila murmured with her hand on my back. "We'll find it somewhere else."

A slow breath left my flaring nostrils. I nodded and turned away. Laila moved her hand around my waist. Then we started to walk across the pathway.

"Aye, that's right," the man called. "Get outta here, ye Angel mutts. Worse than the pointers, ye are!"

All eyes were on our group as we walked across the street. We stayed close as the people watched us carefully. Some had expressions of grief, but most wore looks of disgust upon realizing what we were.

"Are you okay?" Laila asked quietly, moving her hand along my forearm.

I nodded as we made it past the woman we'd watch spiral into a ball of flames. "Yeah, I'm good."

The hustle bustle resumed a bit. A few people still glared our way but most just passed by.

This was how my daughter would always be viewed by her own people. An abomination. They shared DNA but because she had a little more Angel in her, she'd always be a filthy hybrid in her own land.

"That bastard." Kai gasped, stopping and patting his pants. "He's got the jewel. I'd handed it to him inside, right before he gave me the boot."

We all came to a halt.

"Do we have enough to get more?" Laila asked.

"Not if we want to eat. We've only got about a half carat left now," I said.

"I'll go back," Leah said.

"Not alone," Wyatt said. "Clearly the guy's got no issue putting hands on a woman."

"Fine, come with me then," Leah said. "We have to get what we came here for."

Wyatt leaned down to kiss Celena. "But you guys stay here. We don't need a repeat of what just happened."

"Fine," I muttered.

They started back across the street.

"Let me see." Laila touched my upper arm.

I extended my hand to her with a roll of my eyes. "It doesn't hurt."

She moved her fingertips to my knuckle. Then she pressed down a bit. I winced. She pulled back, grinning. "Thought it didn't hurt?"

"Can you just heal it?" I asked.

"But I thought it didn't hurt," she said again.

"Alright, it hurts." A smile came to my lips. "Can you heal it now?"

"Well, since you asked so nicely." She smirked. White light radiated from her palm into my hand. "That was cute though. Defending your lady's honor and everything."

"You should have broken his neck for what he said about Milly," Celena muttered, healing Kai's forehead.

"Yeah, I really should have," I mumbled.

"Is that normal?" Hannah asked with her hand on Kai's upper arm. "Being treated like that?"

"Aye," Kai murmured. "My whole life. Even worse back home if you can imagine. Now ye ken why I like Earth."

"It's strange." Laila glanced down at Milly. "Being the hated minority."

"We're privileged," Celena muttered.

"I said *out!*" the man across the way yelled to Wyatt.

"Either give us the herbs or give us the jewel back." I heard Leah say.

I craned onto my tip toes to see over the crowd.

"I'm not giving you shite," he said, taking a step closer until they were nearly chest to chest.

Wyatt put his hand against his shoulder and pushed him from her. "We just want what's ours and we'll be on our way."

"It ain't yours now," he spat. "Shoulda thought of that before yer pal over there battered me in the lip."

"You took it without offering the service or product we exchanged it for. It's ours," Leah said.

"Ye better control ye wench!" the man yelled.

The festival fell silent again. People began to cluster around them in a half moon. Their curious eyes watched in amusement. But their broadened shoulders cued more than curiosity.

"Sir, we just want what you took from us," I heard Wyatt say, no longer visible through the crowd.

"Ain't nun here yers!" someone in the crowd yelled.

"Ye ain't even Fae!" another voice called.

"Jesus Christ," Laila murmured as she looked over the tense crowd that was gradually turning to a mob.

"Bunch 'a murderers and thieves the lot of ye are!" another voice yelled.

"Bet you're trying to rob the poor old man."

"After beating him bloody!"

"Beasts, the lot of 'em!"

"This is going to get ugly fast," Hannah murmured.

"I'm going to grab them. You can open the portal again for us to go get more money, Kai." Laila handed me Milly.

I cradled her in my arms. Laila was gone before I had time to say bye.

"Alright, everyone, we're leaving." I heard her say from inside the crowd.

"Now the whore's got something to say," the shop owner hollered.

"We're just going to leave," Laila repeated.

The man said something I couldn't hear clearly. Leah, or maybe Laila, said something in response. Then all hell broke loose. The crowd started swaying and their voices raised. I couldn't make out much, but they were definitely insults.

Whore, Angel scum, cunt, wench, poofters, not to mention a hundred others I couldn't say if it was to save my life. Milly started to fuss in my arms. I hushed her, swaying from side to side.

The rushing mob started shifting back and forth, growing louder. I heard Leah yelling and Wyatt nearly screaming. Then all I could hear was Laila saying, "Stop it, we're leaving."

A thud pounded from her shoulder into mine, as if she'd been shoved and hit into something. I was just getting ready to hand Milly to Celena.

Then a heavy *thump, thump* started from down the road.

The cluster of people began to drift apart, but I still couldn't see anything. My heart picked up faster, and Milly's cries grew louder in my arms.

"What the hell is that?" Celena furrowed her brows down the road.

I shifted my head and squinted a bit. As my vision adjusted, my eyes widened.

Straight even lines of men and women in armor marched down the cobblestone path. But the shock came from what trotted at their rear rather than the small army itself.

Just behind galloped a massive wolf. I don't mean large like Wyatt and Celena when they shift. When I say massive, I mean the size of a pick-up truck. It had dusty gray fur with patches of black and soft copper colors. The neck was all white above its gray paws. Other than its size, there was only one major difference between it and a normal wolf. I didn't realize at first, not until I watched its trot turn to a run. Then two large wings curved out of its shoulders and hoisted it from the ground. The man riding it was a mere speck compared to its wonder as it flew toward us.

Once it was flying through the air and no longer blocking my line of sight, my eyes widened in amazement. A dragon, roughly the same size as the wolf, was close at the army's tail. To say the least, I was suddenly captivated. It couldn't have been more than a thousand yards away, yet I could make out almost every detail of its beauty.

Its scales were a brilliant shade of obsidian that reflected hues of green as it moved. There were even hints of blue. It stood on two legs and had a tail so long that it took up near half of the street. On its head sat a large, pointed white horn. Then two large wings the same color as its scales lifted. The army dropped to its knees as the beast began to flap its wings. The air around me spun as the creature took flight.

It caught up to the wolf in a matter of seconds before diving to the ground just in front of us. My body swayed with the quake of the earth.

My breath caught. I clutched my crying daughter closer. The wings were only a few feet from my face as it puffed out a cloud of smoke.

A woman I could only assume was the queen draped gracefully

atop the dragon. On her head sat a sparkling black crown that held a thousand glistening jewels over her long, tight black curls. She wore a purple crop top that curved around either breast and over either shoulder to form an X around her chest. A flowing skirt the same fabric as her shirt with a train as long as a wedding gown rested over at least a quarter of the dragon's back. Thick gold bracelets and wrist gauntlets trailed up her rich black skin, bringing out the silver undertones of her flesh.

She began shouting a firm voice over the mob. The wind spun beneath her, floating her to the ground. Her voice was deep and strong in the heavy Elvan tongue. All of the crowd fell to their knees and bowed their head.

Except for my wife. Even Wyatt and Leah bent their knees in fear, but not Laila. Laila stood there poise as ever while the queen shouted over the people.

"Get down," Kai urged at a near whisper. He grabbed Hannah and Celena's shoulders. They fell to their knees and Kai looked up to me. "On your knee, Jeremy."

Slowly, I lowered myself to the ground. The only sound besides the Queen's voice was my crying daughter. She wailed like a banshee over the woman's strong voice.

Then English left her lips. Rather than the close to Scottish accent I expected, instead I heard a familiar English inflection. Some dialects there sounded close to English, but I knew an accent when I heard it.

It was almost identical to Moriah's. I'd been around the world more times than I could count. I knew accents, and hers was clear as day. London.

She wasn't from here either.

"Is that you, Laila?" Her voice carried and echoed off the buildings. "Surely, you aren't here without Jeremy."

I looked at her under the dragon's perch. She glanced at me, giving the same puzzled expression I wore. "He's behind you."

The queen turned. She crouched to find my gaze beneath the belly of the beast. "What're you doing all the way over there?" A smile pulled at her lips, and she made a rolling gesture with her hand. "This way then."

Back home, we were famous. But communication between the dimensions was slim to none. How did she know us?

I teleported beside Laila. She took Milly from my arms. The queen looked between us.

"What's going on here?" She glanced around the crowd.

The clerk with a bleeding lip beside Laila raised his head. "Do gràs —" *Your grace.*

"Did I say your name?" the queen asked. The man fell silent. "Did I ask you to speak, sir?"

"Forgive me, your grace." The man's hands trembled.

She turned back up to Laila and me. "What's going on here, Laila?"

"We came here for mullock root." Laila's tone was cordial. "We got a hotel, we bought a pram, and we came here. My brother went inside to make the purchase and this man dragged him out by his shirt because of his race.

"He made some comment about bashing my baby's head off the road, and my husband told him to fuck off. Then he called me a whore, so he punched him in the face. We walked away, but he had the last of the jewels we've been using as currency. Without those, we can't get what we came here for. My brother and sister in-law came back to get it and another argument started because he refused to give them our money back or the herb we need."

She turned to the man on the ground. "What is your name, sir?"

"Agnus, do gràs." His gaze was steady on the queen's shoes.

"Is this true Agnus?" He began to speak, but she cut him off. "Think twice before you answer because I do not take kindly to liars."

His gaze was steady with the ground. He gave a slow nod. "Yes, do gràs."

"Now, tell me, Agnus. If I don't take kindly to liars, how do you think I feel about men who call women whores and make comments of beating infant heads off of rock?"

Don't get me wrong, I was grateful for her interference. But that didn't make it any less odd. Why had she sided with us, strangers, over her own people? Was it really just about morale?

Or was it because I was right, and she wasn't from this land? If she'd come from earth, then I supposed it made sense for her to look to us as if we were the kind of people who deserved respect. But if she'd come from earth, how was she these people's queen?

"Forgive me, do gràs," the man pleaded. "I am but a man, I am not without fa—"

"Did I ask for an apology?" The queen's brows fell, and the air swirled around us. It hoisted the man into the air and over the small gathering of people. Then she dropped him to the ground directly at her feet and waited for a response. "Or do you avoid your queen's questions to beg your own?"

"Not kindly, do gràs," the man nearly whispered. "I'm sure ye don't take kindly to the things I said."

"That is correct, sir," the queen said. "That said I'm sure you know that I also don't appreciate any of my people stealing from another on my land. But especially one of our own." She lowered herself to the ground. Her long, ring covered fingers raised the man's chin to meet her gaze. "What is your surname, Agnus?"

"Ròs, do gràs," the man murmured.

"Well, Agnus. Today, you have brought shame to the Ròs name. The Fae stand behind their people, and you not only failed in that regard, but you wished hate upon the next generation of your own kind." The queen looked between his eyes for a moment. "Now is when you beg for forgiveness, sir."

"Please forgive me," the man murmured. "I shouldn't've said those things."

"No. You shouldn't have. Neither should you have refused service to a paying customer who caused your business no harm." The queen let out a slow, even sigh. "Hate crimes are not something that I tolerate, Agnus. You will be punished. You know what the punishment once was for theft, do you not?"

The man began to sob. "I do, do gràs."

"But I do not practice the old ways. Rather than your hand, I'll settle for your night. You'll spend an evening in the prison beneath my castle. Court and fines will be settled at a later date." She brought herself upright and turned to the man sitting atop the wolf. "Asher, take this man back to the keep. I'll return soon."

The queen turned back to us. "I do apologize for your treatment, friends. That was not the example I set for my people."

"Thank you," Laila said.

She smiled and looked at Laila and I with a soft, sweet gaze. "So how is Micah?"

My stomach dropped. "What?"

I could rationalize her knowing of Laila and me. But Micah? Almost no one knew our son's name. How the hell could she? And *why* would she ask about him as if we knew?

The queen cocked her head to the side a bit. She gestured to Milly as the man carried the clerk away. "Who is this?"

Slowly, Laila said, "Milly. This is Milly."

A smile returned to her lips. "Milly, you said."

We nodded, and her smile widened. "Aye, I see. I see. Well, I'm glad to finally meet your acquaintance then. You're looking for mullock root, you said."

"We are," I said.

"Huh," the queen said. "Well, I have a personal apothecary on duty at the castle. You can take some as a gift as well as an apology for the way you've been treated today, if you'd like. Supper will be served shortly, perhaps you and your kin could join us."

I made a face. "Really?"

She smiled. "Unless you'd rather make a trip back to Earth and search for another resource when you return."

"No, we'd rather not," Laila said. "Thank you. Thank you very much."

The queen held her smile. "After me then."

I looked to Laila. *What in the actual fuck?*

CHAPTER FORTY-SIX

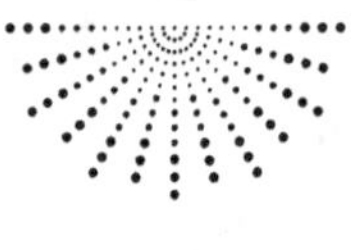

LAILA

I stood inside a large ballroom gazing out a wall of windows that overlooked the gardens on the terrace. The never-ending ocean laid to the left and a portion of the city to the right. Jeremy sat outside with the rest of our family and a few guards.

He sent a smile my way, and I smiled back. Then he turned back to Kai who sat beside him drinking from a goblet. The massive, winged wolf lay on the ground beside the light skinned man wearing a suit of armor with pointed ears that the queen had referred to as Asher in the street.

I was quiet, taking it all in. Why were we here? Why had she been so cordial in the street? Why did she side with us over one of her own?

And how in the fuck did she know my son's name?

"I trust that you're enjoying the view," the queen pulled my attention from the wall of windows.

When I turned to meet her gaze, my brows furrowed a bit. Rather than the bralette and long, open legged skirt, she was now wearing a pair of jeans and a pink T-shirt. Instead of an array of necklaces, bracelets, and rings, only a single purple jewel on a rope chain hung around her neck.

240

She caught my gaze and laughed. "I dress the part for my people, but I prefer comfort to extravagance."

"You aren't from here?" I asked, adjusting Milly against my chest.

"From here, yes. Raised here, no." She smiled and lowered herself to a large marble table to my right. "Part of me wishes that I had been. But I do love Earth. I miss it often. I try to make short trips when I can."

"No shit," I said. "The people, they're okay with that?"

"A birthright is a birthright," she said. "The Open Lands were under another leader's rule when I came along. Things were better here than they are in other places on this realm. Still, the people were ruled by ancient philosophies. When I rose to power, I made it my mission to abolish those concepts. There was uproar for a time. But as with all things, it passed."

"Huh."

Odd. So she was from here, brought to earth, then returned home and took her kingdom back. Why had she left? I supposed people here would know that much. I'd ask Kai.

My gaze shifted over the exquisite room for a moment.

The floors sparkled that same purplish black rock we'd seen all over this realm. An oversized stone fireplace sat in the corner with two large candles on its mantel. A large silver chandelier holding more candles hung above us. The marble table by the window where the queen sat was the only other décor. Official, business-like.

I turned back to her. "What did you say your name was?"

"Oh." She chuckled and pushed long black curls behind her ear. "Avery. Avery Alston. At least, that was my name on Earth. Avery is actually my surname here. But it was the name I gave the police as a child on Earth. My name here is Amaryllis Avery."

"Sounds like you've got a complicated history."

An odd smile came to her lips. "We'll sit down, and I'll tell it to you in grave detail another time."

My squinted eyes stayed on hers for a moment.

She stared at me like we were old pals. She called my son by his first name that only a few people alive knew. And I suppose that some part of me should have been fearful or distrusting at the least. But just as she looked to me like we were old friends, I felt as if I knew her too.

Something was off. But not in the sense that I should run for my life. Just… off.

In the presence of a queen or not, I had to question.

"Ya know, you keep giving me this really weird look."

"Oh? What kind of look?"

"Like you know me." I looked between her eyes, only then noticing their violet color.

One of her brows raised, and she laughed. "You're Laila Callidy. Everyone knows you."

"The others didn't. The shop owners, the people on the street. No one here did."

"Well, I'm not from here." She smiled. "As you just pointed out."

"But you've clearly been here for a long time. I didn't have much of a reputation until two years ago."

A quiet laugh left her lips. "I'm not stuck on this plane, you know. I can travel between them at will, just as you and your siblings can. I do leave from time to time. Never long, but Queens know many things."

"Uh-huh," I murmured. Milly began to fuss and root, so I pulled my shirt to the side. When she began to suckle, I turned back to Avery. "Not many people know my son's name."

Her expression shifted a bit, as if she had to think hard for a moment. Then she spoke again. "I do apologize. I believe that I'd received some misinformation."

"Which was?"

Another quiet chuckle left her lips as she looked between my eyes. I'm sure my puzzled gaze told her that I knew she knew something she wasn't telling me.

I couldn't have possibly wrapped my mind around how we all fit together then. In all actuality, she'd be a hero to us one day. But at the time, anyone who knew *anything* about my son was suspicious.

"I was under the impression you'd brought him home. However, I sincerely apologize for my choice of words on such a sensitive subject."

I licked my teeth for a moment, studying her sincere expression. I supposed it was possible for her to have heard Micah's name at one point or another. The masses didn't know it, but the Chambers may have. Jeremy and his grandparents didn't talk often, but they had briefly discussed Micah and Chris's disappearance. Liam knew it too. Not many others, but I could stretch my mind to believe that at one point, she'd stumbled upon it due to her notoriety.

"Sure. Thanks."

"My apothecary's collecting your herbs now," Avery said. "Should only be a moment or two. Will you be staying for supper? We've got more than we need."

I was curious about Avery. I wanted to figure her out. And if she weren't going to kick me out just yet, I'd stay around for dinner.

"Sure." I smiled.

"If you don't mind my asking, what's the mullock for?" She crossed her arms against her chest. "Not a simple headache, I presume."

"A spell to access mine and my husband's past lives."

She gave a quiet laugh. "Why do you want to know all that?"

"Everyone keeps talking about my destiny," I said. "I want to know what they mean."

"Ah." She stood. "Those spells just show you glimpses, you know. Usually the most formative moments from those lives. The most formative tend to be some of the most painful."

"So I've been told," I muttered. "I've seen some horrible shit though. Lived through worse. I'm sure I'll be okay."

"I'm sure you will," she murmured.

I turned my gaze back out the window as that large, obsidian colored dragon's wing cascaded a few hundred yards ahead. "How does it stay like this?"

"What do you mean?" Avery asked.

"The castle. How does it do this?" I gestured around. "Do other Fae keep it orbiting this mountain?"

"Oh, no." She laughed. Then she stood and joined me at the window, looking out. "This is Elvan magic. A spell cast centuries ago. It uses the power of the volcano. My baby out there," —she smiled at the dragon as its tail whooshed past— "this is hers. And her mother's before, as well as mine, and their mothers before that."

"Why though?" I asked. "Can't be just because it looks cool."

"No, it's not. Although, that was my first thought when I saw it too." She held her soft smile and gazed out over the ocean. "It's set up this way for many reasons. The mountain, of course, is one of them. Like you, I am of the Flame. When needed, I can conjure the lava from within it to use as a weapon. Legend has it that my bloodline was birthed from the fire itself."

"Is that all you control?" I asked.

"I'm Elite. But fire came most naturally for me," Avery said. "But also because it keeps the castle safe. No one has ever penetrated these walls without permission or invitation, and they never will. It also gives us a good perspective. Eyes on the city, eyes on the water. Like a lighthouse armed with incredibly powerful ammunition."

"Makes sense," I said. "So no king?"

She laughed. Her gaze shifted over the man beside the winged wolf. "No. No king."

"Why's that?"

"You ask a lot of questions." She smiled and met my gaze. "But if you must know, kings are a rarity in our culture. Women make better rulers. They always have." Her smile grew a bit odd when she said that last sentence, squinting slightly.

But that didn't make sense to me. Women here wore petticoats. The pram shop owner asked Jeremy's permission to spend my money.

"Women don't seem to be the ones in power here."

"Why? Because they wear dresses? Because they embrace femininity?"

"Well, the attire seems pretty..." I shrugged a bit. "I don't know. This culture just seems relatively conservative."

Something between a huff and a laugh fell from her lips. "If you mean that we don't have prostitutes at street corners, then yes, you could call us conservative. We treasure certain things here. Sex being one of them. But not because it defines us, only because it is a beautiful aspect in life that deserves dignity. It is not the foul thing human culture makes it out to be.

"Women have just as much power as men. And yes, there are certain practices. Men tend to handle finances, they often work away from the home while the woman stays with her children. But you have to understand that there is an equal balance. Not all couples even have children. Not all couples are heterosexual either.

"Yes, some things may seem" —she held up air quotes— "conservative. But it depends on what you define as conservative. If you're referencing the way many women are dressed, then you're looking at us wrong. Many women choose to wear clothing that covers them, but not for the reasons women in your world cover themselves. Not because it is distracting to men, or because a breast is inappropriate.

"Some women feel empowered when fully covered. Some feel empowered bare naked." She smiled. "We respect both perspectives here in the Open Lands."

Huh. Well, I supposed I had misunderstood. Then again, that apothecary owner had called me a whore for virtually no reason, so forgive my confusion.

But I supposed no two people in any world would have identical views on all things. The way the governing entities viewed these things did matter though, and her perspective was in near perfect alignment with my own.

"In regard to the king concept..." Avery looked out into the garden, eyes washing over the red-haired man beside Jeremy. "We aren't opposed to queens marrying. Their opinions always rank behind the queen, but we do marry from time to time. However, tensions have been high between the Elves and the Fae for some time. And the only man I'd want to bind myself to for eternity would not be accepted by my people. Not now, at least. But perhaps one day, a man will sit at a throne beside me."

Oh. So that was her man out there, not just a guard. Interesting.

CHAPTER FORTY-SEVEN

JEREMY

Sitting on that floating courtyard as it oscillated around the volcano was both exhilarating and nerve racking at once. Celena seemed to be having the time of her life hoisting herself from the edge of the cliff only to catch her body in the wind and land back onto the grass. Wyatt, Hannah, and Leah had a blast doing the same. I could teleport and the thought of doing that still terrified me from this height.

Now that I had a kid counting on me, life threatening situations like this weren't something I wanted to take part in for joy. If I had to jump off a cliff to catch one of my kids or someone else that I loved, I wouldn't think twice. But doing it for the rush seemed childish.

They didn't have kids though. Being a father had really changed my perspective on useless acts of fun that could get me killed.

"Aye, thank you, sir." Kai bowed his head as the man handed him a glass of wine.

"Asher, please." He smiled. He extended a goblet to me and lowered himself to the stone bench beside Kai.

"I'm alright. Thank you," I muttered.

"It's juice, mate," Asher said.

Slowly, I accepted the glass with a thanks. To know of us was one thing. But to know not to offer me alcohol was a bit peculiar.

Then again, all of this was. Why had they invited us here? And how did they know us? Because clearly, they did.

Sure, they were royalty, and I could understand knowing our names. But they were so incredibly casual. As if we were all old friends.

Asher was about my height, maybe an inch or two shorter. He had a wide face with a thick red beard over his warm, sand colored skin. Half of his red shoulder length hair was pulled neatly into a ponytail at the back of his head to reveal high pointed ears.

Although near my height, we were built nothing alike. He had broad shoulders and biceps twice as thick as mine. Overall, he looked like the last guy you'd want to pick a fight with. But his tone and demeanor was gentle.

Hannah jumped from the cliff and screamed a higher pitch than she had before. My heart hammered before I saw her shoot back into the air like a geyser. "Jesus Christ." My hand flung to my chest.

Kai laughed. "They're fine, brother."

"Yeah, I know," I muttered. "But God damn, she doesn't have to scream like she's dying."

He laughed again and took a sip from his glass.

The massive dog beside Asher opened his jaws and exhaled a big, wreaking yawn. Then it laid his head to the ground between its huge paws.

I'd seen drawings in books, but they made them out to be vicious weapons used in battle. Looking at that guy though, I couldn't even visualize him tearing someone apart with his jaws.

He was the cutest thing I'd ever seen. Just looking at him made me smile.

His white and gold fluffy fur was at least a forearm's length deep. His eyes had to have been bigger than my daughter's head. The large wings that rested over his back were white and feathery—like that of a dove but on a colossal scale. And his canines were easily a foot and a half long.

But he was sweeter than Tink. Even if he weren't though, I'd still have the reflex to pet him. If I went down getting mauled by a giant fluff ball like him, that'd be a damn good way to go.

I gestured toward him. "What's his name?"

"Zephyr." Asher patted the animal's shoulder.

"He's beautiful," I murmured. "I've heard stories about the pterolycus, but I thought they all died out in the wars."

"Aye, most have." Asher nodded. "We're looking for a mate for him now. He line bred once with his sister a few moons back, but the pups din't make it."

"I hope you find him one." I smiled.

My gaze shifted over the giant canine a moment longer. He looked like I'd taken a picture of a husky and blown it up. In almost all respects, he was a normal dog. His impeccable coat was beautiful mixing shades of gray, white, and warm copper. All four paws, that were about the size of my head, were bright white.

"Be a shame for the race to die out," Kai said. "I remember watching the warriors fly them in the north as a young boy. They were the most beautiful thing I'd ever seen."

"A few up there still." Asher nodded. "They're trying to repopulate. I'd like to stud him out and get a pup or two. Although, what I really want is a breeding pair. Have a few litters and keep them here for the next generations."

I'd heard they could live upward of a thousand years. That they stayed in the family they were born in, passed down generation to generation. But I'd also heard that they were all dead, and clearly, that wasn't true, so I had to ask.

"Are the legends about their life expectancy true?"

"Aye." Asher nodding, patting Zephyr's shoulder. "My father got this ole boy as a pup. When he died in the wars, he flew home and found me. I's only a boy myself then but I thank the realm for him every day. Not sure I'd still be here if not for him."

"Babe," Hannah called to Kai from the edge of the cliff. "You've got to try this!"

Kai laughed. He drank up the rest of his wine and sat his goblet back to the stone bench. "Thank you, sir."

"Asher." The man smiled. "But aye."

He smiled and gave a cordial nod. Then he took off in a jog toward Hannah. I chuckled as they joined hands and took off running toward the cliffside.

Asher chuckled. "To feel that way about life again."

I chuckled. My gaze turned to the wall of windows behind me where Laila stood with Milly in her arms. She spoke with the queen the way diplomats speak at meetings with other foreign leaders. Her gaze was steady, her feet were planted firmly, and her expression showed cautious apprehension. She wouldn't have dreamed of jumping from that cliff side without a good reason either.

"I'm not sure I'd want to feel that way again," I muttered. "Being young and stupid was fun at the time. I'm glad that I got to have those experiences. But these days I have more fun watching TV and holding my daughter."

"Mhmm." Asher huffed. "I miss television. One of the best things about earth."

"You're not from here?" I asked.

"No, I am," Asher said. "But I spent a good chunk of my life on earth."

"Really?" I glanced at his pointed ears. He nodded, and I raised a brow. "Did you wear a lot of hats?"

Asher laughed. "A good Witch did a wee visionary spell on me. Only I could see my points."

"I see," I said. "That isn't common. Traveling to earth, I mean."

"Unusual circumstances. Still, a story too long to tell." He smiled and took a sip from his glass.

I watched him carefully for a moment.

I couldn't figure Asher out. I couldn't figure Avery out either, but Asher puzzled me just as much. He sat beside me as if we'd sat this way a thousand times. He knew not to give me alcohol. And maybe I should have been nervous.

But I was comfortable. I liked him. I felt the same beside him as I felt beside Adam or Brody. Admittedly, I was hesitant. Not scared, but hesitant.

Still, I was curious what the dynamic at play was.

"Care to make a long story short?"

Asher let out a quiet laugh. He shifted his gaze back to the wall of windows where Laila and the queen stood. "Avery needed to know who she was. This place, these people, they needed her. Even if they didn't realize it. So I found her. Helped her learn who she was, how our world works. Showed her how much we needed her. Thought she'd need me to protect her too, but that didn't last long."

That explained her accent then. She was on earth. He grew up here, then he went and found her.

I chuckled and looked over Laila. "Yeah. Yeah, I know how that goes."

He smiled as his eyes moved over Avery. "It's treacherous, isn't it? Being destined to protect someone who is always capable of protecting themselves?"

A quiet huff of a laugh left my lips. "It was for a while. But somewhere along the way, I realized that I'm not here to protect her. I'm not supposed to be her hero. I'm supposed to be the place she goes to feel safe when nothing else does."

CHAPTER FORTY-EIGHT

LAILA

After the apothecary gave me the mullock root, Avery showed us to the dining hall. Standing within its walls felt like stepping into the garden of Eden itself. From the glass ceiling three stories high to the plants budding with fruits and flowers that climbed every column of the room.

Although the palace floated hundreds of feet above the ground, it appeared to have its own ecosystem within this room. Three of the four walls were covered in growing foliage, but the last was a small waterfall that landed in a little pond in the corner of the room. One column in the middle of the farthest wall seemed to be a live tree, still budding new leaves and flowers.

"Hey, you." Jeremy smiled when he saw me walk through the doors.

I smiled back. He kissed my cheek and reached for Milly in my arms. "Where is everyone?"

"They're coming." He brushed hairs from Milly's forehead. "Having too much fun jumping off the cliff, I guess."

I chuckled and gave a shake of my head.

"Dinner will be out soon," Avery said with her hands at her hips. "We don't eat meat here. I hope that won't be a problem."

"No, that's fine. Thank you," I said.

She smiled as she looked between the two of us. "All right then. I'm going to go and fetch the others. Please help yourself to anything you see. Everything here is edible and incredibly delicious. We call the walls our appetizers." She chuckled, gesturing around. "I do insist that you try those blue fruits on the vine by the waterfall there. They are my all-time favorite food. Extraordinarily sweet, also very filling so only have one if you want to enjoy dinner."

"Sure. Great, thank you." Jeremy smiled.

She smiled back as she started from the room. Once at the large, black door, she glanced over her shoulder. "And have a seat wherever you like."

Once she was out of hearing distance, I turned up to Jeremy. "This is weird, isn't it?"

"Yeah, really fucking weird," he said. "But I'm strangely comfortable, ya know?"

"Yeah, I don't think they're bad. But something's not right. It's just... I don't know. She acts like..."

"Like they know us?" he nearly whispered. I nodded. "Asher gave Kai wine, and he gave me juice. And he's not Fae, he didn't read my mind. Did you read hers?"

"A little. She's strong, I couldn't get much. All that I got was emotions. I didn't hear any thoughts."

"What was she feeling?"

"Comfort," I muttered. "Almost happiness but closer to amusement. I don't know, it's odd."

He gave a slow nod. "We need to get some background on her later. Kai probably knows more than we do."

That night, I had the most magnificent dinner of my life. Truth be told, I found myself a bit nervous to even try the foods. Something was strange inside that castle. Beautiful, kind, and loving. But also bizarre.

I waited to watch Avery eat before I touched a thing on my plate. Then I only ate the foods that she ate.

When it was over, I was glad that I had because everything tasted delicious. I ate berries that tasted like jolly ranchers.

The blue fruit on the vine that Avery suggested cracked open to reveal a thick white pulp that tasted like a smoother version of coconut cream pie. The blue juice that puddled in our goblets tasted like a softer, less sweet version of fruit punch.

An important detail that made me comfortable enough to share meal with them was the use made of the thirty-foot table. The maids and cooks brought the foods to it, but instead of scampering back to the kitchen, they lowered themselves to the benches, and dug in. In that moment, I found trust in Avery. That's when I saw that she wasn't only a good leader but a kind one.

Yet, I couldn't get past the look Avery and Asher kept shooting mine and Jeremy's way. It was oddly comforting but still strange. They looked to us with respect and enjoyment. One day I'd think back to that night and laugh when I finally tied it all together.

Avery gave us each a basket and told us to take as much fruit home with us as we could carry. She said they'd die quick once they got to Earth's air, but we could get a few days out of them. I took a healthy handful of the blue fruits because like Avery testified, they were amazing.

Then we teleported back to our hotel rooms and turned in for the night. We agreed to leave in the morning since we'd already paid for the room and no one had much energy left after our long day. After changing Milly and feeding her one more time, she drifted to sleep. Then I lay her down in the bassinet and collapsed next to Jeremy on the uncomfortable lump of fur sewed into a giant pillow these people considered a bed.

"I think I'm ready to go home," I whispered against his chest.

A quiet laugh shook beneath my head. He twirled a piece of my hair between his fingertips. "Not as soft and pretty as the books make it out to be, I guess."

"I can't believe the hate bleeds so deep. It's not like I had anything to do with all those people that died in the war. Hell, Mary probably didn't either. She was too busy popping out kids." I turned to meet his gaze.

He chuckled again. "Yeah, I knew they wouldn't like us. But I didn't expect that."

"Next time we come, we're going to a little town. Maybe it'd be better than the city." I smiled and pushed hair from his face.

"Next time, huh?"

I smiled. "Yeah. I want to come back when they're a little older. When we have Micah back, I mean."

"Sure," he murmured. His arm was still around me, but his distant gaze went to the ceiling.

I rolled onto my side and inched up the bed so that my head lined up with his. "Are you okay, baby?"

He pulled a smile to his lips and shifted to face me. "Yeah, I'm good."

"Are you sure?"

"I'm fine," he said. "Why do you ask?"

"You've seemed a little off for a while." I ran my fingertips along his jaw. "I'm worried about you."

"You shouldn't be." His soft smile slid down at the ends. A slow breath left his nose. "I am a little stressed. Pretty sad sometimes when I think about Micah. But I'm happy too. I'm really happy. I love getting to be here for everything with Milly. And I love getting to be a parent with you. There's just a lot on my mind."

"Like what?"

Obviously, I knew. But I also knew my husband. For me, bottling up my emotions was how I coped. But Jeremy? He dealt with life best when we talked through things. Silence from him was never good.

Another quiet, ironic laugh. Then his smile fell to a gentle, almost fearful expression. "All we keep hearing about is the end of the world, Lai. And I'm scared."

Biting my lip, I gave a nod. My fingers twisted between his. I lifted them to the pillow beside my cheek. His eyes shifted between mine, free hand grazing my cheek.

"If the world ends, we'll pull all of our money out of the bank," I whispered. "We'll buy all the jewels that we can get. And then we'll come here. We'll buy a piece of property big enough for the family. We'll build a new house big enough for everyone we love, and we'll start over."

He let out another chuckle. His gaze shifted between mine in the moonlight. "Oh, so you've got it all figured out?"

I smiled and gave a nod.

His lips fell to a frown. "But what about everyone else?"

"The weight of the world is too much for anyone to carry, Jeremy," I whispered. "We're carrying enough baggage. The entire planet isn't our burden too. I don't care what any prophecy says. We did our job. We saved almost a thousand people. The only thing left that we're responsible for is bringing our family home and killing those three bastards. After that, mission accomplished. The apocalypse isn't our job."

He nodded slow. "We should do that then. Start cashing out our money, I mean. If the markets start to crash, we won't have access to cash. I can build a safe back at the house."

"You really think we need to?" I asked.

His gaze shifted to something behind me. The wheels turned behind those blue eyes for a moment. Then he looked back to me. "I think it's too much to crack up to coincidence. Everyone's scared, and they wouldn't be if there wasn't a reason to be. And I don't want to be ill-prepared. We've made a lot of mistakes because we didn't listen to the signs. The universe is screaming at us this time, and I'm not going to ignore it."

"Then we won't. We'll prepare. But we don't have to be scared until we know for sure. Right now, we get to be happy. We get to raise our daughter. Let's live in the moment while we can."

He moved his head in a soft nod. "Alright."

I cupped his cheek and brought a smile to my lips. "Then smile." Another quiet laugh left his lips, and he summoned a smile against them. "There you go."

Jeremy leaned forward and touched his lips to mine. His hand moved from my cheek to my arm as his lips opened. I closed my eyes and lifted my hand around his back. Then he pulled me over top of him and slid his hands up my skirt.

None of the options laid in front of us were good ones. No route appeared to come to a happy ending. But we had each other. We had our daughter. We had our family and our dog. All that was left to find was our son and the long-lost brother.

I didn't have the energy to care about everything else. Eventually, that would change. But it wasn't going to be any time soon. My family would always be my top priority. The rest of the world would be a close second when the rest of my life was sorted out.

CHAPTER FORTY-NINE

JEREMY

I'd be lying if I said that I didn't feel better about life after getting to fuck my wife that night. Over the years, the first time after she gave birth to our children always stood out. Everyone likes to pretend that sex is just a bodily function, but it always feels like a hell of a lot more than that when you haven't had it in a while.

In the past few weeks, I hadn't been sleeping much. I wasn't having nightmares or anything, but getting my brain to shut off gradually became a harder task. Milly played a part, but it was mostly the impending sense of doom that kept me up. That night though, I slept like a baby. Maybe I just needed a good lay, I don't know.

The plan Laila had was far from ideal. Neither of us wanted to see our planet die. But if it came to that, we'd come out on the other side at any cost. We didn't ask for any of this. I watched Laila hate herself every day for carrying the lives of the survivors on her back. And a little girl was looking up to us now. We couldn't fall into that pit of self-loathing for something we were too small to help.

I smiled down at Milly lying on the bed beside me. Her big green eyes moved between mine. My hand reached out for hers, thumb sliding against the back of her soft knuckles. I held my smile, but a deep breath left my nostrils.

That thought just wouldn't leave my head.

What if the world ends?

She was so little. She was my whole world, but she was so little, and she couldn't protect herself.

What if something happened to Laila and me in this supposed incoming apocalypse? What if we couldn't escape to this realm? Who would keep her safe? Who'd make sure she was okay?

Our family was big and all, but if we didn't make it, there was a good chance they wouldn't either.

I wanted better for her. Better than I'd had, but if the rumors were true, if a war were coming, she'd end up worse than I had.

Maybe that was my family's fate. My parent's, mine, my sibling's, my kid's. Maybe we were all damned to cursed lives.

Laila reached down and lifted Milly to her arms. "Just about ready to head out?"

I blinked hard a few times, bringing myself back to reality. One way or the other, I had to keep my mind on the moment. I had to be in the present. The future wasn't guaranteed, but this moment was. I had to live it.

"Yeah, just about." I stood. "Kinda have to shit, but I think I'm going to wait until we get home. I don't like the communal bathroom thing."

"Yeah, it's pretty weird. Just don't shit yourself when we go through the portal."

"I'm not going to shit myself." I laughed.

She laughed too, hoisting Milly into the sling against her chest. "I hope I don't break the pram when we go through. Might be kind of hard to hold onto it and Milly at the same time."

"I'll handle the pram; you handle the baby. You got the fruit in your backpack, right?" I asked.

"I do. And everyone's souvenirs are in yours." She finished situating Milly in the sling. "Anything we're forgetting?"

"Just everyone else." I smiled. "Leah said she wanted to grab something she saw yesterday for Haley."

A quiet knock sounded at the door, sliding inward. Kai smiled and gave a half wave. "Hey, guys. You can still take me and Hannah to see my old home, right?"

"Yeah, of course." Laila smiled.

"Before we go though." I lifted my backpack over my shoulders and met his gaze. "What's the story on that queen?"

"Amaryllis Avery?" he asked. I nodded. "I only know the rumors. She's been in power here since I was a kid, I know that."

"What do you mean?" Laila said. "She can't be more than twenty-five."

"Aye," Kai said.

"Fae age at the same rate as humans. She is Fae, isn't she?" I asked.

He nodded. "Aye, she is. Look, I don't ken much. But legend has it that when the Open Lands were under attack in the wars, the king and queen sent Amaryllis to earth for safekeeping. They planned to pass through the dimensions with her but died on their way out of the castle. Instead, the King's Guard passed to earth with Amaryllis and his son, Asher. The stories are choppy on what happened after that. All that I do know for certain is that Amaryllis was four when she went to earth. Asher was six. Then two years later, Amaryllis and Asher surface looking as they do now. The Open Lands were in a bad way then. The two of them, with no help from another soul, rose to power. They proved who they were, and they took the Kingdom."

Asher said that he was here and went to earth to find her. Although, Kai did say the story was choppy. Perhaps he tried to pass through, and the portal closed before he had the chance. Then he went back later to find her.

But aside from that, I knew a glossed over version of Fae and Elvan tales. A lot of it was kept secret from our kinds. Not that I blamed them —the Angels decimated the peoples here. They didn't trust us with much of anything, let alone their history. Maybe there was an Elvan spell I'd never heard of that could age someone at an exponential rate.

But the bigger shocker was the fact that the people allowed something like that. To their knowledge, the girl was gone. Then she shows as a grown woman and they just gave the most prominent kingdom in this world over to her?

"And the people just let them?" I asked.

"Aye," Kai said. "They ended war in the land. Abolished death penalties and corporal punishment. People were hesitant at first, but when bodies stopped dropping, their philosophies changed."

"More importantly, how does someone age twenty years in two?" Laila asked.

"You ought to have asked," Kai said. "Seemed pretty friendly with her."

"That was weird, wasn't it?" I asked. "The way they just took us in with open arms?"

"Peculiar, yes. None of that was ordinary."

"Do you think she's trustworthy?" Laila asked. "Because she mentioned Micah so I'm wary."

"She's a good woman." His shoulders lifted slightly. "A wise leader. Very powerful clairvoyant; that may be how she knew of him."

"Maybe," I muttered. "Something still doesn't sit right though."

"I can't say much, but I ken she wouldn't hurt a child," Kai said. "She's been known to kill beasts. But I don't think she's killed a person once. Even to end the wars. She held many captive, easy enough to do when you can control others with a simple thought. Brought western medicine to the realm to help fight diseases we can't heal. She set up welfare systems for the poor. Homelessness no longer exists in the Open Lands because of her. Believe me, she wouldn't have anything to do with what's happened to your babe."

"You know a lot about her," Laila muttered.

"Everyone does. We learned about her as children. She was always in the press sheets," Kai said. "She brought peace to a part of the world that hadn't seen it in decades. And every lad of Fae blood dreamt of growing up and becoming her king."

I laughed, and Laila rolled her eyes with a smile. In fairness, she was pretty hot.

"Hey, Kai, one other thing I was thinking about." I adjusted the straps on my backpack. He nodded, and I said, "You said you knew the apothecary, didn't you?"

"Aye," he said. "Yes, I did. He moved here just before I came to Earth. I visited him a time or two at that shop. I was sure he'd be there. But I barely got a word in before that man was ripping me from the doors."

"Maybe he went back to your hometown."

"That's what I'm hoping."

CHAPTER FIFTY

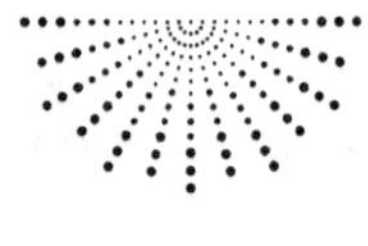

LAILA

I looked at our small crowd. "Do you think we can teleport this many people at once?"

"There's five," Jeremy said. "You take Kai and Hannah. I'll get Leah, Wyatt, and Celena."

"Works for me." Hannah smiled and locked her arm with mine.

"How does this work exactly?" Kai asked.

"Click your heels together and say there's no place like home." Celena gave a playful grin.

Kai made a face. "It isn't fair to make jokes you ken I can't understand."

"It's from a popular children's book about a girl who travels to another dimension called Oz," Hannah said. "We'll read it with Milly if we ever get to babysit."

"Just picture where you want to go." I wiggled my fingers to him. "I'll sense your connection to it and teleport us there. Simple process."

"Alright then." He accepted my hand and closed his eyes.

My eyes closed, images of rolling hills coated in thick, glistening white snow flashing against them. Animals meandered in a small penned off area next to an old wooden cabin with a steep, A-lined roof. Further back, more cottages laid on snow-coated mountains speckled with green pines dusted in white. The air smelled crisp and refreshing, the way ours did on Christmas.

The memory felt quaint and familiar. Though cold, warm in his mind. That village was to Kai what Moe's was to me. Those thoughts brought a smile to my lips beneath my closed eyes. Then we spun through the air.

But before I opened my eyes, the smell told me that it was no longer the place Kai remembered.

The now familiar aroma of charred flesh burned my nostrils. Instead of a small cottage and flock of frolicking animals, all that I saw was a billowing cloud of black smoke in the distance over the white coated land. My gaze shifted around what once must have been a lovely place to live but now appeared to be the remnants of a battlefield.

Where the cottage once sat now rested the burned remnants of what I'd soon realize was Kai's childhood home.

My gaze shifted to Kai. His full lips fell open, and his hand covered his mouth. Those big green eyes filled with tears, quiet gasp leaving his lips.

He pulled his hand from mine and took off to the burned structure. Hannah looked to me with slightly parted, awestruck lips. I held Milly a little tighter as the rest of the family landed close behind us.

Hannah darted through the ankle-deep snow toward Kai.

My chest grew tight, stomach aching. What was he about to walk into?

"This is where Kai grew up?" Celena nearly whispered.

"Where, yeah," Leah murmured as she looked around. "But this isn't what it was like then. I've seen it in his head. Things were peaceful here when he left. There was tension between the Wave and the Elves, but no one thought it'd ever make it to the villages."

"I guess it did," I whispered.

"What are they fighting over?" Wyatt asked.

"What is anyone in the history of any world fighting over ever?" Leah said.

"Religion?" Celena asked.

Leah frowned. "Territory."

"Sounds so stupid when you think about it in such a linear perspective, isn't it?" Jeremy said.

"Because war is pointless," Wyatt said. "Let's just stop destroying each other's shit like a bunch of toddlers and talk about it."

"Some damage is worth fighting for," Celena said.

As they murmured to one another, my chest grew tight with worry. Whatever had happened here would be an awful reality to witness. And I wanted to be there for my brother through it.

I lifted Milly from the sling and passed her to Jeremy. "I'm going to go check on him."

He gave a nod, holding her close against him. "We'll be here."

Before I made it to what remained of the cabin, I heard Kai's quiet sobs. My breaking heart shattered. I closed my eyes. Imagining how he felt in that moment still makes my stomach hurt.

He left this world to start a new life on ours. But leaving a life behind didn't remove the love and comfort that he felt within it. This was his home. These were his people. And all of that familiarity now laid in old, burned piles atop the snow.

When I stepped through the snowy threshold, I followed the sound of Kai's sobs through the remnants of where a hallway once stood. It led to a room with a few knocked over chairs and only one remaining wall. A single column held up a small portion of what was left of the roof. Hanging from it was a torn rope. Then I looked down.

And my stomach dropped.

I covered my mouth. My gaze shifted to Hannah and Kai on the ground next to the body of a middle-aged woman. His crying face rested against Hannah's chest. She soothed his hair and held his shoulders tight to her body.

The woman's face was turned white from snow with blue, frozen undertones. She wore a ratty brown cloak over her long, gray-dusted blond locks. Pointed ears poked through them. Her empty, frozen eyes were wide in fear. Her dead fingers gripped the thick rope at her neck. A single brush of red paint slid from her forehead to the tip of her chin.

I lowered myself next to Hannah and Kai on the snow-covered wooden floor.

Kai never talked much about his life before he came to earth, so I had no idea who this woman was. But it was clear that she meant a great deal to him. After all, he was bringing Hannah here to meet her.

My hand moved to his arm, drifting slowly up and down for a moment. His cries grew heavier as he twined his fingers between mine. His eyes closed, and his head shook.

"I'm so sorry for your loss," I whispered.

He continued to cry with his head against Hannah's chest. She and I exchanged an expression of sympathy, both wishing we could help him. Then we waited for him to regain his composure.

After a few long and painful moments, his sobs softened. He moved his hand from mine and brought himself to his knees next to the body. His eyes closed as his fingers carefully grazed the woman's cold, lifeless face. Another language, Elvan I believe, left his lips for a moment. Then he opened his teary eyes and carefully pulled the woman's eyelids over her frozen gaze.

"Can ye ask the guys if they'll help me bring her to the creek?" Kai asked. "I'll dig the hole, but I need help carrying her."

"I could teleport her—"

"No," he snapped. I swallowed hard, and he took in a deep breath. "I'm sorry but no. This is our way. We carry our dead to their final resting place. She carried me plenty of times, it's my turn to carry her."

I gave a slow, careful nod. "Sure. Sure, of course."

***

Kai spent a few more moments on the floor with his dead friend while I informed everyone of what we just discovered. Then he found a large, soot-covered piece of white cloth that may have been a tablecloth or curtain set once. He laid it out flat on the ground and used the air to lift the woman's body over it before gingerly lowering her to the ground. Then he carefully wrapped her body and whispered more words in another language. Then Jeremy and Wyatt helped carry the woman to the last bed she would lie in.

Before he dug the grave though, he laid her beside the creek. He reached his hand into the cool water, moistened a cloth from the woman's pocket, and washed the red marking from her face. Tears gushed from his eyes as he whispered in the thick Elvan tongue. Once the red was washed away, he lifted her sleeve halfway up her forearm.

There rested a bracelet of some kind, but not one I'd seen before. It wasn't metal of rope; it was green. A thick, forest green vine.

Eyes closed, he murmured to her a moment longer. Then he touched the bracelet. And it grew, climbing up her arm and wrapping around it like a caterpillar to a stick. The twining vines encased her arm, then around her chest, down her torso, around her legs, and then her feet. Last of all was her head.

It was an odd thing to witness, yet so beautiful at the same time. Almost like a beautiful, fairy take on a mummified corpse. I wasn't sure why that was the way they buried their dead, only that it was a beautiful way to send them away.

Then Wyatt and Jeremy held the body in the air by the sheet while Kai pulled enough dirt from the ground to form a shallow grave. The cool winter winds bit our noses as he dug the hole deep enough to submerge the small woman's body. Then he ushered for Wyatt and Jeremy's help lying her into the cold, frozen dirt.

Kai spoke louder, saying words I didn't understand, but in a soft, gentle tone. And strangely, they sounded familiar. Then he wiped the corners of his eyes and cleared his throat.

"What does that mean, baby?" Hannah asked, gently touching his bicep.

"From the ground our flesh has come, to the ground our flesh returns. Rest now; and find your place amongst the stars until we meet once more."

Cool chills crept down my spine. Goosebumps erupted over my skin. Jeremy slid his hand over my arm, tugging me into him.

"That's beautiful," Hannah whispered.

"It's an old Elvan hymn. Traditional to recite at these sorts of things," Kai murmured, looking down into the hole. Then he cleared his throat. "She was my mum's sister, Clarissa. Like my mother, she was incapable of birth. I was the closest thing she had to a son. She's the only reason I was able to make it to ye all. She taught me to travel through the dimensions with the power of her people." He wiped his watering eye, and a quiet laugh left his lips. "I promised ye I'd bring that sister I wanted to know so bad to meet ye when I got settled in. Sorry I'm just getting around to it. I wish ye could have met everyone standing here, Mum."

Hannah awkwardly cleared her throat. Her fingers tightened around his. "She says it's okay.

He turned to meet her gaze. "Ye can see her?"

"I can." Water filled Hannah's irises. "She hasn't been recycled yet. Her soul is still in-between so I can hear her."

His teary eyes bubbled over. "Can ye tell her I'm sorry I didn't come sooner?"

Hannah smiled gently and gave a nod. "She hears you."

"Where is she?"

Hannah gestured beside him. "She just kissed your forehead."

More tears fell from his eyes, but he smiled. "I love you, Mum."

"She loves you too." She smiled, blinking away tears. "And she's happy you found the family you were looking for. She says not to worry about her. We can't live forever but memories will last a lifetime."

He was struggling to maintain his composure.

Shit, so was I. My throat was tight, water running down it from my eyes. It was a heartbreakingly beautiful moment. He may not have gotten the meeting with her and all of us that he'd have liked, but at least he got to say his final goodbyes.

Hannah cleared her throat and wiped her eye. "I'm sorry, I've never mediumed before. This is more intense than I thought it'd be."

"May I?" He smiled and extended his fingers for hers. She smiled and gave a nod. Their eyes closed as Kai delved into her mind. I watched their expressions rotate from joy to grief to love in a matter of seconds.

"I did not know that she could do that," Wyatt said.

"Me neither," I murmured.

"She literally brought us back from the dead," Leah said. "This is nothing."

CHAPTER FIFTY-ONE

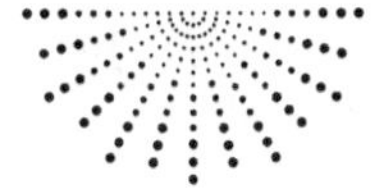

JUNE 21, 2021 - JEREMY

Cool air blew from the register to my arms. The smell of eucalyptus from the wax warmers drifted up my nose. Warm summer sun shined in from the wall of windows, brightening against the dark floors. I glanced at the clock. 11:54. We needed to leave.

I reached for Milly's hand in Laila's arms, touching her fingers. She smiled up at me, plopping her bobbing head back to her mom's chest. I smiled too.

She was gonna be fine for a few hours. But this was the first time Laila had been away from her, and one would've thought she was never going to see her again judging by her tight grasp.

"You cannot take your eyes off of her while we're gone for a second, alright?" Laila looked between Hannah and Celena.

"Nothing's happening to my niece." Celena grinned.

"Yeah, we'll take good care of her." Hannah smiled, playing with Milly's fingers.

"Okay. Okay, I have a bunch of thawed bags of milk in the fridge. I free feed her so if you're worried that she's eating too much, you're wrong. She's just chunky. She does have to burp a few times throughout a feeding though so if she starts to cry, that's probably why.

She usually naps between eleven and noon and again between three and four. But she can nap as long as she wants; you don't have to wake her up. I hope we'll be back in our minds by bedtime, but if we aren't, she falls asleep best rocking in the chair. Then you lie her in the bassinet, and she'll be out for at least three hours."

"Can we give her a bath and put her in her jammies?" Hannah gushed, practically bouncing with excitement.

I smiled. She was so excited to finally get to babysit. Milly practically lived in Laila's arms; this was the first time she got her pretty much all to herself.

Laila nodded. "Yeah, that's fine. She loves baths."

"Her pajamas are in the top drawer of her short dresser." I leaned forward and pressed my lips to her forehead. "And we use the lavender body wash and lotion at night. It helps her sleep."

"The spell will break by midnight at the latest. But if we aren't home by then, she'll want to eat around eleven. She usually goes back to bed right away," Laila said.

"Just make sure you check her diaper before you lie her back down. She's got a habit of shitting all the way up her back around ten thirty. Can't tell you how many times I went to pick her up and had to go wash my hands," I muttered.

Hannah laughed. "Ew."

"Okay, ready when you are, Lai." Celena smiled.

Laila squeezed Milly a little tighter, nuzzling her face against her head. "Yeah, just one second."

"It is getting late, baby." I ran my hand over her back. "Helena told us to be there five minutes ago so we can start the spell at noon."

"So we're five minutes late. It's not like we're going to hit traffic on the teleportation express."

"This is your first time leaving her, huh?" Hannah gave a soft smile.

I nodded and moved my hand along the back of Milly's soft head. Her big green eyes turned up to me over Laila's shoulder with a sweet, innocent smile. I smiled and leaned in to kiss her forehead again.

Damn, maybe it wasn't just Lai. I didn't want to leave her either.

"She's going to be fine, guys." Celena smiled. "Wyatt and Kai are hanging out with us here. Brody, Gwen, and Leah are back at the house. The spell's up, no one's coming in or out until you're back. Don't worry. We won't let anything happen to this little girl."

Laila smiled, closed her eyes, and gave a nod.

We both knew she'd be safe, but that didn't make it any easier to leave her. She was our whole world since the moment she was born. It was especially emotional since the next day would be Micah's second birthday and we still didn't have him back.

But on the other hand, learning about our past lives played some part in breaking the cycle we were trapped in. Whatever the hell that cycle was, anyway. And we needed to find out. We needed to learn more. And that spell was going to teach us at least a portion of what we needed to know.

"Yeah, we know, guys," I said.

"It's just a lot harder than it looks," Laila whispered.

Hannah smiled and gave a sympathetic nod. I smiled back at Milly, running my thumb against the back of her fingers with one hand and brushing hair from her forehead with the other.

"We'll be back in a little bit," I whispered with a smile. Her smile widened as she laid her head against Laila's chest.

I'll never forget how awful that feeling was. We would be back in a few hours and everything would be exactly as it was when we left. Our daughter was safe. But leaving her was fucking terrifying. I'd run out to grab groceries a few times and left her with Laila, but I trusted Laila with anything. After losing Micah, she'd kill anyone without a second thought to protect our daughter. I knew our siblings would too. But they weren't Laila.

As much as they loved Milly, it was nothing compared to the way the two of us did. No one else could fear losing her the way the two of us could.

Although, they may fear losing her because of what Laila would do to them if it happened on their watch. If I'm being completely honest, that's one of the only reasons I felt comfortable leaving.

Plus, Kai and Celena were nearly as powerful as Laila. I knew that Hannah couldn't do much in the ways of keeping her safe. But Wyatt was a boulder. Kai and Celena both had massive offensive abilities and the capability to heal injuries. And Hannah could resurrect the dead.

Realistically, there wasn't a safer place in the world for our daughter in our absence. It didn't ease all of my worries, but we had to go somewhere without her at some point.

"Everything's gonna be fine, Lai." Hannah gave a gentle smile. "I promise. We won't let anything happen to her."

"If she talks and you don't have it on video, I'm killing you," Laila said.

"I doubt our six-week-old who can only hold her head up for more than a few seconds is going to be talking any time soon, baby." I laughed.

"Well, she could. She could be the first baby to talk this early in the history of the world. Would you want to deny the world proof?" Laila raised her brows. "Hmm?"

I laughed again. My gaze turned back to Milly. "You're in charge, little lady. Don't let your aunts and uncles get into any trouble okay, Mills?"

Hannah rolled her eyes. "I hate you."

I grinned and kissed her forehead one more time. "We only have one shot at this a year, Lai. We really have to go."

Laila's eyes closed. She kissed Milly's cheek and carefully lifted her to Hannah's arms. "If anything happens, anything at all. If she gets sick, or if she won't stop crying or, god forbid, something worse happens, you have Helena wake us up. The list for the pediatrician is on—"

"The fridge and you have an entire color coded, personalized child instruction manual on the counter on anything we could possibly need to know." Celena smiled. "We're fine, Laila. Go enjoy your nap."

Laila released a billowing sigh. I tucked my arm around her waist. Milly turned back to me with a smile. She reached for us, and Hannah pulled back a bit. Her big green eyes filled with tears.

It's funny how that memory is so heartbreaking for me, and Milly will never remember it. One day, she'd give two shits less about being with me and Laila. But I can still feel how bad it hurt to leave her, even knowing we'd only be gone for twelve hours.

I teleported before Laila had the time to embrace her once more. Her big green eyes stared up at me with large tears forming in the corners just as Milly had a few seconds before. Water stung mine too. I twisted my arms around her waist. "She's fine. It's only a couple of hours."

"I know." She nodded against my chest.

"Oh, good, you're here," Helena said in the doorway to the formal sitting room. "Let's get to the living room and get started. We don't have much time."

The usually bland, modern living room transformed into something straight out of an occult movie. Where the coffee table and rug once laid now rested a large painted circle covered in small script like writing. A series of triangles connected the larger circle to a smaller circle in the middle where two pillows perched. Four large white candles sat in a perfect square on the edges of the outer circle to face North, South, East, and West. Beside the setup sat a small altar table where Helena had a number of herbs placed out as well as a small blade.

"So how much blood are we going to need to spill for this?" I asked.

"Just a little cut on each hand," she said. "Trust me, the drink's the worst part."

"Alright then," Laila grumbled. "Where do you want us?"

"Get in the circle and sit down," Helena said, mixing something in a stone grinding bowl. "I've just got to add the water and we're good to go."

Laila gave a nod and moved to the center of the circle. "Is this definitely going to last until midnight?"

"It could," Helena said. "Depends on how many lives you two have met each other in before. If you've only met once or twice, it might be an hour. But if you've lived a hundred lifetimes together, it's definitely going to last until midnight."

"Are we going to see a snippet of each lifetime?" I walked beside Laila and lowered myself to the ground. "Or just a couple?"

"You'll see whatever was most important to your soul in your recent lives. Might only be one lifetime though. Might be a glimpse from a thousand. I can't tell you how much detail you'll see in any of them for sure."

Helena made her way to us. She lowered herself to her knees with a small cup in each hand. "But there's a notation on the spell. It said to remind the participants that these are just memories. You are not that person anymore. Whatever you see is not *your* life. They will be nothing more than old thoughts when you open your eyes. The vision of your own death can be detrimental to your mental health if you let it."

Laila laughed quietly.

"We do alright with death," I said.

"Well, let's get it over with then." Helena set the cups on the ground and raised her palm. She whispered something before the dagger gracefully flew from the table into her hand. "Alright. Jeremy, give me your left hand."

I extended my palm toward her.

She murmured something as the blade cut a thick line down my palm. I grimaced. She milked the area for more blood before pulling it over the cup in front of Laila. The crimson puddled into the murky brown liquid. Then she reached for Laila's hand. She carved a similar slit into hers and squeezed the blood into the cup in front of me.

Then Helena took my hand and joined it with Laila's. "Squeeze your hands together and drink up."

"Gross," Laila muttered.

"You suck his dick, don't you?" she asked. "And you realize that urine passes in ejacula—"

"I get the point." Laila sniffed the cup and gagged. "Add drinking my husband's blood to the list of things I never thought I'd do."

"Yummy," I muttered.

I clanged my glass off of hers and held my breath. Then I tilted my head back and gulped.

We won't go into the awful taste; every potion I ever drank was disgusting. Although weird, drinking Laila's blood was still a bit less offensive than drinking Moriah's as we had a few weeks prior.

Laila set her glass to the hardwood. "Magic sucks."

Yeah, witchcraft is gross. I was always so glad that I hadn't been born to a Witch's bloodline.

"Now keep your hands together and lie down on your side facing each other." Helena stood and stepped from the circle. We did as she said, meeting one another's gaze. Then she started speaking in Latin.

Laila's brows pulled together. Her hand clenched tight around mine.

She was scared. Not that I blamed her, I wasn't exactly chipper over this either. But I also had a good feeling about it. Like this would bring us answers of some kind.

I smiled and cupped her cheek in my other hand.

"I love you," she whispered.

"I love you too," I murmured.

I touched my lips to our knuckles. Then my eyes grew heavier than weights. I couldn't keep them open if it tried.

CHAPTER FIFTY-TWO

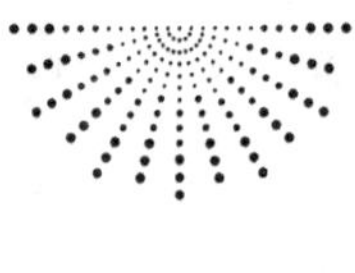

LAILA

Seeing those century old thoughts left me more in tune with myself and Jeremy than I had ever been. I can't say that it was the same as reading someone else's mind. It wasn't even like a dream. To say it was like watching a movie wouldn't be fair either.

The memories were vague, short glimpses really. It wasn't as though I was living most of those moments; it was almost as if my mind was telling me the memories through short flashes. Only a few were detailed.

But I felt like I was her. I couldn't remember every thought and action those other versions of myself lived. But I could remember *being* her.

And I could remember knowing him.

The first memory started out with me as a young French girl on a farm somewhere in the countryside. I never paid much attention in history class but the bonnet and horrible corset that left me struggling to breathe made it clear that we were in a far different time. There were no signs of technology. No cars, no electricity, not even running water. I suppose all of that wasn't relevant anyway.

The relevancy laid in the obvious signs of Wiccan culture within the cabin the girl I was then lived in with her family. In our time, you may describe the décor as boho chic. Dozens of candles, beautiful crystals, an in-depth spice cabinet the old me remembered quite fondly.

I felt a deep connection to the planet as her. She was kind and compassionate. Nothing she did was close to evil, she never hurt a soul. We were different in that respect. She used herbs the way we do now in the form of powders, teas, and ointments like a healer, I supposed. Never would she use magic as a means to hurt someone. But in that time, it didn't matter.

Jeremy, in that life, was named Alder. He looked nothing like the man I married, but somehow, I knew that it was him. He had long blond hair he wore in a pulled back ponytail and chocolate brown eyes, essentially opposite of my Jeremy, but I knew that it was him. I could *feel* him. He mentioned that he was twenty-four, but I'm not sure if I was even out of my teens yet. But I suppose in those times, he was a man, and I was a woman.

I wasn't sure why, as I only saw snippets, but the two of us didn't publicize our relationship there. Neither of us seemed to be married to someone else from what I did see, but we were very much a couple. I didn't see our meeting but from context clues, it seemed like we knew one another from childhood. I got to see our many moonlit runs into the woods hand in hand before we fucked against a tree or on the mud over his jacket.

He seemed to be someone important there. I don't know his title, but I know that he sat on the judge's court during trials. Trials that made my heart race and my palms sweat.

Then he helped carry men and women away as they cried that they weren't Witches before being tied to a burning stake a few hours later or the next day.

For him to be my soulmate, that meant he wasn't human either. Being who he was, whatever that title made him, it kept him in a position to keep both of us safe from the trials. That old concept of outwitting one's enemy by camouflaging themselves within them.

Besides those trips into the woods and the death that followed, the only other clear memory I had was telling him that I was pregnant, as if auto-translating in my mind. His reaction then was relatively similar to how it had been in my life. He was joyful and excited. But then he was panic stricken. Another memory surfaced shortly after of him explaining that we had to leave. All of the details were fuzzy, I'm not sure why he was so insistent, but I agreed almost as quick as he suggested it.

Then the death came. I'm not sure where he was when it happened, but I do recall being ripped off a horse and beaten by a group of men far too big for me to fight off. My powers were minuscule in that body too. No matter how many fists I flailed, I stood no chance.

I didn't get to see a trial. Maybe I had one but if I did, it wasn't significant enough for my mind to reveal. The last thing I remember from that life is fire licking its way up my legs before engulfing my torso. Heat, pain, agony, smoke. That remnant may have been why fire came so naturally to me in my current life.

And then his crying sobs from the crowd. I remember those too. Behind the blinding orange flames, I saw him fighting a group of men that held him from getting to the burning stake I was tied to. He screamed, begging me for forgiveness as I cried out in agony. That look on his helpless face became a recurring theme through those memories.

The next memory was even farther back. That time, we appeared to be in a far different place. There were no trees, only scorching hot sand.

It wasn't as clear as the first memory had been. I didn't even catch Jeremy's name in that life. I may have heard it but found myself unable to identify it, let alone pronounce it.

Either way, the same common theme occurred. We were young. We were beautiful. And all that we wanted was to be together.

But as soon as I became pregnant, I died.

Then another memory would begin. They got faster and faster the further back we went until they were nothing but quick flashes behind our eyelids. Each one took place in another part of the world, speaking a different language, wearing a different body, possessing different features, but some details remained the same in each.

We loved each other. We were kind to others. We were good people that wanted to do good things. We weren't as powerful in any of those lives as we were in this one. But we also wanted to be happy. We wanted to be together and have a family of our own. We wanted a happy fucking ending.

But each time, something went wrong. Just as we were at the edge of what we wanted, I'd die.

I watched a different version of myself die at least a few hundred times during the course of those flashbacks. More specifically, Jeremy watched helplessly as the woman he loved—and his unborn child—left the world before he had the chance to ever call himself a father.

But then, just before I awoke, an image flashed against my eyes. Not a memory with any depth. It was fuzzy, like an old, static engulfed TV. I couldn't make out the backdrop. I couldn't tell where we were.

Just a single frozen image, and one word.

"*Véa.*"

The word came from a man. With big, vibrant, electric blue eyes. Long, flowing black hair on milky skin. His voice was deep, yet soft and melodic. Almost identical to my husband's.

He wore the brightest, widest smile. And two little heads perched over each of his bare, toned shoulders. A little girl with round green eyes, a head of brown curls braided into a crown, and a smile as big as the man who she had her arms wrapped around.

The other little head was a boy. Big blue eyes, waving black hair, and a smile just like the man whose head his rested against.

Micah. I knew it was Micah. That little girl was my Milly. And that man was Jeremy. I knew because of the peace and joy I felt at that image. It was the same feeling I got when I saw him holding our daughter in this life.

But I didn't understand. In all of the memories prior, I died before I had our children. So what was this?

CHAPTER FIFTY-THREE

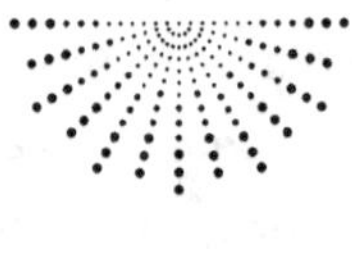

JEREMY

At first, I found myself too angry to grasp what those memories were trying to teach me. What the fuck was the point in all of this if every ending was the same? In every life, she died. She was carrying my child, and she fucking died.

Then I'd find a pretty cliff side, or a sturdy rope, or a sharp enough blade and the cycle would repeat. I'd kill myself and meet her a few years later, and we'd go back to it. For a moment, it left me wondering what we were still fighting for.

But then it occurred to me that this was the first life where we fucking got it.

The theme was the same in each rebirth.

We wanted what we currently had. But in every life prior to this, we died before we made it here. Larger forces manipulated us into our inevitable doom each time.

Yet in this life, both of our children made it to birth. Yes, we lost Micah. But he was still out there somewhere, and we were getting him back. And we had our daughter. We *finally* had our daughter.

We got married almost two years prior. The two of us built our home together. Our daughter was healthy as a horse and stronger than almost anything we'd seen. We were in the midst of every fantasy we'd dreamed of for hundreds or maybe even thousands of lifetimes.

That moment gave me the shred of clarity I'd been begging to understand since it all began. I didn't know it all yet. Figuring out *why* everything happened the way that it did would come later. But one detail couldn't be denied.

In every other life that we met, we hadn't made it past this. More specifically, one or both of us didn't make it past twenty-four. I barely noted that as the memories flashed behind my eye lids but later, we'd make a deep connection with that number.

But the most important similarity? We died in our current lives too. Laila's for the first time just months after our meeting and again after she lost Micah. Then my death came the year before last, when I was twenty-four.

The most important difference between the life we were living and all the ones we'd lived before? Hannah.

She kept us both alive.

That's when it clicked.

Destiny had been searching for a way to let us live for centuries. This time, she tediously lined up each building block. This time, we'd get the resolution we deserved.

She birthed me to a family with the ability to disappear and reappear simultaneously. Then she gave me a sweet sister who loved me and my future wife with every fiber of her being the capability of resurrecting the dead. That pair essentially gifted us with immortality.

Then she put Laila's soul into a bloodline strong enough to fight for our family. Rather than throwing her into a simple Witch, she put her into the most powerful hybrid we'd ever see. She planted her into a suburban existence with life lessons of simplicity to show her what she'd be destined to fight *for* when we found each other.

All this time, we thought that we were fighting destiny. What we failed to realize was that she was on our side. Destiny was fighting for us. She was doing everything in her power to give us the ending we yearned for. It was about time we listened to her.

At least, that's how I saw it then. It really wasn't that simple.

But that brought with it a very important question. If destiny was on our side, why did Mary fight so hard to keep Laila from getting kidnapped only for it to happen anyway? Was her captivity a necessary part of her fate? Was our eternal loss of our firstborn son another unavoidable event in our history? Or was saving him the important part?

Most importantly though, those flashes only saw us the past few hundred—maybe a couple thousand—years of lives. None of them really mattered in the grand scheme. The most important life of all was not revealed in those memories because it was far, far older than we realized.

The first life was the one we truly needed access to.

We slammed forward from the wooden floor just as the clock struck midnight pouring sweat. My hands shook, breaths uneven. Disoriented, I patted around my body to make sure I was really here. I blinked fast, as if waking from a nightmare.

Helena quietly laughed and hit a pipe from the couch in the corner of the room. "Guess you guys have known each other a lot longer than you thought."

Laila's wide eyes met mine. She took slow pants into her heaving chest. Tears pearled down my face as I leaned forward and wrapped my arms around her shoulders. She tucked hers around my back and squeezed as tight as she could. I closed my eyes, holding her so tight I was sure I'd broken a bone or two.

I'd never felt so lucky before in my life. Suddenly, it all felt like it'd been worth it. All that heart ache had a purpose. We were able to feel grateful because we truly understood how much it meant to have what we did. Admittedly, still a bullshit set of cards. And plenty of unanswered questions still remained.

But it was the best set of cards we'd been dealt in an awfully long time.

"I need to go see my daughter," Laila whispered, voice cracking.

Helena chomped down on a handful of chips. Through a mouthful, she said, "You guys alright over there?"

I pulled back. "Yeah. Yeah, we're good. We paid you for this already, right?"

"Yeah, just don't stand up too fast or you might faint. Or puke, and you'll be the one to clean it up. But how'd it go? Did you learn anything?"

"I think so." Laila gave a slow nod. I squeezed her hand tight around mine as I pushed hair from her face with the other.

"You're good though, right?" Helena continued. "Don't feel sick or on the verge of a mental breakdown?"

"A little lightheaded," Laila said.

"And I really have to piss," I muttered.

"But yeah, I think we're alright."

"Just drink a lot of water and get something in your stomachs." She stood from the couch and covered her yawning lips. "But I'm beat so y'all need to get up out my living room."

I gave a smile as I stood. "Thank you for this."

"Yeah, you're welcome," she muttered. "You're so thankful but I haven't seen a review from either of you on Yelp."

Laila laughed as I helped her to her feet. "I'll do that first thing tomorrow."

"Mhmm."

"We'll see you later." I put my hand at Laila's waist.

I closed my eyes, pulled her tight into me, and teleported back home. We landed on the porch with our bodies pressed close together.

Although I'd only seen glimpses of our past lives together, I somehow felt a thousand times closer to her. I suddenly had this broader understanding of who both of us were in the big picture. I didn't know the details of why what we saw in those lives mattered, but it wouldn't be much longer before we started to grasp at least most of the reasons.

"This is the only lifetime where we've had a shot at being happy," Laila whispered. Her watery green eyes turned up to mine. "We're so close to having it all."

I smiled and brushed my thumb against her cheek. "Almost, huh?"

"Is this what he meant by breaking the cycle?" she asked.

"Maybe," I muttered. "It was a dream. I don't have a clue what he meant."

"Maybe saving Micah has always been our destiny," she whispered. "Do you remember what Don said? About how his soul hasn't had many chances to live? Maybe this is why. Because *we* haven't made it far enough for him to live."

"It seems like it," I said. "But I still don't see how he ties into the apocalypse."

"That's not what we were looking for." She pulled away and reached for the doorknob. "We did this to figure out what the cycle was so that we could break it. We did that, we identified the cycle. And we've already broken it. We keep Milly safe. We bring Micah home. Then the cycle is officially broken. Fuck the prophecy."

I wasn't so sure about that. The two had to correlate in some way or another, but nothing we found in those memories overlapped with Christianity and the supposed rapture. In fact, I didn't see any correlation between them at all.

She was right about one thing though. We hadn't done this to bring Micah home. We'd done this to figure out what curse we were under. And now, we knew.

In each life, we died before we turned twenty-four.

I'd just turned twenty-six. And I'd died, but I'd come back. Laila though, she was twenty-three. She had another year to make it through before we were sure we'd broken the curse.

But I wanted to stay in the calm those memories brought for a moment. We'd talk about how we hadn't completely broken the curse soon enough. But for tonight, we should breathe. And hold the baby we'd waited eons for.

I brushed my thumb against her cheek. "Let's go see our daughter."

Her smile widened. As the door opened, Hannah stood from the couch with a finger over her mouth and a gesture to Milly sleeping in the bassinet. I smiled as Laila rushed across the room to our sleeping baby girl.

Me though, I walked to my sister and put my arms around her shoulders in a tight embrace. Kai, Wyatt, and Celena raised their brows as Hannah laughed.

The only way I knew we could break that curse once and for all was through her. Because if something happened to Laila before she turned twenty-four, I had Hannah to make sure she wouldn't stay gone for long.

"I really didn't mind watching her." Hannah chuckled. "She's a lot of fun actually."

"That's not why he's hugging you." Laila smiled, lifting Milly to her arms.

"Thank you for saving us. We wouldn't be here if it weren't for you. Neither would my son or my daughter." I held her tight for a minute. Then I pulled back and met her gaze with watery eyes. "Thank you so much, Hannah."

She smiled softly, giving a slow nod. "Of course."

I swallowed the knot in my throat behind my smiling lip. Then I turned to Milly in Laila's arms. A wave of glee washed over me as a yawn left her little lips and her chubby fist rubbed against her eyelids.

Maybe those past lives played into why I was such an overly emotional guy. I'd watched the woman I loved die a thousand times— give or take a few hundred.

But this time, I wasn't willing to let her go. It couldn't happen again. I wouldn't let it.

I remembered what true loss was now. And I'd be damned before I ever experienced that again.

We were going to get our son. We were going to keep our daughter sheltered from whatever the future had in store.

And I was going to make certain that I never lost the love of my life —or lives, rather—ever again.

The story continues in *The Quiet Army*. Turn the page for a sneak peek, or click the link below to download now:
https://www.amazon.com/gp/product/B095J135H4/

Sign up for Charlie's newsletter and receive a free copy of the Eluding Destiny prequel, *Blood Bar*:
https://liquidmind.media/eluding-destiny-prequel/

If you enjoyed this story, please consider leaving a rating or review on Amazon:
https://www.amazon.com/gp/product/B094KZT5SP/

Join Charlie's private reader group on Facebook and discuss all things Eluding Destiny and Charlie Nottingham:
https://www.facebook.com/groups/661440911724435/

THE QUIET ARMY CHAPTER ONE

MARCH 2022

He was waiting.

Mommy said it'd be a few more days, and Micah was waiting.

Laying against the cool cement, his lips lifted in a smile. He thought about that great blue sky she'd shown him. He thought about that music Daddy had let him hear. He wondered what that big white dog's fur would feel like between his fingertips.

He liked animals; they were sweet. And they never hurt him, not on purpose. Well, the little mouse he'd found at the last place—Stew, Uncle Chris had named him—had bit him once. But it was okay. It didn't hurt that much.

He missed Stew. But it was okay, because soon, he'd meet that big white dog. Just like Mommy promised.

Sleeping was hard that night. He didn't know why; he just couldn't sleep. Uncle Chris was snoring though. He did that a lot. Maybe that's why he couldn't sleep.

It was dark too. He didn't like the dark because he couldn't see much in the dark. And this place was always dark. The last place had more windows. This one only had one, and there wasn't a lot of light at night. He could see the moon though. It was a pretty, almost yellow color. He liked yellow too. It looked happy.

Micah liked happy stuff. He tried to be happy all the time. That wasn't always easy, but it had been the last few days, because Mommy said she was coming. That he'd finally get to go home.

That he'd get to listen to his daddy play music, and that he'd get to meet his sister, and his baby cousin, and all of his aunts and uncles. And Aunt Leah, he really wanted to meet her. Her hair was pretty; it was the first place he'd seen the color purple. He liked purple, too. But he liked yellow better.

He rolled to his side, still looking out the window. He saw something. It was fast; he didn't see it good, but it wasn't a guard—they had short hair.

A quiet gasp left his lips. He scurried to his feet. They were cold, and they scraped against the cement, but he didn't care. It could be Mommy and Daddy.

He craned onto the tips of his toes, squinting out the small, dusty glass.

But there was nothing there.

He frowned. Maybe it *was* a guard.

It was okay though; they'd be coming soon

He heard something. Words, he thought, whispers. He didn't know what they meant, but he heard something.

Maybe it wasn't a guard. Maybe it was the doctor. Micah didn't like the doctor. He did love him, but he hurt him, so he didn't like him anymore.

That was why he couldn't wait to be with Mommy. Mommy would never hurt him, she promised she wouldn't.

Then the big doors clattered open. Bright white lit the room, coming from someone's hands. He squinted.

Another gasp. He smiled wide.

Her long dark hair fell over her shoulders. Two big green eyes glowed above her white hands. Those pretty flowers on her arms reminded him of the ones he'd seen out the window of the last place.

He ran from the window to the middle of the room, starting to the door.

"Mommy?" he asked.

A long breath fell from her lips. The white light in her hands went out. She smiled wide, and he smiled back.

It was her; it was really her. She did it, she made it. Just like she promised. She was here. She was going to take him home and he was going to meet that big white dog and his little sister and all of his aunts and uncles.

"Micah." Mommy took a step forward. But she stopped. Her brows fell, hands touching the opening of the door, but it was like that window. Just like Micah couldn't get through that, she couldn't get through this.

But she was here. She'd figure it out. She promised she would. It was okay; Mommy could do anything.

Then someone behind Mommy turned. And Micah's mouth fell wide open.

He looked just the same too. Like Uncle Chris, but different. His eyes were so big and blue, and his hair was long and black, and he was so tall.

He darted across the floor, yelling, "Daddy!"

Daddy smiled too. But his smile looked a little sad. Like Uncle Chris when he told Micah to close his eyes and not to look. That always meant something bad was going to happen, and he didn't want Micah to get hurt.

"Micah," Daddy said. He reached toward the door too, but it did just the same as it'd done for Mommy. It was like glass. They could see each other, but they couldn't touch.

It was okay though. It'd be okay, they were here now.

White light shined in Mommy's hands. She started talking again, speaking a bunch of words Micah didn't understand.

Just like he thought. Mommy was gonna fix it. That's what she was doing, she was fixing it. She was gonna get through that glass and get him home. He just had to—

A big, strong hand grabbed Micah from behind, yanking him backward. He screamed, heart beating so fast that it hurt. Could a heart hurt? Because his did. It felt like it was falling and hurting at the same time.

Cold metal touched his throat.

Daddy's mouth fell open, both hands reaching out to the glass. Mommy's eyes filled with tears, no longer speaking those strange words. The light in her hands went out.

"You didn't think it'd be that easy, did you?" the doctor's voice said outside.

"Don't hurt him," Mommy said, looking at the person holding Micah. "Please, Amy. Please. Don't hurt my baby."

"We won't," the doctor said.

Daddy turned and stood against Mommy's back. Good, that was good. The doctor hurt Mommy; Micah didn't want him to hurt her again. He didn't want Daddy to get hurt either, but maybe Daddy would keep Mommy safe. Like Uncle Chris kept Micah safe.

"Not yet, anyway," the doctor said. "Nice to finally meet your acquaintance, Jeremy."

"Fuck you." Daddy's voice sounded different than it did when he talked to Micah, he sounded mean. But Micah wasn't mad. He didn't like when people were mean, but the doctor was mean, so Daddy had to be mean back.

"Is that how you're going to talk to the man who holds the fate of your son's life in his hands?"

It got quiet for a moment.

Micah kept looking at Mommy. He'd never seen her look like that. Her eyes were so big, water gushed down her cheeks, and her lips shook.

She was so scared. Micah was scared too, but he didn't want Mommy to be scared.

"Thought so." The doctor blew out one of those long, slow sighs. He did that a lot. "You sure love killing my men, Laila."

Mommy's hands shook, touching that glass wall. She mouthed, *It's okay, baby, it's okay.*

Micah believed her. He always believed Mommy because Mommy didn't lie to him. Mommy loved him; he knew she did.

He was scared, but if Mommy said it was going to be okay, It'd be okay.

The doctor said something else, but Micah didn't really hear it. He just kept looking at Mommy. He wanted her to hold him. He wanted to feel her for real. He never got to touch her for real, and he wanted to so bad.

Blue light shined from Daddy's hand. See, just like Micah thought. Daddy would keep them safe.

"Come on, Jeremy, don't make me do it like this," the doctor said. "Now isn't the time, you have things to learn first."

"I'm not leaving her," Daddy said.

Good, don't leave Mommy.

"You're not," the doctor said. "You have things to learn together. But you're going to be unconscious until I get you into a secure location."

"Just let me hold him." Mommy glanced behind her. "Please. Please let me hold my son."

Micah wanted that too. Maybe she read his mind. The doctor was nice sometimes, maybe he'd let Mommy.

"You will, Laila," the doctor said. "You'll see him soon."

"You won't hurt him if we go with you?" Mommy whispered.

Micah's heart hurt again. He wanted to yell and tell Mommy to stay, but he couldn't. The doctor didn't like when Micah yelled.

The doctor said, "Not yet."

Mommy's eyes started to water again. Her whole body began to shake. Micah's did too. Now he was really getting scared. She wasn't saying it was okay anymore.

"But this gives you more time to try and think of a way to stop me," the doctor said. "Maybe you'll figure it all out and beat me to the punch. You have before. I expected you to be in my custody far longer last time around. This time, I'm not expecting an extended stay."

Did the doctor know then? Was he finally going to let Micah see Mommy? He always said, 'one day.' Maybe that day was today.

"Then why are you doing this?" Daddy said. "Why don't you just stop? You know that we get him back, you've told us this. Why are you still fighting?"

"Because if I don't do this, you don't get them back. I may hate you, Jeremy. But…" the doctor said something else, but Micah didn't hear it. His heart was hurting his ears.

He didn't get that. The doctor always said that, that he hated Daddy. Daddy was nice. Why didn't he like Daddy?

"You're not going to hurt her again," Daddy said.

Good, don't let him hurt her.

"If you want to hurt someone, you hurt me. You don't touch her."

No, don't let him hurt you either.

The doctor said something else, but his voice started to blur into the silent noise of the night. The only things Micah could hear were Mommy's, Daddy's, and that thumping in his ears.

Mommy looked even more scared now. Her legs were shaking so bad, like Micah's did when he was scared. Daddy had his arm around her from behind, and it looked like that was the only thing keeping Mommy on her feet. That worried Micah. Why did Mommy look so scared if she was going to get him out of here?

"What's in it?" Daddy said.

"Oh, you'll know soon," the doctor said. "Don't dump the whole thing in there. Don't want you dying on me."

Daddy was quiet for a second. He said, "What are you giving her?"

The doctor said something else that Micah didn't hear good, but he said, "You're getting the fun stuff."

Micah knew that wasn't true. There was nothing fun here. The only time he had fun was when Uncle Chris and he were alone, and they played games.

"No." Mommy took Daddy's hand. "No."

"I'll be okay." Daddy touched Mommy's back, still holding her up. He smiled, but it looked sad still, not like it did the other times. "It's okay."

Mommy didn't say it that time, but Daddy did. It was going to be okay. Micah felt a little better now; Daddy said it was going to be okay.

The doctor said something else Micah didn't understand, and Mommy shook her head fast. She grabbed Daddy's hand tighter, looking at him now. She was crying still.

But Daddy smiled. "It's going to be okay."

He said it again, that it was going to be okay. That made Micah feel a little better again.

Mommy grabbed Daddy's shirt. He squeezed her back tighter, holding her close.

Micah wanted to be held that close too. He wanted them to hug him. He wanted this to be over. He wanted it to be okay.

Then the doctor came into view. He pushed something into Mommy's arm.

Daddy shoved him away. That made Micah happy; he didn't want him to hurt Mommy again. Daddy would keep her safe though. He'd keep Micah safe too; he said it was going to be okay.

Then Mommy started to fall.

Oh, no.

Daddy caught her though. See, he'd keep her safe. He was nice. He was good. He'd keep Mommy safe. He wouldn't let the doctor hurt her again.

The doctor said something Micah didn't hear again.

Then Daddy said, "Do you have a gurney I can put her on?"

"Your brother will grab the two of you after you're unconscious." He glanced at Micah inside.

What did that mean? What was a gurney?

Daddy glanced at Micah. He looked back to the doctor. "I don't want Micah to see this. Close the doors."

The doctor nodded.

No. No, no, no. They couldn't leave. He liked seeing them, it made him feel safe. They couldn't leave.

"Daddy," Micah whispered. His lip quivered, warm liquid spilling from his eyes. "Daddy, I'm scwade."

"It's going to be okay, buddy." Daddy smiled but tears rolled down his cheeks. "We're coming back for you."

He said it again. He said it'd be okay. That made Micah's heart hurt a little less.

Micah's little teeth began to chatter. "Pwomise?"

"I promise." Daddy smiled a little bigger, nodding fast. "You hang in there. We're coming back—"

"Alright, that's enough." The doors flung shut.

THE QUIET ARMY CHAPTER TWO

OCTOBER 23, 2021 - LAILA

"This is bullshit!" Lydia's voice echoed from the living room of the main house. She stormed into the kitchen. My eyes widened, turning to Jeremy. He pressed his smiling lips together. Ray's voice followed.

"Don't talk to me like that, little girl," he yelled as she stomped past Jeremy to the fridge.

"Well, quit making bullshit rules and I'll quit calling them bullshit." She pulled a tub of ice cream from the freezer.

"It's for your own good—"

"I left with Laila that day because I didn't want to be a prisoner anymore." Lydia slammed the silverware drawer.

Damn, bitch, don't bring me into this.

Not that I blamed her though. I understood being overprotective with children better than anyone, but mine was six months. His was fourteen. She needed a little freedom.

I considered chiming in on her defense but figured it best to do that later. Not in the middle of their throwdown. For now, I'd just sip my warm coffee and continue spoon feeding my wide-eyed baby bites of fragrant bananas.

Lydia's glowing gaze turned to Ray in the doorway. "I've left this house eight times in the past month and a half. You pulled me out of school. I can only see my friends if I have a chaperone. And now you won't even let me go to a party I RSVPed for months ago. Don't tell me that this isn't fucking bullshit, Dad."

"Lydia Marie!" Ray yelled.

"What?!" she hollered. "What, Dad? I'm not old enough to say fuck and shit? Is that what you're going to say? Because I've seen more shit than you have. Quit acting like I don't understand things. I know a lot more than you think I do. I'm not the three-year-old that went missing a decade ago. I'm a few years from being an adult now—"

"If you make it that far!" he yelled. "I'm trying to keep you safe, Lydia. Some madman was standing over your bed in the middle of the night; I can't risk something happening to you again—"

"So, what—You're just going to lock the princess in a tower until a knight in shining armor comes to save her? Newsflash, Dad, nobody's coming. No one's coming to slay the dragon and free me. So why the fuck am I still locked up?"

"Kids still say newsflash?" Jeremy lowered himself to the breakfast nook beside me.

"Apparently," I murmured.

"We just need a little bit more time, Lydia—"

"No, I need to learn how to defend myself," she snapped. "Laila's powerful enough to crack the ground open and drop someone inside of it. She can get in someone's head and make them shoot themselves. I can do that too, but you don't even want me to learn. You want me to be a little bitch who sits around waiting to be rescued."

Eh, she wasn't wrong. She could do all of that, and it was about time that she learned how. But since it was the second time she brought me up, maybe I could help lower the tensions a tad.

Ray's nostrils flared as he took in and expelled a few calming breaths.

"Do you want to go to the mall with me and Milly?" I asked. "I'm looking for something to wear to the survivor's banquet next week. Maybe we can find something for you too. We'll get lunch and try that new rolled ice cream place."

She turned to Ray and crossed her arms against her chest. "Is that okay, Daddy Dearest?"

He narrowed his gaze. "Yes, Lydia. That's fine."

"When are you leaving?" she asked me.

"Probably an hour unless you need longer."

She pushed the lid back onto the ice cream and dropped the spoon to the sink. "I'll go get dressed then." She stomped up the steps.

My gaze shifted back to Ray rubbing his tired eyes. I chuckled. "Teenagers, right?"

"Ya know, when that little girl is putting you through hell, I'm going to laugh at you too." He sat across from us.

I turned to Milly in her highchair and smiled. She giggled, slamming her plastic spoon into the banana mush on her tray. "You're not going to give us any trouble, huh, Mills?"

That was incredibly far from being true. She was going to be hell through her teenage years. But that's a story for another time.

"I get pulling her out of school, but do you have a plan to get her back in?" Jeremy asked. "I get being worried, but seclusion isn't good for someone who's been in captivity. There's no one around here that's close to her age either; that's got to be really hard."

"What am I supposed to do, man?" Ray asked. "Her mother shot her in the chest. The lunatic she's working for held almost a thousand people captive for more than a decade. I woke up to someone standing over her bed. I can't lose her again. Of all people, you should understand that."

"Sure," I said. "But she's right. No one can be her personal bodyguard. She needs to know how to defend herself, Ray."

He scoffed, tightened his jaw, and leaned back in his seat.

"Why are you so against her being who she is?" Jeremy asked. "It's the biggest part of her."

"Because I want her to be safe. I want her to have a normal life," Ray said.

Too little too late. Lydia was never going to be what Ray described as 'normal.'

"Then you should have married a human," I said. "Threats are going to follow her wherever she goes because of what she is. You can't change that. But you can make sure she knows how to defend herself if she has to. Let me work with her. I'll teach her how to keep herself safe. If someone would have taught me to use my powers, my life would look a hell of a lot different than it does right now."

He pursed his lips. "She isn't you, Laila. I don't want her to get overconfident and think that she's invincible."

"If you know what you're doing with powers like that, you almost are," Jeremy said. "But yeah. It's important to know that you aren't."

"And I can teach her that," I said. "I know the importance of that lesson better than anyone. She has to learn, Ray."

"You don't want to look back one day and wish that she knew how to protect herself," Jeremy said. "It can mean life or death. Trust me. You'd be stupid if you didn't let her learn."

Ray ran his hand against the dark five o'clock shadow on his warm, umber skin. He dragged his fingers through his jet-black hair. "I'll think about it. But that party for the survivors, kids her age will be there, right? Kids like her?"

"Sure," I said. "Another friend of mine, his brother and sister are around Lydia's age. Maybe I can introduce them. Emma's kind of a shit head, but they're good kids."

"Alright," he said. "Alright, good. Maybe they could come here and hang out some time if they all get along."

"Maybe." I gave a gentle smile.

"Hey, guys," Jenna called, followed by the front door creaking shut. "Is Adam here? He wasn't at the diner."

"Yeah, he's upstairs with Leah," Jeremy yelled.

"Bring that baby in here first, though," I called.

She came through the doorway pushing the stroller a moment later. Her blond hair was pulled into a messy, knotted bun at the top of her head. She had deep purple bags under her blue eyes behind her messy, rain droplet covered glasses. "He's finally asleep. If you wake him up, he's your responsibility for at least the hour length of his nap."

"That's okay. Huh, Luka?" I grinned, stood, and looked at him sleeping in his car seat. His pudgy little cheeks, his soft blond baby hairs, the sweet blanket framing his face.

"I'm not kidding, dude." Jenna's eyes darted over me. "This baby has colic. He never stops crying."

"Message received." I raised my hands in surrender. "I'll just admire how cute he is when he sleeps. Is that acceptable?"

"Thank you." She sighed, rubbed her temples, and started up the maid stairs.

Milly turned to her cousin and babbled with a gesture to the stroller. "Luka's sleeping. We've got to be quiet." I held my finger over my lips.

Jeremy wiped bananas from her face. "I think she needs a bath."

"Probably a good idea." I lifted her from the highchair. "You're still going to the diner to fix that door in the men's room, right?"

"Yeah." He reached into the diaper bag, pulled out a set of clothes, and a diaper while I made my way to the sink. "Shouldn't take me long though. Maybe we could meet up at the mall for lunch."

"That sounds good. Can you go grab me a towel?"

<hr>

Our day-to-day life had been pretty simple since Milly's birth. Most were like this. Simple, peaceful, and happy.

I hadn't returned to work, but Jeremy had. Max's mom was diagnosed with cancer late in the summer—unfortunately one of the few diseases I couldn't heal—so he had to back down on hours. That left a lot of management issues up in the air. Jeremy seemed happy to take on the work though.

I think in some non-misogynistic way, doing the work that paid for the roof over our heads gave him a sense of pride. Jeremy always struggled with some self-esteem issues, but I think feeling like "the man of the house" was helping him move past them. I didn't mind either. I enjoyed the time I got to spend day in and day out with my daughter.

Aside from the day that we accessed our past lives, I hadn't been more than a room away from her for any length of time. The only exception up until that point was mine and Jeremy's date on our second anniversary. We were only gone for two hours, half of which was spent waiting in the line at Applebee's to get a table. We should have just ordered it because we kept calling Leah and Hannah to check on Milly and spent the whole two hours being nervous wrecks.

Our lives were seemingly normal during those months. But dark clouds still loomed over us from time to time. Many nights were still spent crying on the floor in my shower. However, Milly had a way of shining a light when the clouds rolled through.

We'd been in contact with a higher-level Demon back in August. She made arrangements for us to meet with Lucifer that coming April. Her exact words were, "I'll let you know if there are any cancellations before the scheduled date, although it's highly unlikely."

We reluctantly accepted because we didn't have much other choice. It was the only lead we had. If it would've been someone less important, I would have demanded a sooner appointment. But it was Lucifer. *The* Lucifer. I was in no place to demand shit.

There hadn't been any news on the apocalypse nor information on my missing child and brother-in-law. I wish I could say that I was still searching high and low for a way to find them. But in all honesty, I'd looked everywhere that I could think to. The only chance I had left was literally the devil. I hadn't given up, but I was out of places to look until our meeting.

Transfixed by *The Quiet Army*? Click the link below to download now!
https://www.amazon.com/gp/product/B095J135H4/

ALSO BY CHARLIE NOTTINGHAM

The Eluding Destiny Series

Eluding Destiny

The Horrors That Created Us

Aftershocks

The Precipice

Land of Light

The Quiet Army

Sacred Sins

Flash Back

The Shift

Lost to Time

Gods Among Us

The Cover Up

Blank Slate

Eluding Destiny Prequels

The Last Beginning

Blood Bar

Raven's Cry Series

(MMFM Paranormal Romance)

Raven's Cry

Raven's Song

Celena's Story Duology

(Completed—paranormal romance, urban fantasy)

New Normal: Celena's Story Part 1

Reprisal: Celena's Story Part 2

Origins of the Gods

(Completed Trilogy—fantasy romance, more information on the origins of the Fae and Angels, how life began on earth, where Guardians came from, and—most importantly—a badass forbidden romance)

Origins

The Thrones of Ore and Ice

Creation

Stand Alone Novels

Curse of the Gods: The Bridge Between Origins of the Gods and the Eluding Destiny Series

Sign up for Charlie's newsletter and receive a free copy of the Eluding Destiny prequel, Blood Bar:

https://liquidmind.media/eluding-destiny-prequel/

ABOUT THE AUTHOR

Charlie is a... Okay, talking about myself in third person is weird.

Nice to meet you! My name's Charlie Nottingham, and my whole world revolves around fantasy. When I'm not writing a new book, I'm either hanging out with my dogs, talking with my fans online, or reading some amazing urban fantasy, paranormal romance, or fantasy romance series (always a series, never a stand-alone, because I hate to fall for a character and never see them again). Or re-watching some Buffy or Supernatural. (They never get old!)